A THOUSAND BAYONETS

A THOUSAND BAYONETS

JOEL MARK HARRIS

iUniverse, Inc.
Bloomington

A Thousand Bayonets

iUniverse books may be ordered through booksellers or by contacting:

iUniverse
1663 Liberty Drive
Bloomington, IN 47403
www.iuniverse.com
1-800-Authors (1-800-288-4677)

ISBN: 978-1-4620-3268-6 (sc)
ISBN: 978-1-4620-3269-3 (hc)
ISBN: 978-1-4620-3270-9 (e)

Library of Congress Control Number: 2011912586

Printed in the United States of America

iUniverse rev. date: 08/12/2011

In memory of Michelle Lang, a reporter for the *Calgary Herald*, who died on the outskirts of Kandahar City on December 30, 2009, and for all other journalists who have lost their lives covering conflict.

Author's Note

Except for a brief, fleeting time in the mid-seventies, journalists have never been given the praise they warrant. Indeed, Janet Malcolm famously defamed the venerable profession in her book *The Journalist and the Murderer* in the opening paragraph by saying "Every journalist who is not too stupid or too full of himself to notice what is going on knows that what he does is morally indefensible."

It seems a common view held in today's day and age. Thankfully it has not always been so. The Founding Fathers of the United States recognized a free press as being not only important, but vital to the survival of a healthy and functional democracy. As lofty and ivory-tower-minded as that might sound, I challenge anybody to think of a more important constitutional right. It is a fact that so often and so tragically gets ignored, especially when the military try to bring democracy to countries that have only known iron-fisted rule and propaganda. A free press is imperative for fledging democracies, a fact Napoleon Bonaparte new so well—and used to his advantage and the world's detriment—when he became emperor of France.

Journalists have done much to alter history. William Howard Russell, who reported on the Crimean War for the *Times of London*, changed how the British government treated its troops. Everybody knows how two young eager *Washington Post* reporters brought President Richard Nixon to his knees. It has saved lives as in 1984 in Ethiopia when a BBC documentary woke the world up to a colossal travesty. And more recently it has sparked revolution in Egypt and Libya with the use of social media. These are perhaps the most famous ones, but there are many more examples.

I, however, did not always understand the importance of journalism and how it impacts the way we think and live. As a young writer, I wondered how I could make a buck or two by putting words on paper. It was this pondering that led me to journalism school in the first place. I applied, wrote my entrance exam, but sadly did not get in.

Oh well, I thought. There are plenty of other writing jobs out there. I don't need journalism.

But then I got a call one morning, mid-September in 2005 from a serious-sounding man asking me if I still would like to attend journalism school—or j-school as I learned to call it—albeit a bit late. Somebody had dropped out the first week, and I was asked if I wanted to replace him.

I often wonder what would have happened if I had not received that call. Although I was, of course, disappointed not making the cut initially, I wasn't overly distraught not to be chosen, and probably would have moved on to some other endeavour.

I have to say, journalism school was the most thrilling, happiest, industrious time of my life. My instructors taught me that journalism educates, galvanizes, and informs us. It is the societal watch dog. And excellent journalism is even more imperative now, in our complicated, modern times, than ever before.

Although I learned a lot from all my teachers, I am especially indebted to one: Ross Howard, who continues to train journalists in war-torn countries such as Rwanda, Cambodia, Ski Lanka, and Nepal. He, more than anybody, is the person who inspired me to write this novel.

JMH
Vancouver, BC
June 13, 2011

A THOUSAND BAYONETS

The Shootout

John Webster was hiding in the loft of an old abandoned barn, watching and waiting, clutching his voice recorder tightly. He stared moronically at the red light, watching the numbers count slowly upward, *thirteen, fourteen, fifteen*, willing the red light to continue and praying the batteries would hold out for him.

Below John, five shadowy figures huddled close, speaking in whispers. In the papers, they were known as the Heart gang. Webster knew only two of them by reputation: Kenneth Dzyinski, el capo, the big boss, the head honcho, and Anthony Hewson, the right-hand man. The other goons were big, burly creatures, clad head to toe in leather and silver chains, wearing steel-toe boots. Except for, perhaps, their mousy-grey, badly trimmed beards, they might not have looked out of place in an S&M bar.

"He ripped off two of my earners last week."

"You sure it was him?"

"Shit sure."

A deep, glottal, Eastern European voice said, "Hunter has entered a game he can't possibly win."

Must be Dzyinski, John thought.

Up in the loft, John held his breath, not daring to move. In the distance he could hear the low bawling of a horse, the pitiful howl of a dog, and the chilly wind as it slowly knocked against the barn. And just as he was acutely aware of these sounds, he was suddenly not aware of them at all.

He was transported to a small, colourful bazaar, with cream-coloured buildings on each side. Thick dust particles rose in the tepid air, getting into John's face, into his eyes, up his nose. The bazaar was mostly empty except for a few cautious patrons, moving quickly on their way. John was in the middle of the dusty road, just standing and watching as people bartered for goods, the same Olympus voice recorder tightly in the palm of his hand. During his dreams, John was a regular patron of this place.

John struggled to focus again on the barn. He tried not to be afraid. He refused to think of what would happen if they caught him—probably some halfhearted torture before a bullet in the temple.

He looked down at his silver recorder and the small, constant red light. He felt the straw against his neck and chin. It tickled and scratched his skin, willing him to sneeze, to make some kind of sound. He rubbed his eyes briefly, trying to regulate his breathing.

The gangsters were mumbling again. Would he be able to pick up their voices so far away? Webster wasn't sure. He concentrated on his voice recorder. Then he was safe from fear, from his mind thinking up different scenarios. It was a trick he had learned a long time ago—how to stave off the unwanted.

Who had taught him that? His first thought was his dad, John Webster Senior, but it couldn't have been the old theatre critic. It must have been a soldier—they knew all sorts of tricks, tricks not written in any manual.

He was back at the bazaar, his cameraman, William Russell, by his side. Webster pushed his fake Ray-Bans up on his nose and looked briefly up at the vast, colourless, featureless sky. Every building of any height had been flattened long ago by bombs or by missiles. The surprising result, John found, was that you could look down even a small alley and look on, across the flatness, seemingly forever, like you were looking to the end of earth. And in a way, John figured, he kind of was.

John and William were the only two foreigners there. Everybody gazed at them with dark, opaque, suspicious eyes. William was setting up his camera, installing a new battery, getting ready to shoot live. Webster dug the toe of his shoe into the red dirt—and then he heard the escalating roar of car motors. He looked up to see a caravan of small vehicles arrive. John supposed there must be people in those cars, but all he saw were AK-47s glistening in the harsh light.

Chaos erupted through the bazaar. Screams in Arabic. Suddenly there was an explosion—a mouth of flame engulfing everything. The surrounding houses and buildings tore apart, ash everywhere, blowing and flowing in the stray wind, whipping across, hitting John in the face.

A large crater ripped into the Baghdad street, and it almost seemed as if Satan himself had broken his encasement from hell. Piles of rubble formed, broken and cracked stone. There were cries for help and there were cries for death. Bodies had been flung around like rag dolls. Blood trickled into the gutters, blood trickled down the hill, blood trickled like canals of water, running right past where Webster stood frozen, unaware of time, a roar in his ears.

The casualties seemed endless. Men and women dead. Children dead. A vendor was being dragged away from open flames, his legs torn and shredded so badly they were almost unrecognizable. An old lady had the skin and flesh stripped from her arm, and only glossy white bone was showing. She waved her surprisingly bloodless stump at Webster. The human ash rose and seeped into the sky, filling and choking things, engulfing the world as it was.

And John just stood there, voice recorder light in his hand. William Russell next to him was filming everything, swivelling his camera back and forth. But John couldn't move. Never before had he felt so insignificant, unable to do anything. Shock had settled in, numbing his nerves and mind.

John closed his eyes. He was back in the barn. He could smell the hay and oaky panels.

They are too far away, John thought. *If only there was a way to get closer without being seen.*

He raised his head, clandestinely peering over the edge, his weight on his elbows. He could see them, the light casting their long, shifting shadows against the walls.

One of them said, "This seems very fucking risky."

"All great men took leaps of faith," Dzyinski said.

"Who you like for the job?"

"The Findley brothers."

Suddenly the door swung open, and John saw two masked men with submachine guns step into the room. John glanced at them long enough to know they had bulky shoulders, barrel chests, and baggy clothes. John closed his eyes, buried himself in the straw, and held his breath. If he had known any prayers, he would have started reciting them.

An ominous pause filled the room, seemingly lasting forever. Then a series of unmistakable sounds—an eruption of noise thundered through the barn, seismic in proportion, like the opening of a fault line. Webster could feel, rather than see, the wooden walls shudder around him. It lasted no more than a couple of seconds—nanoseconds maybe—before the cold metallic sounds ceased to be, overtaken by the sound of footsteps pounding the compact dirt and then the loud wail of screeching tires on gravel.

Webster waited before lifting his head. The barn smelled of singed ham. The vibrations rung in his ears. Still, he didn't move, not for a long time. His body was mostly buried in straw. He listened, wondering if anybody was alive down there, but he heard nothing move, nothing stir, only the loud thumping of his own blood in his head.

Maybe they would come back, just to make sure. He waited some more. Eventually he pressed his palms down, lifting his body up. His limbs didn't seem to want to cooperate. Every part of him seemed stiff and numb, frozen. He put his foot on the top rung of the ladder, almost missing his footing and falling forward. The smell became worse. It crawled up his nose, clung to his clothes, his skin, his hair. His stomach wrenched violently in protest.

The sunlight poured through the windows hitting the ground, splintering into white light and blue light. The bullets had ripped the bodies, breaking them apart. They lay spread eagle. Their guns sat just out of reach. Rigid faces leered at him with carrion eyes.

John felt his knees try to give, and he struggled to remain upright. He had to get out of the barn, into the open air. The door stood only a few steps away, but it seemed like miles. He didn't look down. He didn't know how he propelled his body forward, but somehow he reached the door. He grabbed the handle. It took all his strength to try and open it.

The bright sun hit his face, and yet it seemed cold, tangy, and clayish. He closed his eyes and sank to his knees, feeling the broken dirt in his hands. He couldn't feel anything else.

Somewhere in the distance, he heard a low, mournful wail. *What was that?* He realized through his foggy consciousness that the sound was getting closer. Then he recognized the sound. It was sirens. A line of police cruisers appeared over the hilly horizon, speeding along the path, lights flashing, leaving bilious ash-red clouds in its wake, chrome rims spinning around and around in the dirt. They were coming to save him.

The cruisers stopped and then swung around. The police got out, guns drawn, crouching behind their vehicles. John put his hands in the air. The police yelled at John. He laid down, his cheek against the dirt. His hands were wrenched behind his back and handcuffed. He didn't think to protest, to utter any of his usual complaints. He was then lifted up and put into the back of a cruiser

The Office

Charles Dana, managing editor for the *Daily Globe*, picked up the ringing phone. "Dana speaking," he said.

An annoyed voice answered, "We can't get hold of Webster."

Charles sighed heavily. "This Detective Wiltore again?"

"Yes."

"You tried his cell phone, his office?"

"Of course."

Charles sighed again, looking around his small, bleak office, as if Webster would just appear. "Okay, I'll go check around. See if he's here."

"Thanks." Wiltore hung up.

Charles strode out of his office and into the newsroom. The newsroom was a four-thousand-square-foot room with individual stalls and large white pillars; neon-panelled lighting lined the ceiling. Usually it was humming with loud voices, the sound of fingers typing furiously on keyboards, feet pounding on the hard floor. But it was almost seven o'clock, and most of the reporters who had completed their assignments had left—though some remained on deadline pressure—and so the newsroom had only a skeleton crew compiled of mostly copy editors and layout people.

"Anybody seen Webster around?"

Several heads looked up from their desks. "No, boss, sorry."

Charles put his hands on his hips. "Where is he? Has he come in yet?"

There were several automatic shrugs. "Sorry—don't know, boss."

Charles went back into his office and sat down in his chair. His office was painted a cream colour, but needed repainting. A small window looked out across the street, his view comprised of other office buildings.

He had a wall-to-wall bookcase behind his desk. The bookcase was filled with classics written by Dickens, Tolstoy, and Dostoevsky, and textbooks he used to teach his Friday morning class at the University of British Columbia. Newspaper awards lined the wall opposite the bookcase—best editorial, best investigative reporting—dating back through the years and decades. The centerpiece was a framed first edition from 1844.

Charles was proud of his office. It was plain, functional, and not too flashy—not unlike Charles himself. He picked up the phone again and quickly dialled the detective. "Nope, he's not here."

"Get him to phone me as soon as he gets in—and I mean as soon as he walks through that door."

"Of course, detective."

Charles placed the phone back down on the receiver. He got up and went next door to the city editor's office.

Earlier in the day, Charles had gotten a phone call from a Constable Snyder telling him Webster had been involved in some kind of shooting. Charles was confused at first, but the constable filled him in on the few details he knew. Webster had been tipped off to a meeting of the top members of the Heart gang. Subsequently Webster had been taken to the hospital, where he was checked out before being released. He had not been heard from since.

Charles knocked on Robert Smyllie's door. "Where's Webster?" he asked.

Smyllie looked up from his computer. Smyllie was a bald, egg-shaped man with pale skin—probably a result from living a large portion of his life in rainy Glasgow. He spoke in a baritone Scottish brogue. "How the fuck should I know, boss?"

Charles rubbed his eyelids with his thumb and forefinger. "He has a breaking story, a front-pager. Has he sent it to you?"

"What story? Haven't seen a fucking thing."

"Deadline is in an hour."

"You tried his home?"

Charles threw up his arms in frustration. "He's probably at the Palace. Phone them up and see if he's there."

"Yes, boss." Smyllie picked up the phone and dialled. He let it ring, but shook his head. "They're not answering."

"Okay, I need you to go down there and find him. No—wait. I'll do it. You get everything ready to print."

"You sure, boss?"

"Yeah, it's not as if I don't have a thousand things to do."

Charles took the elevator down to the lobby. He thrust his long hands deep into his pockets, waiting as he descended floors. He exited the *Daily Globe* building, an old relic of a structure. It looked like it had been plunked at the foot of Granville Street by mistake, an accident from the past. It was from another time, when newspapers made money and had been an integral part of communal life. Only thirty stories high, the Globe building was a runt among the financial leviathans; but when it had been built, it had been the tallest building in the city and the talk of the town. It was made of brick—now all mossy and weather-stained. The windows were too thin to keep a draft out, and the copper, domed roof always seemed in danger of collapsing.

Charles felt a strange connection to the building. He too was from another age, the golden age of newsprint. When Watergate had hit the news, he had been a young reporter for the *Wall Street Journal.* He had been there for Vietnam—which had irrevocably changed war and war journalism. Those days were long gone now, and every time Charles went in or out of the Globe building, it made him feel old. Someday he would let go of his tight grasp on this profession, but not yet. Not yet.

It was beginning to sprinkle a light misty summer rain, cool and refreshing. Charles crossed the street, looking at the metropolis around him. The city seemed freshly polished, newly minted by the glistening rain. The glass skyscrapers clustered around him, erect, rows upon rows, throwing sharp shadows on to the road. In the distance, Charles could see the looming, angular Woodward's building with the large steel *W* pinnacle against the cloud-smeared sky. To Charles the glowing red *W* seemed like some sort of Babylonian idol, an unnatural attraction in the poorest part of the city. The poorest part of the country. Charles headed toward the Woodward's building as if he were following a trusty navigation beacon.

Sometimes Charles felt he was in an overgrowth of metal, concrete, and glass. Construction hummed everywhere—steel frames nailed together, concrete floors going in, pipes placed, jackhammers thundering away, large machinery excavating mounds of cement and dirt.

Charles passed by men and women dressed in tailored suits worth a thousand dollars, maybe more. They wore slickly polished shoes, golden watches strapped to their wrists, and finely pressed shirts. Almost everybody had a BlackBerry, iPhone, or Palm Pilot in their vanilla-scented palms.

Vancouver had changed so much. These tall skyscrapers, this flood of self-absorbed pedestrians sometimes made Charles feel like he was back in New York, walking along the wide sidewalk of Forty-Third Street—but old New York. Innocent New York. New York before 9/11.

It took Charles ten minutes to get to Palace Bar, on Cordova and Abbot Streets. It was one of the oldest—if not the oldest—bars in Vancouver, and known to be the regular drinking hole of newspaper men, poets, writers, and the occasional broadcaster.

The Palace was small, dark, and dreary, crammed with as many chairs and tables as possible, most of them empty. Loverboy was playing softly on the jukebox somewhere in the corner, and adjacent was a scratched, marked-up pool table, just below several prints of Marilyn Monroe, looking all virginal in her famous white dress.

Charles spotted a reporter for the *Vancouver Times*. The reporter had a flat face and glasses pushed too far up his nose. He got up from his stool. "Hey, Dana," he said. "What are you doing here? Don't tell me you fell off the wagon."

At one point in Charles's industrious newspaper career, he had been able to outdrink anybody at the Palace, but he hadn't had a single drink in ten years. He even remembered the exact moment in time he decided to forever be sober. One dull September day, he had woken up miserable and hungover. His wife put a cold hand on his shoulder and told him he'd better get to work if he didn't want to get fired. Charles laughed at the idea—considering he actually might relish the thought. Charles embarked on his daily commute: the subway from Brooklyn into Manhattan. The rattling pitch of the tracks seemed to make an indentation into his skull. Walking to the office, which was in the heart of the financial district,

Charles got a call on his cell phone from Walker and Thompson, one of the largest PR firms in New York. They wanted to make him an offer. It was almost twice what he was making at the *Wall Street Journal*. Charles said he would have an answer by the end of the week.

He got his morning coffee and then chatted with his fellow editors before going into the morning news meeting. The editors discussed the top stories—international stories, New York stories, and of course, business stories. After the meeting, Charles got another cup of coffee, hoping caffeine would cure his headache. He went back to his desk and made a few phone calls.

"No, no, just meeting somebody here," Charles told the *Vancouver Times* reporter, looking around for Webster, wishing he could remember the name of the reporter.

"Oh, yeah?" the reporter said, his eyes sharpening, smelling a lead. "Who?"

Charles raised two slender palms. "Nobody, just Webster."

The reporter nodded, clearly disappointed. "Well, he's in the corner booth."

Charles went over and slipped into the bench opposite Webster. Webster had his ear against the table, his eyes wide and alert as if he was listening for a heartbeat. Beside him was a half-emptied glass of gin and tonic.

"Webster, what are you doing?"

"I'm off duty—punched my ticket for the night," Webster mumbled.

"How much have you had to drink?"

Webster put a finger to his lips. "I'm listening to the music through vibrations."

Charles stared at Webster, baffled. "But why?"

"Somebody told me Beethoven wrote his music this way … after he went deaf."

Charles had no time for drunken nonsense. "The article, Webster."

"That's why you came down here?"

Charles shrugged. "What else?"

Webster lifted his head and took a sip from his gin and tonic. "Chuck, I just saw five people die."

Charles didn't say anything for a while, unsure how to respond. He was sympathetic, yet he had a job to do. "I can arrange somebody to talk to you."

Webster frowned, gripping his glass tightly as if somebody might try and take it away. "All we do is talk. Talk, talk, talk."

"You want sympathy? I'm the wrong guy."

"You know anyone who has seen people die, Chucky? I mean a violent death, Chucky—it's not pretty. It's slow and painful."

Charles tried not to wince. Everybody in the office called him boss or Mr. Dana; only Webster had the insolence to call him Chuck, or when drunk, Chucky. "I'm sure there are plenty who are well trained in trauma counselling."

"How about you? You do any trauma counselling?"

Charles sighed. The memories were still there, of course. The explosion from the Twin Towers shattered the glass in the *Wall Street Journal's* office. Charles remembered the heat most of all, bright and hot like a supernova. Even now, sometimes, when he stepped out of a building into a hot summer day, he had vivid flashbacks of white ash and silver dust. He remembered walking down the seemingly endless dark, rank stairwell to the bottom. He just thought about getting out of there, going home. His brain was still all fuzzy from the previous night's alcohol. But when he reached the bottom, he wished he could climb back up again. There was mass confusion and mass chaos. Bloodied people everywhere.

It took a couple of months for their office to be renovated so they could move back in. The pit—called Ground Zero, but which was nevertheless just a deep, dark pit—looked ghostly and eerie, especially in the early morning light when Charles got to work. He was staring at the pit when he got a call from the PR firm. The man on the other end of the phone apologized profusely for not calling back earlier, but things had, understandably, been a little crazy.

Charles, for his part, had forgotten all about Walker and Thompson's offer.

"I'm sorry, but I don't think I can take the job," Charles had said, still staring down at the pit, the seemingly endless cavernous hole in the city. It was the unhealed wound from the gunshot that had struck the city, almost fatally.

The PR man expressed his surprise. Charles had seemed so close. Again Charles apologized and hung up, mesmerized by the two towers—the two glistening, symbolic towers that were now only a memory.

Charles hadn't drunk a single drop of alcohol since.

Charles stared at Webster and shook his head. He said softly, "No, but perhaps I should have."

"Amira." Webster said the name in barely above a whisper.

"Who's Amira?" Charles asked. He waited for an answer, but when he didn't get one, he said, "Why don't you let somebody help you?"

"What are they going to do?"

"I don't know, and neither will you until you try."

"She was beautiful, Chuck, unimaginably beautiful."

Charles shook his head. It was no use. Webster was drunk and incomprehensible. "You've done the article, Webster? I have a big hole on my front page."

"I sent it in already."

"Well, we didn't get it yet."

Webster sat back in his chair and rolled his head back. He slowly took out his BlackBerry from his pocket, scrolled through his e-mails, and pressed a few buttons. "Okay, I just resent it to Smyllie, cc'd you on it."

Charles's phone made a gleeful ping, and when he looked at it, he saw Webster's article. He stood up. "I got to get back ... but you should quit the alcohol. It doesn't do you any good."

Webster looked up with giant, drunken eyes. "Sure thing, Chuck."

Hayden

John watched Chuck leave the room, gulping down the last of his gin and tonic. A strange, rotten smell filled John's nostrils, and it took him a while before he realized it wasn't a genuine smell. He didn't know if it was something remembered or something made-up.

He tried to douse the smell with another order of gin and tonic, which dissipated it somewhat, but it still lingered in the back of his nose like a lodged insect.

John looked around at the other patrons in the hushed light. In the corner, there was a woman drinking a martini. She was stroking the neck of her glass and looking around expectantly. Their eyes met briefly. She smiled ruefully. Webster tried a smile back before looking down at his drink.

Somehow the woman reminded John of his ex-wife—with her long dark hair, her olive skin, her big lips, and large eyes. Maybe he would walk over and sit beside her; maybe he would buy her a drink or two. Maybe he would take her home, shut his eyes tight, turn off the lights, and pretend he was making love to his wife again.

He took a last gulp from his glass, which tasted like he had swallowed something rotten—a mixture of ash and dirt. He felt drunk. A headache was coming on, and he tried to remember the last time he had something to eat. He closed his eyes, rubbing his eyelids.

He looked over at the woman who looked like his ex-wife and smiled again. A wider smile this time. She smiled back, shifting her body around the stool into her light, and he realized she didn't look like Hayden at all.

Her skin was much too light and tightly drawn across her face, her nose was too long, her eyes were set too far apart.

"What did Dana want?"

Webster looked up to see Arthur Ransome, a reporter for the *Vancouver Times,* standing over him.

"Oh … hello, Arthur."

Arthur sat down opposite John, the spot Chuck had occupied a few moments earlier. "Is the rumour true?"

John looked down at his empty glass, wishing he had another one. "What rumour is that?"

Arthur pushed his glasses up on his nose. "You were involved in a gang shootout?"

"Where did you hear that?"

Arthur shrugged, looking over at the waitress, as if she might be eavesdropping. "I'm just saying … you might want to be careful."

John automatically sat up. "Why? What do you mean be careful?"

Arthur leaned over the table, speaking very softly. "Well … you know how gangsters are with witnesses."

John couldn't think of anything to say, so he surveyed Arthur drunkenly, trying to decide how serious he was.

Arthur looked back at the waitress again. "You might want to lay low for a while, at least until all this blows over."

John snorted. "You just want to scoop me."

Arthur shook his head and clicked his teeth with his tongue. "Come on, John. Fuck the story. It's not worth anybody's life."

"I didn't see anything. The two men wore masks and body armour."

"Body armour?"

John frowned, thinking he was too drunk to be having this conversation. "I'm not saying any more."

Arthur rose from the table. "Okay, just remember Bernar."

John nodded reluctantly. Ian Bernar had been a journalist for the *Montreal Gazette* who had been shot in his driveway for a story he had done on the mob.

"I'm not worried," John said. "I was in Iraq and Afghanistan, Arthur. These guys don't scare me."

Arthur stood up and reached across to put his palm on John's shoulder. "Just remember, John, these guys are the Taliban of North America."

John paid his tab and walked unsteadily out into the night, back to his apartment. Gastown was once home to sailors, hookers, labourers, loggers, and businessmen, but in the past fifty years or so, it had been infiltrated with yuppies and hipsters and students. It was a bit of an avant-garde place, with a Parisian taste for fresh pastries and organic espresso.

The street was wide, made unevenly with large brick. The buildings were Victorian, with long windows, cobblestone steps, and sloped overhangs. Many of the old hotels had been turned into homeless shelters.

John walked past the old statue of "Gassy" Jack Deighton, owner of the first Vancouver salon, around which the whole of Gastown fittingly sprang up. Poor old Gassy Jack looked like a weatherworn copper-green version of Scarecrow from the *Wizard of Oz*. What would he have thought of the middle-class labourer being replaced by the millennial generation? What would he have thought of the whorehouses being replaced by bistros?

John's building was on the corner of Alexander and Columbia, a loft in a modest four-story building, made of cement and brick and speckled with brown rust and dirt. He had found it soon after he separated from Hayden. It served his purposes well, being both cheap and close to work.

John walked up the stairs to his apartment. He switched on the light. It flickered twice before coming alive. He kicked off his shoes and left them in the middle of the hallway. He felt like a stranger encroaching on his own apartment. Dirty pots and dishes piled up in the sink and on the kitchen counter were from yesterday's dinner. The sink was partly clogged, and specks of pasta sauce had found their way onto the cupboards and along the microwave. He pressed his hand against his chin, surveying the mess. He meant to clean, sometime, someday, but something always seemed to get in his way.

His grey walls were very bare—no paintings or artwork of any kind adorned them, giving the impression this living arrangement was only temporary, and, at first, John had believed that. But as the months and years passed, John came to terms with the fact he wasn't getting back together with Hayden.

John had a hot shower, shaved, and changed his clothes. Feeling refreshed, he picked up an old *Economist* from his bedside table and started to flip through it, but he couldn't concentrate. He thought back to what Arthur Ransome had said, wondering if he should be worried at all. His story would probably be front-page tomorrow, his name neatly under the headline—a perfect calling card for any gangster.

John got up and walked agitatedly around his apartment, only stopping once to stare out the window at a ruddy, blackened building scheduled for demolition. Somewhere in the distance, the steam clock whistled its deep, throaty moan denoting the hour.

John poured himself a glass of gin from the cupboard, got a couple of ice cubes from the freezer, and sat on the old, lumpy couch. He felt cold, unable to move, separated from his body. He wanted to be productive, to do something, but the alcohol in his blood seemed to weigh down his limbs.

Across the hallway, two familiar voices started to yell through the thin walls, arguing about whose turn it was to take out the trash. John stood and listened for a while—actually missing the same arguments he used to have with Hayden. They were a part of coexistence, of togetherness, and they were better than coming home to a dirty, empty apartment.

John couldn't stand it anymore. He knew it was a bad idea—possibly the worst of all ideas—to drop in unannounced, partially inebriated, on Hayden; but the day's events, his apartment, and the voices next door made him feel depressed and empty.

He managed, somehow, to find his jacket again, slip on his shoes, and go downstairs to hail a cab. He climbed into the back, reciting the address to the cabby automatically. He had a purpose again, and the weight he had only moments ago felt had been lifted from him.

Hayden lived in Point Grey, near the university. It was a quiet, affluent neighbourhood filled with high-end coffee shops, fancy restaurants, and large parking spaces. Everybody drove posh cars to and from work, ferrying their kids to private school, manoeuvring to the green or to play racquetball at the gym.

The neighbourhood was filled with middle-aged men and women who wore khakis, Egyptian-cotton shirts, and Jimmy Choo shoes. They ate at country clubs, at tapas bars, and at steakhouses, and drank white wine and martinis in large quantities late into the evening.

The taxi turned up Cambie and then on Broadway until it reached Tenth Avenue. The roads were wide, freshly paved, leading up to elegant, symmetrical driveways; tall green bushes obscured the view of the sprawling big-windowed houses.

Hayden's house was no different than any other. The yard was surrounded by an eight-foot hedge, and John used to sit on the back porch and look out at downtown and the clumped foliage of Stanley Park as it curled up toward the lime-green steel of Lions Gate Bridge, spanning across to the North Shore and beyond the ghostly fingers of Cypress and Grouse Mountains.

The taxi pulled up to the front of the house. In the dark, the house seemed menacing and cold, the windows wide and cavernous looking. John paid the driver and stepped out into the nighttime.

John felt a wave of nostalgia whenever he saw the house, a sense of family again. He imagined coming home after a long day at the office, a waft of simmering charcoal from a nearby barbecue, the fruity crisp smell of an open bottle of wine, the shrill hockey announcer piercing the walls, calling the game.

John pressed the doorbell, looking down the empty street lit only by the tawny street lamps, and wondered how long it had been since he had last seen Hayden and Byron. He couldn't remember. A month? Two? Work had been crazy.

Finally, after what seemed like an eternity, John heard the thumping of quick footsteps. The door edged open, and there stood a short, pudgy nine-year-old. John nodded and tried to smile, but his face muscles failed him. John saw much of his ex-wife in Byron—the way his ears curved, the shape of his small nose, his thick mop of hair.

Byron looked up at his father with keen chestnut eyes and an expectant gaze. John shifted from one foot to the other, and for a moment he was speechless. Finally he said, "Byron, good to see you."

Byron remained silent. His thick neck stretched upward. Maybe Byron wanted something more, something profound, from his mostly absent father. Perhaps he wanted his father to be away on a secret mission for NASA or a deep-sea exploration for the lost city of Atlantis, or maybe he was working for the CIA, the FBI … yes, that was it, that was why his father had not been able to phone or write. He was captured by the enemy and held for ransom until the government paid up.

Again John tried to smile, but the corners of his lips failed him once again. "What? You're not talking to me?" John paused, but all he got was a quizzical expression from his son. John took a deep breath and exhaled. "Would you at least let me in?"

His son opened the door a little more and stepped backward, allowing John to enter. Byron shut the door behind him. A strong waft of lemon cleaner hit John's nostrils, and he looked around at the immaculately kept hallway. The colourfully threaded Persian rug was freshly vacuumed, and Hayden's shoes and boots were neatly placed in a row.

John turned to his son. "What time is it? Shouldn't you be in bed?"

Byron just looked maliciously at his father.

"Come on; don't be childish."

Still silence. Byron's face tightened into several complex knots.

John gave up. "Where's Mom?"

Byron pointed up the stairwell, and just as John turned, he heard an upstairs door close and the soft steps of naked soles on rug. Then she appeared, stepping into the tranquil light. Her wood-coloured hair was long and done up in a loose ponytail; her skin was the colour of dawn. She was wearing capris and a long-sleeved shirt.

"What are you doing here?" she asked.

"Good to see you too."

"What do you expect? A hug and a kiss?"

John shrugged sheepishly. "Work—you know."

"It's late."

John looked down at the Persian rug. "Yeah … I know."

"So you just decided to show up?"

"Well … I had a bit of a stressful day."

"That's too bad; so did I," she said callously.

"Can we go into the kitchen? We can talk like decent people in there, can't we?"

Hayden frowned and then hopped down the stairs nimbly, like she was ten or fifteen years younger, and John couldn't help but admire her dexterity. She had taken up yoga a few years back, and it seemed to do wonders for her.

Byron, still without saying a word, turned and disappeared into the living room. John and Hayden walked into the kitchen, which was silent except for the hum from the fridge.

"I wish he would say something to me," John said, staring down the hall where Byron used to be.

"What do you want him to say? Everything is great and wonderful?"

John shrugged, sitting on one of the stools, hooking his legs around the metal bars.

Hayden leaned her slim arms against the back of the counter, thrusting her chest out. "You know he's very angry at you."

"I … suppose so."

Hayden leaned toward John. "You've been drinking, haven't you?"

"Somewhat," John replied. "Like I said—"

"I know what you said," Hayden snapped. "You had a bad day. Forgive me if I don't drown you in sympathy."

"That's not why I came."

Hayden spread her small palms upward. "Yes, please enlighten me."

John looked at Hayden and examined her high cheekbones, her rigid jawline, and her freckles she always hated. She benefited in the way all children of mixed racial couples did—having dark skin and brown hair from her Brazilian father, but also strong shoulders and mild eyes from her German mother. She was approaching forty, but she hadn't lost an ounce of beauty since she was sixteen.

How a poor, uneducated, unsophisticated journalist had convinced her to marry him, John never understood. Was it his adventurous, cavalier, imperious ways? His refusal to do things like everybody else? His refusal to go to college, get a job requiring a tie?

John asked, "You dating again?"

"How is that any of your business?"

John looked down at his hands. He heard the sound of the television coming from the living room. "What's he watching?"

"God, how am I supposed to know?"

"It's too late to be watching television."

Hayden's mouth dropped partially. "I forgot … You are parent of the year."

"You have anything to drink?"

Hayden's dark eyes widened, and then in a low, strained voice, she said, "Fuck you! You come to my—"

"No, that's not what I mean … coffee, tea, anything."

Hayden didn't move for a moment but then her body slackened. "I don't know … I could put on a pot."

John nodded, knowing he was taking advantage of her good nature but not caring.

Hayden turned and took out a can from the cupboard.

"You know," John said, "I was remembering when we went to South Africa together. I don't know why …"

With her body still turned, Hayden stopped moving. "Please don't, John. I can't do that."

"Do what? Remember what happened?"

"You seeing a psychiatrist yet?"

John clenched his jaw, remembering the conversation he had with Chuck. "We've been over this."

Hayden took a couple scoops of coffee and dumped them into the machine. She pressed the on button, and the machine started vibrating. "What about your nightmares? The little boy?"

"They're gone—he's gone."

Hayden turned, leaning her body against the counter. She tucked her chin against her chest, looking at John. "I don't believe you."

Webster stared at the coffee machine as it poured water through the grinds. "You know … I often try and remember what the order was … but I have trouble, you know—I forget. I don't know what came first. Who was the one to stop kissing the other when they came home? Who was the first one to stop suggesting we go for walks?"

"Stop this, John. It's not healthy—the way you ruminate on this." Hayden put her hands up to her temple. "This won't put things back the way they were."

"Who's your boyfriend?"

"He's a lawyer—that's all I'm going to say."

"What's his name?"

Hayden waved her hands up in the air. "Forget it."

"What type of law? Is he your lawyer?"

Hayden seemed tired all of a sudden. "I'm not having this conversation with you."

The coffee finished brewing. Hayden didn't move, and so John got up and got out a mug that had Baywater Realty Co. printed on it, Hayden's employer, and poured a cup. He drank it black. John sat back down, looking at his cup of coffee. He took a sip, gripping the mug around the base. The coffee was suddenly unappealing, tasting of ash. He pushed the memories of the bazaar back down.

Neither Hayden nor John said anything for a while. John was content just to be in the presence of his ex-wife, to be in the same room as a warm, breathing body. He loved the familiarity of everything surrounding him—cupboard handles, the white tile, the granite counter, the tawny lighting.

Hayden spoke after a while. "You haven't made any support payments in over three months."

"Really? You should have reminded me."

Hayden raised her eyebrows. "Oh, so it's my problem?"

"No, but a friendly reminder."

"John, we haven't been friendly in years."

"Please, Hayden. I've had a bad day, and I don't want to think about that. Tell me about your day."

"My day? When have you ever cared about *my* day?"

"Come on, that's unfair."

"You want me to get my lawyer on your case?"

"The one you're dating?"

Hayden frowned. "I think you should go."

John took another sip of his coffee and then poured the rest down the sink. He placed the cup in the dishwasher. He turned and looked at Hayden, who had her hands crossed tightly across her chest. "I saw five people die today."

Hayden put her hand over her mouth and turned away, her slender shoulders hunched. "You can't just say that. It's so unfair, John. So unfair."

"I'm sorry … but I have nobody else to turn to."

Hayden shook her head. "What are you involved in now?"

"It was a gang thing."

"And now you're stuck in the middle. They're going to kill you next, John."

John reached out to touch Hayden's shoulder, but she slapped his hand away. John tried to reassure her. "I'll be fine."

"My God, John … You can't just run back to some safe zone. You think just because you're a journalist …"

"I don't think that, Hayden. I'll be careful. I promise."

"You told me you got out because it was a young man's game."

John nodded. "Yeah …"

"So … then why go back?"

"This isn't Afghanistan."

"No, this is worse. You don't have any protection here."

John said, "I'm going to say good-bye to Byron."

Hayden nodded curtly. "Be safe … I don't want a funeral."

John shot Hayden a look, but the day had been too long and he didn't want a fight. Instead, he went into the living room. Byron was sitting in the dark watching a cartoon show. John stood in the doorway, watching the television, trying to discern the plot, but as usual, he had trouble figuring out what was going on. There seemed to be a lot of fighting and killing.

John stood as if frozen, waiting to see if Byron would say something—because he couldn't think of anything. It struck John he didn't really know anything about his nine-year-old son. What did he like? What were his interests? What movies did he like? Did he hang out at the mall like his dad used to do? John didn't know. Finally, after seeing enough of the television show, he walked over to his son and looked down. "I'll see you soon, Byron. You should go to bed soon." John rustled his son's hair, but Byron didn't respond, not even a grunt. John frowned and walked out of the room and out of the house.

He called a taxi and waited in the cool summer night. He sat on the stone steps, pulling his knees up to his chin, looking out at the quiet, serene street. He wanted to go back inside and yell and shout and make a disturbance, something he had failed to do when he was married. But no, he had a hard time speaking harshly to Hayden.

The Mole

John took the clunky elevator up to the top floor. He had a copy of the *Daily Globe* tucked neatly under his arm; a picture of Ken Dzyinski was on the front page, with John's byline underneath. It was still early, and John had the elevator all to himself. He looked up, watching the numbers light up, thinking about a dream he had last night.

He was standing on a large, sandy, dusty street, possibly Baghdad. He was unable to move, and there was a boy standing several feet in front of him, just out of arm's reach. The boy was no older than Byron. He had on a dusty white shirt, sandals, red shorts, and a hat. Thick ropy hair was sticking out, uncontained by the hat. His face was smeared with blood and dirt. He was reaching out with one arm to John, crying out for help, but John was unable to move. His feet were planted, rooted to place like he was in cement. Suddenly the boy burst into flames. He dropped to his knees, writhing in pain, unable to extinguish the fire. And John was still unable to move, unable to help the boy. The only thing he could do was watch as the boy burned to death.

The elevator door chirped cheerfully and slid open. John walked out into the newsroom. He knocked on Charles Dana's office, but he was not there. John found Dana in the boardroom with five sectional editors, going over the day's stories.

John waited by the door as each editor in turn told Chuck the stories they had for that day; Chuck listened, his skinny legs crossed daintily, his long arms crossed against his chest. Chuck had on a blue tie, a red and green striped shirt, and a brown suit. He wore thick-rimmed glasses that gave him a slightly bug-eyed appearance.

Stilson Hutchins, the foreign editor, said, "We have that riot in Shanghai and that plane crash in Egypt.

"Okay, we will probably lead with the riots," Chuck said, and Hutchins scribbled it down on his notepad. Chuck then asked, "What else do we have?"

"Elections in Edmonton."

"Okay, that will probably jump onto page two," Chuck said. "How is the Tanner investigation going?"

Robert Smyllie shifted uncomfortably in his seat, looking down at his notes. "Not too good—not much new on that front."

"Okay, tell them to keep pressing. Something will come up."

Smyllie nodded. He looked somewhat relieved at not receiving a tongue-lashing.

Chuck adjourned the meeting, and the editors quickly dispersed. John approached Chuck, who was checking his e-mails on his phone.

"I need to see you," John said.

Chuck frowned, pocketing his phone. "Okay, in my office, but make it quick. I have a meeting in two minutes."

They walked to the end of the newsroom, where Chuck's office was. Chuck opened the door for John.

"Good article yesterday. You have a follow-up in mind?"

"That's what I wanted to talk to you about."

"Okay—but you should be talking to Smyllie."

John sat down opposite. He looked across at Chuck's desk, at the silver name tag that read "managing editor." During the first Gulf War, when John had been young and ambitious, he had looked up at the Baghdad night sky, smeared with luminous reds and oranges and yellows from the oil fires. He used to dream of becoming a publisher or an editor of a national newspaper, with the ability to reach minds across the country, to dictate the coffee-break conversation.

But John had given up dreaming long ago. He saw the political suaveness and the patience Charles Dana needed, and he knew he would never possess those qualities. He could not deal with the board of directors worrying about stock prices. He could not deal with the constant infighting from the Pommeroys—the family who owned much of the paper. As he grew older, John's restlessness didn't wither, and his nose hadn't turned any browner.

"Dzyinski's funeral is scheduled for Tuesday."

"Good. Who's taking over the Heart gang?"

"I think they're dead in the water."

Chuck put his hands together, his bushy eyebrows raised unconvinced. "Find out who the players are. There's always some hotshot with big ambitions."

"I want to find the shooters."

Chuck frowned. "You don't want to concentrate on the Heart gang?"

John looked down at his lap. He could feel the intense gaze of his boss on him. "They're yesterday's news. Ernest Hunter is taking over."

Ernest Hunter was Ken Dzyinski's big rival in the drug trade.

Chuck nodded. "You know Cochrane has a crime blog going?"

"So I've heard."

"A million hits last month. Why don't you have something going like that?"

John looked up. "I don't know.... A blog?"

"You need to start adapting, John. You're not old. You can still learn."

"A million hits?"

Chuck nodded solemnly, taking off his glasses and folding them before placing them on a stack of papers. John was certain Chuck just wore the glasses to look more editorial. "The police talk to you yet?"

John shrugged. "Yeah, a little bit."

"A Detective Wiltore phoned me. Seemed pretty eager to speak with you. Wanted me to phone him when you came in."

"What did he want?"

Chuck shrugged. "I'm guessing he wants to know how you knew about the meeting and he didn't. I want you to talk to Mack before the police, got it? He'll be able to tell you how to play this."

"Sure, Chuck."

In many ways, Charles Dana reminded John of his father: the same didactic tone, the same confidence, the same way they occupied space—sparingly yet with great force. Neither man was particularly abrasive or loud or obnoxious. But nobody forgot them at a party either.

John pursed his lips, pushing the thoughts of his father out of his mind and instead thinking back to what Hayden had said.

He said to his boss, "I almost got killed yesterday. I can't stop thinking about it … I don't know … I've had close calls before, but this time seems different."

Chuck nodded understandingly. He leaned forward, putting his bony elbows on his desk and cupping his hands together. "You're not as young as you once were back in Afghanistan and Iraq."

John frowned, confused. "What does that have to do with anything?"

"I think you've reached a stage in your life when you realize you're not invincible."

John shook his head. "No, I don't think it's that.… You know the Who song?… "Meet the new boss … same as the old boss."

"Sure."

"I feel like that has been my life. Regime change? Meet the new boss. Biggest gangster in the city gets gunned down? Meet the new boss. I can't seem to get it out of my mind."

Chuck flattened his moustache with one hand. "You want me to put Cochrane on this? She feels it's her story after all."

"No. No. I'm fine—I have things under control."

"You sure?"

John nodded, not really sure, but knowing if he said no, the story he worked so hard on would be swooped up from under him and given to Elizabeth Cochrane, who usually had the crime beat.

Chuck continued. "The police will probably subpoena you for your notes. I don't think this detective mucks around, so be prepared."

"No problem, boss."

"I need to see results, Webster," Chuck said. "If I don't, Cochrane is going on it, okay?"

"Okay, boss."

John left the office, but instead of going back to his desk, he went downstairs and across the street to a pay phone. He looked around at the cars as they slowly made their way up Granville Street. The sun was climbing slowly in the milky-white sky and shining an incandescent light that hit the sidewalks and reflected off the passing traffic. The rain was gone, and there was no trace of puddles anywhere.

John watched as people passed by, but none of them seemed to pay him much attention. Was he being paranoid? Maybe, but after his conversation with Chuck, he was feeling a little on edge.

He slotted three quarters into the phone and dialled a number he knew by heart. A croaky, boozy voice answered.

"Drake? It's John."

Drake McMillan was his informant in the Heart gang.

"I have nothing to say to you," Drake said. There was a click and then a dial tone. John cursed and fed another seventy-five cents into the machine and dialled again.

"Drake—listen. You want me to go to the police?"

There was a pause. Then Drake said, "What do you want?"

"What happened? It turned into a goddamn Wild West shootout."

"Fuck if I know."

"Did you tell anybody else?"

"No, why would I?"

"You told Hunter, didn't you?"

"That's a lie. Did you hear that somewhere? It's complete lie." There was panic in Drake's voice.

"There was a leak somewhere."

"Not from my end."

John was still surveying the street for anything strange, not really sure what he expected to see. "Dzyinski is going to kill Hunter, but Hunter strikes first. A strange coincidence."

"Like I said, I know nothing about it."

"You wanted me to see that. Why?"

"The only reason I told you is because you ride my ass. You're fucking bad for business, John."

"Can we meet?"

"I can't be seen with you. There's a whole bunch of heat on now."

"How did you find out?"

"Anthony Jung let it slip while he was high."

"Who else was there?"

"Nobody, just me and Anthony."

"Who's going to take over now?"

"I don't know—everything is in disarray right now. Nobody knows which way is up."

"You tell me once you hear something, okay?"

"Fine."

John put the phone back down on the receiver. He looked around once more, feeling skittish—almost as if he was back in Afghanistan—before reentering the Globe building.

The *Daily Globe* was part of Dominion News Corporation, which was primarily owned by the Pommeroy family. The Pommeroys were one of Canada's oldest, largest, and most powerful families.

John was thankful he had only met one of the Pommeroys—an unmemorable man at an unmemorable function. Oxford educated. A rowing champion. He was a cousin or something of the great John Pommeroy. Charles Dana, of course, had introduced them. John had made polite conversation for a few moments before returning to his slightly more vulgar, slightly more uncouth colleagues.

John stepped into the elevator, wondering if he should be more cautious. Hayden was right: there was no safety zone he could disappear into. No bodyguards here.

John ran into Elizabeth Cochrane in the hallway. She was dressed in a dark suit and dark stockings, her platinum-blonde hair tied up into a tight ponytail; her skin was pale as a ghost's. Her large eyes were liquid blue and convex. She had on perfectly applied blood-red lipstick, giving herself a vampire look.

John gave her a thin smile. "You trying to steal my story from me?"

"I have contacts. What do you have?"

"I have the story—only thing that matters."

Liz shrugged as if to concede, but John knew her better than that. "Who's your source?" she asked.

"Why? So you can write about it on your blog?"

"Everybody and their pet has a blog, John. Why are you so resistant?"

"Because it's not real journalism."

"Tell that to the person who gets all their news from their iPhone."

"I hear anything about my story on your blog, I will get you fired. You understand that?"

Liz grunted and sauntered away. John watched her go before heading back to his desk. He phoned Mack's office and got his secretary.

"Could you tell him to give me a call when he gets in?" John asked, hanging up.

John worked the phones for a couple of hours. He phoned everybody he could think of in connection to Dzyinski—police, gangsters, family members. Nobody wanted to talk. Calls to the Dzyinski residence went unanswered. The phone just kept ringing and ringing. John thought it strange there was no voice mail.

John typed up what Drake had said—not much, but he did his best to turn it into a story. He then took his Olympus voice recorder out from his drawer and placed it on his desk. He stared at it, running his hands through his hair. He had been putting the recorder off, but he knew eventually he would have to listen to it. He plugged in his earphones and played the last few moments of Ken Dzyinski's life.

Most of it was a jumbled mess of undistinguishable noise, with the occasional voice cutting through.

What was the last thing Dzyinski said?

John stopped the recorder and rewound it several seconds. He said something about the Findley brothers … who were they? John had never heard of them before.

John got up and walked over to Liz's desk. She was concentrating on her screen, typing away furiously. He stopped suddenly and listened. Liz wasn't the only one typing; the entire newsroom was pounding keyboards. The hard *click, click, click* reverberated off the pillars, the walls, the floor. Everyone was trying to meet deadlines.

John said, "Hey, Liz … I apologize about what I said earlier. I'm under a lot of stress."

Liz didn't look up. "Hey, look around you. Fucking everybody is stressed."

John looked around at the faces in the cubicles, staring at their tawny computer lights. Liz was right: everybody had their teeth clamped tight, their eyes squinted, their backs hunched over.

John frowned. He didn't like to apologize twice, but this time he needed to suck up his pride. "Okay, I'm sorry."

"Some friendly competition never hurt anybody."

John took a deep breath. "What do you want from me?"

"For you to stop being such an asshole."

"Okay, fine … your wish is granted. Now I need some information."

"Sorry, John, I'm on deadline. Come back later."

"You heard of the Findley brothers before?"

Liz stopped typing and swung her chair around, looking intently at John. "You know the boss. He's kind of prone to exaggerating things."

John, who had never known Chuck to ever exaggerate anything, grunted in flat incredulity. "You always thought you were better than me—all you j-school graduates do."

Liz tilted her head. John tried hard not to admire the bone work of her neck. She gave him a supercilious smile. "Oh, come on now, just because I'm younger, more adaptive, and learned … but you know how to actually write."

John struggled to remain calm—hard for him considering the circumstances. "I actually decided I don't need your help. There's this thing called Google, you see." John turned and walked back to his desk.

"Oh, come on, John," Liz called after him. "It's a fucker of a story. You think you can handle it?"

"See, I'm adapting!" John yelled across the room at her.

Liz got up and went over to John's desk. "Come on, I've been on this beat for seven years. Just admit it. You need me."

"It's my story, Liz. My contacts. I grew this thing from the ground up."

Liz bit the bottom of her lip. "What ship are you on, John? This isn't some fucking harbour cruise. It's a man-of-war. You got one good story. Good fucking job. I'm happy for you. But now you have to do the legwork over again, and I'm saying you need an extra pair."

"Who are the Findley brothers?"

"You mean Thomas and Jeffery Findley? They own a garage on Second and Main. Tough fuckers. Run with the Dzyinski crowds. Allegedly Dzyinski's top hit men—although never been proven, of course. I think they spent some time in jail for B&E but not too sure."

"I suppose Dzyinski doesn't need them anymore. What do you suppose they're up to now?"

Liz shrugged. "Your guess is as good as mine. Probably scrambling right now."

Around three o'clock, John popped into Smyllie's office and told him he was going out to get a quick bite to eat and to follow up on some leads.

"What do you got, Webster?" Smyllie asked.

John told him about the Findley brothers.

Smyllie frowned. "You'll be okay? You want me to send somebody with you—at least a photographer or something?"

"No, I'll be fine. I'm going to their garage. I'm sure it's okay."

Smyllie nodded, not reassured. "Okay, just check in with me when you get back. So I know you're safe."

John parked across the street from the garage on Second Avenue. He locked his car and walked into the office. It was small and cramped. The neon light flickered overhead. A man with a scruffy, unkempt beard was eating McDonalds on the counter.

"Can I help you?" he asked through a mouthful of hamburger, dripping ketchup on the counter.

"My name is John Webster. I'm a journalist for the *Daily Globe*. I'm looking for the Findley brothers."

The man swallowed and took another bite from his hamburger. "Man, you don't go looking for the Findley brothers."

"Why not?"

The man shrugged, looking away.

"Look," John said. "Are they around? I need to talk to them."

The man shook his head.

John leaned on the counter looking around the office. There was a beaten-up door behind the counter, and John wondered where it went and if the Findley brothers were hiding out back there. He sighed, trying hard not to appear frustrated, but he was getting nowhere. "When will they be back?"

"They come and go, depending," the man said. "Now if you don't mind, I need to get back to work."

John took out his card and put it on the counter. "Do me a favour and tell the brothers I want to talk to them about Ernest Hunter."

The man glanced down at John's card, but didn't touch it. "Okay," he said dubiously. "But if you knew what was good for you, you would take that card and put it back into your pocket."

John smiled and turned toward the door. "Have a nice day."

Investigation

Detective Wiltore slammed the phone down. He was sure Charles Dana was screening his calls. He phoned Webster's line again, but predictably, got no answer.

"Hi, you've reached John Webster, reporter for the *Daily Globe*; please leave me a message."

Wiltore slammed the phone a second time and turned to his new partner, Detective Tamara Lewis, and said, "Let's just go down there. I'm sick of this shit."

Lewis nodded once and stood up. Wiltore was unable to tell what she was thinking, and he didn't like that in a partner. She was wearing black pants, a man's oxford shirt, and a thin headband that kept her long, thin hair in place. Wiltore, for the past month, had tried to figure out what he didn't like about her and had come to the conclusion it was because she didn't look like a cop. She was too small and too cute, her face was too round, and her voice was too high-pitched. Wiltore, who had a cop's thick neck and a father and an uncle who were in the force, had grown up around cops.

"Unless you have a better idea? I'm open to suggestions," Wiltore said testily. He was feeling tired and was in the mood to pick a fight.

Lewis, however, wasn't having any of it. She shrugged and said, "No, it'll be good to meet John Webster anyways."

They grabbed their jackets and headed to the elevator.

So far their investigation wasn't going very well. Forensics had been up and down the barn, but hadn't found much physical evidence—nothing helpful anyways. These hit men were professionals. That was clear.

The barn and surrounding six-acre property were owned by Anthony Jung, one of the gangsters who had died in the gunfight. His wife, Tiffany, had been in the house four hundred yards away, having a bath, halfway through a bottle of wine and listening to her iPod—or so she claimed. Wiltore had wasted hours knocking on the neighbours' doors, but nobody professed to having seen or heard anything.

A burned-out Honda Civic, presumably the one used as a getaway car, had been found under the 232 Street underpass, several kilometres from the barn. By the time the firefighters had gotten to the scene, there wasn't much left of the car, and lifting prints from it had proven fruitless.

Wiltore had run the licence plate and found the car had been reported stolen by a Larry Field two days ago in downtown Vancouver. Not a big surprise.

Wiltore was intrigued by the getaway car: burning it was unusual in a targeted shooting. Gangsters usually weren't so sophisticated; usually they ended up quickly dumping the cars in a mall or a car impound. These gangsters were calm, collected, cool. They knew what they were doing and didn't panic.

As they walked to their unmarked Ford, Wiltore wondered if organized crime was getting smarter, or if these hit men were a new, special breed. Either way it didn't bode well for the investigation.

The only other substantial lead was the .45 ACP cartridges the gunmen had used. They were, as Wiltore expected, wiped clean of prints before being littered all over the barn floor. The cartridges were common enough, probably coming from a Heckler & Koch submachine gun; such guns were, unfortunately, easily obtainable and were used by many police and armed forces around the world.

Wiltore unlocked the door, and Lewis walked around to the passenger seat. She sat cross-legged, head rested against her seat back. There was an unspoken rule: Wiltore always drove. The car was old—the alternator had just been replaced—and needed a good vacuuming. Soda cans and plastic Dasani bottles littered the floor.

Wiltore's old partner, Marcus King, had taken early retirement to work in security management down in Arizona. They had worked together for over five years clearing cases, and they were good at it. Wiltore had begged Marcus not to do it, but he could not be persuaded from a pension, the constant sun, and a lackadaisical lifestyle. Wiltore's heart sank when Marcus was replaced by Tamara Lewis, who had just transferred to Integrated Gang Task Force.

Wiltore took the car out of the garage, and they drove over the Cambie Street Bridge, past the recently remodelled B. C. Place, an imposing structure shaped like a giant crown, behind it a canvas of blue sky. Wiltore was hoping to get away to a few more B. C. Lions games this year, but it was tough with his work schedule and his wife really wasn't much of a football fan. He used to go with Marcus. They turned right, down Seymour, and stalled in a little bit of traffic. The sun lit the sky up, reflecting down on to the pavement. Along the sidewalk were trash cans overflowing with garbage, beginning to rot and stink.

Wiltore sighed, looking into the rearview mirror as the cars lined up behind him. They were wasting their time. *If only Dana was cooperative,* he thought.

Lewis turned toward him. "You play last week?"

There was an intersquad soccer game played every Tuesday night at the UBC gym. It was not much more than a beer leaguer really, but a bunch of the IGTF guys had gotten a team together. They had yet to ask Lewis to play, and Wiltore wondered if this was her way of trying to get them to include her.

Wiltore gave a tight smile. "Beat them 17–0."

Last week had seemed so long ago, ages ago—before the biggest criminal organization on the West Coast of Canada had been crippled. Wiltore knew what this meant, of course: more bloodshed was to come, as now all the other two-bit criminal organizations would jockey for position in the drug hierarchy.

Lewis frowned. "Who did you play?"

Wiltore shrugged. "I don't know—some traffic cops, I think."

"My boyfriend is a traffic cop."

Wiltore found a parking spot right at the foot of Granville Street. "There we go. Rock star parking." Wiltore paused outside to light a cigarette. He put away his lighter and inhaled, feeling the smoke burn in his lungs.

Lewis shook her head. "I don't understand how you can smoke and play soccer at the same time."

Wiltore smiled. "Well, I don't do it at the same time …"

A flash of annoyance passed through Lewis's eyes. "You know what I mean."

"You know, I didn't actually take it up until I became a detective. Passed the exam and got paired with Marcus. He was a big smoker, and for some reason, it only seemed natural that I started." Wiltore paused for a moment to reminisce. "We spent a lot of time together. Cracked a lot of tough cases."

Wiltore extinguished his cigarette on the pavement and, with Lewis, went inside. They took the elevator up. The cables groaned as if they were about to snap.

Lewis looked nervously at the floor, as if it was going to give from under them. "You couldn't have let up after, say, 10–0?"

Wiltore looked at his partner in surprise. "You still thinking about that? Was your boyfriend on the team?"

Lewis shrugged. "I'm just thinking how much it would suck losing 17–0."

Wiltore tucked his thumbs into his belt, staring at Lewis. "I can't believe you would date a traffic cop. There's no excitement in traffic."

Lewis nodded. "No drama either. I like it that way."

Wiltore grunted just as the doors slid open to the large newsroom. For a moment he felt overwhelmed by the energy of the floor. Gangly, unfit people were running down the aisles with pens, paper, and books. There was a full-blown argument going on in the corner of the newsroom— about what Wiltore couldn't understand. And over this, CNN was blaring loudly.

The secretary pointed the two detectives to Webster's desk. Webster was a tall, broad-shouldered man with short dark hair. He wore whitewashed jeans and a white collared shirt, wrinkled and a little threadbare. Wiltore studied him critically. He was boyishly handsome, with large, dark, mischievous eyes.

Oh, he certainly has his secrets, Wiltore thought.

Wiltore introduced himself and Lewis. Webster smiled thinly, as if he was trying to mask something, shaking both their hands with a strong, powerful grip.

"How's the investigation?" Webster asked, sitting casually back down in his chair.

"We have a few leads," Wiltore said, holding the journalist's gaze.

Lewis said, "You mind taking a ride down to the station with us? We'd like to ask you a few questions."

Webster leaned back in his chair, staring up at them with almost a Medusa-like stare. "If you don't mind, I have a deadline."

"Actually we do mind," Wiltore said, irritated. "We also have a deadline."

Wiltore expected Webster to protest a little more, but instead he just nodded and said, "Let me phone my lawyer first."

"You don't really need a lawyer," Lewis said. "We just want to ask a few questions."

"I feel it would be best," Webster said, dialling.

Lewis frowned. "You have something to hide?"

But Webster wasn't paying attention. He was talking to somebody on the phone. "Yes, just get him to come down when he gets back … thanks."

The car ride was a silent one. Webster rode in the backseat. When Wiltore stopped at red lights, he glanced up at the rearview mirror, watching Webster, who had one elbow against the window and was staring out at the sidewalk lost in thought.

Lewis was the first one to break the silence. "You wrote that book about Thomas Ronkin, didn't you?"

Thomas Ronkin was a convicted serial killer who preyed on prostitutes from the Downtown Eastside, Vancouver's poorest neighbourhood. Although not directly involved, Wiltore remembered the case well. It was a failure of all levels of government and police forces.

Webster turned his head to look at Lewis. "You read it?"

"A long time ago," she said, smiling shyly, showing big white teeth. "It was a good book … thoughtful."

Webster asked, "You guys the lead on Dzyinski now?"

They turned into the police garage, driving down a ramp. "That's right."

They parked the car and got out. They took the elevator up to the second floor and then passed along a series of narrow, low-ceiling hallways. Webster had to stoop to pass. They arrived at the interrogation room, which was bleak-looking, with only a small overhanging light. Wiltore closed the door behind them. Webster sat down casually, barely looking around. Wiltore could tell this guy would be tough to break. "I did some research on you," he said.

Webster shoved his hands in his jean pockets. "Please, tell me what you found out."

"Your father, John Webster Senior, was killed in a car accident when you were seventeen. Shortly after, you dropped out of school and got a job at Reuters. You've covered a number of wars—both Gulf Wars, Afghanistan ... I even heard you chartered a plane—using your own money—to fly into some African country."

Webster stared back at Wiltore. "I flew to Khartoum."

"Where?"

"It's the capital of Sudan," Webster said, fixing his gaze on Wiltore.

Wiltore shrugged, dismissing it. "We have a few questions to ask you."

"Not before my lawyer gets here."

Wiltore unbuttoned his jacket, folded it once, and placed it on the corner of the table.

"You really want to play it this way?" Wiltore asked. "Our jobs are hard already. Why make them harder?"

"Let's just say I would feel more comfortable."

They waited. Wiltore went and got some coffee from the vending machine in the hallway. It tasted bitter and stale, but he drank it anyways.

Eventually Mack Carrington arrived. He wore orange pants and an orange pullover vest. He was in his mid-fifties, with faded reddish hair, a few wrinkles around his mouth and eyes. He moved to greet the two detectives with a slight waddle.

Wiltore frowned, puzzled over the lawyer's attire.

"Sorry, I was on the golf course when I got the call," Mack said.

"Can we just get on with this?" Webster asked.

Mack sat his hefty body next to Webster. He was a slightly ridiculous-looking figure, and Wiltore wondered how this clownish man ever became the leading expert on libel.

Mack turned to the police officers. "Why is my client in an interrogation room? Is he a suspect?"

Lewis shook her head. "No, it was just a quiet spot where he can talk in private."

"What's this all about?"

"The Dzyinski murder. Your client was at the barn where it happened."

Lewis sat on the edge of the table, leaning her small body forward, looking at Webster. "I know you already gave your statement to the RCMP, but can you run us through it? Even the smallest detail can be helpful."

Webster told them how he had hidden up in the loft and saw two masked men enter with machine guns.

"You didn't hear a car approach?" Wiltore asked.

Webster shook his head. "No, I guess they parked near the street and walked up to the barn."

Lewis looked over at Wiltore. "That might explain why they were wearing masks. In case a neighbour looked out the window."

Wiltore nodded, wondering how these two men in broad daylight had not been seen by anybody. He supposed when you lived next to gangsters, you learned to turn a blind eye. "How did you know about the meeting?"

"I have a source."

"Who?"

Webster shook his head. "Sorry, I can't tell you that."

Wiltore glared at Webster, wondering what his breaking point was. "Somebody inside of the Heart gang—must be."

"I'm a journalist. I have to protect my sources."

Wiltore stood up. "Even if your sources are no-good scumbags?"

Webster nodded, his eyes large and cold. "*Especially* if they're no-good scumbags."

Wiltore frowned and started to pace the room, but after several laps stopped abruptly. He wasn't thinking. He wasn't being very smart about this interrogation. He turned to Webster. "I'm certain you know who killed Dzyinski or have evidence that could lead to an arrest and conviction. Either way, you're in my way of catching these criminals."

"My reputation is at stake here. If I give up my sources, I might as well become a corporate lackey."

Wiltore sighed, sitting back down. He and Lewis had been chasing these guys for almost three days straight with little sleep, and he was beginning to feel the effects. He decided to try a different tactic. "You were shot in the leg in Afghanistan, weren't you?"

Mack spoke up first. "What does that have to do with anything?"

Webster frowned, putting a hand on the lawyer's shoulder. "It's okay … Yes, I got caught in a battle with the Taliban."

"Wouldn't you like to see the person who shot you brought to justice? Made to stand up in court?"

Webster seemed to shrink in his chair, and Wiltore felt he was finally getting through to him. But, instead, Webster shook his head. "No, I wouldn't … It was war."

Wiltore was confused. "Yet you were an innocent bystander. There's a reason we have international laws."

Webster looked down at the table. "I don't blame them for shooting me—not really. A war correspondent's job is not to bring anybody to justice for anything … it's as a recorder, a sort of mediator."

Wiltore sighed, taking a slow sip of his coffee. He didn't really understand what Webster was saying about being a mediator, and he didn't really care either. "Let me ask you this then … you have some sort of death wish?"

Webster tilted his head. "Why do you say that?"

"Because unless we catch them soon, they will kill you."

Mack half-raised his large body off his seat. "Are you threatening my client?"

"No, just stating a fact—but I don't need to remind him." Wiltore turned to look at Webster, who sat emotionless in his chair. "He knows that already."

"You know how many people were killed during the Sudan civil war?" Webster asked.

"I'll ask the questions," Wiltore snapped, growing irritated at getting nowhere with this interrogation.

Webster shrugged and looked down at the ground.

Wiltore said, "I'll give one last chance to answer my question."

"I'm not giving up my source."

Wiltore drained the rest of his coffee and sat back in his chair. There was a long pause. "We'll put you in police protection. You can't survive out there by yourself."

Mack said, "Are you trying to bribe my client?"

Webster looked straight at Wiltore. "Are we done here? Because I really do have a deadline I need to meet."

"If you want me to do it the hard way, I can," Wiltore said. "I will get a subpoena, drag you in front of a judge. And then you will hand over your notes, I can guarantee that."

Webster sat undaunted. "Do what you must, but I'm not giving you my source."

Wiltore tried not to appear desperate or frustrated. "You'll have no choice."

Mack stood up, signalling Webster to follow him. Webster stood up to his full height, towering over everyone. He looked at the two cops, his eyes deep and intense. "Two million," he said.

Wiltore looked at him. "Sorry?"

"Two million," he repeated. "Two million were killed in the Sudan civil war."

Wiltore opened his mouth to respond, but couldn't think of anything to say.

After Mack and Webster left, Lewis got up, surveying the one-way glass. "Well, that could have gone getter."

Wiltore shrugged. "He'll break ... he has to. Otherwise he'll end up like Dzyinski."

The Funeral

The priest was dressed in a dark suit, his tie forgettable. Truth be told, he didn't look much like a priest, maybe a downtrodden salesman, down on his luck. He had thinning greyish hair and a round wrinkled face. His hands and legs were neatly pressed together in a pose of solemn regard. He read from the Old Testament. "To everything there is a season, and a time to every purpose under the heaven," he said in a deep, harmonious voice that echoed throughout the church.

Above, the sun spilled over the rafters, through the stained-glass windows, and on to the pulpit, sending luminous shards on to the mourners, dressed all in black.

John sat in the back, between two bulky women with chunky thighs and droopy cheeks. They were crying, tissues pressed to their faces. John wondered who they were and their relation to Ken Dzyinski. John supposed even callous, malevolent men had someone to weep over them.

Dzyinski's picture was up front, propped on a stand in a wood-tarnished frame. He was younger, handsomer there than in actual life. His hair was cropped short, and he had a supercilious smile on his thin lips. Strangely, he was wearing a black and white tuxedo. *Maybe the photograph was from his wedding*, John thought.

There seemed no mention of a criminal menace, no mention of his killing, of his breaking bones, of selling drugs to addicts. If John listened to the speakers, Dzyinski was a perfect citizen, holding a nine-to-five job at a construction company.

John shifted his weight between the women, his tall muscular frame feeling squashed and confined. He looked down the aisle at all the different people collected together. There in one corner were Dzyinski's parents, trying their best to appear stoic and pragmatic; and over in the other corner was Dzyinski's wife. She was probably in her mid-forties, beautiful and slim, atomic blonde; and next to her were her two boys, sharply dressed, hair all matted down by gel and neatly parted with razorlike precision.

John stared at the backs of the two boys. They sat tall, rigid, almost emotionless. A life of drugs and murder had left these two boys fatherless. John had been a little older when he had lost his father—a car accident in the snow, a drunk driver coming from a New Year's party.

John remembered the funeral vividly. He remembered his mother wore the pearls his father had given her for her birthday. He remembered the oak floorboards. He remembered afterward, at home, looking at the family album. His mother was in her room sobbing.

As he flipped through the pictures, John thought he hadn't really known his father. Look, there was a younger version of John Webster Senior sitting on a Parisian park bench, the Eiffel Tower a sublime backdrop; and look, there he was in the first apartment he owned; and look, there was an out-of-focus composition of the hefty Scotsman in the bleak *Times of London* newsroom. Life, it seemed, only amounted to a series of snapshots.

John turned his attention back to the priest. He felt out of place, an impostor. He didn't belong among the grievers, but he felt a great journalistic need to record this immense seismic process. It was a togetherness of people so unlike anything else—a strange spectacle if one really thought about it, one that only the extinguishing of a life could produce.

"A time to kill, a time to heal, a time to break down, and a time to build."

Eventually the funeral ended, and the crowd shuffled slowly out the front door. John sought shade underneath the branches of a pine tree. The bright summer sun and fluorescent green grass were incongruent to the dark, mournful atmosphere inside the church.

John watched as the steady throngs piled out, a tidal wave of sorrow, as people dissipated toward their cars and on with their lives. Dzyinski's wife appeared at the doorway, reeking of spray-on beauty and wearing white balancing-act stilettos, clutching her two sons by their elbows, a determined look on her face. Maybe she just wanted to forget.

Police presence wasn't far off. They milled around restlessly across the street, monstrous zoom lens at the ready. They took pictures of everybody, prepping them for profile. John didn't doubt that his image was being filed away somewhere.

The press corps was out in force too, adding to the muddled chaos, circling like sharks in a feeding frenzy. They surrounded Dzyinski's wife and children, but the Dzyinski family strode stoically on.

That was when John saw Ernest Hunter appear from the church. He was together with about half a dozen hoodlums. John didn't have to have particularly keen eyes to recognize them as dangerous men, tall, powerful, and purposeful. All the reporters left Dzyinski's wife and swarmed Hunter, but his hoodlums shoved all the cameras and microphones aside.

Strange—John hadn't noticed Hunter or his posse inside. John watched them as they looked around with an aggressive alertness before heading toward the parking lot. Hunter was clandestinely talking to a tall, squarely-set man, their chins close together. The cameras snapped open and shut, open and shut in rapid progression, lapping it all in, *click, click, click.*

Meet the new boss … same as the old boss. He was different than Ken Dzyinski, not so muscular, and except for his posse maybe—not so inauspicious. Yet their demeanours weren't far off from each other—their bitterness, their anger at the world displayed plainly on their shoulders.

The reporters had moved on to somebody else, one of the other luckless mourners, and John had a split second to decide what to do; but before his mind fully processed the pros and cons, his legs were in full gear. "Mr. Hunter?" he yelled.

The entourage stopped abruptly. All eyes pivoted toward John, the lone figure, somehow different from all the other reporters. Hands went inside jackets; feet galvanized for action.

John put his palms up. He didn't want to be shot by an overly jumpy gangster. "John Webster from the *Daily Globe.* I just want to talk to you for a second."

Up close, Ernest Hunter was no more than five feet, with a round face with pale, flecked skin. He was wearing a black suit and grey tie. His face narrowed as he studied John. One of the henchmen whispered something to Hunter.

"You were the one inside the barn, weren't you?" Hunter asked.

John nodded, suddenly unsure of what he was trying to accomplish.

"Then you saw who killed Dzyinski?"

John looked sideways toward the platoon of police, unsure of what to say, but his mouth acted before he had time to think it through. "Yeah, I saw them. I know they were your men."

Hunter smiled. It was an ominous smile that reached no further than the tips of his cheeks. "You a gambler, Mr. Webster?"

"You mean cards?"

"I mean cards, slots, horses, dogs, fights, hockey."

John shook his head. "I wouldn't call myself a gambling man."

Hunter nodded. "But you do gamble, don't you? Not being a gambling man isn't the same as not gambling."

John shrugged, wondering where this was going. "I suppose I do gamble on occasion, Mr. Hunter."

Hunter smiled again, showing a row of yellowish teeth. "It's Ernie."

One of Hunter's henchmen whispered something into his ear again, but Hunter waved him off. "I thought so, Mr. Webster. You look like a gambler. I pride myself on being able to spot one, size people up, read them. I can always tell a gambler when I see one. I say, 'There goes a gambler—someone who doesn't play it safe.'"

John looked at Hunter's posse, who were looking around at the police toward the parking lot. They were obviously getting antsy, and this made John nervous. "Can I ask you a few questions, Ernie? About Dzyinski?"

"Sure, come take a ride. I have a meeting I need to go to." Hunter nodded toward his SUV.

"I'm not going anywhere with you."

Hunter smirked. "Why not?"

"You know why."

This seemed to amuse Hunter. "You don't think you're safe? The police just a shout away?"

"Did you kill Ken Dzyinski?"

Hunter shook his head. "You disappoint me there. I thought you knew how to play it close."

"Where can I find you?"

"I have a place, a casino out in Richmond called Andromeda. I'm usually there. You may—I don't know—go home lucky."

Hunter laughed loudly and abruptly, showing his large teeth again. He then turned away. His posse followed him. They all got into large black SUVs with military-like precision.

John watched them go. The last gangster to climb in was an ugly man, pock-faced with a flat nose and Spock-like ears. He turned just as he was closing the door and looked at John. He pointed his index finger and cocked back his thumb into an imaginary gun. He smiled and then pressed his thumb down, firing an imaginary bullet. He laughed, closing the door behind him.

The engines came to life, a powerful ripple of noise. The SUVs sped out of the parking lot and down the street, turning left onto the main drag. John wondered where they were going, what appointment they had to keep. John stuck his own hands in his pockets and looked over at his mushroom-coloured Toyota, briefly contemplating following them but realizing they were too far ahead.

John unlocked his door. It whined as he opened it. He sat there, his head resting against his seat, his old car smelling of stale crackers, wondering where he was going with this story. What chance did he have of catching Ernest Hunter? The police had all their resources and all their manpower, and even they weren't smart enough to put Hunter behind bars.

The church had emptied out now, and the police and the press were beginning to pack away their things and leave too. John watched them dissipate. He should go too, he thought. He had his own story to write, but he didn't feel like going back to the office quite yet. So he sat there, not really thinking about the time, but knowing every second he sat motionless was one less second he had to finish his story.

Something made him look back at the church. A tall woman dressed in a white coat had just closed the wooden door behind her. She looked around, as if she was expecting to see someone or something, before walking hastily toward the parking lot. John watched her. She was beautiful and thin, with wispy brown hair—a jagged, knotted mess held together by a gazillion hairpins. She walked past John without noticing him sitting in the driver's seat. She got into her own car, a navy-blue Ford Fusion.

John suddenly sprang into action. Dashing across the parking lot, he tapped on the window. She looked at him startled, a hand creeping up to her chest before recovering. She then leaned over and rolled down the passenger window.

"Have a pair of jumper cables?" John asked.

"Jumper cables? ... Uh, no, don't think so," she said in a soft voice.

John pointed his finger back to his car. "I think I left my lights on ... now my battery is dead. You mind giving me a lift?"

The woman frowned, her cheeks colouring. "I don't know—I'm kind of in a rush." The woman glanced sideways in embarrassment. It was obviously a lie.

"Just to a bus stop? I'm going downtown. You can drop me off anywhere."

The woman looked toward the road, knowing she was trapped. "Okay, sure. Get in."

John opened the door and climbed in. The car smelled strongly of lavender perfume.

"John Webster."

The woman looked over at John, as if still unsure of this foreign presence in her car, but finally said, "Michelle Lake."

Michelle turned onto the road. John watched her drive. She had several silver earrings on her right ear. "You knew Ken well?" John asked.

"No, not really. Went to school together."

John frowned. It was obviously another lie, but this time she tried to cover it up by saying, "He was ... in my brother's grade—they were friends."

John watched her reaction closely. "Your brother didn't come?"

"No ... They fell out of touch."

"But you stayed?"

"I don't know ... Not really."

There was something reserved about Michelle—that went without saying, but there was also something more than that. She spoke in a quiet, songbird voice. And she seemed to be privy to many secrets. Why John thought this, he didn't know, but it had something to do with her sharp cheekbones and dark eyes.

John looked at her and said, "I don't understand."

"I just thought … I don't know," she said in one exasperated breath. "How did *you* know Ken?"

"Worked with him, construction."

Michelle didn't say anything after that, but looked straight ahead, her jaw clenched.

John drew in a lungful of air and held it, knowing he had to ask the next question. "How did you *really* know him?"

Michelle slowed down, tightening her grip on the steering wheel. "What are you saying?"

"I'm saying I think you're lying to me."

Michelle frowned. "You don't even know me."

"I'm good at spotting liars."

Michelle pulled over to the side of the road. "You're a cop, aren't you? You look like a cop."

John suppressed a laugh. "A cop? No."

"Please get out of my car," Michelle said, looking down at the dash.

"Come on; don't be like that."

"What's it to you anyways—how I know him?"

"Nothing really—just interested."

"Get out of my car."

John got out and closed the door. He watched as she turned back into traffic, cutting off a truck. John stared thoughtfully for a moment before calling a cab.

Ernest Hunter

The house looked like the White House. It was east-facing and looked very presidential with its white columns, ornate windowsills, turn-of-the-century American-colonial style. In some ways, this house was the president's house—except he was the leader of the underworld, not the free world.

John was in the middle of Shaughnessy, one of the most expensive pieces of real estate in Vancouver per square inch. He stared out at the immaculate green lawn, the rows of colourful rhododendrons, and the immense wrought-iron gate.

John hated stakeouts. When he had been young, he had romanticized them. He had always imagined himself at his best waiting for somebody to appear—something to happen. But now there was always just too much time to think. Now John liked to be at the computer typing out his story, minutes before deadline. Then there was no time to wonder about Hayden, about Byron, about the little boy who haunted his dreams.

John crossed his arms and leaned back in the tanned leather seat. The car smelled of leather cleaner. The mats were freshly vacuumed, leaving no remnants of the previous driver. He had rented a Lexus for the morning. Nobody would believe an old rust-speckled Toyota had any business parking on the winding roads of Shaughnessy, with Hollywoodesque boulevards and tall elm trees casting jagged shadows.

An aqua-coloured Ferrari sped past. John couldn't see the driver through the dark windows, but he worried he had been there too long already. Would somebody call the cops? How would he explain that to Wiltore and Lewis? He imagined himself back in the bleak interrogation room, staring at the one-way mirror, the weary reflection of himself.

The morning passed uneventfully. Very little of substance occurred on Angus Drive: A woman in tight whitewashed jeans walked by towing a white Bolognese, a man in a charcoal-grey suit came out to check his mail, a chequered taxi drove slowly down the street as if looking for an address.

At ten thirty, the gate to Ernest Hunter's house swung open, and two black SUVs floored it out of the driveway. John was almost caught off guard. He fumbled with the ignition, afraid he was going to lose them. His car grumbled to life. He pressed down on the gas, lurching not so subtly into action.

They went around Shaughnessy Park, turning off onto Tecumseh Avenue. Would they notice they were being followed? John dropped back several car lengths just to be sure. He nervously watched as the two SUVs came to a stoplight. John was three cars back. He tapped nervously on the dashboard and fiddled with the radio dial.

He followed the SUVs as they went east on Twelfth Avenue until they reached Commercial Drive. There they turned left, down the Drive. The large vehicles stopped several blocks down, and Ernest Hunter and his posse jumped out and went into a coffee shop appropriately called Don's.

John found a parking spot around the corner in a residential area lined with old wooden houses with large covered decks. Commercial Drive was an interesting mix of hippies, Italians, pot smokers, South American immigrants, and Rastafarians. In the 1800s, it used to be the main Vancouver business district, but now it was the artistic hub for young painters and writers.

John found a vantage point on the street opposite Don's. He could see Ernest Hunter and his gang in the corner of the coffee shop. Hunter seemed much too casual and relaxed. John waited. He knew he couldn't get too close and risk being seen.

A fat, earthy-skinned Italian wearing a black apron—possibly Don himself—came over and shook hands with Hunter. They talked for several minutes. Hunter laughed, and then the Italian waddled away.

Then John saw a familiar figure walk quickly from around the corner and step into the coffee shop. John knew the man well: Drake McMillan, his informant. Drake was certainly not pretty to look at. He was short, hollow, pedestrian-looking, working class through and through. His head was slightly egg-shaped, and he was almost completely bald. He wore black track pants and a white undershirt. Even from across the street, John could see coarse armpit hair.

John watched Drake greet Hunter with a fist rap and then order a coffee. John cursed under his breath, wishing he could get close enough to hear what was being said, but he knew that was impossible. The coffee shop was busy—music playing loudly, the hiss of the espresso machine, people laughing.

John quickly walked down the alleyway, looking for a back entrance, hoping he could sneak in unnoticed, but the rear door was locked. He walked back around to the front again. Should he risk getting closer? He saw Drake and Hunter. They seemed to be discussing something serious now—their expressions hard and their brows rigid.

John watched them like he would watch a silent movie. Their mouths moved, but he was unable to hear anything. John stuck his hands deep into his pockets, feeling the frustration build, wishing he could read lips.

Eventually Hunter stood up; his posse did the same. Everybody rapped Drake's knuckles again, and the gangsters shuffled out. Hunter was on the phone again. John ducked underneath an awning, hiding in the shadow until the SUVs rounded the corner again and Hunter got in.

Drake was alone now, sitting on a wide bench. He seemed to be lost in thought. John wondered what he was thinking. Now his gangster façade was gone; a sadness seemed to have crept into his mouth and eyes and hunched shoulders.

John entered the coffee shop and slid into the seat across from Drake, where Hunter had been only moments ago. Drake looked up from his coffee, showing no surprise at John materializing.

"So you're switch-hitting now?" John asked.

Drake gave a rueful smile. "Just having a friendly conversation."

"About what?"

McMillan slouched in his chair. His skin was pale, his muscles droopy, which gave him a slightly famished Irish look. "Oh, you know … the Canucks … who they're going to sign in the off-season."

John frowned, looking back at the big Italian owner who had said hello to Hunter earlier, wondering how well he knew Ernest Hunter. Would the Italian owner report their conversation to Hunter?

John said, "Maybe we should take a drive."

"I have nothing to say to you."

"Some people would be very interested to learn about your meeting with Ernest Hunter."

Drake frowned, unconcerned. He knew John was bluffing. "A man's got to eat."

"You wanted me to see Dzyinski get executed, didn't you? You set the whole thing up. Why?"

"You have no idea what happened."

"Then tell me," John said. The Italian owner was looking over at them now, frowning. He was staying too long; he knew it. "You wanted a bigger piece of the action."

"I had nothing to do with Dzyinski's death."

"The police are going to subpoena me for all my notes. Your name comes up quite often."

Drake frowned. "What's that supposed to mean?"

"It means what am I supposed to do when they come with a court order?"

Drake's skin seemed to go even paler in the low-watt panel lighting. "They'll kill me. You can't let them get my name."

"Then help me out, and I might feel inclined to burn my notes."

"It was Anthony … he was the one who told me about the meeting. Said he would bring up some of my grievances with Ken."

"Did everything go through Anthony?"

"Sure … I couldn't speak with Ken directly."

"Okay, this is good. We're getting somewhere. What else?"

"John, I've got to go." McMillan stood up, but John grabbed hold of his arm and held him down. He only hoped he wasn't causing too much of a scene.

"Give me something I can print."

"That's not my problem."

"It will be soon enough."

Drake sighed heavily, glancing over at the owner. Maybe he too was worried about what the owner might tell Hunter. "What sort of leads do you have?"

John shrugged his shoulders. "Nothing really. There were two men with submachine guns they had masks on and looked like they had body armour."

Drake dipped his pinkie finger into his cup, scooping up the remaining foam. "You could try Sid Lowe. He dealt weapons for Ken a couple of years back, but now is doing time in Seattle. He might be willing to help you—bit of a long shot maybe."

John stood up, suddenly eager to go. "At this point, I'll take anything."

Washington Correctional Facility

John got up at five o'clock and drove his old Toyota along the I-5, thinking about the dream he had the night before. In his dream, in every dream, he had been back in the long wide Baghdad streets. He remembered the hot sand whirled around him, getting into his hair, into the corners of his eyes, up his nose, into the crevices of his hand. The particles stuck to him like static electricity.

Once over the border, John changed the radio to a Washington news station. The traffic was light, and so he made good time. At around eight, a light summer rain started, and the road had a fresh oiled look.

In Seattle, John stopped at a gas station to fill up and bought a *USA Today* and a coffee to wash the taste of last night's beer from his mouth. He hadn't been down to Seattle in several years, and it struck him how it hadn't changed much, how stuck in time it seemed. He got back into his car and continued on the highway, passing through Seattle, happy to leave the city behind and travel across the open land. Snow-tipped Mount Rainier loomed luminously ahead, like a blue beacon calling him. He had forgotten how much he liked road trips, the mobility and freedom of the car. He pressed down on the pedal, feeling his engine vibrate as his speedometer climbed. He watched as the little quaint American towns passed by, the ruddy happy signs wishing him well in his coming and going. He gradually forgot his Baghdad dream and fell into a pleasant trance. He turned off the I-5 at Olympia and headed along the 101 Highway.

John found the jail easily enough. He parked and got out, stretching his legs. After talking to Drake, John had been on the phone for almost the rest of the day, trying to get access to Sid Lowe. It hadn't been easy. He had gone through several department levels, filled out an application form, and talked to Sid's correctional officer before he was granted permission.

John walked down a long gravel corridor, lined with small well-pruned bushes. At the gate, the guard studied John's driver's licence dubiously before he was allowed to enter. He walked through a metal detector and was then frisked. His phone was confiscated. The guard then took John's voice recorder and held it in front of him as if he'd never seen anything like it before.

"I need that," John said.

The guard grunted and handed it back to him.

John was led into a small room, painted a slimy colour that reminded John of an old high school cafeteria.

The guard told John he only had ten minutes with the prisoner and then left.

John sat down on the bench and waited, looking around. He wondered if the prison would record their conversation. He didn't care either way. Let them listen.

Several minutes later, Sid Lowe entered the room, escorted by a guard. Sid was a small-eyed man with incongruent features. His hair was thin and grey and knotted. He smiled and gave John a limp handshake before sitting opposite him. Sid put his elbows on the table and said, "So, you're a journalist?"

John nodded. "That's right. I'm writing about Ken Dzyinski."

Sid frowned and lowered his head. "Yeah ... I heard."

"You ran guns for him?"

"So the judge said."

"Where did you get them from?"

"Down here you can pick a gun up at a superstore ... take your pick."

John tried not to appear frustrated. "I'm talking about a Heckler & Koch."

"You ever stop to consider what you're doing?"

"What do you mean?"

"Well, you drove, what? Three, four hours on some scant lead. A hope I might give you something?"

John remembered all the half conversations he heard in Afghanistan, the rumours on top of the rumours. "I've followed scanter leads before."

Sid smiled, showing small, pointed teeth. "Pretty desperate, aren't you? If you're making the drive to talk to an old-school gangster like myself."

John shrugged. "Sure. I'm hoping you can help."

"What can you do for me?"

"Depends on what you give me."

Sid laughed again. He seemed to be enjoying this excursion from his dreary daily routine. "How about flavoured water? Black currant or something."

"How about a chance to do something good for a change?"

Sid shook his head. "You sound like the fucking priest in here."

John looked up at the clock on the wall impatiently. He only had six more minutes before the guard came in to collect him. He didn't want to waste any of his time. "I keep all my sources confidential. I promise nothing will get back to you."

"You know my father wrote for a car magazine?"

John shuffled restlessly on the hard bench, trying hard not to groan. "Can we get back to Ken?"

"He took me for rides in some of those fancy cars he got to test out, you know? My first ride was in a Camaro convertible, sixty-seven—first year they were built. Man, those were beautiful cars—big, spacious, V8 engine."

John glanced back up at the clock, taunting him. He couldn't help himself. "I drive an old Toyota. Gets me around, doesn't break down on me."

"My father loved those cars, loved them more than anything else, more than money, more than his family." Sid shook his head as if he couldn't quite believe it himself. "We couldn't afford any of those beautiful cars he test-drove. He bought an Edsel Ranger. Secondhand."

"He ever get his Camaro?" John asked in spite of himself.

Sid shrugged. "Don't know. One day he quit his job, just got up and left. Sold his Ranger and disappeared. Never saw him again. I scoured magazine articles for the next two years hoping I would see his name. Truth is, I don't think he ever had it in him."

"Had what in him?"

"To take a chance. He preferred to lament down at the bar rather than go get it. He probably drank himself to death in some shitty town."

"I'm sorry," John said. It was the only thing he could think of saying.

"You remind me of my father. If you're not careful, you'll end up just like him."

John frowned. He hadn't expected this. "I'm trying to find Ken's killer."

"You think the cops give two shits who killed him? What resources are they giving him? He's not the prom queen, not the football star."

John sighed. He obviously wasn't going to get anything from Sid. "You miss the point. It's not just about Ken."

"What's it about then? Stopping the bad guys? You know you can't stop them."

John leaned forward on the bench, wondering if what Sid said was true or not—you couldn't stop all of them, but he'd uncovered his share of evil men in his time. "You want me to find your father?"

Sid looked up in surprise. "No—good God, no. I don't care about him. He can ride in his Camaro all the way to hell as far as I'm concerned."

"But you admire him, don't you?"

Sid seemed to think for a moment. "I suppose, in a way. I admired him and hated him at the same time. I admire you for your obsession."

"I see people outside my apartment hopped up on drugs, and I think, how can it not be an obsession?"

Sid shook his head sadly, as if he was in front of a small child. "Man, you can't stop a junkie from getting his fix. You should know that. Dealer or no dealer."

"That's just what you use to justify your actions," John said.

Sid was saved from answering by the guard who came in and said time was up. Sid and John rose. They shook hands. John supposed Sid was right—it was a long shot. He wondered what he would do once he got back to Vancouver.

Sid walked toward the guard, but stopped halfway and turned back toward John. "There's a man named Carl Dewitt. He supplies Ernest Hunter."

"How can I find him?"

"Time is up," the guard grumbled again, taking hold of Sid's arm. For a moment John thought Sid would turn around and punch the guard, but instead he just meekly nodded his head and followed.

The Findley Brothers

The garage looked quite ordinary from the outside—stucco white, a small blue sign on top that read "Findley's Garage" in large block letters. There were several cars parked in the lot, a barbed-wire fence surrounding it. The faint vibrations of a classic rock station floated from an open window.

Wiltore pulled up across the street from it, surveying it. He and Lewis sat quietly in the car for a while, not saying anything. Wiltore rubbed his face, suddenly realizing how tired he was. "I had a birthday party for my cat yesterday. I tried to get out of it, but …"

Tamera Lewis looked over at him with raised eyebrows, and for the first time in their shift, Wiltore smiled. He realized how crazy he sounded.

Wiltore cut the engine and again looked out across at the garage. What he was hoping to see or find, he didn't know, but still he sat there, leaning back against the headrest. Lewis didn't question him. *At least she knows when to be quiet*, he thought.

"My kids have all moved out. So my wife started adopting cats. Now I hate cats, but I don't say anything because I know she's kind of got this empty nest syndrome what with the kids gone and stuff. And she absolutely loves these cats. There's nothing I can do. She put a little party hat on her. Put the pictures up on Facebook."

Again, Wiltore waited for Lewis to say something, but she just stared at him, waiting for him to continue. Wiltore didn't know why he was talking about his wife's cats. What had gotten into him? Wiltore took a deep breath and said, "You should see them; they do look very cute—like those calendar pictures."

A mechanic looked up from the car he was working on and stared out at Wiltore and Lewis. They had been spotted, even in an unmarked car. Wiltore knew it wasn't too hard to spot a cop—especially if you are well versed in the art.

Wiltore watched as the mechanic stretched, put down his tools, and casually walked into the office. "What do I tell her? That she embarrasses me? How can I do that?"

Lewis looked over at Wiltore. "I'm not sure if I'm really the right person to ask."

Wiltore shook his head and then said in a quiet voice, "Twenty years of marriage … and I feel like we don't have anything in common anymore."

Lewis hesitated, her face strained. "Maybe you should see somebody."

Wiltore nodded. "You ready?"

"Sure."

Wiltore turned the ignition. The car rumbled to life. Wiltore released the break and pressed the gas, and the car lurched into action. He cut across the traffic and parked diagonally across the driveway.

A fat, grisly man in a Slayer's T-shirt appeared from the office, waving his arms madly. "Sir, you can't park there. You're blocking the entrance."

Wiltore and Lewis got out. They flashed their badges at him. "Police," Wiltore yelled. "We can do whatever the fuck we want."

The grisly man stopped. He had tattoo sleeves up his arms. "But our customers …"

"I don't care about your customers. What's your name?"

The man stared wide-eyed. "My name?"

All the mechanics had stopped and stared at the commotion.

"Yes, your name," Wiltore barked.

"Mike Caudron," the man in the Slayer's T-shirt stammered. For all his intimidating looks, he seemed quite scared. The goal was to keep them off balance. Then they were easily controlled, easily manipulated.

Wiltore made a big show of taking out his notepad. "And how long have you been working here?"

"Two … two and a half years."

Lewis went around and wrote down all the names of the mechanics.

"You can't do this," one of the mechanics complained.

"You want us to arrest you instead?" Lewis asked. "Obstruction of justice."

"You can't do that. I know my rights, lady," the mechanic said.

Wiltore walked over and stood close to the mechanic's face. There was fear in the mechanic's eyes. "You may think you've learned everything from an episode of *Law & Order*, but trust me, you don't know the first thing about what rights you have. So you either cooperate with us or we arrest you? Got it?"

The mechanic swallowed and nodded.

"Okay, name?"

"Blair Gennaro."

Wiltore smiled and turned back to Mike Caudron. "Is either Tom or Jeff around today?"

Mike shook his head. "No. They're not in today."

"Where are they?"

"Don't know, sir," Blair said.

Wiltore was beginning to feel annoyed. "Well, give them a call. Tell them they are wanted back here."

Mike looked down. "I can't do that; I'm sorry."

"Why not?" Lewis asked.

"They'll fire me."

"Well, it's a crappy job anyways—working for a gangster."

Mike looked up. "They're good people. You keep harassing them because they have the wrong friends, that's all."

"Yes, you keep believing that."

Lewis stepped forward. "Look, you either give them a call or we hang around, blocking your garage until they show up."

Wiltore smiled. "Don't suppose they'll be too happy when all your customers decide to take their cars elsewhere."

Mike held up his hands. "Okay, okay. I'll give them a call."

Mike disappeared quickly into the office, and the mechanics went back to work. The radio was now playing the Rolling Stones' "Sympathy for the Devil."

Thirty minutes passed by. Wiltore and Lewis questioned the mechanics, but they had very little to say about the Findley brothers. Apparently they didn't make much more than a token appearance. The last person they interviewed was Blair.

"I've only met them, like twice," he told the police officers. He seemed hesitant to cooperate, but he looked defeated.

Lewis asked, "And what was your impression of them?"

"I don't know. They seemed like decent people. They pay me on time. That's all I ask."

"You're aware they are connected to drug trafficking and the murder of six people?"

Blair shrugged. "Can't believe everything you read in the papers."

"In other words, you just don't care."

Just then a blue, mud-stained pickup pulled right up against the police car, blocking the sidewalk. A big, burly man with long hair and a beard jumped out. "What the hell you think you're doing?" he yelled.

"VPD, Mr. Findley."

He strode over to the two cops. He towered over both of them by a good six inches. "I don't care who the fuck you are. Get off of my property."

"We need to ask you a few questions."

"You're wasting your time. I don't know anything."

Wiltore smiled. "You don't even know what we're going to ask you."

"It doesn't matter—I don't know it."

"I have some information you might want."

Findley seemed to have calmed down. "What?"

"Inside your office."

Findley hesitated but finally nodded. They went inside. The office was small and in need of a paint job. A calendar from last year still hung on the wall. It had pictures of fifties' muscle cars on it.

Findley sat down behind his desk and crossed his muscular arms across his chest. The two cops sat down opposite Findley.

"Which brother are you?"

"Tom," he said, almost with a sneer.

Wiltore asked, "What do you know about Ken Dzyinski's murder?"

Findley shrugged his shoulders. "Don't know anything."

Wiltore leaned forward. "Cut the crap, Tom. You know who killed him."

"Honestly, officers, I don't, but if you want to leave me your business cards, then I will phone you if I hear anything."

Neither of the cops said anything for a while. Wiltore rubbed his chin, fully aware Findley was mocking them. They had no leverage and Findley knew it. "You know that journalist?"

Findley frowned. "Which one?"

"The one that saw who killed Ken."

Findley's large eyes flicked between the two cops uncertainly. "What about him? He saw nothing."

"He went down to see Sid Lowe this morning."

Findley's frown deepened. "How do you know that?"

Wiltore smiled, enjoying this edge. "I have connections everywhere. Even at the Washington Correctional Center."

"So? Why are you telling me this?"

"Just wanted to let you know. He may be on to something."

Findley scuffed, but he looked worried. "Sid Lowe has been in jail for years. What's he going to say?"

"I don't know. You tell me."

"He came by the office. I wasn't here."

Wiltore frowned. "Who did? Webster?"

Findley nodded. "Yeah … wanted to speak with me or my brother."

"What happened?"

"Nothing. He left his card with Brad and said he would be back."

"Okay, thanks for your time, Tom."

Wiltore and Lewis left Findley's garage and drove back to the police station. They drove back in silence. The only sound was the low rustling engine and the police dispatcher on the airwaves. After a while, Lewis reached over and turned the radio off. She looked out the window, one elbow on the windowsill.

They parked the car, and Wiltore locked the doors. They walked to the elevator.

"What was that about?" Lewis asked.

"What do you mean?"

"Why tell Tom Findley—Dzyinski's top hit man—about Webster?"

Wiltore shrugged as if it was no big deal. "Give him something to think over."

"You might as well have put a price on Webster's head."

"Findley would have found out anyways."

"It was how you said it, Jesus, Clint!"

"Look, we have nothing going on this investigation. The VP expects something … We've worked all week without one decent lead. Christ, Webster was there already. He's ahead of us!"

"I'm sure he's got nothing; otherwise, it would be in the papers already," Lewis said.

Wiltore frowned. "I hate reporters."

"Nobody likes them, Clint, but what you did back there …"

"Really? You were fawning over him in the car."

Lewis glared at Wiltore. The elevator door *dinged* as it opened, and the cops stepped inside.

Neither of them said anything for a while as the elevator hummed and rattled its way up. Finally, Wiltore said, "I just wanted to light a fire under Webster's ass; if Dzyinski's crew is after him …"

"Look, Clint, that's not the way … the subpoena will come through."

Wiltore looked down at the dirty floor. He felt angry and frustrated. She had just been transferred in and was already telling him how to do his job … yet in the back of his mind somewhere, he knew she was right. He said, "You know as well as I do … days count on this."

"Let's just hope Webster doesn't find out about this."

A Tree Falling

John walked past Liz's desk. She was concentrating on her computer, typing furiously. Her back rigid, her arms extended outright, posture perfect as if she was practicing for a part in a movie for a 1950s' receptionist.

John made himself a new cup of coffee in the lunchroom, adding a ton of cream and a heavy dose of sugar. He sucked it back listlessly, leaning on the table and looking out the window.

"You should be working on your article, not hiding out in here."

John turned to see Robert Smyllie standing in the doorway. He had cloud-white hair shaved in military fashion. He wore a thin, cream-coloured oxford shirt and pants hiked up on his large belly. For somebody named Smyllie, he very rarely smiled.

"I'm working on it, Rob," John said.

Smyllie got himself a cup from the cupboard. He inspected the stains around the rim disdainfully, but poured himself some coffee anyways. "Good. I'm glad. Because here I just thought you were daydreaming."

"No, just thinking about the article."

Smyllie nodded. "Oh, thinking? I thought you got paid to write what people tell you—not think."

"How does your wife stand you, Rob?"

Smyllie raised his eyebrows, not very amused. "The boss wants to put Cochrane on this with you."

John let out a low groan. "Tell him I've got it."

"She's got the expertise, John."

John took another gulp of coffee. "Well, tell Chuck he can put her on it when I get arrested."

Smyllie nodded. "Okay. You talk to the Findley brothers yet?"

John shook his head. "No, haven't been able to get hold of them. Doesn't look like they spend much time actually working."

Smyllie shoved his hands in his pockets, nodding his head slowly. "Well, keep at it. They have to show eventually. And my offer still stands, if you want somebody with you."

John nodded, "Okay, thank you."

John left the lunchroom and went over and sat on the edge of Liz's desk. Liz didn't look up, but kept typing.

John said, "I don't want to be your enemy, Liz."

"You're not my enemy, John. I've accumulated enough of those already without adding another one," she said without looking up from the computer screen.

"Can I talk to you for one moment?" John asked.

"We are talking, aren't we?"

John waited. She eventually stopped typing and swung her chair around, looking intently up at John. She was dressed in a slimming blue business suit. Her minty hair looked like it had been hastily wrenched back into a ponytail. She had superfluous amounts of skin toner on, but, John reflected, she was one of those rare women who appeared beautiful no matter what they did to their face.

"I need your help again."

"The Lord helps those who help themselves—the Bible might have been the first handbook for journalists."

"What are you talking about?"

"I'm talking about a byline."

"Forget about it."

"Here's an idea," Liz said. "Why don't you finish something that's on my rack ... I've got a lovely ninety-year-old rape story you can do."

"No, thank you."

Liz's posture suddenly seemed to melt away. Her shoulders slumped; her chest collapsed. "I'm tired of this shit, John."

John studied her. "I think you're more fragile than you seem."

Liz raised her eyebrows. "There's no such thing as a fragile journalist. It just doesn't work. You know that."

"Some stories just get to you more than others."

Liz sighed, looking back at her computer. "What do you want to know?"

"You know a Carl Dewitt? An arms dealer."

Liz snorted. "Oh sure, I have drinks with him every Saturday."

"Liz … seriously."

Liz didn't say anything for a while. "He was charged once—thrown out of court. I haven't heard of him for a while, though. I could ask around. See if he's still a player."

"That would mean a lot."

"But if I miss my deadline, I'm blaming you."

John got up from the corner of the desk. "Bet you've never missed a deadline in your life."

Liz smiled. "Being a suck-up doesn't suit you, John."

John laughed despite himself. "That's why I avoid it as much as possible."

Liz suddenly sighed and cast her crystal-blue eyes down. "You ever feel like … I don't know—giving it up?"

John looked at Liz. He wanted to tell her, only about every morning, every time he imagined himself still with Hayden, every time he thought about what he had given up for the job. But there was something that prevented him. There was something funny in her voice, as if she was lowering her guard, lulling John into a false sense of security, and so he said, "And do what?"

"I don't know—PR or something."

John shook his head. "No. You'd miss it too much. The rush, the adrenaline. It puts you at your best."

Liz nodded her head slowly. "You're probably right," she said, although she sounded unconvinced. She turned her pale face away suddenly, her sharp profile casting a shadow against her cubicle wall. "It's just … sometimes I feel it's hard to look at myself in the mirror. I feel like a vulture sometimes."

"Why?" John asked, surprised.

Liz looked back at John. "Don't you?"

John rested his body against the cubicle wall, not saying anything for a while. "I don't dwell on it too much."

Liz spread her hands. "I mean, look at us! We're pathetic."

John tried to smile, but only managed a weak grin. "Speak for yourself."

"You know sometimes I want to go home at five, have a great dinner at an expensive restaurant with some handsome doctor or something, and not worry about anything."

"We have our trade-offs. There's nothing like having your name at the top of an A1 story. It beats everything ... and sometimes we do the occasional good too."

Liz laughed. "Don't get too ahead of yourself there." She paused, burying her forehead into her hands. "You sure you don't want to take this one off my hands? ... She was gang-raped by a bunch of teenagers ... stupid fuckers. Posted pictures of the whole thing on YouTube. Can you believe that? ... I wonder what would be worse ... being raped or being humiliated over the Internet."

John didn't answer right away. What could he say to that? Liz had done dozens of rape stories, dozens of murder stories, dozens of horrifying stories. She had worked on stories about serial killers—Thomas Ronkin, women who had been mercilessly tortured, their bodies cut up and fed to dogs. Even now it was too brutal to think about.

Liz had been the first reporter on the scene when Ronkin had been arrested. She saw the police photos; she had heard the testimony. If John had picked a time for her to crack, it would have been then, but maybe it was all a delayed reaction: an accumulation of all those stories built up in her psyche.

John thought back to all the stories he did in Iraq and Afghanistan. "I think everyone has one story in their life that gets to them. I have one ... Her name was Amira."

But Liz cut him off. "You know what? I don't want to fucking hear about it."

John nodded. "Nobody does—that's the problem. Nobody will publish it."

Liz didn't say anything. John was about to leave again when Liz asked him, "John, if a tree falls and nobody is around, does it make a sound?"

John frowned. He didn't understand what she was getting at. "No, I guess not. Why?"

"But isn't it the same action whether somebody is around to hear it or not?"

John looked up, thinking back to his high school science classes. "Sound is technically the interpretation of vibrations. Without a conduit, those vibrations are just that—vibrations."

Liz looked at John, her mouth slightly open in surprise, probably not expecting anything so intelligent to come from his mouth. But then she looked away and muttered, "When did you become a fucking scientist?"

John looked at her blankly, unsure of how to respond.

Liz returned to her computer, reading the lines she had written on the page.

"What's this all about sound, all of a sudden?" John asked.

"Just forget I asked it," Liz said.

John nodded, still confused, and returned to his desk.

The Library

The Vancouver Central Library was incongruously shaped like the Roman Colosseum. John climbed the stone steps toward the glass entrance. He always thought it was a strange design—modeling a modern building of learning and knowledge after an ancient place of depravity and death.

The library was forty metres high, and each of its nine floors was supported by massive concrete pillars, a welcome change from the average Vancouver skyscraper. It was a sandy-red colour, like the sun at dawn, and its thin oval walls made of glass and concrete, simulated the rustic, dilapidated, decaying killing ground of centuries ago.

John took the elevator up to the fifth floor to the nonfiction section. The room was expansive, with shelves and shelves of hardcover books. It was busy for a weekday afternoon. Natural white light from the ceiling-high windows flooded on to the burgundy carpet, giving the whole place a vibrant, buoyant feel.

But Webster never felt completely at ease in the library. He didn't know why, but he felt as if some imaginary crowd was jawing, booing him. He avoided it whenever possible, but he had to find Elizabeth Cochrane's book about the rise of the drug trade in Vancouver. He wasn't sure how helpful it would be, but maybe he could quell the editor's call for having her on the story if he knew a little more about the history. He was determined not to be outmanoeuvred by her.

John went over to the computer and found the book's call number. He wrote it down on a piece of scrap paper and then went over to the stacks to look for it.

That was when he noticed a slightly heavy-set man with greasy shoulder-length hair across the room, browsing a rack of magazines. The man was wearing a black T-shirt with a red flame on it and a pair of worn jeans. He looked out of place from the other patrons. When John had been in Iraq and Afghanistan, he had learned a knack for spotting a person who looked suspicious, and there was something off about this man. Or was he just being overly jumpy?

John decided to casually walk down to the end of the shelf. He picked up a random book and pretended to examine it. Sure enough, the man put down the magazine and walked toward the stack John was occupying. John wondered if he had seen him before. He didn't seem particularly menacing and he was in a public place—but then again, most gang-related shootings happened in public places.

John looked over at his shadow again. The man was pretending to look at a row of books now, seemingly ignoring John. John put down the book in his hand and walked quickly to the other end of the floor.

The man followed slowly. John abruptly turned—maybe a little too abruptly—and stared at the man, who also stopped abruptly. His eyes widened for a second before he gave John a wicked smile. He then turned and walked quickly toward the escalator.

John ran after him, but the man moved quicker than John would have imagined, pushing a couple over, escaping down the escalator. John stared after him and shouted, "Who are you? What do you want?" But the man had already disappeared among the thicket of patrons.

John checked out Liz's book and left the library, feeling a little shaken. He decided to catch a cab back to the office, hoping to shake off anybody who might still be tailing him.

He sat in the back of the taxi, trying to read the first chapter but finding it impossible to concentrate on the words in front of him. He wondered what the man with the greasy hair meant. John decided he must be one of Ernest Hunter's men, sent to scare him. Well, he wouldn't let Hunter—or anybody else—intimidate him.

Then he thought maybe he was being foolish. Perhaps the man had only recognized him from television or from the newspaper. Maybe the man hadn't been following him at all.

The taxi dropped him off at the *Daily Globe* building. He took the elevator up and collapsed into his chair, feeling a little weak and exhausted.

"What's wrong?"

He looked up to see Liz peering at him over his cubicle wall.

"Nothing. Just a little tired."

"You have my book there?"

"Huh?" John looked down. He had forgotten he still clutched Liz's book in his hand. Now he was embarrassed.

"Yeah, I was going to burn it, you know, so nobody could read it from the library."

Liz raised one pencil-thin eyebrow. "I guess I'll just have to burn my notes along with it."

"What?"

"I found something on Carl Dewitt."

"Okay, I take it back."

Liz smiled. She was pretty when she smiled. "That's better. He owns a strip club on Pender Street and Jackson Avenue. Real classy place called Rocky Moon."

"Thanks, I owe you one," John said.

"How about a byline?" Liz asked, leaning closer over the cubicle wall. Her earlier melancholy seemed to have disappeared.

John smiled. "Not that much."

"Jackass," Liz said, taking a swipe at him, which John easily dodged.

John made a few phone calls and then went to his car. He drove east, along Hastings Street. When he stopped at a traffic light, he looked out his window at the haggard-looking people pushing shopping carts, looking worn and dried-up. John drove on a little more, past Main Street. He was now in the worst part of the city, two-square kilometres of absolute squalor, everything permeated by drugs and despair and illness.

John watched a skinny couple walk slowly—ever so slowly—across the street. They had droopy skin, bulging eyes, and thin, tangled skin. They looked like they were holding each other up. The woman was scratching at her neck fiercely where there was a large red welt. John followed them with his eyes, contemplating how in the twenty-first century in one of the richest cities in the world, two people could be so poor and downtrodden.

John was always saddened at what the Downtown Eastside had become; it had once been the lifeblood of the city, but now was rotting inch by inch—despite the government, which poured buckets of money into it.

When the light turned green, John turned left and then right onto Pender Street. He drove past a Donair takeout stand, past a movie theatre with a neon-pink sign, past a smutty-looking pawnshop, past a porn shop with a blow-up in the window, past a few crumbling brick buildings with smashed windows, past a small park littered with broken glass, past cheap tourist shops, past a butcher shop with animal carcasses hanging in the window.

John parked his car one street over from Jackson Avenue. The day had suddenly turned heavy and oppressive and stale. The afternoon sun, high in the sky, shone down on to the pavement and illuminated the shop windows. A smell of garbage wafted from the alleyways. There was no wind.

Almost immediately a thin man with a long grey beard accosted him for change. John dug into his pocket and gave the man a couple of spare dollars. The man nodded in thanks and shuffled on his way. John walked along, watching a man sift through a dumpster, looking for something of value.

Despite the poverty, John loved the area and the people, even the hastily scrawled graffiti on the walls. Everything was intensified here, almost as if the entire neighbourhood was under a large magnifying glass. A strange kind of kinetic energy seemed to flow through the streets, washing everything, coating the entire neighbourhood with emotional residue. Down here, life was more real, more intimate, closer to the edge. John felt as if the skin of society had been peeled away from the Sunday afternoon dinners, from the drunken office parties, from the bus ride to work, and replaced with hard-core reality.

John found Rocky Moon on the corner. It was an exhaust-stained brick building with black awning. A billboard above the flashy Rocky Moon sign said Dandy Daisy was performing for the next week.

John hesitated before he pushed the large doors, and then stepped into a dark hall. Immediately John was bombarded with a loud, dumb-ass beat. Two monstrous-looking bouncers searched him and then took his picture.

John climbed a short set of steps and entered into a large glossy room with advertisements on the walls. The stage was in front of him. Two rose-coloured girls were dancing methodically to the beat. They had long spidery legs, their stomachs flat and hard.

The girls danced, grinding their pelvises. They danced wrapping their legs around the pole. They danced dead-eyed. They danced flinging around their long, luscious hair. They danced under the megawatt lights with their perfectly symmetrical breasts that didn't bounce.

John watched for several moments, and it struck him that the dancers all had the same dimensions, measured like cattle. Circumference of bust? Thirty-six. Circumference of waist? Twenty-four. Circumference of hips? Thirty-six. Height? A little leeway there—maybe five six, five seven.

John watched the girls without much emotion. It had been years since he had been to a strip club, and the primal nature of the whole performance struck him as ritualistic, a sacrifice to the soul.

For an afternoon, the place was busy. There was some hooting and hollering, catcalling in a drunken savagery—beastly really. The crowd, of course, was filled with stereotypes: the businessman, his tie loose; the construction worker in his overalls; the geeky teenager who probably used his brother's ID; the long-haired, thick-whiskered university student in a vest.

John badly wanted a drink, so he ordered a glass of whiskey from the bartender. The bartender was boyish-looking and had long hair that curled in front of his eyes. With the awkwardness of an aardvark, he poured John a drink and slid it over to him.

John asked him, "Is Carl Dewitt working tonight?"

The bartender looked at him blankly. "Who?"

"Carl Dewitt. He owns this place. He in?"

"I don't know who you're talking about."

John took a sip from his glass, wondering how old the bartender was. "How about the manager? He's around, I presume."

The bartender nodded hesitantly before disappearing into the back. When he came back, he told John the manager would be out shortly. John waited around for about thirty minutes. He grew bored of the continual dancing, of the thrusting and pumping, and so he just continued to drink. He had a few and then a few more, feeling the alcohol warm his throat and dowse his senses. As he waited, the seats began to fill up.

Eventually a broad-shouldered man appeared from the office. He was dressed in a suit and tie and had a scar across the bottom of his chin. He wore thick golden rings on each of his fingers. He appraised John with big, hard eyes. "You want to talk to Carl?"

John finished his whiskey and stared back. "Who are you? "

"My name is Keith Dowell," he said, crossing large, thick arms. "Who the fuck are you?"

"My name is John Webster. I'm a reporter for the *Daily Globe.*"

Dowell snorted. "What do you want to talk to Carl about?"

"His involvement in the death of Ken Dzyinski."

"He knows nothing about that."

John looked incredulously at Dowell. "Really? You asked him, did you?"

"Carl is a respected business owner and an upstanding citizen."

John looked around him. A bouncer dragged a drunken man from his chair. The drunkard was kicking and putting up a fuss. John said, "Yes, I'm sure he is."

"Well, Carl is very busy, but if you leave a card, then he will call you."

John nodded reluctantly, seeing he wasn't about to get any further, frustrated that all the waiting had resulted in nothing. He took his card from his wallet and handed it to Dowell. John was sure Dowell would rip it up as soon as he left.

John said, "Tell him I have a source that says he sold Ernest Hunter the guns that killed Ken Dzyinski."

Dowell nodded. "I will, but empty threats don't make much of an impression on him."

"It will when he reads about it in the paper tomorrow."

For the first time, Dowell looked concerned. "Tomorrow?"

"Well, my deadline is today, and I have to write something."

Dowell eyed John coldly. He then turned to the boyish bartender. "Mr. Webster's drinks are on the house tonight." He then turned and disappeared back into the office.

John got up slowly and walked to the door, but before he got there, he saw a waitress who looked familiar. She had dark brown hair pulled loosely to the side in a schoolgirl ponytail. Her lips were large and dark and fleshy. Her face was narrow, and she had a long neck.

John watched her. She wore a skirt that reached mid-thigh and a tight red top. She moved along, collecting empty beer bottles and money like a ghost, invisible, it seemed, to those around her.

John walked over and touched her on the elbow. "Hi, Michelle."

Michelle almost dropped the tray of empty bottles. "My God, you scared me." She tried to smile, but failed miserably. "What are you doing here?"

"Can I talk to you for a moment?"

"I threw you out of my car for a reason."

"And left me stranded. You owe me."

She looked down at the ground. She was wearing long silver earrings—too classy for a strip club. "What do you want?"

"I want to talk to you about Ken."

"Why are you so interested? You sure you're not a cop or something?" Michelle looked him over, appraising him.

"No, a reporter for the *Daily Globe*."

She seemed to consider this. "That might be worse—I'm not sure."

She turned to go, but John caught her by the forearm. She turned back, her face stretched in fury. "I can get you kicked out, you know, so don't fucking touch me again."

John held up his hands. "Sorry—sorry. I didn't mean to do that."

"Now, I've got to get back to work."

"I was there, you know."

Michelle stopped, trying hard not to be intrigued. "Where?"

"At the barn. I saw Ken die."

Michelle slowly turned back. Her face was cast in shadow from the stage. "That was you?"

John nodded slowly.

Michelle didn't say anything for a while. "I read about it in the newspaper …" She frowned and glanced over at the bar. "Okay, meet me in the back in fifteen minutes."

John bought another drink—this one he paid for—and downed it before he went around to the alley. It smelled like garbage and urine. He watched a man and woman crouching in the corner of the alley, shooting up.

The sun was decaying slowly toward the horizon, giving off a harsh tawny light, spilling its warmth on to the city and alleyway, but John felt no warmth. The brick and cement around him seemed to suck up the heat, leaving him close to shivering. John could still hear the dance music muffled by the back door. He felt he needed another drink, but he didn't want to miss Michelle.

John heard some shouting and swearing not too far off and then the loud echoing of sirens.

Eventually Michelle came out, closing the door behind her. She was holding a large leather purse in both hands. She looked up at John, not saying anything. She dug out a pack of cigarettes and put one gently in her mouth. She then took a lighter and, cupping the cigarette, lit it. She inhaled slowly, closing her eyes, and then blew a long wisp of smoke. She seemed tired, maybe wanting to be transported somewhere else—anywhere other than a gritty back alley.

She suddenly looked old, crow's-feet around her eyelids, her forehead creased. John allowed himself to imagine her as an ex-stripper, doing the pole routine, gripping that bar with her narrow thighs, spinning around and around, flipping her long chestnut hair around, casually, nonchalantly slipping out of her exotic clothes.

John finally broke the silence. "You were having an affair with him, weren't you?"

Michelle opened her eyes, genuinely surprised. "With Ken? Good God, no."

"Then why were you at his funeral?"

Michelle seemed to mull the question over. "You know … I don't think you were very fair with him in your article."

John took a step toward her into the barely discernable light. She took another slow drag from her cigarette. John stared at her and said, incredulously, "I'm sorry—wasn't fair to a mass murderer?"

"You shouldn't be here, you know."

"You mean here? At Rocky Moon?"

Michelle nodded. "They see you as a menace—maybe even bigger than the police."

John snorted and raised his eyebrows. "Who thinks that?"

Michelle offered the cigarette to John. "You smoke?"

John shook his head. "No, I quit."

"Too bad. I don't trust a man who doesn't smoke."

"Why did you lie to me back at the funeral?"

Michelle crossed her slender arms. "Same reason you did, I guess."

"Carl runs guns for Hunter, doesn't he?"

Michelle shrugged. "I just keep my nose down. It's not good to get into that sort of thing."

"You know what 'on background' is?"

Michelle shook her head. "I'm not helping you out; forget it."

"It's when I can write what you say but not attribute it to you."

Michelle dropped the butt of the cigarette and stomped it under her boot. "They'll find out, trace it back to me."

"I promise they won't. I do this for a living."

"I'm sorry, John," Michelle said, flattening her ridiculously short skirt.

"You were friends with Ken, weren't you? You can at least tell me that."

Michelle shook her head distractedly, listening to the music or something beyond the music. "No, I wouldn't have called us friends."

"Don't you want to see his killers come to justice?"

"You don't understand, John. If Carl knew I was even at the funeral, he would kill me," she said. "Look, I have to get back to work."

Michelle opened the door and was about to slip back in, as quietly as she came, but John took hold of her wrist. She stopped and looked down at his fingers, as if she couldn't quite believe he had touched her again.

"Why didn't you wear black?"

"I'm sorry?"

"At the funeral ... If you wanted to blend in, why didn't you wear black like everybody else?"

Michelle hesitated, looking at the hallway in front of her and then back at John. "It's stupid."

"What is?"

"I told him—I promised him I wouldn't."

John wanted to ask her more questions, but she slipped out of his grasp and shut the door on him, leaving him alone in the alley. John walked around to the front to his parked car. The sound of car engines and cars once again became loud and obnoxious.

He sat in the darkness of his car, feeling wetness around his neck and forehead. He hadn't even been aware he was perspiring. He wiped the sweat off with the back of his hand. He then started the engine, smiling to himself. She knew something that she wasn't telling him—but that she wanted to tell him. That was certain. What also was certain was that if he kept slowly chipping away at her, she would crumple.

Subpoena

"Charles Dana?" a voice asked from the deep shadows of the *Daily Globe* building.

Charles stopped just outside of the front door and looked at the man calling his name. He was dark-skinned and dressed in a handsome blue suit, his wavy hair cut short and gelled back.

"Yes? Can I help you?" Charles asked. Who was this guy? He suddenly remembered the warnings he had given Webster and wondered if he shouldn't have heeded his own advice. Charles looked at the door and then back at the man. The man didn't seem particularly menacing in his expensive clothes, a small brown suitcase in his hand. But then how did he expect a gangster to look?

The man in the suit stepped up and handed Charles a legal-sized envelope. "You have just been subpoenaed to hand over all documents and evidence related to the murder investigation of Ken Dzyinski."

Before Charles could say anything, the man turned and walked away. Charles watched him disappear into the crowd of businesspeople. He then took out his cell phone and quickly dialled Webster's number.

"Hey, what's going on?" Webster replied.

"Where are you?" Charles asked.

"Just coming back to the office. Why? What's going on?"

"Okay, good. No … wait…. Don't come back here."

"Why? What's going on?"

Charles looked around the street. Everybody seemed to be looking at him—eyeing him suspiciously. Groups of well-dressed people stopped at the light. The light changed from red to green, and with it the motion of traffic changed. Somebody honked their car horn angrily, and it reverberated down the sidewalk. A cold westerly breeze hit Charles's face. "I've just been subpoenaed, and I'm guessing you're next."

"Okay ... but what should I do?"

Charles knew if the court couldn't serve Webster the subpoena, then it couldn't force him to reveal his sources. Charles looked around again. He still felt the eyes on him. He turned and walked into the *Daily Globe's* darkstone hallway with its cavernous ceiling. It wasn't very crowded. People he didn't know walked through the glass door, their quick footsteps echoing through the hallway. The security guard smiled at Charles, but the smile quickly faded as the guard probably sensed something wasn't right with the editor. The damp coolness over his head from the old, damp building felt good—reassuring. He leaned his head up against the wall.

"Not home ... Let's meet somewhere. We can discuss things."

"The Palace?"

Out of the corner of Charles's eye, he could see the security guard walking over to him. "No, someplace people wouldn't think of looking for you."

There was a silence on the other end. "How about the Celtic? It's over on Commercial Street."

"Okay ... sounds good." Charles hung up, put his phone in his pocket, and turned to reassure the security guard that everything was all right. "I was just feeling a little dizzy, that's all."

Charles almost ran to his car. He didn't know if it was from fear or adrenaline. He dug into his pocket, struggling to get his keys out. He looked around, wondering if anybody was following him. Was this whole thing a setup?

He pulled out into traffic. He glanced into his rearview mirror. How could he tell if anybody was following him? He briefly thought about phoning Webster and asking for pointers. Charles drove around the block a couple of times, constantly looking in his mirror but not sure what he was looking for. Finally, feeling silly and a part of some spy movie, he drove over to Commercial Street.

Charles parked close to the Celtic and walked over. He pushed the stained-glass door open and looked around. It smelled stale and oaky. The pub was packed with young, supercilious people, yelling and shouting at each other over the fluting and fiddling. The men were all strong-shouldered and steep-jawed and the women all slim-hipped and big-breasted. They were dancing and jigging in one inebriated mass.

Charles found Webster sitting at a corner table. He looked surprisingly relaxed, if a little tired. Charles sat down opposite, looking back, seeing lawyers everywhere.

Webster had a glass of whiskey on the rocks in front of him. "Let's see it."

Charles placed the vanilla envelope on the table. Webster stared at it for a moment, and then turned it around and opened it. He studied the legal document. A ruddy-looking waitress came around, giving Charles a suspicious look, perhaps because he was the oldest person in the pub. "You want anything to drink?" she asked.

"Just a soda water."

Webster put the subpoena back into the envelope. "How long do you think I can hide from them?"

Charles shrugged. "I don't know. You have anywhere to go?"

"I don't know ... I can find somewhere."

The waitress came back with the soda water. Charles took a listless sip before saying, "You can always stay with us."

Webster shook his head. "No, they'll suspect that. I'll find someplace."

Charles asked, "You think you can finish your article by the time we go to court?"

Webster shrugged. "I'll do my best. You worried?"

Charles shook his head, smiling weakly, trying to appear more confident than he felt. "No, I'll tell them I don't know who your source is, that I don't know where you are ... They can't put me in jail for that."

Webster finished his whiskey and ordered another from the waitress. His eyes followed her through the crowd. Neither Webster nor Charles said anything for a while, each lost in their gloomy thoughts. They knew if they didn't give the police Webster's source, they probably would be thrown in jail. On the other hand, Charles had never risked jail for a newspaper article before, and the idea kind of thrilled him.

He listened to the music, and after a while, it was hard not to enjoy the communal goodwill feeling that infused the Irish pub, and Charles felt his spirits lift. He felt the fiddling and the stomping vibrate somewhere in the bottom of his stomach. The Irish always knew how to dance their way through a problem—no matter the severity.

The waitress placed Webster's drink in front of him. Webster looked up at Charles, as if he was expecting a disapproving glare, but when he didn't get one, he shot the liquid back.

Charles looked at the band playing up front. There was a congestion of people jumping up and down, swaying and dancing with every last ounce of vigour. Charles was struck how people could come here and escape the humdrum, the monotonous, the grinding routine of life. Their spouses left them? Dance. Their mothers had cancer? Dance. They had to work in some shitty warehouse for minimum wage? Dance.

Charles craved a drink more than ever. His soda water just wasn't doing it. Why was he tempted now? Was it the subpoena? The people around him? He didn't have an answer. He thought he could walk into a pub and not feel the ten years of absence so heavily; he felt tightness in his shoulders and tightness down his back. It was a problem only alcohol could cure, but alcohol also managed to wreck him at the same time. He was able to function much better as an editor, as a husband, as a father, sober.

It wasn't often Charles was surrounded by young people. A couple stumbled past them, the man's hand probing underneath the woman's skirt. The woman halfheartedly swatted at him. This primal behaviour made Charles think back to his own wanton teenage years. Of course, his greatest act of rebellion had been smoking behind the garage. Life had changed much since he had been young. He continued to think back.

"You know, my father was a priest," Charles said.

Webster looked incredulous. "A preacher's son?"

"Yeah, you ever believe in God?"

"No," Webster said, shaking his head.

"He made me go to Sunday school, to church—listen to his sermons.

He talked about God, about faith. I suppose I never had much faith—had too much of a sceptic's heart."

"Journalism is a good field for you then."

Charles nodded. The day Afghanistan was invaded, Charles phoned his father up for the first time in over twenty-five years. He answered on the second ring, sounding just as youthful and vigorous as the last time Charles had spoken to him. Charles didn't understand why he decided to try and patch things up with the cantankerous old man that day. But he knew it had something to do with thoughts of war and warmongering and its inevitability.

Charles asked, "You think more about that blog?"

Webster shrugged. "It may be the future, but I still believe newspapers will be where you'll find the best journalism ten, twenty—a hundred years from now."

Charles nodded. "Let's hope so."

Webster looked hesitantly down at his drink. "Chuck … I can't run forever."

"Then you better finish before they get your notes."

"It's frustrating—the stonewalling."

"What are you going to do?"

"Don't know. Keep snooping, I guess." Webster paused, and his shoulders sagged. "I talked to Liz today …"

"Oh yeah?"

"I think she's having a crisis of faith … And I'm not talking the spiritual kind."

Charles nodded. "We all get those from time to time."

Webster swirled the ice around in his glass. "I'm not afraid of jail."

"I know you think you're tough—going through those wars—but this is different, a different kind of toughness, a different kind of fear."

"Sometimes I wonder if I'm doing the right thing."

"You're having doubts about withholding information from the police?"

Webster pressed his palm against the bottom of his eyes, pulling his eyelids down. "I don't know. Maybe. I don't know what I think anymore. I haven't been getting much sleep."

Charles drank the last of his soda water. "Remember when you did that story just after 9/11?"

Webster shook his head. "Which one?"

Charles sat back in his chair. He thought back, shaking his head. "It was an insane time. Everybody was scared. The world was no longer what it had been. People would get on the bus, line up for coffee, and eye the person next to them as if they were a terrorist. Osama Bin Laden had proven that the great American machine was not invincible. We could be defeated. We became scared of everything. You couldn't fly with nail clippers, ballpoint pens. You couldn't fly with pencils, with hand cream. You couldn't even take a plastic poppy onboard an airplane. Imagine holding the whole plane hostage with a poppy!" Charles paused, setting his mouth into a frown.

"And I remember before you went off to Afghanistan, you decided to fly down to Seattle with about twenty banned objects. I remember you wanted to take a Swiss Army knife—but I told you not to. I had visions of you being strip-searched and locked up in jail as some sort of extremist, and I would have to plead with the authorities to release you."

Webster smiled. "They confiscated my water bottle, but I got through with my Swiss Army knife."

Charles shook his head. "One of the many times you ignored my advice. I remember you got home bursting with pride. And I was proud of you. You did what you thought you had to do. You followed your instincts. You pushed the boundaries, questioned authority. You didn't—still don't—let anybody tell you what's right and wrong. That's journalism. That's what being a reporter is all about."

Webster nodded, turning away, but Charles could tell his words were impacting him. The truth was, Charles hadn't meant to make such a long speech. It was the sort of thing he said to his class, not to seasoned professionals like Webster. It had just sort of tumbled out, but even Charles needed to remind himself sometimes why they did the things they did.

The band took a break, and there was a sharp silence before the DJ took over. The sudden cut of noise—even if only momentarily—relieved the strain on Charles's ears.

"Chuck," Webster said after awhile, "you think it even matters who killed Ken Dzyinski? I mean, as Sid said, he's no prom queen."

Charles sat back in his chair. "You think the police feel that way?"

Webster shrugged. The waitress came over, and Webster said they would take the bill. "They aren't putting many resources into it."

"Well, maybe that gives you a chance of cracking it first, before they do."

Webster snorted. "Don't give me too much credit."

"Why not? If the police had any good leads, they would be tracking them down instead of subpoenaing you."

Webster didn't say anything. In the background, the DJ was pumping up the crowd. Charles asked, "You need some money—for a hotel or something?"

"No, no, I'll be fine," Webster said. He paused, and Charles felt he was on the cusp of saying something important so he waited. "Maybe there is something in my notes, you know … that the police could use. I'm not smart—I didn't even finish high school, but what if the police could catch the killer based on something I wrote down?"

"It's not your job. Remember, the police have had the same opportunity to gather the same information as you did."

Charles insisted on paying, placing a crisp fifty-dollar bill on the table. "You'll need all the money you have in the next couple of weeks to stay out of jail."

They stepped outside into the fresh humid evening. Silver moonlight poured through the clouds and on to the city. The music still seeped through the cracks in the door, and the boisterous, mutinous shouts and previous laughter seemed so close. But that was all behind them—as 9/11 and Afghanistan were also—and now they looked out to the tranquil streets.

Charles searched the long shadows for mysterious lawyers, subpoenas at the ready, and he wondered how long it would be before he stopped looking for some clandestine menace. He wondered if this was how Webster, coming back from the Middle East, felt all the time.

Charles turned to face Webster, who seemed lost in his own thoughts. "You know what you have to do on this one?"

Webster nodded, looking beyond Charles, down the street.

"You sure you don't want Cochrane's help on this one?"

"I've got it covered—I'll be fine."

Charles reached out and put a hand on Webster's large muscular shoulder. The act seemed to surprise both of them. Charles was by no means a sentimental man. "You know, there is an old Irish saying that goes, 'May you have hindsight to know where you've been, foresight to know where you're going, and insight to know when you've gone too far.'"

Webster smiled wearily. "I'm Scottish—we never did listen to the Irish."

Charles nodded, smiling back at him. "I know, but be careful nevertheless."

They shook hands and parted. Charles watched as Webster stuck his hands in his pockets, turned, and quickly walked down the street. Charles smiled, despite himself, and turned to head back to his car.

The Casino

The lights blinked ceaselessly, almost dazing John as he stepped through the large glass doors, through a metal detector, and into the casino. John continued down a wide hallway. He heard the sound of slot machines first—the cha-ching and other computerized sounds. Then he heard the spinning of the roulette wheel, the shouts of card dealers, and people screaming for good fortune. His feet tread softly against the blood-red carpet floor. He entered a cream-coloured room. No clocks were on the walls denoting time. Things stood still in the casino, a vortex of time and space. John supposed that was part of the lure. In here you never grew old, life was stagnant, and becoming a millionaire was only a roll away. The room was packed with an endless progression of gamblers, people with a dog-eyed gaze, their jaws slack and gaping.

John passed the slot machines. A mesh of colourful gimmicks littered the place. Neon lights were everywhere, casting grotesque shadows across strained faces. John felt he had stumbled onto the set of an apocalyptic zombie movie.

John steadily made his way around the large windowless casino, watching people play their game, pull that lever, roll the dice, flip those cards. Sagging weary men and women weighing their luck. They were dressed halfheartedly, without much thought or care—ties loose, laces undone, heels kicked off, shirts not tucked in, yesterday's powder still on.

John took note of the hundreds of surveillance cameras and the security guards trolling the room. You would have to be crazy to try anything.

John cashed in about a hundred dollars worth of chips and sat down at the roulette table, feeling very James Bondish—only dressed more poorly. He stayed there half an hour, his money dipping and rising, until eventually he wandered over to the bar and ordered a whiskey from a woman wearing a low-cut black dress, her cleavage very much on display.

John sat on a stool. A woman with boyish-short red hair smiled at him from across the bar. She had on a leather jacket and black stockings. John smiled back but then turned his attention to his drink. He was not there for complications.

John had checked into the hotel adjacent to the casino, a forty-nine-story building with all the usual amenities: king-sized bed, cable, a swimming pool, and a sauna. He had specifically requested a westerly-facing room with a perfect view of the casino. He had moved the desk so it was underneath the window and had set up his laptop so when he typed, he could just look up and see Andromeda Casino in all its brazen glory.

A little while later, John was tapped on his shoulder. John turned and saw the Spock-lookalike standing looking severely down at him. He looked like he was wearing the same suit he had worn at the funeral.

"Mr. Hunter wants to see you," he said, his voice gravelly and husky.

John nodded toward his drink. "Can I take it with me? Normally I wouldn't mind … but fifteen dollars seems a little steep."

The Spock-eared man didn't seem amused. "If you want," he said.

John stood up, needlessly dusted off his pants, and smiled at the henchman, trying to disguise his anxiety. He grabbed his glass and followed the henchman through the crowd. They walked to the very back of the casino. The henchman opened a door, which led to a narrow, poorly lit corridor. At the end stood two security barrel-chested guards, who reminded John of two Minotaurs. The security guards stepped up to John and told him to spread his arms. They patted him down quickly and professionally. They took out his wallet and looked at his driver's licence. In John's other pocket, they found his Olympus voice recorder.

One of the security guards said, "We're going to hold on to this for a while."

John shrugged, biting back the urge to say something really snarky; he had learned the hard way sometimes it was best to keep his mouth shut.

The guards nodded and stepped aside. The henchman opened the door, and John followed him.

Much like the man himself, Ernest Hunter's office was small and plain-looking. It was well-lit with harsh light, and on the wall were several watercolour landscape paintings. Hunter was sitting behind a small wood-stained desk. He was bent over a bulky computer screen.

He looked up when John entered and gave a wide smile. He was dressed casually in a white crew-neck shirt and a pair of ripped jeans, looking more like a liberal arts student than a gangster. He stood up and shook John's hand. In the dark room and yellowish light, Hunter looked even paler and scrawnier and disjointed than at the funeral.

"I've been watching you," Hunter said, seemingly very amused at himself. "I knew you were a gambler."

John gave his own version of a pencil-thin smile, sitting in a worn leather seat opposite Hunter, crossing his legs. The Spock-like henchman leaned up against the back wall. He crossed his arms and looked at his boss. John looked back at him, wondering if he was about to get a bullet in the back of the head.

"Don't worry about him," Hunter said, as if he could read John's mind. "He's harmless."

"If you say so," John replied.

Neither said anything for a while after that. Hunter leaned back in his chair, pressing his hands to the top of his head. Hunter's dark eyes were searching him, trying to access him, find out what he was made of. But John wouldn't give anything away. He remained silent, knowing he would only let slip his nervousness.

John turned to face Hunter. "My editor knows I'm here. Just in case anything happens."

Hunter seemed amused by this, and the tension in the room suddenly relaxed. He leaned forward, putting his boney elbows on his desk. "You win any?"

John took a slow sip of his whiskey, more for show than anything. "I don't know—why don't you tell me?"

Hunter grinned, glancing toward his Spock henchman. "Hard to not like somebody like him, isn't it?" Hunter turned his attention back to John. "You grew up on the eastside, didn't you? What year did you graduate?"

"I didn't—didn't make it past tenth grade."

Hunter smiled widely, turning his palms upright. "Me neither. We have something in common. Shows a man doesn't need education to be successful, doesn't it?"

John frowned, wondering what sort of game Hunter was playing. "Are you having me followed? Saw somebody trailing me the other day."

Hunter sat back in his chair, a smug look on his face. John cursed himself for letting Hunter get under his skin.

Hunter said, "Why would I have you followed?"

"I think you're scared of me."

Hunter tried to act surprised but failed. "Scared of a journalist?"

"Trust me, it's better to have a dozen cops on your ass than one journalist."

Hunter grinned again. He seemed to be enjoying himself. "Trust me, if I wanted you followed, you would never know about it."

John cocked his head and raised his eyebrows. "You think so, do you? When I was in Afghanistan, I was followed for three years by the CIA, by the Afghanistan government, sometimes by Al Qaeda—those people knew something about tracking a person. They had satellites at their disposal. They had armies. So forgive me if I laugh at your bravado."

This seemed to finally vex Hunter. John had gotten to him. Hunter shifted irritated, wiping at his nose. "You're the one with too much bravado, Mr. Webster."

John gave a saintly grin. "I just report what people tell me, that's all."

"Don't play naïve; it doesn't suit you."

"Is that all you got? You just wanted to taunt me?"

Hunter bit his lower lip. "You're the one who walked into my casino."

"I was just enjoying a nice drink at the bar when I was rudely interrupted by your lackey," John said, hooking an accusing thumb over his shoulder toward the Spock henchman.

Hunter put his hands together. John sensed the old-school gangster was studying him. After another lengthy pause, Hunter spoke. "It's sad how little you know about Ken Dzyinski's murder."

"Why don't you enlighten me then?"

Hunter gave a low, rumbling laugh. "Wishful thinking, my friend."

"Why did you summon me here then? If not to talk about Dzyinski?"

"To warn you."

"To threaten me, you mean."

Hunter put up his palms and frowned as if deeply offended. "No, I don't threaten—make friendly reminders, maybe."

John laughed, despite himself. "What do you want to remind me of?"

"This path you're going down. I know you think you're helping people, those druggies, maybe, I really don't know, but you're just putting yourself in jeopardy."

John felt the blood drain from his body and prayed he wasn't turning white. He was scared, despite everything. "If that isn't a threat, then I don't know what is," John said.

"I already told you, I don't threaten anybody. What do you take me for?"

John stood up. His legs felt numb. He had listened to Hunter enough. "I know you ordered somebody to kill Dzyinski, and I will eventually find out who."

Hunter's smile suddenly disappeared from his face, and he tilted his head forward, glaring at John. "I would have thought somewhere in that fucking medieval country somebody would have taught you some fucking manners."

John turned and walked out before things escalated. He expected somebody would stop him, but nobody did. He walked until he got to his car. There he sat, unable to move, as if paralyzed. John tried to breath regularly. A throbbing pain started at the base of his skull. Eventually he fumbled for his keys in his pocket before realizing they were in his lap. He started his car, and the engine sputtered into action; the noise seemed to snap John out of his comatose state, and he drove out of the parking lot.

John had grown increasingly worried about some documents he had on his computer at work, some of which incriminated Drake McMillan. He wondered if the police would be able to confiscate them. He realized he had to go back and erase them. It was the only way to be completely safe.

John took Highway Ninety-Nine back into the city. The sky was dark and grimy except for the remnants of a streaky pink sun as it disappeared behind a gloomy cloud. The scenery rolled on and on before him, passing him, disappearing in his rearview mirror.

He thought about his interview with Ernest Hunter. He was perplexed and frustrated. How deeply was Hunter involved? And how could he ever prove anything?

John crossed the almost-barren Granville Bridge, and English Bay rippled sluggishly before him, melting outward into the night. John turned right, and he could see the Woodward's *W* almost directly before him, shining brightly, six thousand pounds of LED lights, rotating slowly around and around. John stopped at a red light and looked up to admire the domination of the skyline. The incandescent *W* seemed the most radiant beacon in the night, a hopeful pinnacle looking on to a dreary monolithic construction of wrought iron, sheet metal, and glass.

John rolled down his window and let in a draft of warm summer air. He inhaled deeply, as if he could smell the whole city. He hadn't been sleeping well lately. It was the stress of the article and the police subpoenaing him, and he was having terrible nightmares—worse than normal.

John parked in the underground lot. It was dark and empty and eerily silent. As John locked the car, he felt a strange kind of dread in his stomach, a feeling drawing him back to his days in Iraq and Afghanistan, a feeling he often followed but now ignored. He was perfectly safe in Vancouver, he told himself. There was nothing to fear in the garage. Even so, he looked around into the gloominess. Somebody could be hiding behind the large cement pillars, but the parking lot was quiet as ever.

John walked quickly to the elevator, looking all around him. In the Middle East, he had trusted his instincts, but here in Vancouver it seemed a little silly to be ducking for cover from some imaginary threat.

The elevator doors shut, and John felt himself being lifted off the bottom level. He felt better in the bright compartment—safe from his fears. The doors opened on to the newsroom, which had slowed down from its usual pace. Only a few interns were working the graveyard shift. He just needed to pick up a few notes, and then he was gone. He wouldn't talk to anybody. Hopefully he would go unnoticed.

John was walking quickly between the cubicles when he heard a familiar, abrasive voice. "You better fucking call me back, Alex. I'm doing the story with or with you, you hear?"

John looked over to see Liz slamming the phone down and suddenly spinning her chair around. She gave him a look of embarrassment. "Don't you hate it when people ignore your calls?" she said, looking down at her skirt, trying to straighten it before looking back up at John. She looked tired. Her blonde hair was in disarray, her thick layer of mascara was all smudged, and bags were around her eyes. Yet despite all that, she was still girlish and pretty. "What are you doing here anyways? I thought you were in hiding."

"I am. Came to pick up a few things."

Liz nodded. "Sure, under the cover of darkness. What do you think the boss is going to do?"

John shrugged. They were only a few feet apart, and he could sense she was tense and distraught. "I don't know. Lie, I hope."

"You think they'll put him in jail?"

John shook his head. "No, they can't prove anything." He leaned up against the cubicle wall looking at Liz. "What are you doing here, anyway? It's late."

Liz rubbed the corners of her eyes. "I know … I'm just following up on some leads for my story. It's not going very well."

"Is this for the rape story you're doing?"

Liz shook her head. A smile was on the tip of her red lips. "No, different one now. Paul Gibson was murdered this morning—shot on his way to work. I'm on it."

John frowned. "Paul Gibson? The name sounds familiar."

"It should. He was the CEO of Gibson Investments—which owns about half of the commercial real estate in Vancouver. I was trying to get hold of his brother, Alex Gibson, but he's not returning any of my calls."

John nodded, trying not to feel envious—realizing the competitiveness juices were swelling up in his chest, but also realizing Liz deserved a good story after the raped woman. "Any leads?"

Liz sighed and took a sip from her coffee mug. "Ugh. I don't know why I keep drinking cold coffee." She put the mug back on her desk. "Nothing so far. But it's early. The police think it is a professional hit. Probably fucked with the wrong person."

"Liz, anybody warn you about your trucker's mouth?" John said.

Liz laughed. "Yeah, probably once or twice."

"Well, good luck." John turned toward his desk.

"John?"

He stopped and turned. He was only half paying attention, realizing his article would have to be something extra special to knock Gibson's murder off the front page. "Yes?"

She was playing with the sleeve of her shirt, a nervous habit that made it no less endearing. "You ... ever been on a blind date?"

John frowned. "Sorry?"

Liz repeated her question. John shook his head, wondering at the strangeness of the question. "No, why?"

Liz looked back at her computer screen, as if the words on her screen were beckoning to her. John stood there, waiting to see if she would say anything more. After a while, she continued, "I met this guy on the Internet. We've been talking back and forth for about a week ... I don't know why I'm telling you this ... but maybe you should try it."

John frowned. He thought Liz was the last person to give him dating advice. "I'm an old-fashioned journalist who prefers the old-fashioned ways."

Liz dropped her jaw, showing two rows of big white teeth. "Oh, come on. The only people we meet are criminals and scoundrels."

"Not true; I met a real nice girl the other day."

Liz looked up at him, her big blue eyes searching his. "What's her name?"

"Michelle."

John didn't know why he suddenly thought of her. He had only met her twice and had no romantic intentions toward her, well, at least not overtly.

Liz sat very still, her face emotionless. "Where did you meet her?"

"Does it matter?"

"She's not some gangster's wife, is she?"

John shook his head. "No, I met her at Ken Dzyinski's funeral."

Liz frowned, sitting back in her chair, gripping the armrests. "Be careful, John."

"Don't worry, I am," John said.

"What does she do?"

"What is this—twenty questions?"

"I'm just trying to look out for you, that's all."

John paused, looking out across the newsroom. "She works at Rocky Moon."

Liz tried to stifle a laugh, putting one hand over her mouth. "At the strip club? You can't be serious."

"She's a waitress—not a dancer or anything."

"Not the type of girl to bring home to your mother."

"I'm past the mother-approval stage."

Liz turned back to her computer. "She's the last thing you need right now."

John shrugged, but knew what she said was true. He watched Liz type, expecting her to say something else, but when she didn't he went to his desk.

John turned on his computer. It hummed slowly to life. He transferred all the documents he needed on to a USB stick and then wiped his computer clean, hoping a police computer expert wouldn't be able to extract anything. He then shut the computer down and went back to his car.

He drove back to his hotel, careful to check if anybody was trailing him. He parked and got out of his car, slamming the door shut. The temperature had fallen drastically, and John felt cold with only a light jacket. Again he felt uneasiness creep up in his stomach. He looked across the parking lot, across the stretching darkness and the green grass that inhabited the meridian. He saw nothing.

Convinced he was being paranoid, John went upstairs and had a shower in his room. He felt refreshed afterward and sat in front of his computer. While he waited for it to boot up, he wondered how many hours in the day he spent sitting, staring at his computer. He clicked on the Internet and before he realized what he was doing, he began surfing dating websites. He looked at women's profiles and stared at their pictures. They all looked more or less the same.

His mind wandered to Liz. After a while he got up and restlessly went to the window, looking out at the casino's bright lights blinking against the night. He missed his own apartment, the noise from the streets, from his neighbours, even the yelling matches. Here, in the middle of suburbia, all the rooms had double-paned windows and thick walls. It made him feel utterly alone. He turned the television on for some static noise, flipping through the channels—sports, news, sitcom, infomercial—but even that didn't help.

And then realizing he hadn't had anything to eat since the morning, he decided to go downstairs to the diner, but the hotel restaurant was closed and everybody had long gone. He stood in front of the locked door wondering what to do. He didn't particularly feel like leaving the warmth and comfort of the hotel, so he went across to the bar that was attached to the casino.

The bar was mostly empty, and half of the chairs had already been placed upright on the tables. A melancholy piano was playing quietly over the speakers, and the bartender was sweeping behind the counter.

John ordered a drink and stared down at the clear liquid, feeling slightly pathetic and sad. The piano probably didn't help, he reflected. He wanted to tell the bartender to put something lighter on, something upbeat.

Had it really come to this? John thought. He could picture his father sitting next to him. He would have said something like, "Junior, you're still young and handsome; stop wasting your time." He didn't feel like he had a lot of time. He didn't feel like he was young anymore. Then the strong presence of his father fell away and was replaced with the boy from the bazaar. The boy was always there, hiding in his subconscious. He downed the last of his whiskey and ordered another one, struggling with the fact that he was hiding away in a hotel with no place to go except for his own computer.

Paul Gibson

"You didn't talk to him?" Wiltore asked.

Carl Dewitt shook his head.

Wiltore and Lewis were sitting in Dewitt's office. It was a dark, cramped, stuffy room with no windows. There was a whole row of slutty posters on the walls, which Lewis looked at disgustedly. Dewitt said, "Apparently he came here looking for me, but I didn't talk to him, no."

Carl Dewitt wasn't particularly imposing, but he had a definite presence about him. He shaved his blond hair short. His head was bumpy, and he had a large pimple in the middle of his forehead. He wore a white shirt and white tie. He sat back casually in his seat, his hands pressed together, looking as if cops interrogated him daily.

Wiltore asked, "What did he want to talk to you about?"

Dewitt shrugged, scratching his head. "No idea. Talk to my manager, Keith. I think he talked to him."

"Ken Dzyinski?"

Dewitt held up his hands. "You know I had nothing to do with that."

Wiltore raised his eyebrows and said a little incredulously, "I'm glad. You don't know how reassured that makes me feel."

Dewitt shook his head, frowning. "I don't know why you always have to give me a hard time. I'm a legitimate businessman with nothing to hide."

Wiltore sighed, looking past Dewitt at a poster of one of the airbrushed girls with large come-hither eyes. It had already been a busy day. At seven in the morning, the deputy chief of police, Benjamin Ervin, had pulled him and Lewis into his office and demanded results. Not a good way to start. Wiltore could only promise he would find out more when Charles Dana and John Webster were dragged before court.

Wiltore knew Ervin was having a bad couple of days. There would be plenty of political pressure to have him solve the Gibson case. And in the back of Wiltore's mind, there was the nagging feeling Gibson was connected to Dzyinski.

Wiltore asked, "You know where he went after he left here?"

"No idea. Sorry."

"You are friends with Alex Gibson, are you not?"

Dewitt shrugged again. "I would say acquaintances—not really friends."

"What do you know of his brother's murder?"

"Only what I see on television and read in the paper."

"You haven't spoken to him?"

"No."

Wiltore tried not to let his frustration show. "I know Alex Gibson came here."

Dewitt tilted his head. "I don't know—maybe he did. I don't keep track of all my customers. Again, you should be talking to Keith. He would know better than I would."

"When does Keith get in?"

"Probably around three or four."

"Okay, we'll be back."

Wiltore stood up and buttoned his jacket. Lewis followed his lead. It was obvious Dewitt wasn't going to be any help. Wiltore said, "You know, Carl, I will solve Ken's murder."

Dewitt nodded. "I look forward to that day. Until then, good luck."

Wiltore and Lewis walked out of the office and into the empty bar. The bartender was washing dishes, getting ready for the nightly ruckus. He was thin and a little gangly and looked young. Lewis tilted her head toward him, and Wiltore nodded. They walked over.

"How's it going?" Lewis asked, giving her most girlish smile.

The bartender looked up. He had weedy eyes, and his mouth hung slightly open. "What do you want?"

Lewis said, "You saw the journalist in here? John Webster?"

"No, I wasn't working."

Lewis leaned her elbows onto the bar. "What's your name?"

"Simon."

"How old are you, Simon?"

"Twenty."

Lewis looked over at Wiltore. "You enjoy your job, Simon? You enjoy watching the dancers take their clothes off?"

Simon smiled weakly, but a flicker of uncertainty crossed his face. "Yeah, of course."

Lewis gave a fluttery laugh. "I don't blame you." She then leaned real close in. "What if we tell your boss, Carl, that you have been talking about him?"

Simon snapped his body back. "I just work here, keep out of trouble."

"Then you'll help us out."

Simon looked uneasily around, but the bar was empty and Dewitt showed no sign of leaving his office. "That guy—the journalist—seemed to be talking to one of the waitresses."

"Which one?"

"Her name is Michelle Lake."

"What were they talking about?"

Simon shrugged. "I don't know."

Lewis said, "Come on, Simon, you were doing well there for a while."

"I guess he was asking her questions. That's all I know."

"Okay. Where can I find Michelle now?"

Simon looked down at the counter. "No idea."

Lewis looked at Wiltore. "I guess we go back and talk to Carl."

"Okay, okay … She works during the day at Scotty's on Southwest Marine Drive and Boundary."

Lewis and Wiltore nodded. "Thank you."

They went back to the car and drove to Scotty's. The traffic was bad, and Wiltore longed to flip on the siren and speed past everyone.

"What do you think Webster knows?" Lewis asked, crossing the bridge.

"If I knew, I wouldn't be chasing him," Wiltore replied testily.

Neither officer said anything for a while. Then Lewis, perhaps to break the silence, asked, "You playing soccer this week?

Wiltore shook his head. "No, I'm just too tired what with this case ... And I've barely seen Christine."

The traffic wasn't getting any better, and so Wiltore eventually decided to get off Marine Drive. He drove along the side roads, bypassing a couple of signs that said "Local traffic only." Lewis gave him a sharp look.

"What?" he asked. "If we stay on Marine Drive, we'll never get anywhere."

Lewis asked, "You think Gibson and Dzyinski are linked?"

"It's connected somehow ... maybe not directly. A professional hit."

Scotty's was a well-known fifties' diner, where you could get a dollar cup of coffee and free refills and pancakes with real maple syrup all day long. Wiltore remembered going there as a kid with his dad after Sunday school. Scotty's was one of those rare places that never seemed to change.

They drove into the parking lot, stopping underneath the huge neon sign. They locked the car and walked past a dirt-flecked pickup with a bumper sticker that read "Jesus is white." Lewis and Wiltore looked at each other with puzzled expressions.

They flipped their badges at the hostess at the front. The restaurant had floral wallpaper and badly upholstered booths. The restaurant was only half-full, and conversation seemed muted. All the servers seemed to be wearing ugly yellow dresses and white aprons. Wiltore felt the nostalgia in his throat. He could almost see his kid self in the corner, his father in his blue police uniform sitting across from him.

Lewis said, "We're looking for Michelle Lake."

The hostess, a small Filipino woman with fading curly hair, pointed to one of the servers in the corner. The two cops walked over.

Michelle was tall, statuesque, and had long earthy-coloured hair tied up with hairpins. She could have been the prettiest woman in the entire restaurant except for the bored, glazed-over look she wore on her face.

"Mrs. Lake?" Lewis asked.

Michelle turned and tried to smile, but it seemed too much effort and the muscles in her cheeks fell. "Hello, officers," she said.

Wiltore looked at Lewis and then back at Michelle. "Well … yes. We were wondering if we could ask you a few questions."

"About what?" Michelle asked innocently. She placed her pad of paper in her apron pocket. "I'm kind of busy here."

"Does your boss know of your other job?" Wiltore asked.

Michelle sighed and looked beyond the two police officers out to the street, to the traffic passing by. "I think I'm due for a smoke break anyways. Wait for me out back."

The two police officers went back out to the parking lot. They watched as an obese man and woman struggled out of their car and hobbled toward the restaurant. Wiltore could smell the stink of the dumpster in the corner. Wiltore kicked at the gravel, trying to be patient. His back and shoulders were stiff, probably from the stress that had built up. He longed to curl up, go back to bed, cling to the warmth of his wife. The coffee he had drunk about an hour ago wasn't helping.

He looked over at Lewis, who was lost in her own thoughts. "How's your traffic cop?"

Lewis shrugged. "We're on break."

"What? When did this happen?"

"Yesterday … last night, I think—I don't remember anymore." She rubbed her eyes. She was obviously also tired. The investigation was taking a toll on her too.

"What happened?"

"Apparently I've become too irritable to live with."

Wiltore sighed. It was a common enough complaint among police officers' spouses and significant others—one he had heard more than once. "Sorry," he said to Lewis.

They didn't say anything more until Michelle stepped out of the back entrance. She was no longer wearing her apron. Her bright-yellow dress was stained with grease and other food. She was holding a pack of cigarettes and a lighter. She offered the pack to the cops, who shook their heads.

"Why doesn't anybody smoke anymore?" she said, shaking her head sadly. She tapped a cigarette out of the pack and put it between her pink lips.

"I saw you at Dzyinski's funeral," Lewis said suddenly.

Michelle nodded. "Yeah."

"Why did you go?" Wiltore asked.

"Pay my respects." She cupped the cigarette and lit it with the lighter.

Wiltore gritted his teeth. "I mean, how do you know him?"

Michelle crossed her arms under her small breasts. "He came to the club sometimes. Was a good tipper."

Wiltore shook his head. "Doesn't make sense. He could never go to Rocky Moon. That's Hunter's hangout."

Michelle shrugged. "I don't know any Hunter."

Wiltore took a step closer to Michelle, who backed up against the wall of the building. Nevertheless, she looked unafraid. Wiltore stared at her. "Don't play games with us, Michelle. We know your boss runs guns for Hunter."

"If that's true, why don't you arrest him?"

Wiltore let out a low sigh through his teeth. "What did John Webster want with you?"

"You mean that reporter?"

Wiltore nodded.

Michelle hesitated, trying hastily to cover it up by taking a drag of her cigarette. "Same thing as you, I guess. He wanted to know about Ken Dzyinski."

"You know where Webster is?"

Michelle shook her head. "No. Why would I know that?"

"We need to talk to him, and he's disappeared."

Michelle shrugged.

Wiltore glanced at Lewis and then switched topics. "You know Alex Gibson?"

Michelle took her time in answering, tipping a clump of ash onto the ground. "Sure; he comes into the club sometimes. He's also a big tipper." She paused, looking from Wiltore to Lewis. "Haven't seen him in a while. Heard his brother was murdered."

"What do you know about that?"

Michelle shrugged. "You think the two are related?"

"Why would they be related? Nothing connects the two."

Michelle crossed her arms. "You were just insinuating, that's all."

"What's the brother like?"

"Flashy guy. Wore expensive suits, always had an entourage with him."

Wiltore handed Michelle a business card. "If you talk to John Webster again, please give me a call—I don't care what time."

Michelle peered at the card uncertainly. "He's in big trouble, isn't he?"

"Just give us a call."

"Why should I do that?"

Wiltore frowned. "Because if you don't, I will walk into your restaurant and tell your manager that you moonlight at a strip joint."

Michelle stared at Wiltore before pocketing the business card. She then extinguished her cigarette underneath her heel and went back inside.

Gangsters

The boy again. He stared at John with large dusty-brown eyes—innocent, accusing eyes. John knew what was about to happen. He tried to run. But he couldn't. He looked down at his old army boots, trying to move his feet, but there was nothing he could do. He tried to yell out to the boy, tell him to run, but his tongue seemed larger than his mouth, and he swallowed his words.

The boy stretched his arms out toward John, mouthing the words, "Help me." But John was helpless. John watched as the boy burst into flames, slowly falling to the ground, writhing until finally he was still. And he burned some more. He burned until he was nothing but white and black ash. John tried to turn his head, to close his eyes, but he had no eyelids. He couldn't do anything.

John woke. At first he didn't know where he was, but then his eyes adjusted to the dark and he saw the glow of the digital clock beside his bed and remembered he was at the Andromeda Hotel. He sat up, digging his hands into the unfamiliar down pillows, kicking the fresh silk sheets. He immediately reached out for his phone but then remembered he had turned it off, just in case the police could track him with it.

He rubbed the corners of his eyes, stretching out his bare feet. The room was large, and there was a flat-screen television in one corner and beside that a window with the blinds drawn. The room smelled faintly of lemon cleaner. He wondered what time it was. He looked again at the bedside clock. It read one fifteen. He had only been asleep for less than thirty minutes. How was it possible he felt perfectly rested, as if he had slept eight hours?

He put his hand out on the other side of the bed, feeling the cold sheets. He hated waking up to an empty bed with no one beside him to comfort him, to tell him they were just nightmares, half memories, the boy gone now.

He thought about phoning Hayden, waking her up, but what would he say to her? That he wanted to hear her voice? She would just hang up on him.

He thought about phoning the Rocky Moon and asking for Michelle. He went over to his computer and looked up the number. He scrawled it on the notepad by the phone. He stared at it. He would have to make something up.

You want to go out sometime? … go for coffee? … get a drink?

No, he couldn't do that. She worked at a strip joint. She was a source in his story. He could think of a thousand reasons why he couldn't ask her out. He thought of her slender face, her high forehead, her small nose.

Then he thought, *What's the worst that could happen? Why am I afraid of phoning?* Summoning up a bit of courage, he dialled Rocky Moon. The phone rang three times.

"Keith Dowell speaking."

John quickly hung up. He stared at his phone, ashamed of himself. He pulled on his jeans and a T-shirt and went outside into the temperate summer night. The air was still and calm, and he looked up at the overcast sky. The cumulous clouds were a faint plum colour. John looked for stars, but the city lights and the clouds blocked any remnants of their existence. John thought it was very sad, almost like the death of something immense and powerful.

John dug his hands into his pockets and walked toward the casino. There were about six or seven smokers congregating under the overhang, laughing and talking loudly. For just a moment, the moon peeked out from a flat blanket of clouds. It was high and almost full, spilling a moody light on to the casino. But then the clouds shifted and covered the light from the moon. John walked past the smokers, breathing in the fizzling caramel smell of their tobacco.

He took his mind off of Michelle by playing the slots. In the corner, there was a group of about eight or nine handsomely dressed men having a debauchery. One man was flinging chips around like Frisbees and tipping the tight-skirted waitress in twenty-dollar bills. Another of the group put about a dozen chips on a number, and when the ball landed on his square, he jumped and pumped his hand into the air. Their good humour and laughter both mesmerized and disheartened John. When had he been able to do that? Where had all his fun times gone?

John played the slots a little longer. The flashing lights and rhythmic clicking mesmerized him for about ten minutes, curing him of longing—until, that is, he ran out of chips to feed the machine.

He slid off the stool and wandered over to the bar and ordered himself a whiskey. He looked around at the other people in the bar. Most of them were overly dressed and overly drunk. He talked to an old, hippie-looking man for a while, but the conversation was a bit one-sided. The old man just nodded and swayed back and forth, dangerously close to falling over.

John saw a pretty young woman drinking alone, and so he went over and introduced himself. She had long, dark hair tied back, curvy lips, and tanned skin. He bought her an apple martini. She smiled and they spoke for a while, but their conversation seemed dull and boring—or maybe it was him; by that time John was too tipsy to tell.

The woman gave John a hug and left, and he sat alone again for a while. Then there was a commotion at the front of the casino, and all eyes were drawn to it. A tightly-knit group of tight-shirted men had just entered. They all looked the same—chests thrust out, arms swaying by their sides, weaving like weapons. There were flashes of photography and the quick click of shutters. A woman tried to shove something—a picture maybe—into the group.

John beckoned the bartender over. "What's going on?" John asked.

The bartender snorted. "Oh, that's the fighter Wally Couldhard and his entourage. They come in here a lot."

"Boxer?" John asked.

The bartender smirked, tight-lipped. "No, MMA—where have you been, man?"

Piano music started to play from the speakers, and somebody asked what was playing. John heard another voice answer, "Moonlight Sonata."

John listened to the music over the quiet chatter in the bar. He then called the bartender over again and ordered another drink and asked if he could use his phone. He could feel the warmth of the alcohol in his cheeks and forehead.

"Sure thing, boss," the bartender said, reaching behind the counter and giving John the phone. John dialled Rocky Moon again. Keith Dowell answered again, but this time he found the courage to ask for Michelle.

"Who is this?"

"John Lake—her brother."

There was silence on the other end, and for a moment John thought Dowell would call his bluff, but instead he said, "Just a moment. I'll see if I can find her."

John waited for what seemed like a long time. He could hear the techno beat on the phone and classical in the other ear, creating a strange, dizzying sensation. Finally Michelle answered.

"It's John," he said, clutching the phone tightly.

"What do you want?" Michelle said, sounding annoyed.

"I need to talk to you—it's urgent."

"Brother? Seriously?" she hissed. "You can't just phone here."

"I'm sorry, but it could be important."

"Can't you just tell me?"

"Not over the phone." This wasn't going anywhere near as planned. What would he say when he saw her?

"I can't—I'm sorry."

"I've found a key piece of the puzzle."

There was a long pause. John closed his eyes and held his breath.

Finally Michelle said, "The police were here looking for you. What did you do?"

"Nothing—it's nothing. They want to serve me with a subpoena so they can drag me before court."

There was a long pause and every moment John thought she was going to hang up, but finally she said, "Okay … I'm not off work for another hour. Where should I meet you?"

"How about I meet you at Rocky Moon?"

"No—you can't come here," she said quickly. "Where are you? I'll meet you there."

John paused, unsure of what he should tell her, but finally he said, "I'm at Andromeda's Casino out in Richmond. I'm at the bar."

"Andromeda? What are you doing there?"

"Hiding."

"Talk about being in the dragon's den."

"Exactly. Nobody would think of looking for me here.

"Okay, I'll see you there." She hung up.

John gave the phone back to the bartender. He looked around. His hippie friend had gone. John started to order another couple of drinks, but the bartender informed him they were closing. "But I'm waiting for a friend."

"I'm sorry, but we're closing in ten minutes."

John nodded and paid with his credit card. He stood up, feeling the blood rush down his body. He walked unsteadily toward the door.

He continued out of the casino and toward his hotel. The other patrons from the casino trickled out behind him. Their voices carried through the calm night: a congealed recap of the night's winnings and losses, triumphs and sorrows. John stopped at the edge of the building and leaned up against the wall, excusing the action by watching the evaporating crowd.

Somebody called his name, and he instinctively turned toward the voice. Instantly he knew it was a mistake. A clandestine figure with a hoodie drawn over his face, wearing baggy pants, walked toward him. John's instinct kicked in, and he turned and ran.

There were several loud pops. A woman screamed. A car window shattered, spraying shards of glass everywhere. John dove to the ground and crawled behind a car for protection. He flattened his body against the ground, trying to make himself as small as possible.

His adrenaline was pumping, seething through his body. The alcohol seemed to have disappeared from his body altogether, replaced by a different drug. The world suddenly seemed small and genuine.

John heard the scuffle of sneakers on pavement, and he knew he had precious little time. He lifted his head and saw the door to the hotel.

He crouched low, behind a row of cars, and ran. An eruption of bullets echoed across the street. He stumbled and fell. He lifted his body and crawled awkwardly behind the wheel of a Ford pickup truck. He looked around. He was disoriented. Where had the shooter gone? He peered out but couldn't see anything. He thought it best to keep moving, so he continued to crawl. The cold sound of gunshots still rang in his ears, buzzing. He listened, gathering himself in, focusing on what the soldiers had told him.

He could see big black boots. The gunman was standing between him and the hotel. John waited, his heart pounding in his chest. The gunman shifted his weight, clearly getting inpatient. He didn't seem to know where John was hiding and was waiting for John to make some kind of move. John decided to slowly back up, putting distance between them. He crawled toward the parking lot where his car was. If he could just get there, he would be safe.

Somewhere nearby, John heard an engine spurt to life and then a screech of tires. The sound seemed to reverberate off the pavement and the walls of the cars, coming from all directions, a vortex of sound. The gunman sprang to life, firing several shots at the car as it swerved to the exit. The windows seemed to explode simultaneously, and the car skidded and slammed into a post. John could see the profile of the gunner perfectly, and if the gunner had turned his head, he would have seen John crouching behind the car, but he was fully concentrated on the car. The gunman stood perfectly motionless for a moment and then slowly walked toward the car.

John quickly analysed his options. The gunner would soon discover that the driver wasn't John, and then he would be trapped between parked cars. John felt his only chance was to run, and so he summoned all of his energy and, keeping his body low, he made for it.

There was a loud crack of gunfire. It seemed so close he thought his eardrums would burst. The warm night seemed to be slipping away from him. If he stopped, he knew he would be dead.

He reached his Toyota. Somehow he unlocked the car and fell in. He tried to slow his own breathing. The gunfire had stopped, but he barely noticed. John slouched so he could barely see over the steering wheel. With what seemed like a Herculean effort, he turned the keys in the ignition, released the hand brake, and pressed the gas, easing the car forward.

He stretched his neck over the steering wheel to see the exit and made for it, slowly feeling his car accelerate. The gunfire resumed again, and suddenly there was a loud pop and a hiss. John felt his car swerve and he wrenched the steering wheel, but he overcompensated and hit a parked car. John was thrown sideways, hitting his head against something. His vision blurred. Everything was spinning around him. He closed his eyes, touched his face with his hands, and suddenly felt like he would just like to lie still and not move. As he contemplated sleeping, his mind strangely wandered back in time. He thought of Byron, and suddenly he saw a doctor in aqua-blue scrubs, his hands between Hayden's legs.

He's coming out ... Look, there's the head ... Push! Just a couple more.

The vivid imagery was enough to snap John back to reality. He opened his eyes and stared into a blank greyness before realizing he was, in fact, looking at the ceiling of his car. He forced himself upright, back into the driver's seat. He threw his car into reverse and pressed the gas pedal, but nothing happened. There was only a slow cough and a choking sound.

He blinked and was suddenly aware of a sharp prick between his shoulders and neck. What happened? He reached back with his right arm and felt a warm flow of liquid, and when he looked, he realized his hand was covered in blood. He tried to get out of the car. It took a few tries, but he finally managed to force the door open and tumble out. He tried to get up, but he fell down.

He lifted his head and looked around. He felt on the verge of vomiting. He was on a wide street, and on either side of him were large, uninteresting buildings. A row of street lamps cast long spidery shadows on to the pavement. John tried to run, but he couldn't move. There was no pain, only stiffness.

He looked around for the gunman, but he couldn't see him. There was a lot of blood now. His shirt was soaked in it. He took a couple of slow steps, somehow making it to the hotel doorsteps, but he collapsed before he could open the door. He looked up for the doorman, but he wasn't at his desk. In fact, the whole interior of the hotel was black.

John rolled over onto his side, coughing and choking. He heard the soft scuffle of footsteps slowly approach. He was sure it was the gunman to finish him off. Instead, when he lifted his eyes, he saw a small boy. He was wearing a white shirt and white pants. He had auburn skin and thick curly hair. His small round eyes stared at John with interest.

"Help me," John rasped. "I think ... I've been shot."

But the boy didn't move. He just stared at John from the shadows. John couldn't see his face, but he looked familiar from somewhere, but he wasn't sure.

"Please ... help."

Still the boy didn't move. John couldn't place him. He was thinner, frailer looking than Byron. Maybe one of Byron's friends? But John didn't remember meeting any of Byron's friends.

"You ... know ... Byron?" he called out. John felt each breath become more difficult, and speaking was laborious. John felt a cold wind pass over his body, and he became extremely cold. Where did that wind come from? Wasn't it summer? Why was he so cold? John wrapped his good arm around his chest.

John struggled to keep his eyes open. He raised his body upward. He took hold of the railing and got to his feet. He turned his back on the boy, who was still staring blankly at him, and pushed the hotel door, but it was locked. He forgot they locked the door at night. He dug into his pocket for his key card, struggling to remain conscious. Where was everybody? Why was nobody around? He sank to his knees, the world closing in around him. He managed to slide his key card from his pocket, but he didn't have enough strength to raise his arm to slip it into the slot. He fell onto his back again. He looked behind him and saw the boy still standing there.

All John wanted to do was close his eyes and rest. He knew it was a bad idea, and he tried to keep his eyes open but they were too heavy.

"Come help me up," John mumbled, but he was almost talking to himself. He was mouthing the words. Finally, he fell into unconsciousness.

The Hospital

John woke and stared upward at the white panels and the neon-yellow lights. They were bright and hurt his eyes. He pressed his eyes closed and tried to move, but he only had a vague sense of his body. He lay there in the darkness for what seemed like a long time, but may have only been a few minutes. He had no sense of the seconds ticking away. After a while, he slowly opened his eyes again. The lights made an irritating low humming sound.

I need a drink, John thought.

He let out a gasp and a gurgle and shifted in the bed. Or at least he thought he shifted. He looked down at his hands, but they felt distant. What had happened? He remembered being at the casino, having a glass of whiskey at the bar …

He turned his neck to see a green, threadbare curtain drawn across the small room. There were no windows anywhere, just dull-grey walls illuminated by the light. He heard the urgent sound of footsteps on linoleum and a voice over speakers, but he couldn't make out what it said.

Was he back in Germany? In Afghanistan? He was pulled back to that inescapable place. Had he just been airlifted out? He squeezed his eyes tight and then opened them again. No … The voices were speaking English. His memory gradually came back to him in flashes like fuzzy snapshots. The Taliban hadn't gotten him. He wasn't back in Afghanistan. He had been in a car crash. He had been shot in the shoulder.

John managed to raise his head, but he felt nauseous, the world spinning away from him. He lay back down and closed his eyes, and in a few minutes he felt better.

Somehow he fell asleep again, and when he woke, he saw a mousy, greyish-haired nurse standing over him, smiling.

"My name is Susan, Mr. Webster," she said brightly, showing gummy teeth. "Don't worry; you'll be okay."

John struggled to sit up. He could feel the blood in his feet and arms. He thought of asking the nurse for a whiskey or a beer, but he knew she would never give him one. "Where am I?" he asked. His voice was hoarse and seemed foreign.

"Richmond Hospital."

John didn't reply. He looked at the bedside table, which had an old digital clock on it. It read three o'clock. He looked down at himself. He was wearing a thin cotton gown. His legs were bare. What had they done with his clothes? He needed to collect his things and go. He couldn't stay. They would find him.

Susan took a step forward. She seemed a towering presence. "Can I get you anything? Some juice or something?"

"When can I leave?"

Susan frowned suddenly. "I'm afraid it might be a while."

John shook his head adamantly. "No, you don't understand—"

"Mr. Webster, are you aware of what happened to you? You can't leave until you're stable enough. Understood?"

John nodded curtly.

Susan leaned over John, smiling again. "Okay, now, can I get you anything?"

John knew the nurse had defeated him. He suddenly realized he was hungry. "Maybe something to eat?" he asked.

Susan returned with a snack from the cafeteria. After John was finished devouring the food, he fell back asleep. For the first time in a long time, he dreamt of nothing. Just a pleasant darkness. He woke feeling refreshed. The grogginess of the other day was gone. He tried to get up from his bed, but a cord of pain went through his chest and he collapsed back into bed.

Somebody had put the *Daily Globe* next to his bed. John picked it up and looked at the front page. There was a large picture of him—a younger, smoother-faced version. Underneath was the headline "*Reporter gunned down outside of casino*," by Elizabeth Cochrane. John read the article and then flung it across the room in disgust. The newspaper fell apart in midair and floated to the ground. He sat back down, and after a while, having nothing else to do and unable to retrieve it, he regretted his rashness.

A doctor entered and looked down at the scattered newspaper. "What happened here?"

John gave an embarrassed smile, but didn't respond.

The doctor, a handsome, steep-jawed man with thin greyish-blond hair, sighed heavily and stooped to pick up the paper, crushing it in one hand. "You want to read this?"

John nodded once, but tried not to appear too eager, lest he give the doctor a sense of satisfaction.

The doctor placed the paper on the bedside table and then did a checkup on John.

"It's good to see you in stable condition," the doctor said. "It was a bit touch-and-go when you first came in. You had lost a lot of blood."

John lifted his eyebrows. Touch-and-go? What did that mean? He almost died? The thought suddenly sank deep into his gut. He had been running on adrenaline and never considered the possibility that he had almost died.

The doctor continued his examination in silence, and John was too afraid to say anything else. Finally, the doctor straightened up. "If all goes well, we should have you out in the next couple of days. I just want to keep an eye on you."

The doctor left. John tried to read the jumbled newspaper, but he couldn't concentrate on the print or the pictures in front of him. He eventually put the paper aside. He felt it was some sort of word puzzle and he was missing all the vital clues.

John had nothing much to do, and he became increasingly agitated—the quiet chatter outside, the droning voice on the speaker system, the chemical smell in his room were all becoming sources of irritation. He was restless, but every small movement was uncomfortable and brought pain. He wanted to go, to leave the hospital, to be back in his apartment, which had never quite seemed like home but now he longed for it.

A tall, thin man in a suit appeared at the curtain. He had on a thick silver tie and his smoky-coloured suit. "John Webster?" the man asked. John lifted his eyelids, which were suddenly very heavy. There was nothing immediately threatening about the man in the doorway, but his sombre tone and his lack of a smile were slightly insidious.

"Who are you?" John asked, trying to hide the panic in his voice.

If the man pulled out a gun or a knife, there would be nothing John could do about it. He could barely move, and to defend himself would be all but impossible.

Instead, the man placed an envelope on the bedside table. "You have just been served."

John looked over at the envelope and sighed heavily, barely aware of the man's departure. John turned the envelope over and opened it. He studied the subpoena but he wasn't able to make much sense out of it, and so he returned it to the envelope and fell asleep.

John's next visit was from detectives Wiltore and Lewis. Wiltore was dressed in a black suit and crinkled green-striped tie, while Lewis looked dashing with her long blonde hair tied back into a bun. She wore a white blouse and blue dress pants.

"Hope you're feeling much better," Wiltore said, trying to hide his smugness.

John managed to sit up. "You missed your friend."

Wiltore nodded to the envelope on the table. "Yes, I can see he made a delivery. No more hiding from us."

"I was on vacation."

Lewis raised her eyebrows and said incredulously, "In Richmond?"

John tried a deep breath, but pain spread across his body. "So you delivered the subpoena. What else do you want from me?"

Wiltore took out a notepad. "We are here to take a statement from you."

John looked suspiciously from one cop to the other. "I don't know how much help I can be ... I didn't see much of anything."

"Did you get a good look at the shooter?"

"No. It was too dark, and he had a hood on." John described to the police what happened, but stopped abruptly and then asked, "What happened to the other guy? The guy in the car?"

Wiltore and Lewis looked at each other. "He didn't make it. Shot through the neck. Died instantaneously on scene."

John sank into his bed, looking up at the ceiling. "The gunner ... he thought I was in that car."

"It wasn't your fault," Lewis said gently. She took a step closer and smiled sympathetically.

John said, "It was that bastard Carl Dewitt."

Wiltore scrawled something in his notebook. "Let's not jump to any conclusions. You've pissed off quite a few people recently."

Lewis asked, "You hear anything about the Paul Gibson murder?"

"No. Why?"

Lewis and Wiltore glanced knowingly at each other before turning to look back at John. John raised his eyebrows at the cops. "What?"

Wiltore finally answered. "You can't print this ... but we think either he or his brother got involved with Dzyinski's gang."

"What sort of involvement?"

Wiltore shrugged. "Not sure yet. That's why we're asking you."

Lewis asked, "Did you notice anybody following you?"

John shook his head. "No, nobody followed me."

Wiltore tilted his neck. "You sound certain. You always watch for tails when you're on vacation?" The incredulity crept back into his voice.

John suddenly felt very tired. He closed his eyes. He remembered seeing the boy at the entrance of his hotel. He had seemed so vivid, so lifelike. What was happening to him? Was he going crazy?

Lewis asked, "Did anybody know where you were?"

"No."

Lewis gave Wiltore a knowing glance before turning her attention back to the journalist. "Forget the subpoena for a moment. Obviously the gunner knew you were there. He must have gotten the information from somewhere."

"No ... I didn't tell anybody."

"Not even your editor? ... What's his name? Charles Dana?"

John thought about his call to Michelle. "No, I didn't tell anybody—not even he knew."

There was a pause. Over the speakers, a doctor was being paged. Lewis crouched next to John's bed so they were at eye level. She had large, solid-blue eyes like a cat's. They stared at each other. Lewis looked grim, her mouth pursed tightly across her face. "John, I seriously think you should tell us who your source for the barn shooting is. For your own safety. Did it ever occur to you that maybe your source was the one who shot you to keep you quiet?"

John shook his head. "No, it wasn't him."

"There's no way you can be sure. These are psychopaths you're protecting. They don't give a fuck about you."

"I'll see you in court," John said, leaning his head back onto his soft pillow.

Wiltore shook his head sadly, as if he was scolding a small child, and said, "You have two weeks before you see the judge. What do you hope to accomplish in the meantime?"

"More than you will, that's for sure."

Wiltore gritted his teeth, and the veins in his thick neck bulged. "Webster, why do you have to be such an asshole?"

Lewis glanced at her partner before turning back to John. "You should think about hiring some security. Get your paper to pay for it."

John closed his eyes and smiled, trying to appear more confident than he felt.

"Okay," Lewis said. "But we'll be back."

After the detectives left, John slept. He had no concept of time. He drifted in and out of consciousness. The pain came and went. Sometimes John heard Susan's friendly voice asking him how he felt. She increased his morphine, and for a while he felt better.

John woke up to find Hayden sitting on a small stool across from him. She sat perfectly motionless, one leg crossed over her knee, a fist underneath her slender chin. She was dressed in a black suit and leather boots, her large brown eyes mysterious and darkened by mascara.

John struggled to sit upright, but Hayden remained reptilian still, barely even registering John's movement. Her face was passive, her lips drawn-out. John realized his hands were shaking. He looked down at himself embarrassed and dug his hands into the bedsheets.

There seemed to be some emotional void between them. He looked at her shyly. What was she doing there? She hadn't moved, and for a moment, John thought she was a mirage of his imagination—just like the boy.

John waited for her to say something, but when he realized they were in some kind of stalemate, he asked—rather moronically, he knew—"Is Byron here?"

"He's in school," she said.

"You never seem to get any older," John mumbled, lowering his eyes.

Hayden still didn't move, and John wasn't even sure if she had heard him. Finally, Hayden sat back, uncrossed her legs, and stared down at John. "It might be because, unlike some people, I haven't been shot."

John frowned. "Is that a joke?"

"No, it's not a fucking joke."

John stared at her in shock; Hayden never swore. John couldn't think of anything to say in reply.

Hayden continued, "You might as well have pinned a great big sign on your back. What were you thinking? Writing a story about ... about those people. You're nothing but an annoyance to them. You think you're this great big hotshot writer."

"That's not true. You know that, Hayden. It's just what I do. I can't help it."

Hayden was silent again. John could hear her breathing and he felt like she was just gathering herself up for another attack, so he decided he would say something before she could gather momentum. "I've been thinking a lot about you—you and Byron."

Hayden shook her head. Her exterior defence was broken. Her eyes began to swell up. "I hate seeing you like this, John."

"I'll be all right. Afghanistan was worse."

Hayden nodded her head once, wiping her face with the back of her hand. She got up abruptly and walked over to the bed. "You remember when I came to see you in hospital on the base in Germany? I was so distraught they almost didn't let me on the plane. I had to explain that you had been shot in Afghanistan. The flight attendants all thought you were a soldier. They told me how heroic you must have been, how you were fighting for your country ... I think I even imagined you as a soldier. It almost seemed true at the time ..." Hayden sighed heavily. She put a hand on John's forehead. Her hand felt warm and moist. "I never told them you were a journalist … I think I was too embarrassed. I didn't want to tell them you had been running away."

John didn't look at Hayden. He didn't know what to feel. Should he be angry? Sad? Disappointed? He supposed it was just another point showing how their marriage had been: years of misunderstanding and miscommunication.

Hayden withdrew her hand from John's head and tucked her chin into her neck. "What are you going to do when you get out?"

"You asking me to quit?"

"William got out."

"Yeah—but I have no business sense."

"You've never tried it before. How would you know?" Hayden seemed to enjoy talking to John as if he was a small child—perhaps it had something to do with being around Byron. Neither of them said anything for a while. "Byron saw you on television," Hayden said after a while. "It made him very upset. I didn't know what to say to him. What do I say? Defending the people of Afghanistan is at least easy. I could have done that."

John suddenly felt resentful—not just at Hayden, but at the doctors, the nurses, the whole world generally. "I didn't ask to be on television."

Hayden pursed her lips. "That's real hypocritical coming from you."

John thought back to all the times he had filmed people who hadn't wanted to be filmed. He closed his eyes, feeling himself lose this argument like he lost his other arguments with her.

Hayden continued on her lecture. "John, you're too old to be playing cops and robbers."

"It's not a game, Hayden."

"Then why do you treat it that way? Who's on the front page? Who gets the byline? It's juvenile, John." She pronounced his name like a prison sentence.

John wanted to protest, but he was too tired, too weak. He heard the sound of something—a stretcher perhaps—rolling down the hallway, rumbling louder and then falling away into the distance. Somebody coughed in the adjacent room, and it was a startling reminder they weren't alone.

John kept his eyes closed. When he opened them, he hoped Hayden would have disappeared, but he still heard her soft breathing.

"John," she said, "I've made up my mind. I'm not letting you see Byron anymore."

John's whole body became rigid, and his mouth went dry. He tried to swallow, but he couldn't find any saliva. He looked up at Hayden, his teeth gritted from the sudden, sharp pain in his shoulder. "What do you mean? But I'm his father."

"In name only … You stopped being his father a long time ago."

"That's unfair," John said, struggling to remain calm. "Maybe I haven't always been there for him, but that doesn't mean I don't love him."

"You were never there for him."

"That's not true."

"Name one birthday, one play, one game you've made of his."

"I'm sure there was … I just can't remember right now."

"You were always too busy with Afghanistan, with Iraq, and now with these criminal gangs. I thought once Afghanistan ended, things would be different … but you seem to have created your own little Afghanistan war right here."

"You can't stop me. I'll take you to court."

"And what will you tell the judge, John?" Her voice was once again patronizing. John hated that tone. It was worse than yelling. "That you're behind on child support? That you lead a dangerous lifestyle? That you have seen Byron only once in the last four months?"

John was at a loss for words. "But I'm his father," he said again, although this time more pathetically.

Hayden collected her purse and slung it over her shoulder. She looked at her ex-husband smugly, knowing she had won. "If that's your only defence, I'm afraid you're going to be in trouble. I'm ready for a fight."

"No, wait, let's talk about this rationally," John said.

"I have a house to show in half an hour," she said, turning. But John wouldn't let her have the last word. He swung his legs over the side of his bed. The blood drained down his neck, and he saw large, black hexagon specks in his vision, and he almost fell back onto the bed. But with great control, he steadied himself. He pulled the IV out of his wrists and tried to stand, ignoring the weakness in his knees. The machine next to him made a dull, listless whine.

John took a step, but it was finally too much. He crumpled to the floor, landing on his injured shoulder, letting out a scream. Somebody—a nurse perhaps—rushed in and helped John back to bed.

"What were you trying to do?" the nurse asked sharply. She was a small Filipino woman and spoke with a slight accent.

It was Hayden, who still stood by the door, her face a little pale, who answered. "He was being his usual stubborn self."

Michelle Lake

John checked and rechecked the address against a scrap of paper he held in his good hand. He paid the cabbie, got out of the taxi, and walked up the sagging wooden steps, which let out an agonizing, baritone groan under John's feet. He was at Michelle Lake's house on Pandora Street.

He had been discharged only hours ago. The doctor had pronounced him in stable condition and given him some painkillers to take home. John exited the hospital and walked out into the fresh air, expecting the world to be fundamentally different, but everything seemed the same and in place.

He took a taxi back to Andromeda to collect his clothes and computer and found that his bill had been paid by management. He sat in the lobby collecting his thoughts, watching people come and go, paying him no attention.

He then decided he needed to talk to Michelle so he phoned a friend he had at the phone company, a guy named Phil Leslie. Phil was actually more of Hayden's friend—had gone to school with her, in fact—but he genuinely liked John and so he helped him out on occasion in getting phone numbers or addresses.

"Thanks, Phil, I owe you," John said, hanging up.

John looked around Michelle's house. The fence surrounding the property was broken and mangled, and the lawn hadn't been cut in weeks—maybe months. Ugly, grotesque, dull-coloured weeds tangled with a few scattered flowers still miraculously surviving in the hostile terrain. The lawn had more rubble, pebbles, and small boulders than blades of grass.

It was one of those old houses on an old street that nobody paid much attention to, least of all the residents who lived there. The house was narrow and slanted, and John expected to see a few rusted tires or a car up on blocks.

John rapped his knuckles on the door, and while he waited, he looked around nervously, stuffing his one good hand into his pocket before taking it out and pressing it up against his side.

It was ten o'clock in the morning and the summer sky was slightly overcast, but behind the pink-and-woolly-looking clouds, the sun shone, offering a promise of warmth.

He touched his shoulder gingerly without thinking. It didn't feel all that bad, but he was heavily doused up with painkillers. John heard the sound of heavy footsteps approach. The door opened slowly. A middle-aged man with a dirty brown shirt stood at the entrance.

"What do you want?" he said. He had a lumpy face and was bald, except for a ring of curly hair around the base of his skull.

"Does Michelle live here?"

The man looked quizzically at John for a moment and John thought he was going to slam the door in his face, but instead he asked after a while, "Is she the MILF?"

John looked down, suddenly embarrassed. "I don't know. She's tall, brown hair. Last name is Lake."

"Hold on a second," the man said. He closed the door. John heard him yell for Michelle, and a few minutes later the door opened again. Michelle stood there in a flowery, strapless dress. She wore no makeup, and her hair was tied tightly back. She looked so different in daylight, John barely recognized her.

Michelle frowned, gripping the edge of the door. "How did you find my address?"

John smiled despite himself. "A journalist has his ways."

Michelle reached out and touched John's shoulder, which was in a sling. "My God. I heard … you okay?"

John shrugged as if it was no big deal. "I've been worse off. I was shot in Afghanistan in the leg."

Michelle leaned one arm against her doorframe. Her concern

disappeared, and her face became unreadable. "What are you doing here? I told you everything I know."

"Can I come in?"

"How did you find where I lived?" She looked at John, her jaw tight with annoyance. "I know the club didn't give it to you. Was it the diner?"

"I have a friend who works for the phone company. He comes in very useful sometimes," John said.

A child started crying in the background. "Sorry—it's Ella ... Please come in."

John stepped in and closed the door behind him. He was in a dark, rank-smelling hallway. He could hear the television coming from the room directly on his left, and the hazy glow from the screen spilled out on to the dark wooden floor, changing and morphing.

John waited, looking around the walls. There were a couple of cheap landscape prints hanging. He watched a fly buzz around and then land on a candlestick that didn't have any candle. Michelle came back with a baby in her arms.

"This is Ella," Michelle said. "You have any kids?"

John nodded. "Yeah. A boy named Byron. But I was always—let's say I wasn't around much. My own father died when I was young and ... so I guess ..." John paused with embarrassment. Why was he talking to Michelle about this? Was it because his argument with Hayden was still too raw? Did he feel he needed to justify himself to somebody—even if it was a waitress at a strip club?

Michelle smiled understandingly, making her cheeks look small and dainty. "It's okay; I hardly know you."

John shrugged, but a moment of understanding passed between them. He looked away and saw a small, frameless picture on the wall next to the landscapes, of Michelle and Ella and a tall, handsome-looking man with faded, kinky hair. His feet were spread apart, and he was smiling widely and confidently toward the camera.

"This Ella's father?" John asked.

Michelle nodded slowly. "Yeah ... James."

John stared at the picture, feeling a strange pang of jealousy. "What does James do?"

"He's not around ... You want to come into the kitchen?'

John nodded and followed Michelle into the kitchen. It was no better than the hallway—dishes were piled up in the sink, the stove had dried pasta sauce covering it, and it smelled of yesterday's meal. They sat at a small wooden table in the corner. Michelle turned a switch, and the overhead light begrudgingly flickered on.

Michelle asked, "What's your next story going to be about?"

"What do you mean?"

"Your next story ... or are you going to take some time off?"

John shook his head. "No time off for me."

Michelle raised her thin eyebrows, her mouth shaped into an *O*. "You're not going to, you know, stop? Even after they tried to kill you?"

"Michelle, I thought you knew me enough to know I don't write articles about the old lady down the street who lost her dog or the boy who had leukemia."

"Why not? Everybody loves dogs."

The question baffled John. He couldn't tell if she was sincere or not. "Why don't I? ... I dunno, it's just not in me, I guess. It's not what I do."

"Coffee or anything?"

"You have a beer? That would be nice." John had been craving one since he had been in the hospital.

Michelle raised her eyebrows, but nodded. "Sure—at least I think we do."

John nodded appreciatively.

Michelle said, "Hold Ella for a second."

John tried to object, but before he could say anything, he had Ella in his lap. Ella looked up at John and then let out a low sound, like the hissing of a tire, before nestling into John's arms. John's heart thumped loudly—so loudly, in fact, John was sure it would disturb the baby and she would collapse into another crying fit. But instead, Ella closed her eyes and her body relaxed.

She smelled of soap, and his breath of onions. A strong, bitter wave of nostalgia swept through John as he looked down, reminded of when Byron was just a baby. He mostly remembered saying good-bye as he left for the airport. Kissing Hayden dutifully on the mouth and then getting into the taxi. For the first time, he wondered if he had been running away instead of going to something. Responsibility, he supposed, was something he had never been very good at.

John asked, "Where did you get the name Ella?"

Michelle took out a beer from the fridge, popped the tab, and handed it to John. "After Ella Fitzgerald, of course. When I was pregnant, I thought if there was one talent I could bestow on her, it would be to sing."

"You can sing?"

"I used to—when I was younger. Jazzy stuff mostly. But I also did musicals. Was in *Rent* when I was in my twenties. I can't anymore—too much partying."

John smiled encouragingly. "Bet you were real good."

Michelle smiled thinly. "You want me to take Ella back?"

"I'm fine … that is, if you're okay." Ella had closed her eyes and was breathing deeply, peacefully. She looked half-asleep, and John kind of liked having the warm body against his chest.

Michelle nodded. "John, why are you here?"

John didn't answer for a while. He didn't want to disturb the peace he felt, the goodwill Michelle had extended to him. But there was no use putting it off either. "How did you know Ken Dzyinski?"

Michelle took a lighter and a pack of cigarettes out from her pocket and placed them on the table. She took a single cigarette from the pack and lit it. She then took in a long drag and nodded toward the cigarettes on the table. "Still don't?"

"Nope."

"Ken came to the club sometimes."

"Michelle, we both know that's a lie."

There was silence. John heard the soft pitter-patter of somebody coming down a stairwell, and then a woman appeared in the kitchen. She was wearing a thin white nightshirt and yellow panties. The woman opened the fridge and grabbed a Coke. She had mousy blondish hair and a pretty face with too much mascara. She made no motion to introduce herself. She stared at John and then Michelle, unsmiling, seemingly unembarrassed by her partial nudity. She popped the can open and disappeared into another room.

John said, "Tell me about Ken Dzyinski."

Michelle looked back at the room the woman had just disappeared into, seemingly troubled by the demand. Finally she said, "I didn't know him very well. He tipped well, always had a bunch of people around him."

"Do you go to the funeral of all great tippers?"

Michelle seemed to struggle to come up with some sort of lie, but then she smiled and said, "No."

John became increasingly agitated by her lack of cooperation. "I want to know who you told where I was."

"I didn't tell anybody. I told you—I had to get off work. I showed up, but by that time …"

John handed Ella back to Michelle so he could drink his beer. Ella seemed not to notice the change of hands and was as peaceful as ever. John watched as Michelle cuddled Ella in her arms. John took a short sip of beer, careful not to appear too greedy. It tasted good going down his throat. "You were the only one I told. Even my editor didn't know where I was."

She stared at him. "I didn't tell anybody—I swear."

John sighed. The trouble was he wanted to believe her. But—perhaps for the first time—he didn't trust his own instinct. Was it just because he was attracted to her? Was it just because she was pretty and had a feminine vulnerability to her? He searched for other options. "Was it possible somebody was listening in on our conversation?"

Michelle shrugged. "Don't know. The club? Possibly. It's not known for its privacy."

John tried not to sigh again. It was the booze—skewed his judgment. He should never have phoned Michelle from the casino. Something he never would have done when he was younger. "You didn't tell anybody where you were going afterward?"

"Maybe somebody spotted you there and made a phone call? You were hiding out at a casino. You don't think maybe that wasn't the brightest idea?"

John had to admit she was probably right. He had been right under Ernest Hunter's nose, after all. He had probably seen him on one of the thousand surveillance cameras, or one of the security guards had picked him out of a crowd.

John took another sip of beer. He desperately wanted to take it with him, but knew he couldn't. "Okay," he said. "I should probably go."

Michelle looked up at him and nodded. "Okay."

John collected his coat and put on his shoes. Michelle followed him into the hallway, watching him silently. As he opened the door, she said, "John …"

John turned to look at her. "Yes?"

"You a big traveler?"

John frowned, confused. "Not really anymore. I used to when I was younger … for work mostly. My first job was with Reuters. Went places only a desperate young reporter would go—Congo, Ethiopia, Ivory Coast … Why do you ask?"

Michelle shifted pensively in her spot. "You ever go to India?"

"No, but I've been to Pakistan. The east side—not close to India."

Michelle looked down at Ella. "The only place I've really been is New York—when I was just a girl. You've been to New York, I suppose."

"Of course. Many times. It's my favourite city."

Michelle nodded as if she was barely listening. "I would like to go to India. Learn how to be a yoga instructor."

John frowned. "You like yoga?"

Michelle smiled, slightly embarrassed. "I only just started, but yeah …"

John nodded, unsure of what to say or why she was telling him. "Good luck," he finally managed.

John went home thinking about all the mysteries Michelle had. Perhaps that was why he liked her so much. He knew he should have been harder on her, pressed a little more, but much to his chagrin, she had clouded him with her long legs and luminous mahogany-coloured eyes.

John pushed the door open to his apartment without the use of his key: the lock was broken again. He climbed the creaky steps to his unit. He threw his keys carelessly on the kitchen counter and looked around at the clutter, the half-eaten pizza on the counter, and the grubby floors. It was just as bad as Michelle's home, if not worse.

How long had he lived like this? It seemed like only a couple of days and not years since Hayden had kicked him out of their house. So where had this mess come from? Had it just suddenly arrived?

His arm was throbbing again, and he laid down on the couch and tried to go to sleep. He knew he couldn't afford to rest. He needed to find Ken Dzyinski's killer before he was dragged to court, but he was too groggy to do much of anything, let alone put together some sort of plan. Would he throw Drake McMillan to the police? No, he couldn't do that. His whole reputation as an investigative journalist would be gone—the reputation he had spent his entire professional career building. But the alternative was jail. If he had been younger, the thought of jail wouldn't have troubled him, but now …

He wondered what would happen if he went on the lam again. But he knew the answer to that one. A warrant would be issued for his arrest. He wouldn't get very far—two, three days of freedom tops.

He phoned his lawyer, Mack Carrington. Mack answered on the third ring.

"Hey, Mack, it's John. Can you get the court date pushed back, stall a little? I need more time."

"John, I'm sorry," Mack said in his deep Scottish accent. "I will try, but I'm just about out of moves."

"So what? You're just giving up on me?"

"I've filed everything I could. This thing is going ahead."

John gave a deep sigh. "Okay, thanks, Mack," he said and hung up.

Susan Dzyinski

It was an act of desperation, no doubt about it, but the two detectives had little choice but to rehash old territory. With that thought in mind, Lewis pushed the entry bell. It made a high-pitched whine like the slow boil of a kettle. The detectives waited in the driveway, their unmarked cruiser parked diagonally across the wide driveway.

"Yes?" came an unfriendly voice through the speaker.

They looked at the monstrous mansion through a fifteen-foot iron fence. The mansion had several green gables, a double oak door, aluminum siding, and a four-door garage. It was painted a sombre maroon colour.

"VPD. We've come to see Mrs. Dzyinski."

"I'm sorry, but she's sick and not seeing anybody today."

Lewis asked, "Did we not make ourselves clear? Vancouver Police. We don't make appointments."

There was hesitation on the other side. The man was obviously weighing his options. "Let me see how she's feeling."

They waited, and as they waited, Wiltore peered at the cameras on top of the bars. The house was more of a fortress than anything else. It sat well back on a flat, expansive piece of luscious green grass, trimmed and well-manicured. Thick deeply-rooted spruce trees lined the driveway up to the house.

The cops had spent the day casing Andromeda Casino; they had talked to the patrons, the dealers, the managers, even Ernest Hunter. But the cops didn't learn anything new. None of the witnesses professed to getting a good look at the gunman.

Hunter had provided the security tapes with surprisingly little protest. But even the tapes hadn't shown anything particularly useful. They recorded Webster gambling a little and drinking at the bar.

Eventually the gate doors swung open, and the two cops got back into their car and drove up the driveway. Two bulky-looking men came out of the house to greet Wiltore and Lewis. The two men—both over six feet tall and at least two hundred and fifty pounds—had authoritative looks in their dark eyes. They had ear pierces and shaved heads, and wore charcoal-coloured suits.

"Credentials please," one of them asked.

The two cops showed their badges. The security guards wrote down their badge numbers on a notepad and then handed the badges back. "Okay," they nodded. "Detectives, please follow us."

Wiltore and Lewis found themselves in a cavernous white-walled hallway, a crystal chandelier overhead, a pine-coloured wooden floor underneath their feet. Wiltore tried not to stare at any one thing for too long. There was a carpeted stairwell to their left, but directly in front of them was a long hallway that the security guards directed them down. Hanging on both walls were large acrylic paintings with ornate, golden frames.

They entered a dark room painted a blood-red, with a large shag carpet and several large cushioned seats. At the far end was a long oblong mirror overlooking a bar, table, and clutter of stools. On the bar was a careful arrangement of alcohol. Along the walls were posters from classic movies—*Scarface, Taxi Driver, Magnificent Seven, Casablanca.* The whole room looked like it was based on a seventies' New York disco club.

The two security guards offered the detectives drinks, but they declined.

One of the security guards said, "Make yourselves comfortable; Mrs. Dzyinski will be here soon."

Wiltore nodded politely, but nobody moved. Nobody relaxed. Lewis walked over to a bookcase next to the bar and started opening a photo album.

"Hey," the security guard said. "You can't be touching that."

Wiltore stepped in front of the huge security guard, hoping he looked braver than he felt. "Don't go telling her what she can and can't be looking at."

The security guard hesitated, unsure what to do, glancing back at his partner who was standing by the door. "You got a warrant?"

Wiltore said, "Hey, we were invited in, remember?"

Lewis shut the album and put it back on the shelf. "It's okay. I'm done."

A couple minutes later, Mrs. Dzyinski entered from the left, closing the door behind her. She was barefoot and moved quickly and quietly, almost as if she was floating. She was wearing pink sweats and a pink hoodie that cut off at her stomach, showing muscular, tanned abs with a silver-studded belly ring. Her long blonde hair was shiny and shimmered when she moved in the light. Her eyebrows were plucked and trimmed down to pencil-thin lines.

She floated over and shook the detectives' hands. Her grip was light, almost nonexistent. "Pleasure to see you again, detectives," she said, although her eyes were void and apprehensive, betraying it was no pleasure at all.

She collapsed into one of the large chairs, as if her legs couldn't hold up her body weight anymore.

"This used to be my husband's favourite room," she said. "I thought it appropriate to meet here."

"We are terribly sorry to inconvenience you again, Mrs. Dzyinski."

She inspected her French nails, putting her feet up on the cushions. She seemed strangely detached. Wiltore looked at her closely. The skin around her eyes was slightly whiter than the rest of her face. Botox maybe.

"Please call me Sue," she said, barely above a whisper. She raised her eyes. "Were you offered a drink?"

"No, thank you, Sue."

"Pity …" She looked over at the bar. "I don't know who's going to drink all this alcohol."

Wiltore took a step forward. "We'd like to ask you a few more questions."

She looked around the room as if she hadn't heard him. "You like movies? Sometimes Ken would spend the entire day watching them. Not very many people knew he was a walking encyclopaedia about everything Hollywood. He could tell you when all the old pictures were made. We used to go to the movies every Friday. That was before we had kids, of course."

Wiltore looked around the room, saying nothing. He had a hard time imagining Ken Dzyinski watching *Gone with the Wind*.

"You find them? The people who did this?" Her voice was pitiful enough to make Wiltore and Lewis look down at the shag carpet.

"No, madam, not yet."

"But at least you're close?"

"Well … we are hoping the journalist will help with the case once he appears before the court. We served him a subpoena."

"Which journalist?" Sue asked, her eyebrows raised.

"His name is John Webster; you may have heard of him."

Sue didn't say anything for a long time. She was staring at Humphrey Bogart. "You're saying the journalist knows more than you do?"

Wiltore glanced towards the bar to hide his annoyance. "Sue, we don't know what John Webster knows. But he was shot outside of a casino the other night. You know anything about that?"

Sue raised her body in her seat. A flash of anger crossed her eyes. "Why would I know anything about that?"

"Please, don't play games with us. I'm not in the mood today. We know you still have connections."

"I never got involved with anything like that."

Lewis asked, "What do you know about Paul Gibson?"

Sue thought for a moment. "He the real estate guy?"

"That's right."

Sue shrugged. "I don't know—nothing."

"But he's been over at this house?"

Wiltore looked at Lewis, wondering what she was getting at, before turning his attention back to Sue. She was obviously wondering the same thing and took a while to answer. "I don't know … maybe."

Lewis suddenly seemed very intense. "Please, think back."

Sue glanced at her two bodyguards. "Possibly. We threw a lot of parties."

"Why would an upstanding, honest businessman be at one of your parties?"

Sue frowned, squinting her eyes. Amazingly she still had no wrinkles on her face. "I won't have you insulting me in my house."

The two security guards took this as a cue to negotiate the two police officers back to the door, but neither Wiltore nor Lewis would have any of it. "Were they in business together?" Lewis asked.

"I already told you, I knew nothing of my husband's business dealings."

Lewis nodded, seemingly satisfied with this answer. "Thanks for your time, Mrs. Dzyinski."

The security guards guided the police officers back to their car. As they were driving out onto the road, the gate closing behind them, Wiltore asked Lewis, "What was all that about?"

Lewis smiled smugly. "While I was looking through the photo album, I saw several pictures of Paul Gibson."

"So what? Maybe he was like his brother and just liked hanging out with gangsters."

Lewis looked over at Wiltore. "There was one with Dzyinski's arm around him."

"You think they were in business together?" Wiltore asked.

Lewis nodded slowly. "Their deaths were no coincidence. Hunter was after both of them. We just need to find out why."

The Fighter

The gym was in a generic strip mall, with a green awning, an incandescent sign, and large paneled windows. It didn't look like anything out of the ordinary. John told the cabbie to stop at the far end of the parking lot. He watched the entrance for a moment while the taxi sat idling. He got out a twenty-dollar bill and handed it to the cabbie.

John walked across the parking lot and opened the door to Wally Couldhard's gym. The air inside was stale and lifeless, coated with sweat. All around him were punching bags, speedballs, free weights, and skipping ropes scattered across the gym floor. There was a soft neon glow that reflected off the mirrors. On the far wall there were great boards of advertisements. John noted one was for Andromeda Casino. According to several newspaper reports he had read, Andromeda was a major sponsor of Couldhard.

John looked for a receptionist, but there was nobody around. In fact, his entrance had gone unnoticed by a group of perhaps fifteen or twenty men who were crowding around a ring in the far corner of the gym. There was a sudden eruption of cheering and jeering.

John, curious what the exhibition was, peeked between the crowd and saw two topless, sweat-soaked men trying to manhandle each other. One was in red shorts and was rubbery-looking, bald, slightly flabby, and stubby-armed. The other man was in black shorts, and he was a little taller and muscular, with a darker complexion.

Despite Black Shorts' height and strength advantage, Red Shorts seemed to be winning on quickness and technique. Red Shorts took two small steps forward and threw a punch combination while his opponent, Black Shorts, backtracked, begging for time. Black Shorts had obviously taken a beating: he had a bloody eye and was panting hard.

They circled each other like birds in a cockfight. The crowd egged them on, willing the fighters to smash each other. Black Shorts kicked at Red Shorts' ankles, trying to regain some momentum, but his kicks were ineffectual. Red Shorts kept throwing punches, which Black Shorts tried to block. Then, with one step, Red Shorts darted in and connected on the temple. It wasn't a hard punch, but it knocked Black Shorts back against the ropes.

John pressed up against the crowd to get a better look. He rubbed up against a burly-looking man with some sort of tattoo engraved on the back of his neck. John smelled a mixture of breath mints and nicotine. He could feel the excitement in the crowd, a low rattle of electricity, and the thick swell of anticipation. All eyes were fixed on the ring, almost hypnotised. Nobody seemed to notice or care about John, who stuck out like a sore thumb among the tattooed, shaved-head, wifebeater-wearing men with golden earrings.

Red Shorts gave a roundhouse kick that just barely missed his fatigued opponent. Black Shorts counterattacked, but Red Shorts dodged easily. Black Shorts seemed to gain a little of his breathing back and started attacking, but then Red Shorts threw a bit of a wild punch, but somehow managed to land on his opponent's jaw. Black Shorts spat a glob of blood onto the canvas, stumbling backward against the grey ropes, struggling to stay upright. Red Shorts threw a classic left jab. His opponent went down in a heap, and in a moment Red Shorts was on him, punching him in a fury until the referee called the fight.

The crowd went crazy, arms thrust up into the air, some wildly cheering, some cursing and swearing too. Money begrudgingly changed hands and was quickly pocketed. Not until it all died down did John ask the double-chinned man where Wally Couldhard was. The man looked at John strangely, only now noticing him.

"You're shitting me, right?"

"No …" John said, wishing he had pulled a picture of him from the Internet.

The man with the double chin pointed to the man with the red shorts who was still doing small victory laps around his opponent. "That's Wally," he said.

John nodded. "Thanks."

He pushed through the crowd until he was right up against the ropes. Wally looked like he had taken his fair share of beatings. His face was flat and ugly, and his nose was incongruously shaped like a *Z*—broken, replaced, broken again. Wally smiled, and John could see two golden fillings.

John felt a tap on his shoulder. He turned and saw the man with the double chin frowning at him. "Who are you anyway?"

"My name is John Webster. I work for the *Daily Globe.*"

"Somebody fucked up your arm?"

John sized the man up. "I just want to talk to Wally."

The man glared at John, his eyes seeming like two unripe grapes. "Maybe he doesn't want to talk to you."

John ignored him, turning his back on the man—perhaps not the smartest of moves, but John took a chance the man wouldn't sucker punch him—and tried to catch Wally's attention.

Wally's opponent was being treated by two unimpressive-looking men—certainly not doctors and probably not even medically trained, but nevertheless, they were patching the fighter up, checking for broken bones, fractures, giving him some water and some pills, bandaging his cuts. Amid all the commotion, the referee had gotten a towel and was on all fours, trying to wipe the blood off the mat.

Wally, seemingly ignoring everything around him, ducked under the rope and walked toward a door at the end of the gym. John followed, the double-chinned man close behind him.

"Mr. Couldhard, can I talk to you for a second?" John called after him.

The double-chinned man spoke for Wally. "No, he's busy, can't you see that?"

Wally stopped and turned to face John. The sweat made his muscular body shiny. He was breathing heavily.

"Who are you?" he asked.

"John Webster from the *Daily Globe.*"

Wally appraised John, nodding toward John's sling. "You were the one who was shot?" he asked. This fact seemed to garnish some respect with the ultimate fighter.

"You were at the casino when it happened," John said.

Wally nodded. "Come into the change room with me."

The man with the double-chin protested. "Wally, you can't just be talking to reporters like that—not without being prepped first."

Wally said, "Don't mind him, man. He's just my manager, Leon."

The three of them entered the change room. Wally opened a locker and brought out his gym bag. He unwrapped the bandages on his feet and hands and slid on a shirt. "You know, I was almost killed once," Wally said. "Back when I was younger, I was part of a gang. We did a whole bunch of stupid shit, man. Thought we were the Crips or something. We would shoot up other gangs' houses, man. And, of course, they would retaliate."

"Is that how you know Ernie Hunter?" John asked.

Wally stopped abruptly and looked up at John. "No, no, man."

Again Leon protested. "You don't have to answer, Wally."

Wally glared at his manager. "Shut up, Leon."

John continued, "But you're good friends with him?"

Wally shrugged and put on a pair of sweatpants. "We have a business relationship, man. He sponsors me, man."

"Apparently you are in his casino a lot."

Wally shrugged. "I suppose, man. I make my appearances."

"You know he's linked to organized crime?"

Again Wally shrugged, closing his locker. "People say a lot of things."

"I think Hunter tried to kill me that night."

Wally smiled, showing his golden teeth. "Come on, man. Why would he do a thing like that?"

"Did you see anything suspicious that night?"

Wally laughed. "When I'm there, I have people coming up to me all the time asking for my autograph, talking to me. I don't have time to notice anything suspicious."

"Do you know Carl Dewitt or Keith Dowell?"

Wally hoisted the gym bag over his shoulder. "What do you want from me? You think I'm going to rat out my friends?"

"Nobody will know. I'll use you on background—nobody will know. Please, Mr. Couldhard, just give me something I can print." John felt slightly embarrassed sounding so desperate.

Wally and Leon exchanged significant looks. Wally then turned back to John. "Look, I admire you—getting shot, man. You're hard-core, no doubt about it, but man, I can't help you. But, hey, if you ever want tickets to any of my fights, phone Leon here."

John left the gym feeling frustrated. He walked to the street, hoping to catch a taxi. If not, he would have to call one. But as he was walking, a man came toward him. He had on dark clothes and a Diesel beanie pulled tightly down on his face. He had thick golden earrings in his ears. John thought about running, but if the man was going to shoot, John thought, he would have done it already.

John's fear must have shown in his face because the man said, "Don't worry; I'm not going to hurt you."

John asked. "Who are you?"

"I'm your friend. I have some information you might want."

John peered at his face. He seemed familiar somehow. "What sort of information?" John asked.

The man glanced nervously back at the gym. "Not here. Come with me."

John shook his head. "No, I don't think so."

The man shrugged and started to waddle away. John hesitated. The attack at the casino was still fresh in his mind. What if it was a trap? But if this man really did have important information, could he afford to let him walk away? He glanced toward the road and the cars that hurtled past him. The engine noise, although close, seemed muted and irrelevant and might as well have been a thousand miles away. If John got into trouble, nobody would be able to save him.

John gritted his teeth. He had to chance it, figuring if Ernest Hunter wanted him dead, then he could have just shot him dead in the parking lot. Why set an elaborate trap? John caught up to the man. "Okay. Where to?"

They walked around to a dark alley at the back of the gym. There John hesitated again. The alleyway had no lights and smelled of sewage and grease.

The man turned back to John. "Come on. I don't have all day."

John followed. They passed through the alleyway to another parking lot, which was empty except for a plain white van. The man opened the sliding door and got into the back.

John asked, "Can't we talk out here?"

"I don't want anybody seeing us."

Reluctantly, John stepped into the back of the van, and the man closed the door. The man turned on a small rooftop light, and when he did so, John recognized him. He was the man who had fought Wally. Now that the man wasn't moving around in a blur of kicks and punches, John studied him closely. He had a small mouth, hollow cheeks, a day's worth of stubble, and a scar above his left eye. His right eye was black, and he had bloody tissue stuck up his nose. His pale, reddish skin made him look old, but John put him at no more than thirty.

The two men sat on plywood planks. John looked around at his surroundings. The van smelled of rotten eggs and stale tobacco. There were tools and scraps of metal scattered everywhere, so John had to be careful where he put his feet.

The man leaned his head back against the door. He was breathing deeply through his mouth. He seemed content to just sit there.

"What's your name?" John asked.

But the man just smiled—it was the tiniest of smiles. Several of his teeth were missing. "I'm just a concerned citizen."

"Okay, what do you know?"

"You go to many fights?"

John shook his head. "No, I don't follow."

The fighter grabbed an ice pack from a cooler in the corner and placed it over his eye. "I recognized you from the television," the fighter said.

John knew by experience sometimes he couldn't rush things. People got around to what they wanted to say only in their time. "I guess I'm famous now."

"Tell me … what's it like being shot?"

"I don't know … At first it doesn't feel like anything, and then there's a lot of pain."

The fighter let out an unsatisfactory grunt. "Heard you were asking around about Ernest Hunter."

"You know anything about him?"

"Sure, know he runs the Andromeda Casino."

"What else?"

"He's supposedly some big-time gangster."

"You don't think so?"

The fighter shrugged. "I try to keep out of those things."

John studied the fighter carefully. "But you know something."

"Ernie used to sponsor me … but people say I'm past my prime. Wally is the up-and-comer. Going to make it big-time, supposedly. Ernie likes his ultimate fighting."

John waited for the fighter to continue. Eventually, after a long pause, he said, "You can't quote me. I don't want anything I say in the papers."

John nodded. "Okay."

"There was a rumour going around that Ken Dzyinski wanted to build a casino."

"A casino? Where?"

"Get this—five blocks away from Andromeda."

John gave the fighter an incredulous look. "Really? How would he ever put that through the city? Surely they wouldn't allow two casinos in the same area?"

"Apparently it was a done deal."

John thought for a moment. "Where did you hear this?"

The fighter shrugged, switching the ice pack over to the other eye.

"You're not going to tell me?"

"No."

"I won't print it."

"Even so, some things are best left alone."

John weighed his options and came to the conclusion he better not push, but also knew he would have to get somebody else to substantiate it before he even wrote a single word. John shook his head irritated. Again he thought about his court date as it loomed over him. How would he finish his article in time?

John said, "And Hunter couldn't allow that to happen?"

"You know how much money he makes from that casino? But the real reason is all his drug money gets washed through there. It is invaluable."

"But why would Dzyinski do that?"

The fighter shrugged. "Probably as a direct challenge to Hunter ... or possibly just to fuck with him."

John suddenly remembered the Paul Gibson murder. "You know anything about Paul Gibson?"

The fighter shook his head. "Was he the real estate tycoon who was murdered?"

John said, "The police think perhaps the Gibson and Dzyinski murders were connected. Maybe Gibson was going to finance the casino for Dzyinski."

The fighter shrugged. "I don't know. Possibly."

John stopped for a moment. Something didn't add up. Then he realized what it was. "How do you know this about Dzyinski anyway? I mean, you're Hunter's man."

The fighter spat a glob of saliva and blood onto the floor. "Hey, I'm nobody's fucking man."

John held up his hands. "Sorry, I didn't mean it like that. But you traveled in his circles. How did you hear this rumour about Dzyinski? It doesn't make sense."

The fighter glanced down at the plywood, shifting his body, embarrassed. "Does it matter?"

The fighter looked up at John again. There was a guilty look in his eyes, and in that very moment, John guessed it. "You were buying from Dzyinski, weren't you?"

The fighter tilted his chin back. "Only a little bit ... for the pain."

"You didn't go to Hunter?"

The fighter shook his head. "His people wouldn't let me. Said if I get caught, it would be the end of my career."

"Maybe that's why Hunter dropped you."

"If Hunter found out, he would have dropped a lot more than just my contract."

"Bet Dzyinski was more than happy to oblige," John said. "What did he give you?"

"Well, at first it was just Demerol ..."

John shook his head. He imagined Dzyinski destroying Hunter's prized fighter just out of spite. "Bet he never charged you a penny for it, did he?"

The fighter glanced away, and that said everything that needed to be said.

John thanked the fighter, climbed out of the van, and went back through the alley to the strip mall. He walked along Third Avenue for a while, walking aimlessly, trying to gather his thoughts, but at the same time trying to gather awareness of his surroundings.

There was the general city noise—a jumble of cars and machines, the wind tunnelling through the buildings. The streets were straight, and there were telephone poles like rows of soldiers standing at attention, giving the illusion of order and rule.

John kept walking until he reached Minoru Street, and there he turned left. The general organization of the traffic lights and the city should have had a settling effect on John's mind—but in fact, it had quite the opposite. He felt a mixture of fear and dread. Was there someone waiting for him out there? Was this where he bought it? Not in some war-torn country, as one might suppose. A rush of blood reached John's head, and he looked around him as if a marksman would materialize from nowhere and within seconds, everything—the problems with Hayden, his article, the subpoena—would all be over.

John dug his hands into his pockets and kept walking. He felt he was back in Afghanistan and Iraq—the old queasy feeling of never being completely at ease, never being able to completely relax; as if he was tracking down some half rumour of Al Qaeda or the CIA or some other militant group and not just after some drug lord, some trafficker of women. It wasn't that the tall, decaying, ruddy buildings of Gastown or the concrete of Richmond were like the bright, sun-soaked ones in Baghdad or in Fallujah. It wasn't that the despondent Vancouver homeless compared in any way to the white-clad Muslims. No. There were deeper connections that John didn't understand, a deeper psychological link.

John realized he had recreated this scenario. Why? Was it because he fed off the feeling of living in life's grey area, the proxy to death? Or was it the nostalgia he felt whenever he had a lead? A subconscious longing to be back there, not just covering the great American blunder, the story of our time, but to be in a riotous world, in another turbulent time, when his body wasn't broken and his muscles didn't ache, when he still had the remnants of a marriage and happiness was just dangling spectacularly out of reach—before the epiphany that fate had seen another path, when he clung to some useless naivety that his life's work wouldn't be a continual downward spiral of disappointments.

Comparing Notes

Wiltore and Lewis walked into Fusion Coffee Shop. They ordered, and as Wiltore waited for his drinks, he looked around the store. It seemed to be run by young men and women wearing bowler caps, hipster shirts, and unnecessarily large glasses. Whatever misgivings Wiltore had about the place, they certainly had the best coffee in town.

Wiltore was in a good mood, a rarity recently. The subpoena had been delivered to Webster, and now it was only a matter of time before he divulged his sources. Wiltore was slowly choking the journalist, squeezing him from all sides until he had no choice but to divulge everything he knew about the gangsters.

Lewis came back from the washroom. She adjusted her ponytail. "Cliff …"

Wiltore looked at her. She seemed to be gaining some courage to ask something. "Yes?"

"I'm curious … Somebody said—I forget who, that you went down to New York after 9/11 to help with the cleanup."

Wiltore frowned in confusion. He hadn't thought about that for a long time. "What about it?"

"Well, what was it like?"

Wiltore's good mood was quickly evaporating. "Why do you want to know?"

Lewis shrugged, staring past Wiltore, out the window. "I don't know. I'm curious, that's all."

Wiltore felt an anger swell in his throat. It came suddenly and unexpected. "It was ten years ago. I helped clear some rubble. That was it."

Lewis gave a curt nod. "Sure." There was a long pause. She looked down at her black shoes. "Cliff? Is there something you don't like about me?"

Wiltore raised his eyebrows. "What do you mean?"

Lewis didn't say anything for a while. Instead, she looked out the window, her eyes glazed over. Wiltore waited for her to continue, and finally she did. "I mean, why were we put together?"

Wiltore suppressed a sigh, longing to be back with Marcus. Marcus would never have asked about cleaning up Ground Zero. He would have had the good sense to shut up. "Why? The answer is simple enough. I needed a new partner, and you needed somebody to show you the ropes."

Lewis nodded, and they waited in uncomfortable silence until they got their lattes and went back to the car, sipping on their drinks as they drove back to the police station. Wiltore drove into their parking space and killed the engine. Lewis got out of the car, but Wiltore didn't move.

Lewis looked back. "What?"

Wiltore didn't look at Lewis, but stared straight ahead into the dark, cavernous garage. "I didn't mean to be so … harsh, I guess. It's just some things are best left where they belong."

"Sure," Lewis said, although she sounded uncertain. "Is that it?"

"And I'm sorry if I haven't … warmed up to you as I should. It's just that Marcus was, I don't know, very different. We understood each other, I suppose."

"What do you want? An apology because I'm a woman?" Lewis asked.

Wiltore snapped his head toward Lewis in surprise. "No, it's nothing to do with that."

Lewis shrugged, slightly incredulously it seemed to Wiltore, as if to say it didn't really matter.

They took the elevator to a conference room on the sixth floor. They were to meet two detectives, Sergeants Devin Blake and Damon Cook, who were on the Paul Gibson case. Wiltore had worked with both of them on several other cases as part of the Integrated Gang Task Force. Both were good cops.

Lewis asked, "You really think this will do any good?"

Wiltore shrugged. "Who knows? But they seem connected, don't you think?"

"Yeah, I suppose—I don't know."

"Worth a shot, at least."

Both Blake and Cook were small-neck men with crew cuts that had gone out of fashion in the early nineties. They greeted Wiltore and Lewis with tough cop-like handshakes. They had large dark circles under their eyes—a look Wiltore was all too familiar with.

"What? You didn't bring us any?" Cook asked with a smile, indicating the lattes. Wiltore forced himself to smile.

All four officers sat down behind the large pseudo-oak vinyl table. Wiltore and Lewis sat facing the large window that looked out on to downtown and the ambitious, audacious skyscrapers, and beyond that, the curling tip of Stanley Park and the local mountains, which were the colour of unpasteurized milk.

Blake and Cook sat forward in their seats. They wore conventional greenish-brown American-style suits that were popular with a lot of detectives—made them seem a little more cavalier, Wiltore supposed.

Cook looked from Lewis to Wiltore, and asked, "What do you got for us?"

Lewis told them about the photographs in Dzyinski's house. This seemed to intrigue Blake and Cook, who gave each other knowing glances. Wiltore suddenly realized he was envious of them. It wasn't just that they got the better case, but it was the connection they shared—that he used to share with Marcus. And he realized maybe he didn't like Tamara Lewis all that much, not for what she was, but for what she wasn't.

After Lewis had outlined the Dzyinski investigation, Wiltore asked how the Paul Gibson case was going. The details had all been over the paper: Gibson had been driving to work early in the morning in his BMW Coupe when he had stopped at a traffic light. A large SUV (some said blue, some said grey) pulled up beside him and pumped him and his car full of bullet holes. The SUV had sped off, almost hitting a red Neon. The SUV had been found a couple of hours later underneath the Arthur Lang Bridge, burned to a crisp, just like the getaway vehicle for the Dzyinski shooting.

Blake and Cook sighed simultaneously. Blake spoke first. "Not much to go on ... Sure, Gibson had some enemies, sure, some pissed-off landlords, but nobody with the motivation or the know-how to pull something like this off."

Wiltore leaned forward in his chair. "No descriptions?"

Blake shook his head. "Nothing."

Wiltore shook his head. "People today ... too engrossed in their cell phones to be any fucking good as witnesses."

"And what makes things worse is the brother, Alex Gibson, has skipped town. His lawyer won't tell us anything—only that he is on a personal leave of absence."

"You think he maybe ordered the hit?" Lewis asked suddenly.

Blake and Cook both shrugged. "We don't know. Maybe. What we know is they were on good terms, or so it seemed. We checked into his finances, didn't find anything irregular in his bank account or the company's, but with these rich motherfuckers, who knows?" Blake said.

Wiltore said, "Maybe he's at the bottom of the Fraser Arms."

Cook nodded. "It's possible. We just don't know at this point."

Blake turned toward Wiltore. "This is our first real lead ... if you can call it that."

Lewis, who had her head lowered, suddenly asked, "What was the calibre?"

".45 ACP. Why?" Cook asked.

Lewis smiled. "Same as our guys."

"Shit." The four cops sat back in their chairs, each lost in his or her own thoughts.

After a while, Wiltore said, "The shitty part is we know almost certainly who's selling the weapons ... a guy named Carl Dewitt."

Blake said, "Yeah, I've heard of him. Owns that classy strip joint down on Pender or something."

"You figure he's the weak link on this?" Lewis asked. "What about the Findley brothers? Maybe we should go after them instead?"

Wiltore shook his head. "Webster seems to be concentrating his efforts on this Michelle Lake."

Lewis threw up her hands in frustration. "Why are you so concerned about him? I still don't understand what you think Webster knows."

Wiltore bit down on his lip, again trying to control his temper. Why was Lewis always trying to make him mad? "He has a source inside the Dzyinski gang. Somebody who could blow this case wide open. What do you not understand about that?"

Lewis shrugged but tactfully didn't answer, leaving the cops to all sit silently around the table. Finally Wiltore spoke. "You think Ervin will authorize surveillance of Rocky Moon?"

Blake and Cook both nodded. "The chief is holding our balls on this one. He wants it cleared."

"Okay, we'll put in a request, and hopefully we can get lucky."

As Wiltore and Lewis went back to the elevator, Wiltore's phone rang. Wiltore looked questioningly at Lewis before answering it.

"Hey, Wiltore, it's Ervin. You have a couple of minutes to come up to my office?" Wiltore frowned. It was unusual for Ervin to be calling him.

"Sure, what's going on?"

"We'll talk when you get here."

Wiltore ended the call and frowned again at Lewis.

"What?" Lewis asked.

"I think we're in deep shit," Wiltore said.

They took the elevator up to Ervin's office. It was a spacious room with a view overlooking South Vancouver and beyond that Richmond. Ervin was a tall, handsome man with faded chestnut-coloured hair, mixed with a touch of grey. They shook hands, and Ervin told the two detectives to take a seat.

"What progress have you made with the case?" Ervin asked.

Wiltore explained the connection to Paul Gibson and their theory, hoping it would be enough.

"But you're not close to making an arrest?" Ervin asked, leaning back in his chair.

"Well … no," Wiltore admitted.

"When do you think you will be?"

Wiltore frowned. He didn't like Ervin's tone, and he risked a glance toward Lewis, who sat quietly with her face showing no emotion. "I don't know, sir. It's rather complicated. We're talking about the mass murder of one of the major crime syndicates by professionals. We knew finding the killers was a long shot at best."

Ervin nodded slowly, folding his hands in his lap. He worked his jaw around as if he wasn't sure what to say next. "Wiltore, you're a good cop. I've know you what? Ten, fifteen years? I consider you a friend, so I'll give it to you straight. The chief wants you off of this. He doesn't think you can handle something of this magnitude."

Wiltore sat up straight, gripping his knees to resist the temptation to punch Ervin. *Couldn't handle something of this magnitude?* Was he serious? He had been clearing difficult cases for the INTF for ten years, and all of a sudden he couldn't handle it? But Wiltore didn't say any of that. He took a breath and instead chose a more diplomatic tone. "I don't understand. Why? What have I done to piss him off?"

"I don't know … You have that journalist. He's making us look like fools."

Wiltore tried to smile, to show it was of little consequence, but he just sat there, his face rigid in disbelief. "That will all be over in a couple of weeks. He can't duck us forever."

Ervin nodded as if he wanted to believe Wiltore. "He doesn't like how you handled it so far. It took forever to subpoena him."

"That was not my fault, sir, and you know it. He was hiding from us because some idiot served the editor first and he tipped Webster off. What I need is more manpower."

"You're not going to get it, Wiltore. You know that."

"But you're willing to give Cook and Blake anything they want?"

Ervin frowned, tightening his fists. "I'm not talking about that case— completely different circumstances."

"How is it different? If anything, that case should be easier."

"Like I said, I'm not discussing that. I fought for you, Wiltore. I bought you some more time." Ervin sighed. "That journalist better sing for the judge, or I'm putting somebody else on the case."

"But, sir!"

"I'm sorry, Wiltore, but the decision has been made."

Lewis stood up first. "Thank you, sir."

Wiltore looked from Ervin to Lewis, who had a pleading look on her face. Wiltore slowly got up from his seat as if he was being forcibly ejected, glaring at Ervin as he left.

Wiltore and Lewis got into the elevator. Wiltore looked like he was about to be sick. When the door closed, he smashed his fist into the wall.

Lewis stepped forward and grabbed his wrist. "Stop that—the cameras. They will suspend you."

"I don't fucking care. How could they do that to me?"

"So this is about you, is it?" Lewis said angrily.

"Fucking right it is. I'm the head investigator."

"Whatever happened to being a team? Maybe that's why he wants you out. You're not a team player, Cliff."

Wiltore stared at her, unsure of how he should handle her sudden anger. "Look, Lewis, nothing against you, but I have ten years of experience on you and—"

Lewis cut him off. "No, I'm finished with your bullshit. I can't be in this elevator with you. You want to piss your career down the fucking drain—fine with me. Destroy this elevator. See if I care. I'm going to go write that report. I'll see you in a couple of hours, and then maybe we can go back to Rocky Moon and retread old ground." She pressed the button for the next level down. The doors swung open, and before Wiltore could say anything, Lewis stepped out and walked down the hallway.

The Date

There was a naked woman up on stage, but John wasn't even looking at her. His eyes were on Michelle Lake. He watched her as she served beer to her customers in her skirt and red top. She smiled a soulless smile and in true showmanship style, stuck the money into her bra, or alternatively she would run her hand up her dress and stick the money in her silk stocking. When she turned, her face was unreadable, a Houdini mask.

John was sitting in one of the dark corners, nursing a glass of whiskey. He had promised himself he wouldn't drink too much, but he had been there for only fifteen minutes and he was already on his second drink. The alcohol was humming pleasantly in his head.

Michelle looked stunning—a little cheap, but stunning nevertheless. Maybe it was her cheapness that attracted John, her sense of easiness. He could feel no guilt with her, no struggle. He had won Hayden over, wooed her good and proper; but as he got older, he found he had little energy or patience for that sort of thing anymore. John took another sip from his drink, chastising himself for thinking such things.

It was a weeknight, and the place was mostly empty; there were only a few dedicated followers. The strippers looked like they were just going through the motions. No swank. A group of teenagers in the corner were making the most noise.

He didn't even know what he was doing there. He should have been pouring over his notes, doing interviews, cold calling. Instead, he was here, and with only some vague notion of asking Michelle out. He didn't know exactly what had come over him. He supposed it was some feeling of connection, the same feeling that had come over him when he had told Liz he had met somebody.

But what could he say to her? Had she even noticed him? She must have. He had been there for fifteen minutes. She must be ignoring him on purpose. Was it just because he was here, in this place? Why hadn't he just phoned her like any other normal human being would have done? He had just been walking by on his way home, had seen the sign, and walked in.

Four uniform cops came in, and instinctively John sat back in his chair. He watched as the cops looked around the place, casing it, John supposed, for known faces. For once, all eyes weren't on the pinkish flesh on stage. The police headed to the bar and talked to the bartender for a while. John relaxed a little.

"What are you doing here?"

John looked up and saw Michelle standing over him. She was using the distraction of the police officers.

"What are you doing tomorrow night?" he asked.

Michelle rolled her eyes. "You can't be serious."

"If I wasn't serious, I wouldn't be here."

"Meet me in the alleyway in ten minutes."

Keith, the bar manager, was now talking to the police. He smiled politely and was nodding his head. A couple of the cops were slowly looking around the bar, their hands on their waists. John pretended to concentrate on the dancer. One of the cops went into the washroom and then came out again, joining the other officers. After a while, Keith shook hands with the cops, and the cops left. John breathed a sigh of relief. He didn't know why he was wary of the police; he just knew he didn't want any altercation with them.

He paid for his drinks and then went outside. Michelle had a light jacket on and was smoking, leaning up against the wall. She looked different somehow—a lone, stern, statuesque figure in silhouette. She didn't even look up when John approached.

"You can't come back here," she said.

"I know," John said. "I don't know why … it was on a whim."

She looked up with concern across her face. "No, really—you can't come back. They will kill you without even thinking about it."

"I'm not afraid of them."

"You're crazy."

John thought there was some hesitation, an uncertainty in her voice, and so he pressed. "What if we just talk? Get to know each other better?"

Michelle was silent for a while, inhaling her cigarette quickly. "You don't want to get to know me better. I'm not a good person."

John let out air through his nose. "Are you insinuating I am?"

"I think you try to be ... and that's the difference between you and me ... I don't even try."

"Don't say that ... just because you work at a strip club. It's good money. I get it."

Michelle stubbed out her cigarette underneath her heel. "Look, I have to get back. My break is over. I don't want anybody coming looking for me."

"Just dinner. No expectations, nothing fancy." John didn't know where he was getting the audacity to talk to her like that.

Michelle opened the door. "Okay, one dinner, and then you'll leave me alone?"

"I promise."

"And you'll drop this Dzyinski nonsense?"

For a moment, John almost promised, knowingly lying, but he stopped himself. "I can't promise that."

Michelle made a noise, almost like a grunt, still holding the door open. "I think I liked you better when you lied to me."

John unexpectedly felt hurt by her comment. "I'm honest when it comes to personal things."

Michelle nodded, and John thought she smiled a little—the first genuine smile he had seen her give all evening. "Okay, give me a call later. I'm off at midnight."

An Unexpected Visitor

John heard a noise. It was an unfamiliar sound, and at first he wasn't sure what it was; but then after a while, he realized it was his apartment buzzer. It had been such a long time since anybody had used it, the sound was strange to him.

For the past thirty minutes, John had been settled down on the couch reading *The Secret Man* by Bob Woodward, but he was having a hard time concentrating. His mind seemed to be on another wavelength, a chaos of thoughts. He kept going back to the different pieces of the puzzle—casinos and professional fighters and strippers and tycoons. He thought if he could just give himself some rest, he would be able to think clearly and come up with some answers. But so far, it hadn't worked.

The buzzer sounded again, seemingly louder this time. John went back to his book, but the person at his door was persistent. The doorbell buzzed again. He looked at the clock; it was 11:30 p.m. John sighed, put down the book, and went to the door. He pressed the intercom.

"Yes?"

"Hey, it's Liz."

"What are you doing? It's late."

"Oh, nothing ... having a drink downtown with a friend. I remembered you lived here." She sounded strange. Something was not quite right.

"Hold on a moment." John went to the window, peeled back the curtains, and looked down at the road for a watchman or a getaway car, but it was empty and dark except for the yellowish glow from the street lamps. Again he felt a trap in the pit of his stomach. Maybe somebody had a gun to her back, using her to get him downstairs in the dark. He went back to the intercom. "You alone?" he asked.

"Just let me up." She laughed—naturally enough. A hard thing to fake. So John pressed a button that opened the door.

He waited by the door, hearing her high heels click against the old staircase. He wondered again why he was so jumpy. Liz knocked aggressively, and John let her in. She almost tripped entering. Her face was flushed, and her eyes large and lucid. John led her over to his couch and plunked her down.

"You've been drinking?" It was more of a statement than a question, and he realized that was why she didn't sound her normal self.

"Maybe a glass or two."

"What are you doing here?"

"I was wondering if I could crash here. I drove downtown, and, well …"

She was wearing a red dress that came down to mid-thigh, a long bead necklace, and a leather jacket overtop. Her brassy blonde hair curled over her shoulders, and her bare, pinkish legs came together at her knobby knees. John was astounded at how different she looked outside the office, in something different than her plain business suit.

John rubbed his eyes with his thumb and forefinger, suddenly feeling tired, overwhelmed, and the urgent need to rid himself of her. "Where do you live? Perhaps I could drive you?"

"No, no, that's too much trouble. I'll be fine in the morning. I just need a couple of hours to sleep it off."

"How did you remember where I lived? I'm surprised."

"I had to wake up the boss to get it." With great difficulty, Liz struggled out of her jacket and flung it over the armrest, but she missed and it slid slowly down to the floor. John picked it up for her, folded it once, and placed it on a nearby chair.

"You woke up Chuck to find me and ask if you could sleep on my couch?" John asked incredulously. "How drunk are you?"

Liz looked around with a frown on her face, as if she was just noticing her surroundings. "This place is an absolute mess."

John snorted. "You're one to criticize. I've seen your desk."

"Do you have anything to drink?"

"I think I have some beer or some whiskey."

Liz smiled. "Whiskey it is, then."

John wasn't really sure it would be a good idea to give Liz any more alcohol, but nevertheless he went to the cupboard and got out two glasses and a bottle of whiskey. "On the rocks?"

"Just straight."

John poured two glasses and gave one to Liz. He sat down on the opposite side of the couch.

Liz asked, "How can you bring anybody home with your place looking like this?"

"I don't have much company. My son once in a while …"

Liz slid over so she was sitting next to John. He could smell her fruity perfume and the tinge of alcohol on her breath. "How about women? You must bring a woman home once in a while."

John smiled, hoping it covered his embarrassment. "Liz, why don't I take you home?"

Liz put her head on John's shoulder, and her hand slid up on the side of his thigh. "But we've just started drinking. I don't want you to be pulled over."

"I'm fine," John said, taking Liz's wrist and putting it in her lap. "What's the matter with you anyhow? Who were you with that just left you like this?"

Liz sat up. "Oh, I was on a date with a guy I met on the Internet."

"Didn't go very well, I take it?"

The question seemed to trigger something in Liz, who burst into tears, buried her head into her hands, and sobbed uncontrollably.

John wanted to comfort her, but was afraid of touching her. "It's nothing. It's one date. Those things are supposed to be awkward and terrible," he said.

"No, no, it wasn't the date. I just feel depressed about things, that's all."

"What things? You should stop drinking. It'll just make things worse."

"Please, you're one to talk," she said, getting up and stumbling to the washroom. John watched her struggle, afraid she would fall and hit her head, but also afraid what might happen if he tried to help her.

While John waited, he poured himself another drink, which he knew was a bad idea but he couldn't help himself. He heard the toilet flush, and the bathroom door opened. When John turned, Liz was standing there, supported by the doorframe. She had washed her face, and all of her makeup and mascara were gone.

Liz asked, "You think I could have a glass of water?"

John went and got Liz a glass of tap water. "I think you look better without all that makeup."

Liz stepped into the shadow. "You think so?"

"Sure."

John handed Liz the glass, which she thirstily chugged back. She handed John the empty glass back, and he went to get her another. Liz collapsed back onto the couch and stretched out her legs. Her dress was creeping scandalously up her thigh. "Sorry about everything—coming here, drinking your alcohol."

"No problem."

"After this Gibson story, I've cleared my plate. I'm going to travel to the Mayan Riviera. I looked at prices—cheap. And I'm going to find myself a nice cabana boy to fuck my brains out."

John sat down on the armrest. He looked down. "Is this all because of a single date?"

Liz sighed heavily. "I swear I'm never going on a blind date ever again."

"If you're looking for some kind of advice, you've come to the wrong person."

There was a long pause. For something to do, John got up and topped up his drink. He looked at the caramel-coloured liquid and then drank it. Liz was breathing heavily. She smoothed her skirt down her thighs and put her head back against the cushion. She stared at John with big puffy eyes. "What was it like? In Afghanistan?"

John put one hand on his forehead. They had never spoken about it before, and he wondered why she was asking now. "It was like stepping back two hundred years," he said.

"Were you afraid?"

John didn't answer right away. He went over to the window and pretended to look out. A police siren howled in the background and then dissipated into the distance. The tawny streetlights in the coal-coloured darkness made the scene look like old London. When John turned, she was still looking at him, expecting an answer. He let out a heavy sigh. "Every day."

"Is that why you came back?"

"I came back because I had been shot."

"I don't believe you. What was the real reason?"

John looked at Liz, startled at her assurance. "It was the reason ... that and I missed my family. I had been an absentee father and husband."

Liz nodded and closed her eyes. John stared at her. Her breathing started to regulate. But then she asked, "What was the worst story you've ever covered?"

"Worst in what way?"

"The one that keeps you up at night."

"Why do you ask?"

"The rape story ... I can't get it out of my head, John. That poor old woman. She sounded like my grandmother. I don't know what it was about her, but talking to her ..."

John drank the rest of his whiskey and poured himself another glass. He was surprised at how little was left in the bottle. "I haven't told many people this story." He waited, but Liz didn't say anything.

"When I was in Iraq, there was a restaurant close to the American compound—where I was staying. It wasn't a particularly good restaurant, but it was close and the owner of the place, Omar, was a kind, older gentleman. I would go there every couple of weeks with my cameraman, William Russell, and our security team of former British SAS agents. Omar ran the restaurant by himself. His wife did all the cooking—not that it was much of a problem because most nights his restaurant was pretty empty. The customers he did have were all Americans and a few Brits.

"Omar was rumoured to have this absolutely gorgeous daughter. She apparently washed the dishes in the back, but none of us ever saw her; we would sit around and talk, just out of earshot of Omar, about this mythically beautiful daughter. I did see her once. Briefly. Her name was Amira. She was as beautiful as I had heard—more so. She must have been around sixteen or seventeen and had this dark, thick hair. Her skin was the colour of tree bark. The one time she ventured out to the front of the restaurant, the entire security team stopped eating and stared at her. She just looked shyly back. I think she was just interested in seeing us foreigners—that is, until Omar ushered her into the back again.

"A couple of months later, I heard from someone that Amira had been kidnapped walking back from the market. One of the kidnappers phoned Omar the next day asking for fifty million US dollars to return Amira.

"'Fifty million dollars? Where am I going to get that type of money?' Omar asked the kidnapper.

"'Sell your restaurant; get it from your American friends. I don't fucking care,' the kidnapper told him.

"'Let me at least talk to Amira. Please. At least I want to know if she's alive.'

"Amira was put on the phone.

"'How are you, dear?' Omar asked.

"Amira whimpered an incomprehensible reply.

"'Amira, listen to me closely. Did they take your honour?'

"Again Amira whimpered an incomprehensible reply, but Omar was persistent.

"'Amira, honey, did they violate you? Did they rape you?'

"'Yes, Daddy,' Amira sobbed.

"'Okay, Amira, don't worry. Everything will be all right. Put them back on the phone.'

"The kidnapper came back on the phone. 'We have a deal?'

"'Keep her, you piece of shit,' Omar replied. 'I don't want her back.'

"Amira was found a week after in an alleyway, her throat cut."

John paused in his story. He looked up at the ceiling, his eyes roaming as if he was looking for something. He felt something warm and hot in his hand, and when he looked down, he was surprised to find Liz's hand within his. She was staring at him. Large, silent tears were rolling down her cheeks. He looked away, afraid of holding her gaze.

"I went back to the compound and cried. It was the first time I had cried about anything in that country—I had seen so much, and I cried over one person. It seems silly looking back at it. After everything, it was one person who got to me. It was Amira. The tears just kept flowing, and I cried so much I felt sick. I went to the bathroom and threw up."

There was silence. John looked at Liz as if he expected some sort of response, but she just looked sad and pathetic. He didn't blame her for not saying anything. What could she possibly say? The only recourse was for John to get up to get another drink. He was feeling drunk now, draining the whiskey bottle into his glass. When he turned around, Liz was standing right in front of him. She leaned over and kissed him, pressing her lips against his teeth, forcing her tongue into his mouth. John backed away, gasping, "What are you doing?"

Liz touched his cheek. "Just don't say anything."

Her other hand rubbed against his shoulder and chest. She led him back to the couch. John bent his head back, and then she was on him, straddling him. Her dress was bunched around her waist.

The alcohol seemed to numb his senses, a kind of vertigo experience. What was going on? Was this all really happening? He protested again, but it was just a small whimper. He felt he wasn't all there, as if he was made of liquid and was melting away.

"I know you want to fuck me," she said in an unnaturally low, growly voice. "So fuck me."

As she ground into him, she hoisted her dress over her shoulders and pressed her breasts to him. Her skin was unnaturally pale. When John put an arm around her waist, he expected her to be cold and hard, but she was warm to the touch. He kissed her tentatively and was surprised by the surge of pleasure it gave him.

Liz slowly, haphazardly, undid his brass belt buckle, digging her nails into him, and he bit his lip in surprise. He looked up at her. Her breathing was rapid, but her forehead was creased and a frown set upon her mouth.

John closed his eyes, feeling the blood pulse through him. "Be gentle with me; I'm old," he said.

Liz seemed to laugh—it seemed unnatural, a canned TV laugh. "Not so old," she said.

This seemed to galvanize John, who suddenly grabbed her and turned her around, bending over the couch. He put his hands on her waist. She egged him on, screaming, moaning, screaming some more, burying her head into a pillow. He went faster and faster until he eventually collapsed back on the couch. They both lay there motionlessly, not saying anything, breathing together rhythmically. Liz dangled one leg over his stomach and put her head on his chest, her long hair loose and crumpled on his shoulders. John could smell her fruity shampoo. It was a woman's smell—something so fleeting and so foreign to him now.

Feeling exhausted, John drifted asleep. The boy came back. Of course, the boy again. He was staring at John with large dark eyes, his thick hair blowing in the windless sky. He had on the same long white shirt and pants and a brown belt, and his feet were bare and dirty. John's cameraman, William Russell, was pointing his small HD camera at him, as if Will was expecting the boy to do great and unprecedented things. All around them, the fire from the blast was raging, unquenchable. The dead and the dying were there too, of course—the torn limbs, the broken bodies, the ribbed guts. Blood ran down the gutters like rainwater.

The boy reached out to John. "Help me," he said. His voice was strangely void of emotion. The camera was rolling, capturing the movement.

John tried to take a step forward but couldn't. Little bits of sand hit his face, digging into him like glass shards. "I'm going to help you; don't worry."

"I'm going to die," the boy said.

"I'm going to put you on the news," John said. He looked down, trying to pick up his feet, but they were somehow stuck to the dirt.

The boy asked, "How will that help me?"

"You will be famous. Everyone will want to help you."

The boy suddenly panicked. He fell to his knees, covering his face with his hands. His cries were pitiful. "No—you don't understand … Help me. Take me away from this place."

John wanted to run, to snatch the boy up, tuck him in his arms, but he couldn't. Suddenly he was sinking like he was in quicksand. He tried lifting his legs, but his body wouldn't move.

The boy took his hands away from his face and stared at John. Everything became silent. The boy was still kneeling, as if he was praying.

He then burst into flames, combusting from within, and John was forced to watch as the boy withered away, screaming in pain. The boy seemed to melt away until he was nothing but hot ashes. John tried to turn away, but he couldn't. He could only watch in horror.

John woke up with a start, his heart pounding. He rubbed his eyes and looked around him. Liz was gone, but her warmth still lingered, hovering around him. He wondered how she had gotten home after all that. He got up, and the feeling of her body slipped away. He realized he was feeling regret all too soon.

He wiped perspiration away from his forehead and concentrated on steadying his breathing. He looked around the cold, empty apartment. The only proof that Liz had ever been there was her glass, half-empty, sitting on the small coffee table. John tilted the liquid down his throat, put the two glasses in the sink, and tried to forget about what had happened.

City Hall

John called a cab to take him to City Hall. He put on his shoes and coat and went downstairs, feeling as if he couldn't stand his apartment for a moment longer. He descended the stairs feeling groggy and dehydrated, remembering the previous night with a feeling of dread and self-loathing. What had happened? Why hadn't he resisted her? Was he really that weak?

It was already warm. The sun was rising. John stuck his hands in his pockets. The streets were busy with people heading off to work. A tourist stopped to ask John directions to the Steam Clock.

The cab pulled up, and as John got in, he thought about the transportation tab he was running up and wondered how long it would be before he could drive again. He still couldn't move his arm without tremendous pain. The doctor had told him it would be six months before he would be able to remove the sling. He sighed at the thought.

The driver was a young East Indian man who was blasting Fleetwood Mac on his stereo. He turned it down and said, "Hey, you're that journalist, aren't you? The one who was shot?"

John nodded reluctantly but was saved from any further conversation by his phone; it was his mother.

John said, "Hello, Mom. How are you doing?"

She asked him, as she always did, about Hayden and Byron. John answered in the generic, not wanting to worry her about him or his once-family. John felt bad cutting his mother short, but he had little choice in the matter.

His mother asked, "You'll phone me, okay?"

"Of course."

Next, John phoned Gibson Investments, but only got a recorded message that the office had been shut down until further notice. He tried pushing zero, star, and every other button to try and get through to a real person, but without any success.

John looked out the window, watching all the businessmen trying to act like Manhattanites with their blue suits, golden cuff links, and sixty-dollar haircuts. All the while, John was trying to summon up enough courage for his next phone call to Liz. The taxi turned onto the bridge, and John got a stunning view of the buildings reflecting off the water in pastel colours. John watched downtown fall away in the distance, feeling slightly melancholy that the longest day had come and gone and the summer's final orchestration of brilliance—the final converging encore—was upon him, before the curtains of a colourful, lukewarm autumn were to fall.

He then remembered Michelle. He was supposed to call her last night. Fighting off the urge to swear, he took his phone from his pocket and called her.

"John, you were supposed to phone me."

"Yeah, sorry. I got caught up with work."

"I waited for you."

"Look, I'm sorry. I'll make it up to you. Promise." John hated lowering himself, saying sorry, but he did it if it helped the situation.

"No, I told you, one shot at this. You've had your chance."

"Come on, Michelle. I think we could be good together. Why don't you give me a chance?"

"You really don't see what's going on, do you? I thought you called yourself a reporter."

John was taken back and surprised at how much her comments hurt him. Often he thought he was immune to criticism, but every once in a while, he was reminded how attached he was to other people's words. He didn't say anything for a while, but recollected his thoughts. There was something wrong with this whole conversation, something a little bit off, but he wasn't sure what it was. He said, "I don't think you're really angry at me."

This seemed to flabbergast Michelle. "What?"

"You don't sound like you're angry. I think you're intentionally pushing me away. Why?"

Michelle seemed at a loss for words. "John, you don't know me. You think you know when I'm angry and when I'm not?"

"Michelle, if there is one thing I pride myself on doing, it's reading people."

"John, we're just not right for each other. Let's leave it at that and move on."

"I can't do that, Michelle. I won't accept that, not until we've tried. So why don't I take you for dinner?"

Michelle let out a long sigh. "You don't give up, do you?"

"Wouldn't be much of a journalist if I did, now would I?"

Michelle hung up. John looked down at his phone. He decided not to call her back right away. Instead, he phoned Liz. *Might as well get all the difficult calls out of the way*, he thought. The ringing seemed to go on forever, until finally Liz answered. "Hey, how are you doing?" he asked, feeling his voice was unnaturally upbeat.

Liz let out a groggy groan. "Why are you asking me that?"

John found himself apologizing, which only made her angrier. "You made it into work?"

"Look, John. I was drunk and lonely. Let's just pretend it didn't happen, okay?"

John took the phone away from his ear for a moment to stop himself from saying anything he regretted. "Sure, fine. I actually phoned to ask you if you'd gotten hold of Gibson Investments yet?"

"John, what the fuck?"

Again her anger seemed to erupt from nowhere.

"No, Liz, I ..."

"You trying to steal my story? What is this? Revenge?"

"Revenge? Revenge for what?" John was confused. He looked straight ahead so as to avoid eye contact with the driver.

"Good-bye, John."

"No, wait, listen to me. There might be a connection between Gibson and Dzyinski. My source said Paul Gibson was working on building a casino. I want to confirm it."

But Liz didn't appear to be listening. "John, I didn't think you could be this fucking low, but apparently nothing is beneath you."

Then there was a dial tone as Liz hung up. John listened to it for a second or two, his nerves raw and unhinged. He stared at his phone in stunned disbelief.

"We're here."

John looked up from his phone. The driver was staring at him.

"Huh?" John said.

"I said, we're here."

"Oh, okay … Thanks."

John paid the cabbie and got out. City Hall was a grey, block, Art Deco building built in the mid-thirties. It had an uncouth neon-pink clock at the very top. The building was twelve stories and wind-worn, with mud stuck to the crevices. As old and as ugly as it was, the building still managed to convey a sense of authority and clout.

John found the planning department easily enough. A middle-aged woman with strawberry-red hair sat behind a much-too-large oak desk. The woman glanced up with large injudicious eyes as John entered. She seemed the type of person to enjoy her small sphere of power.

John greeted her with a smile and introduced himself. "I was wondering if Jared Fraser was available?" Jared Fraser was the manager of the planning department.

The secretary frowned. Her eyes wandered to John's sling. "I'm afraid not. He's in a meeting."

"When does he get out? It is imperative I talk to him, and I'm on a bit of deadline."

"Not until eleven."

John looked up at the clock on wall. It was almost ten thirty. "Okay, I'll wait for him."

The secretary frowned deeper, looking at her computer. "I'm not sure he'll be able to see you. His calendar says he has another meeting with the West End Business Association."

"I'll take my chances."

John sat down on one of the chairs along the wall and waited, and as he did so, he checked his e-mail and messages. He phoned Michelle back but only got her answering machine. He waited, trying not to let his anxiety show.

A little while later, Jared Fraser blew jauntily into the office. He was a scarecrow-looking man, tall, with thick-rimmed glasses and sucked-in cheeks. His glasses and his slick-backed hair gave him a slightly malnourished Buddy Holly appearance. He was talking on his cell phone, and in the other hand, he had a black leather briefcase. He nodded curtly to his secretary, who smiled and mouthed a hello.

John got up. "Mr. Fraser? May I speak with you?"

John followed Fraser past the secretary's desk and down a hallway, ignoring the secretary's calls to stop. "Sir? You can't go back there. Sir!"

John followed Fraser into his office. It wasn't until Fraser turned to close his door that he realized John was behind him. His eyes widened in surprise. He said in the phone, "Larry, I'm going to have to phone you back." He put his phone back into his pocket, looked up at John, and said, "May I help you, sir?"

"John Webster from the *Daily Globe*."

Fraser broke into a smile. "That's right. I saw you on the television." Fraser offered his hand, which John took.

John said, "You have a couple of moments? I would like to talk to you about something."

"Sure, have a seat." Fraser pointed to a chair in the corner. Fraser's office was small, with a glass-topped desk. There was a small window that overlooked a cement parking lot. In the corner was a waist-high bookcase that appeared to be filled with reports and engineering manuals.

Fraser settled behind his desk. "I don't know how much help I can be. I read your last article ... I don't know what's happening to our city." Fraser shook his head sadly.

"I actually wanted to talk to you about Gibson Investments."

Fraser leaned forward, putting his skinny elbows on his desk. "Paul Gibson? I heard he was shot—don't know much about the circumstances. Is he mixed up in this?"

"Was he planning on building a casino?"

Fraser frowned and rubbed his chin. "I remember ... he did put an application in. What does that have to do with anything?"

John watched Fraser closely. "He wanted to build it close to Andromeda, didn't he?"

Fraser sat up. "Well ... there were several locations. It was just in the beginning stages; I don't remember anything by the Andromeda."

"Gibson did mainly condos and office buildings. Why a casino?"

Fraser shrugged. "I don't know. You'll have to ask them that." He stopped, and then thoughtfully asked, "You think Gibson was killed because of this casino application?"

John shrugged and told Fraser his theory about how Ernest Hunter killed Dzyinski and Gibson because of the casino. "Casinos are big business—millions of dollars. People have been killed for less."

Fraser sat back, stunned. John let him process the information. Finally Fraser said, "So you think Ken Dzyinski was the driving force behind the casino?"

"I don't know for sure, but Gibson would have to get somebody to run it."

Fraser's eyes suddenly lit up as if he had just realized something. "You going to write this in your paper?"

John shook his head. "Say one of the biggest and most respected companies in Vancouver has mob ties? No, not likely—not without more evidence."

"I wish I could be more help."

John rubbed his face, thinking. "What were some of the other locations proposed?"

"Well, the most likely site was on Lancaster Avenue and about Seventy-Fourth Street. Gibson Investments owns a couple of blocks of old industrial warehouses there. Probably wouldn't be too hard to convince the council—what with Gibson's clout."

"I'm sorry ... Did you say Lancaster Avenue?" Lancaster Avenue was in southeast Vancouver, an area known for its ethnic gangs.

"Yeah, why?"

"Oh, nothing ... It's just I grew up close to there—it's where my mom lives. You think it would have gone through?"

"Well, it's impossible to say—depended on how the council would have voted. The area could use some revitalization. Some jobs. Probably wouldn't hurt the area."

John almost felt as if he was being personally attacked. The thought of his mother living around the corner from a casino was too much. John said, "Except bring organized crime into the area," he said angrily.

Fraser looked down at the table, surprised by John's outburst. "You take the bad with the good, I guess. Can't really stop organized crime by refusing to build a casino."

John stood up before he said something he regretted. Suddenly everything took on a more delicate tone, as if all his boyhood memories were about to be ripped away from him. "Thank you for your time, Mr. Fraser. You have been most helpful."

Fraser nodded as if he was unsure of himself. "I don't know if I was helpful, but you're welcome anyways."

The hallway back to the lobby seemed longer and darker than before. He didn't understand how—or why—he felt so paternal about the area. He hadn't lived there for over twenty years, but somehow it was still home—more so than his Gastown loft, more so than even his house with Hayden. He supposed no one really gets over the powerful nostalgia of his or her childhood home.

By the time he got back to the Globe Building, he had regained his composure and felt better. The newsroom was in its usual state of frenzy, almost zoo-like. People were shouting and running between desks, phones ringing, lights flashing, and the harried sound of desperate fingers pounding on keyboards. Sometimes John loved to stop—when he himself wasn't stressed and on deadline—and soak in the pace, the energy, of the room.

John went over to Liz's desk. She was on the phone, and John hung back at a respectful distance until she was done. When she hung up, she stared at John with big, angry eyes. "John, not now."

"Look, Liz, I'm not trying to steal your story, honest. I think there's a connection between the two murders—honestly I do."

Liz turned back to her computer. "I said, not now. I'm working on this."

John took her chair and swung it around so she was facing him.

Liz sighed. "Fuck, you don't take no as an answer, do you?"

"Please hear me out. Then you can go back to whatever you are working on."

Liz didn't say anything for a while but just stared at John. He took it as permission to continue. "Let's work together on this thing. Why do we keep fighting each other?"

John somehow expected Liz to throw her arms around him or smile or fist-bump, but instead she just sat perfectly still, her legs crossed, her arms on the tip of her armrests. "No … I don't think so."

John was stunned. "No? Do we, or do we not, work for the same newspaper?"

"Yes, but make no mistake: we are competitors. For the best stories, for the front page. You wouldn't let me help you out with Dzyinski, and now when I've got the better story, suddenly you want to collaborate? I don't think so."

"Aren't you listening to me? They are one and the same. Whoever killed Dzyinski killed Gibson. We find one killer, we find both killers."

Liz tilted her head. "Really? What makes you think so?"

John took a deep breath and explained how he met the fighter, how Gibson was planning on building a casino so Dzyinski could run it.

"Interesting, but you only have the word of an unknown MMA fighter and some vague theory. Not exactly compelling evidence."

"Yes, that's where I think we can help each other."

"I'm sorry, John," she said, not sounding particularly sorry at all. "Maybe if you had shown a little willingness earlier …"

John sucked in a large amount of air through his teeth. "Okay, you don't think the two are related? We'll see who gets the story first. I bet I sweep it from right under your tiny, little nose."

Liz scoffed. "How are you going to do that in jail, John? All I have to do is bide my time. The boss has already promised me both stories."

John bit the bottom of his lip so hard it started to bleed. "What did you say?"

Liz turned back to her computer in an effort to end the conversation. "Forget it—nothing."

"When did Chuck tell you this?"

"I said forget it."

John turned and strode with his long legs over to Chuck's office and, without even bothering to knock, flung the door open. Chuck was sitting at his desk, talking on the phone. John walked over and brought both of his large hands down on Chuck's desk. "You're giving my story to Liz?"

He looked up from the phone, the loud thwack of John's palms against the oak barely registered. Chuck spoke into the phone. "Gordon? Can you hold for one moment?" Chuck calmly pressed the hold button and placed the phone down on the receiver.

John said, "How could you do that to me?"

Chuck shook his head exasperated. "It's a backup plan, John."

"I'm not going to prison."

"Let's hope not, but who knows what the judge will decide?"

"But give it to her? Of all people?"

"It's not your decision, John."

Chuck went to pick up the phone again, but John was quicker; he snatched the phone and said, "He'll have to get back to you," slamming the phone down onto the receiver.

Chuck frowned. The corner of his mouth twitched. "You realize you just hung up on the premier of our province?"

John raised his eyebrows and stared at Chuck, wondering if Chuck was being facetious—but no, Chuck wasn't the joking type. "What were you doing talking to him?"

"John, I'm managing editor of this newspaper. I talk to a lot of people."

John signed and took a seat. He told Chuck his theory about how the two murders were connected.

"So, isn't that even more of a reason to give it to her? She wants it. She has brains and guts—just like you."

"She is nothing like me. She's walking on the edge—I don't know why nobody can see it."

"And you're telling me you're perfectly fine? How much are you drinking these days?"

John sat back in his chair, stunned. John stared at Chuck furiously, trying to control his anger. "You have any idea—" He stopped suddenly, realizing he was only feeding into Chuck's argument. Chuck just sat there, fully composed, and that only made John angrier. John said, "Fine; do what you want."

John took the elevator down to the lobby. The ride down gave him time to cool off and allowed him to feel slightly childish. He pushed the door open into the daylight.

Mother

"You still having those nightmares?" Mary Webster asked her son. She was sitting in an old oak rocking chair. She was thin and frail, her shoulders hunched over and her hair dyed jet-black. She was wearing a pink blouse and purple sweatpants.

John frowned. "I told you about those?"

Mary shook her head. "No, Hayden did."

John didn't say anything for a while, and his mother seemed content with the silence. John could hear the traffic drone from Southwest Marine Drive. "How often do you talk to her anyways?"

Mary looked down. "I don't know—not often."

John gritted his teeth. He pictured them on the phone together, laughing and talking about him.

John was sitting on his mother's old porch. The sliding-glass door was open a fraction. The sun shone down in splotches between alder grove trees and the stucco buildings. The wind would pick up now and then and peck at their clothes and hair. They drank Earl Grey tea from an old acrylic pot that his mother had used seemingly forever.

John looked out on to the yellowish-brown lawn, the same one he used to play in as a kid. It was narrow and cut uneven, a four-foot hedge that surrounded it giving them little privacy. He wondered who his mother got to cut the grass.

John suddenly remembered how, on summer day weekends, he would take his hockey stick and a tennis ball and would shoot it at the hedge until his father would yell at him to stop destroying the plants. His childhood seemed so long ago and filled with false memories. Had he really been that young? It seemed most of his brain was filled with periods from Iraq and Afghanistan and Africa; his innocence had been nonexistent, and so it startled him to remember he had once found simple pleasure in destroying his father's plants.

John asked, "You remember an application for a casino?"

Mary nodded. "Yeah, sure, in the old industrial zone. I was all for it."

John closed his eyes. As she got older, he found it more difficult to remain calm around his mother. "All for it? It was going to be run by gangsters, Mom."

Mary seemed unperturbed by this news. "The whole city is run by gangsters, dear—that mayor of ours is a crook if I ever saw one." Despite the fact she had been living in Canada for over half her about fifty years, she hadn't lost—or refused to lose—her Glaswegian accent.

"Mom, I'm serious. You know the one who was recently killed? The one I did a story on?"

"I never read the news, you know that, dear."

John tried to keep from sounding exasperated again. "And I never understood that—you used to when Dad was alive."

"Yes, but he probably never would have spoken to me if I hadn't."

John sighed and took a sip of his tea. His mother made the best tea he had ever tasted. Whenever he made tea at home, it never was quite the same. Maybe he needed to get a real teapot.

"What do you know about the application to build the casino?" he asked.

Mary stared at her son. "Is this why you came? To shake me down for information?"

"Mom, you know that's not why. I can find out about the casino from anyone."

"You don't visit me in, what? Three, four months? And suddenly you come with all these questions."

John resisted rolling his eyes. "It hasn't been that long."

"How much trouble you in anyways?"

"What do you mean?"

"You have gangsters shooting at you. I never understood you. And neither did your father."

"My father wrote theatre reviews."

"You say that like it's a bad thing."

"No ... It just wasn't journalism."

"What do you call it, if not journalism?" Mary asked. "I honestly don't see the difference. He worked for a newspaper—so do you."

John sighed. It was the same argument he had with Hayden. The same argument he always had, and he didn't feel like revisiting it again. "Please, can you tell me about the casino?"

"I went to one of those meetings at the community center. A lot of people showed up, I remember that."

"Was there anybody who you recognized?"

Mary shook her head. "No, although one of the city councillors was there—can't remember who. Some guy came around door-to-door asking for support. I signed." John frowned at her. Mary said, "What? It's not like I have anything better to do with my Saturday nights. Especially if my only child doesn't visit me."

"Mom, it's not about a night's entertainment."

"Well, how am I supposed to know it was going to be run by gangsters?"

"Maybe if you read the newspaper."

Mary waved her hand and scoffed. "All murder and rape. I'm old, John. Got to hold on to what's good in life."

"It's not all bad news, Mother." John defended his profession automatically, but he wondered how much of what she said was true. He thought back to the stories Liz was doing, the stories he did.

Mary got up slowly. She moved fragilely ever since her hip replacement. She collected John's cup and the teapot and went inside. John followed her. The kitchen hadn't been renovated since John had left home. It had pink linoleum counters, yellow cupboards, and an old stove. John watched his mother wash up the dishes. "I should get going," he said.

"Okay, but could you see if you could fix my computer before you go? Damn thing won't get onto the Internet."

John nodded. He went into the living room where his mother kept her connection to the outside world. Her computer was old and clunky—much like the ones John had at work. He turned it on, and while he waited for it to boot up, he played with all the cables. Eventually all that he needed to do was reset the network.

John went back to the kitchen where his mother was still washing dishes.

"When your arm heals, maybe you could look at the leak in the bathroom?" Mary asked.

John repressed a sigh. "Sure, Mom. I'll see you around, okay?"

Mary turned and wiped her hands on the towel. "Okay, be careful. I don't want to lose you too."

"Mom, you're not going to lose me."

His mother turned to look out the window so John couldn't see her face. "I've come very close twice already," she said. She sounded far off, her voice glum and despondent.

John went over and kissed his mother on the cheek. "I'll be careful, I promise," he said, trying to sound cheerful and upbeat. He hated to see his mother so sad.

Mary looked at John. Her old face seemed even more wrinkled and creased than usual. "I know you'll be careful. That's not what concerns me."

"If you remember anything more about the casino, you promise me you'll call and tell me?"

Mary nodded and then stopped suddenly, remembering something. "There was somebody else at the meeting." She frowned in concentration, and her forehead creased. "A man named, I think, Alex Gibson—I think he was the developer."

"Alex Gibson was there?"

"Yeah, why? You know him?"

John nodded. "Yes. He's the owner of Gibson Investments. They own the Tokyo Tower downtown, you know the one."

"They own that?" Mary said, clearly impressed.

"What did he say?"

"He spoke about how great the casino would be for everyone."

"What else did he say?" John asked, intrigued.

"Oh, I don't know, dear. It was so long ago."

"Please think; this could be important."

"He talked a lot to the city councillors."

"Was his brother with him?"

Mary frowned. "Who?"

"Paul Gibson, his brother."

Mary shook her head, lapsing into silence, thinking. "No, I don't think so. That Alex Gibson spoke to a man a lot. He never addressed the crowd directly."

"You know his name?" John asked.

"No … He was dressed well, suit and tie, if I recall. Older, with greyish hair."

John tried to prod his mother for more information, but that was all she could recall. John kissed his mom again, put on his jacket, and called a cab.

News

Clifford Wiltore took a lighter from his jacket pocket and carefully lit up another cigarette, watching the rain drearily roll down the edge of his porch and listening to the loud, thick pounding on top of the roof. It was one of those summer showers that would last about an hour and then clear up and the sky would be clear and blue again. Wiltore took a long drag from his cigarette—for some reason, it tasted strongly of bitter apples—and slowly exhaled a steady stream of pale smoke. He picked up his beer and took a long gulp, trying to wash the taste away.

Wiltore's cell phone started to ring. He brought it out of his pocket and looked at the call display: Tamara Lewis. He turned off the ringer and shoved it quickly back into his pocket. Wiltore stood up and leaned over the porch, reaching his palms out to touch the rain. It felt good—warm and smooth. He splashed the water on his face, running his hand through his thinning grey hair. *He wasn't that far from retirement*, Wiltore reflected. He had about five good years left before he would start to fade away into the bureaucracy of the force. It would swallow him up, and he would be left with a comfortable but boring desk job. He had about that much time to prove to them he was police chief material.

Operation Angel was supposed to do that. It was his baby. His plan. He had conceived it. For two years he had begged for funding, and finally after brown-nosing the right politicians and police officials, he had gotten it—the largest police operation in the history of the city, spanning across every regional police force on the west coast: from Vancouver, Surrey, and

Langley, to the Seattle police, even the FBI. It had cost over ten million dollars, a hundred and fifty-six full-time police officers, and countless man-hours.

Operation Angel was ambitious in its scope—designed to cripple the drug trade, lock up Dzyinski and all of his lieutenants, deport all the foreign drug dealers, and make Vancouver a respectable city again. Wiltore had obtained warrants to bug homes, clubhouses, and bars; he had twenty-four-hour surveillance on Dzyinski and his six lieutenants; he had undercover officers—and not one single arrest was ever made. After ten months, the police chief had declared Operation Angel a failure and shut it down.

Wiltore again pleaded with the policy makers, but to no avail. He had had his chance. The next couple of months he had drifted through his job a defeated, torn-up man. There were even rumours he would be replaced as head investigator of the Integrated Gang Task Force.

Wiltore had resorted to spending his days sitting on the porch, staring vacantly out on to the quiet street, where the raggedy neighbourhood kids would play street hockey or soccer until the light grew dim and they were all called away for dinner. Wiltore felt an odd comfort watching the gangly, awkward kids, as if he was presiding over them, protecting them from the purple sedans and large Cadillacs that he had sometimes seen or imagined—he didn't know which—roaming the streets like careful cheetahs stalking their prey.

Wiltore heard the screen door open and close behind him, and from the corner of his vision he saw his wife, Christine, slowly approach. She was thirty-eight, fifteen years younger than Wiltore, and was approaching middle-age beauty—the type of beauty that resided in personal confidence and contentment in life and the changing, uncontrollable world. Her eyes were soft and understanding and her face was beginning to show the appearance of a few worn lines, but it only made her more beautiful. She was slim-hipped, had light brown hair, and wore a long jean skirt and a baggy white blouse that swayed elegantly when she moved. She looked down at her husband.

"You out here again?"

Wiltore put a hand around Christine's waist. "I can't help it."

Christine didn't say anything for a while. "Don't forget Ivan is coming back to town on Friday."

"Did you write it on the calendar?"

Christine nodded. "Of course."

Wiltore took hold of his wife's hand briefly and said tenderly, "Then don't worry; I won't forget."

Christine sighed. "You should really stop smoking."

Wiltore flicked the cigarette out onto the damp lawn and watched it as the orange glow slowly fizzled out. He had always looked young for his age—sure, he had the grey hair and the moustache, but he had always had a smooth, wrinkle-free face and a full set of thick hair. It was only in the past year that he had begun to look older: his cheeks had hollowed out, his hair faded and thinned, and large creases had appeared on his forehead.

"You still angry about that reporter?"

"I don't know—maybe."

Wiltore finished his beer and tossed the can on the deck. Christine watched as it morosely rolled off the side and into the garden. "Phil wrote me and asked me to co-sign a loan. Is it okay if I say yes?" she asked.

Wiltore frowned. "What does he need the money for?"

"His friend is selling him a car—a Civic, I think."

"A Civic? What does he want a Civic for?"

Christine raised her eyebrows and said in a single drawn-out breath, as if this conversation was beneath her, "I don't know, honey."

"He's supposed to find a wife in a Civic?"

Christine frowned. "Oh, come on, plenty of women like Civics."

"Maybe so, but not the men driving them."

Christine walked to the edge of the porch. "You know, I hate it when you say things like that."

"What? I'm just saying the truth."

"Not everybody wants to be macho."

There was a long pause, and Wiltore was afraid he had really pissed his wife off. But when she turned, he saw in her face that she wasn't angry, but she did look concerned. "What's going to happen now? With your case—I mean."

Wiltore sighed. "Well, John Webster—the journalist—is scheduled to go before a judge on Monday, and I guess we'll see."

"You think you'll be able to crack the case then?"

Wiltore longed for another cigarette, but he didn't dare light another one up in front of his wife. "I hope so."

"Then stop feeling so goddamn sorry for yourself."

Wiltore gave Christine a surprised look. She almost never spoke to him like that, usually leaving him to wallow alone in his thoughts. "It's not how I wanted it. Spent years tracking Dzyinski down—millions of dollars trying to put him in jail, and somebody just comes along and kills him."

Christine ran a finger through Wiltore's hair. "Okay, so you don't get the credit you wanted and it's a shame those men were murdered, but the end result is the same. You should be happy."

"What am I doing, Christine? My whole job just seems so irrelevant."

Wiltore's cell phone began to vibrate in his pocket.

Christine heard the shallow sound and asked, "Aren't you going to answer it?"

Wiltore didn't say anything; instead, he stared out across the street at the small brown bungalows that lined up in a row like dreary hills. He slowly got up, went inside, and got himself another beer from the fridge. Christine sat down in Wiltore's chair and waited for him to return, thinking wistfully of many different memories, like fragments of a broken mirror. Times they used to walk in the park holding hands, eat omelettes for breakfast, drink languidly in the warm night.

Wiltore opened the screen door and smiled, almost leeringly, at Christine. Christine turned to look at her husband, but it made her shiver. Wiltore leaned against the railing, again looking out at the neighbour's house. The curtains were closed and there were two dull-yellow lights on, looking like scary, gleaming eyes, and the house one gigantic flat face, peering back at Wiltore.

"What do you think of our neighbourhood? Nice and quiet, isn't it?" Wiltore asked.

Christine clenched her fists. Her jaw wrenched open. "You have to stop it. Stop it this instant," she cried.

Wiltore half turned, surprised. "I was just saying—"

"No, you weren't. You always do it, and I'm tired of it. You make me feel guilty because we don't live in the middle of some goddamn drug- and prostitute-infested neighbourhood."

"That's not what I meant at all."

"Fine—good then."

"When was the last time you were in the Downtown Eastside?"

"Stop it."

"It was just a question. Ten, twenty years ago?"

Christine shrugged, turning her body away from Wiltore so her face was cast in shadow. "I don't know."

"I go there every day. If you went, you wouldn't be so judgmental." Wiltore finished his second beer and threw it off the porch.

"Nobody can live like this, Cliff." Her voice was pleading.

Wiltore tightened his grip on the porch railing. "Some of us have to, Christine. I think everybody in this city should be required to spend an afternoon every month there … see what it's really like."

"Isn't that what that journalist is trying to do?"

Wiltore frowned at the reference to John Webster. "I think he's a vigilante—trying to make a name for himself."

"It seems to me you both want the same thing. Shouldn't you be cooperating?"

Wiltore turned to face his wife. "I don't think he gives a rat's ass who killed Dzyinski."

"Language, sweetheart," Christine scolded softly.

"Sorry, honey—I've tried, but he won't budge."

There was a distant rumble, and then a big van turned the corner, disturbing the quiet street. The van was large and clumsy and had a satellite dish on the top and the words "CBC News" printed in large red letters on the side.

"Not again," Wiltore groaned.

"I thought they were finished," Christine said.

Wiltore watched the reporters wearily.

"They better not," Wiltore said, threatening nothing but the thick, pinkish evening.

They watched as the van parked across the road. Two men jumped out into the summer rain, one with a large camera, the other with a tripod and microphone. The one carrying the camera was dressed in a pair of old jeans and a worn T-shirt. The one with the microphone was more carefully groomed; he had light brown hair, a sharp jaw, and a light blue jacket with a bright red tie.

"Don't even think of taking a step onto my property," Wiltore yelled.

"Sir, we just want to talk to you about Ken Dzyinski," the man wearing the suit said. The two men stopped at the edge of the sidewalk and stared up at Wiltore.

"No comment."

"Detective Wiltore, sir, if we could just have a moment of your time." The man wearing a suit had put down the tripod, and the man with the camera had turned it on and connected it with the tripod.

Wiltore released his grip from the porch and went down the stairs.

"Cliff, don't," Christine pleaded, stepping in front of Wiltore, but he just brushed her aside.

"Don't even think of filming."

"We're on public property."

Wiltore with definitive strides stepped up to the camera and pushed it over. Before he could be prevented, he stomped down on it, smashing the lens, sending parts and bits across the sidewalk. The man wearing the suit pushed Wiltore backward, and then Wiltore punched him in the jaw and he flopped onto the ground like a dying fish. For a moment, Wiltore stood over him feeling victorious—and only slightly ashamed. A few small droplets of sweat were running down his moustache; his heart was racing and his chest heaving.

Wiltore turned to look at the cameraman, who wasn't moving and was staring stunned at his partner on the cement sidewalk, who was rolling around clutching his face. Wiltore snorted and without a word strode back into his house, past Christine who had folded her arms across her chest, her jaw slightly clenched.

The Racetrack

The track smelled of hay and manure and musty oak. Old, cracked sheds and stables lined the outside of the wrought-iron railing. John could heard the sound of galloping horses against the compact dirt, pounding like a fierce bombardment of musket fire, and the announcer commentating on the rising action over a loudspeaker.

"It's Breaker in front. Tycoon just a nose behind. Mouse is gaining!"

John shuffled through the summer crowd. People sat forward in their chairs, the men dressed in Hawaiian shirts and khaki shorts and the women in long flowery dresses that exposed their white calves. The air was warm and moist and humid and had the consistency of vegetable broth.

John had tried phoning Gibson Investments again but had no luck. He had even gone to Alex Gibson's house, but there was no answer when he knocked.

Frustrated, John had gone through the *Daily Globe* archives for any mention of Alex Gibson and had stumbled across a profile of him in the business section. Alex Gibson, the younger brother of Paul Gibson, was the more public, outgoing one. He owned a yacht, had just recently donated ten million dollars to cancer research, and loved horse racing. In fact, he kept three horses down at the Hastings Racetrack and purportedly spent much of his free time there.

There were worse places to start, John thought, and so he went down to the track and found himself amid several thousand jeering, riotous spectators, trying to find Alex Gibson, unsure if he was even there and with only a vague idea of what he looked like.

John approached anybody who would give him a moment, asking if they knew Alex Gibson. Most people stared at him as if he was some kind of creep and moved quickly on. John even talked to the security guards and the bookies, but they just shook their heads.

John walked up and down the grandstands, which were congested with people on this bright and sunny day. The sky was cloudless and pure blue and seemed endless. It was the type of day good for gambling—what was a week's or a month's pay?

Combing the stands like a hotdog vendor made John feel tired, and he realized how weak he still was from his time in the hospital.

A wind swirled around the racing grounds; around the magnificent proud horses; around the stables; around the officials in navy blue uniforms stamping tickets; around the grandstands, whipping the flags back and forth; and around the hungry-eyed gamblers, clutching their stubs.

Discouraged, John decided to rest, and so he sat down in one of the seats in the upper levels. From there, he watched as the horses took their positions at the starting gate. A man in a brown suit passed through the aisle, and John got up to let him through. The man thanked John and took his seat. John stared after him, thinking he looked familiar.

The race started, and John got caught up in the shouts and cheers from the crowd. John tried to peer through the conglomeration of people, but it proved virtually impossible to see anything until the race ended. When it did, John glanced sideways and saw the man in the brown suit staring at him. He had his peppery-grey hair slicked back, and his face was blocky but handsome. The man nodded toward John and then smiled.

John decided to leave. He slid out of his seat and went down the stairs to the exit. When he looked back, he saw the man had gotten up from his seat and was trying to make his way to the stairs.

John walked quicker, trying to lose the man in the crowd. He ducked into a tunnel that went underneath the grandstands. There were only a few naked light bulbs every few metres, casting an eerie tangerine glow through the tunnel. John walked on. To his left there was a door that led to washrooms and another that led to storage of some kind and further down, change rooms. John looked back. He could see nothing in the darkness, but he started to run nevertheless.

He ran until he came to the end of the tunnel. He climbed up and over a fence, one-handed, and onto the racecourse, almost tripping and falling. He allowed himself to look back and saw several burly-looking security guards running after him.

John ran across the track and into a little gap between a large brick building and the fence. He ran along the building looking for escape and found the entrance to Happy Jack's, a small bar. The tacky sign, hanging just above the double-door entrance, had neon lights. The inside was about twenty-five feet wide, with plywood floors, tables and chairs close together, and a wall full of television screens showing the oval and the odds on the races. There was a long bar to the right, where people could mill around, order drinks, and shoot the shit.

The patrons were drinking and talking and watching replays of the races. Nobody took much notice of John, who walked quickly to the back, careful not to draw too much attention. He found a hallway that went to the washroom. He pushed the washroom door open, and found it was empty. He looked around for an escape route. The lights were cheap neon tubes, and the floor was made of brown tile, cracked in places. John tried to open the window with his good hand, but it wouldn't budge. He cursed his useless right arm. He looked at the window and saw it had been painted shut. He grabbed the top of the frame and tried forcing it open without any success.

"Sir," a voice came from behind John. John turned and saw three security guards had entered the washroom and spread out in some kind of attack formation. They were all over six feet tall, with large stomachs flowing over their belts but with muscular arms.

"Somebody is after me," John said.

"Sir, you will have to come with us," one of the security guards said.

John looked at the three men and nodded. He had no choice. The guards escorted John to a bleak room, sat him down, and then left him to wait. He felt exhausted, his whole body strained, but then a feeling of total and utter anger washed over him—so quickly and so intensely he didn't recognize it as such.

What had he done? They had no right to hold him. But then he realized it was larger than that. He wasn't just angry at the security guards, but at everything, for his whole situation: Hayden for trying to take Byron away from him, Liz for her selfishness, Ernest Hunter for trying to kill him, Wiltore for trying to lock him up, even Chuck for being his boss. He knew it was an unfair anger, but it was totally and utterly immobilizing. He had never felt anger like it before.

Eventually one of the security guards came back with a notepad and asked John questions. Name? John told him. Occupation? John told him. Why was he running?

"You don't understand. Somebody is trying to kill me," John said. He pointed to his sling. "I was shot by some gangsters."

The security guard nodded, seemingly uninterested, and scribbled something on his pad of paper. "You're a reporter for the *Daily Globe*?"

John nodded and dug his press pass from his wallet. The security guard scrutinized it dubiously before he passed it back.

The security guard asked John a couple more questions before he stood up. "Okay, we're not going to press charges, but we are banning you from the premises. If you come back here, then we will have you arrested. You got it?"

John frowned. He couldn't believe it, but he decided he didn't want to argue. John was escorted to the park exit. There the man in the brown suit was waiting for him, his hands dug into his pockets.

"He was the one chasing me," John told the security guards.

The security guards looked at the man in the brown suit. "You mean Mr. Ireland? He's the one who convinced us not to press charges."

Security turned and disappeared into the crowd of gamblers. John turned to face Mr. Ireland. He had his hands in his pockets and was smiling. "I don't want to hurt you, Mr. Webster. My name is Don Ireland. I'm an attorney for the Gibson family."

John shook hands with the lawyer, feeling slightly stupid.

Ireland said, "I was wondering if I could have a word?"

John hesitated, looking back at the security guards, who had disappeared back behind the large steel gates.

Ireland frowned. "You are jumpy, aren't you?"

"Having the mob after you can have that effect."

Ireland nodded, understandingly. "I need your help."

"Help? How?"

They slowly walked around the outside of the park. Hastings Racetrack was surrounded by dried grassy hills and ancient spruce trees. Beyond the city, through some sort of trick in perspective, the local pinkish mountains seemed perilously close, like they could be touched. The Pacific Exhibition Park was just east of the racetrack, and the steel, rust-flecked amusement rides rose into the white sky. John could hear the whoosh of the carts and the laughter and the screams through the clear day.

"What I say is off the record," Ireland said. "My name gets into print, and I will sue your ass for all it's worth. Clear?"

John nodded. "Of course; you know I protect all my sources."

Ireland nodded. "Yes, I heard about your subpoena. What are you going to do?"

John shrugged. He didn't like to be reminded. "What can I do? It's out of my hands."

Don Ireland stopped abruptly and looked north toward the mountains, deep in thought. Clear days were rare in Vancouver, and the mountains were usually draped in rain or fog. In the summer months, most Vancouverites were surprised to see exactly how close they were to nature's impressive peaks.

"I'm concerned for Alex," Ireland said.

"You should be. He's deeply involved in organized crime," John said. "He got his brother killed."

Ireland turned toward John. He seemed to be choosing his words carefully. "I don't know if that is entirely accurate."

John studied the handsome lawyer. "How much do you know?"

"I must remind you I have an attorney-client privilege."

"Saying that means you already know too much. Forget Alex—I would be worried about yourself."

Ireland stopped again. His shoulders went rigid, and his neck stiffened. Apparently it hadn't occurred to him he could be in danger as well. "As far as I know, neither Paul nor Alex did anything illegal."

"Neither did I, and look where I am now."

Ireland looked at John's shoulder. "Alex was always the cavalier one. He loves gambling, loved the thrill, I suppose." Ireland seemed hesitant to say more.

"You know, attorney-client privilege doesn't cover illegal activity."

"Don't try and tell me the law," Ireland snapped suddenly.

"I'm just saying if you know of any illegal activity, you are compelled to go to the police."

"Alex had always had this dream of building a casino, but he had no idea about how to run it. That's when Ken Dzyinski approached him. Gibson Investments would provide the capital cost." Ireland waved his hand in the air as if to indicate he didn't know the details. "They had some profit-sharing agreement."

"And it would provide a legit business for Ken to run all his laundered money through," John said.

Ireland held up his hands as if to profess his ignorance. "That had nothing to do with me."

Sure it didn't, John thought. "You think Paul was killed because of his connection to this casino? It doesn't make sense. Why Paul, not Alex?"

"I think it was a warning to Alex. Paul didn't want to do it. He was against it from the beginning."

"Where is Alex?" John asked.

Ireland shrugged and looked down at the ground. "Don't know—on sabbatical until all this blows over and he's fit to return."

"Come on, Mr. Ireland," John said, staring at the lawyer. "You've been so truthful up until now."

Ireland bit his bottom lip, and his eyes narrowed. "He's not really in any condition to see anybody—let alone be interviewed."

"He gets the same deal I made with you. He wants to find his brother's killer, doesn't he?"

Ireland stopped walking, and John stopped with him. The crowd was cheering as the announcer introduced the horses in the next race.

Ireland nodded. "Okay. I trust you … which is kind of funny."

"Why?" John asked.

"I've never trusted a reporter before." He then paused to consider this statement. "I'll take you to him," he said.

They walked to the parking lot. Ireland drove a navy blue Lexus LS 600HL sedan. The doors automatically unlocked, and John slid into the passenger's seat. The car smelled fresh and herbal, and the floor mats were groomed without a fleck of dirt on them. They drove out onto Highway One out to Burnaby. The car hummed along beautifully, and John felt as if he was just floating along, the lampposts flying past them in flickers of light. Ireland had his radio turned to the news station. The anchor was listing the ups and the downs of the week's markets. Ireland listened intently and then relaxed when the commercials came on.

They traveled along for a while, turning north on Sperling Street. The houses were all boxy, with boxy lawns and small, pruned hedges. Sperling Street was a wide street that slowly ascended. In the distance, to their right, Simon Fraser University rose up on Burnaby Mountain, a cluster of grey-slab buildings, miserable and gloomy, saved from utter desolation by the surrounding patches of evergreen trees.

Ireland asked, "So you think Dzyinski's murder is connected to Paul's?"

John nodded. "I can't prove it yet, but I hope I will be able to soon."

They drove on a little while longer.

"You can't tell anybody he's here," Ireland said, shifting gears. "Especially not your colleagues. I don't want any sort of media frenzy."

"He's hiding from Ernest Hunter?"

Ireland nodded. "Yes—and a lot more as well."

John waited for the lawyer to elaborate, but when he didn't, John figured he would learn more when he saw Alex Gibson.

The single residential houses eventually dissipated, and they turned left into a gated community of low-rise buildings. Ireland nodded to the security guard, who pressed a button and opened the gate.

"This is where Alex is?" John asked incredulously.

Ireland shrugged. "Good a place as any. Away from prying eyes. And it's under my name. Nobody will find him here."

They drove along a narrow, winding road until they almost reached the end, where they stopped. They took the steps to the third floor. Ireland stopped at room 503. He looked back at John. "I have to warn you that he's not altogether well."

"What do you mean?"

Ireland fumbled for his keys. "He's ... well ... he's on antidepressants for one thing."

John shrugged, not really understanding. "Okay."

"He took the death of his brother hard," Ireland said as he inserted the key into the lock and turned the doorknob.

John wasn't prepared for what he saw. They stepped into a room completely black. Ireland closed the door behind them, and for a moment John was terrified; his throat became constricted, and his chest contracted. Something flashed before him—a small person dressed in white, but then the mirage disappeared and his eyes adjusted to the room. He was in a hallway, and in front of him was a kitchen. Then he realized why it was so dark: all the windows had been boarded up with plywood.

John groped in the darkness. "Can you turn on some lights?"

Ireland shook his head. "No, Alex unscrewed all the bulbs." Ireland found a light switch and demonstrated.

"This because of his brother?" John asked.

Ireland. "I don't know ... He's become paranoid."

"Has he been to see a doctor?"

Ireland shook his head. "I can't get him out of the apartment."

"Surely you can get someone to come look at him?"

"He refuses. Bars himself into the bathroom."

John looked around, getting over the shock. He had seen this once before, in Iraq. A *New York Times* journalist named Robert Capa had holed himself up in an abandoned building. He had boarded up all the windows and hid in the closet, and when a team of US Marines had gone in, Capa had refused to leave, saying he was working on a story about termites.

John followed Ireland down the hallway to the end. Ireland motioned for John to hold back. He then turned and knocked on the door.

"Alex? ... It's me, Don."

There was no answer, and so Ireland stepped into the room, telling John to wait. "I'll just be a moment."

John crept up to the door. He heard voices but couldn't make out what was being said. After about ten minutes, Ireland opened the door a crack, looking tired and exasperated. "He will see you now."

John nodded and stepped in. The bedroom was small and boarded up like the kitchen. There was a bookcase in one corner but it was empty, and overhead was an empty light-bulb socket. The bed was a queen-size with silk sheets. Alex was so motionless, he seemed to blend in with the bed. But then he slowly unravelled himself, kicked back the sheets, and sat up. He was in striped pyjamas, he had a lengthy, unkempt beard, and his greyish-auburn hair was wild and uncut.

John studied Alex closely—or as closely as the low light would permit. Alex seemed to be at least aware and coherent. If anything, he looked slightly sleep deprived, as his eyes were a little red and puffy.

Alex attempted a smile, but he appeared just to grimace. "Dan tells me you're a famous journalist."

John glanced at Ireland, who stood emotionless, his face partially masked in the darkness. "No … infamous, maybe."

Alex nodded, gripping the side of the bed. "Sometimes I look on the Internet to see if those fuckers have been caught yet." He sighed heavily, leaning backward in his bed. "I don't know what I'm going to do."

"You can't stay cooped up here. If you're so scared, go away somewhere— down to Palm Springs or Mexico."

Alex snorted. His eyes glistened in the darkness. "Palm Springs? Mexico? That would be the worst place to go."

John frowned. "Okay, so maybe Mexico is a bad idea, but somewhere … Not this boxed-up apartment."

"You don't understand what you've gotten yourself into, do you? Ernest Hunter has contacts all over the world. He'll find me no matter where I go. I'm safer here."

"You know who killed your brother," John said, staring closely at the real estate tycoon.

"Not for sure, I don't," Alex said, wiping his nose with the back of his hand. "I was having dinner with my brother at the Vienna Café when I was approached by a guy named Carl Dewitt. You know him?"

It was Alex's turn to stare closely at John, who nodded slowly. "He owns a strip joint down near Gastown."

"He sat down next to my brother like they were all the best of friends and said if we didn't stop with the casino application, then he'd kill us."

"Did you tell this to the police?"

Alex shook his head. "You crazy? Of course not. The police are all mobbed up."

John grunted, incredulous.

"No, really. Dzyinski boasted he had half the police force on his payroll. I'm sure Hunter has some in his pocket as well. I couldn't take the chance."

John pursed his lips. He was sure Dzyinski was lying, and he wanted to get back to the incident at the restaurant. "Okay, how long ago did Carl Dewitt threaten you?"

"About a month ago."

"Did anybody else see you there? Can anybody verify your story?"

Alex frowned and snapped, "I don't know—why don't you ask the fucking waiter?"

John held up his hands. "Okay, okay. I'm sorry ... How did you react?"

"We were really shaken, of course. We paid and left right away." Alex shook his head and ran his fingers through his hair, giving another grimace. "The poor manager was in conniptions because he thought we didn't like the food."

"Okay, what did you do after that?"

"I talked to Ken Dzyinski, of course. Told him what happened. He seemed pretty upset about it. He told me not to worry about it, that he could handle it ... That was the last time I spoke to him."

John thought. "What did you do after Dzyinski was murdered?"

"We agreed to halt the plans for the casino. It wasn't worth it."

"You make it public?"

Alex nodded. "Yes. Sent out press releases, the whole works."

John looked back at Ireland, who still hadn't moved. "Okay ... but there is one problem. The whole thing doesn't make sense. Why would Hunter have your brother killed if you had already decided to stop with the casino plans?"

Alex shrugged, leaning his head against the backboard. "Maybe the plan was already set in motion; maybe he just did it because he's crazy. I don't know."

"When was the last time you saw your brother?"

"It was the night before he was murdered. He seemed worried."

"How so?"

"We were both greatly shaken by Ken's death. I wanted to talk to Ernest Hunter, but he said it was best to leave Hunter alone. He didn't want anything more to do with it."

"Is there anything else you can tell me that you think might be helpful?"

Alex shook his head. "No, I don't think so."

John nodded. "Okay, thanks for your time."

John turned toward the door and Ireland followed him, but Alex called them back. "I don't understand one thing," he called out.

John turned to face the tragic-looking figure. "What's that?" he asked.

Alex didn't answer right away. Instead, he crumpled the bedsheets up in his tiny, frail hands. "How are you not afraid?"

Through the light from the cracks in the boards, John looked toward Ireland and then back at Alex. Alex had stopped playing with the sheets and had tucked his neck slightly back into his shoulders. He stared hard at John, his eyes wide, interested, reflecting what little light there was in the room.

"I am afraid," John said. "Every second, every moment of the day, but you control it. You don't let it overwhelm you."

Alex nodded hesitantly, seeming unsatisfied with the answer, but he didn't seem to know what to say and so John said good-bye and left. Ireland followed him.

John and Ireland left the building and stood in the sunlight, not saying anything, letting their eyes adjust from the darkness. The apartment complex was quiet. A fat American shorthair cat scampered from under a car to the dumpster.

Ireland was the first to speak. "What do you think?"

"I think you need to go to the police."

Ireland frowned unhappily. "I can't. He told me in confidence ... There was no law broken. Legally I am bound to attorney-client privilege."

"The police might be able to arrest Carl Dewitt with that testimony."

Ireland scoffed and pointed back at the building. "And how reliable is that testimony? Any lawyer in this city would tear him apart."

John shrugged. "At the very least, you should get him into a hospital, get him to see a doctor."

Ireland shook his head. "Not before Ernest Hunter is put behind bars."

"You believe Hunter still wants to kill him?"

Ireland shrugged. "How can I take that chance? If somebody puts a knife into him, how will I ever forgive myself?"

Ireland drove John downtown in his Lexus, the motor purring along barely making a sound. John looked out the window, lost in thought. "Where should I drop you?" Ireland asked.

"Anywhere in Gastown would be fine," John said, still staring out at the blue mountains.

Ireland asked, "You believe what he says about the police? I mean, being in Ernest Hunter's pocket?"

John shook his head. "This isn't Afghanistan—he's paranoid, like you said."

Ireland shook his head. "Sometimes I think his paranoia is rubbing off on me."

"Yes, it can be contagious."

Carl Dewitt

John swiped his key card to gain access to the Globe building. He nodded to the security guard and went into the elevator. The doors closed, and the elevator lifted him up off the ground floor. He felt weightless, as if he had no body. He looked at himself in the wall mirror. He looked hollow and translucent—as if he'd aged ten years in the last month. His mind was preoccupied with Alex Gibson and Don Ireland and different scenarios.

He thought about how little sleep he had been getting lately. Last night he had slept for maybe two—three hours tops. After a while he went to the fridge and got a beer. He had about a dozen or so before he was able to return to his bed. His dreams had been crazy and frightening.

The elevator groaned like an old battleship, and the neon light was bright and orangeish. It made John's throat dry and his chest contract. Was that just the effects of the alcohol? Was he getting worse? He looked at himself in the mirror again. His one arm was in a sling, and the other was shaking a bit. Or was that just his imagination? He couldn't tell anymore.

The elevator door opened into the gigantic newsroom, and he immediately felt at home. The claustrophobic effects dissipated. He went to his desk. The entire day was filled unproductively. He phoned Michelle, phoned Rocky Moon to try and get hold of Carl Dewitt, and went downstairs to the pay phone to call Drake McMillan, but nobody answered and he didn't expect any of them to return his calls.

He sat down at his desk and pounded out a story, feeling the minutes tick away to his court date. He found it hard to concentrate, but he wasn't sure if it was apprehension from the subpoena or from his drinking binge.

At lunchtime, John knocked on Chuck's door. Chuck was in his office working diligently away like usual, his skinny shoulders hunched over his computer.

As John entered, he got immediately to the point. "We haven't talked about the subpoena recently—what we're going to say."

Chuck sat back in his chair. "I'm going to say I don't know who your source is. There is nothing to prove otherwise."

"And what am I supposed to say?"

"Only you can decide that."

John frowned and sat down in a chair. He looked down at the floor. When he looked up, he saw Chuck was still staring at him with his piercing glare. "You look terrible," he offered.

John forced a smile. "I'm going to jail—how should I look?"

"I don't think the courts are ready to infringe on freedom of the press quite yet—have a little faith."

John sighed. "Sure. Although I would probably feel better if I knew we got through to the readers."

Chuck folded his scrawny arms across his shallow chest. "You remember when Michael Jackson died?"

"Of course."

"You remember the media coverage he got? The circumstances around his doctor and what he prescribed?"

John frowned in confusion. "What are you trying to say, Chuck?"

"Michael Jackson's death received way more attention than the war in Afghanistan ever did."

John shifted in his seat, feeling that his boss was trying to bait him, but not sure why. "You trying to reassure me? These are your words of wisdom, Chuck?"

Chuck shook his head sadly. "When did you ever need to be reassured, John? Tell me that."

John half-rose in his chair. He wasn't going to argue, but Chuck wasn't going to let him get away that easy. "Sit down, John."

Obediently John sat back down. "People just care more about Michael Jackson than Afghanistan, is that it?"

Chuck used his thumb to push back his glasses. "Look, all I'm saying is you need to put things in perspective. You do your job, sometimes it helps, most of the time it doesn't. Don't get all reminiscent."

John nodded. "It was Carl Dewitt who murdered Ken Dzyinski and Paul Gibson."

Chuck stiffened in his seat. "What? How do you know that?"

"I don't … Can't prove it anyways. I spoke to Alex Gibson. He said Dewitt threatened him and his brother … next thing he knows, Paul Gibson is killed."

"And it was over this casino licence, of all things?"

John nodded. "Seems so."

"Well, you should write what you have. We'll put it in tomorrow's edition."

John shrugged. "I promised I would use him for background only."

Chuck nodded. "Okay, anything you can use?"

"I need to verify some things before I can finish it."

"It will be ready for tomorrow's edition?"

"It will have to be." John rubbed his jaw. "It might be the last article I write for a while."

Chuck smiled. It was such a rare act for him, it seemed unnatural on his usually severe frame. "Don't worry. They wouldn't dare, and I will make sure I do everything in my power to stop it."

John left Chuck, sat down at his computer, and again tried to type out a comprehensible story. His one good arm was growing tired from using it all day. He looked around the newsroom, hoping to see somebody he could dictate to, but everybody was busy. John gave up and shut down his computer. What did he have to say anyways? Nothing. Nothing to go on, no sources, no one to go on record.

John went to the washroom. That vacant feeling he felt in the elevator seemed to return, and he splashed some water in his face, hoping it would make him look less ghostly.

He decided to go outside to the pay phone and give Drake McMillan one more try. John hadn't believed Alex at first when he had said the two main gangs bribed police officers, but he wanted to ask him about it anyways. It had been slowly gnawing at him since the morning, and he didn't know why—perhaps it was just his reporter's instinct for a dirty cop story.

John was surprised when Drake answered, especially since he sounded so jovial on the phone. "John, haven't heard from you in a while. What's up?"

"I need some information."

"Of course, you do. What do you want to know?"

"Did Dzyinski have any cops on his payroll?"

There was a pause and John thought Drake might hang up, but he didn't. "I have no idea. Why would I know a thing like that?"

"You're lying to me, Drake."

"I swear I'm not."

"Drake, I have a court date on Monday; and if I tell them even half of what you've told me, you'd be going to jail for a long time."

"You're going to hang that over my head forever? I don't know anything."

"How about Hunter? You seem pretty close to him now."

"It's only business. Nothing more—and he wouldn't tell me anything."

John clenched his jaw. He was getting angry. "You better get me something I can use, or I'm going straight to the police."

"Okay, give me time. Let me see what I can find out, okay?"

"Thanks, Drake, you are a real pal, you know that?" John said, disgusted, and hung up.

John went to a walk-in clinic on Corral Street several blocks from his apartment. It had a red neon sign in the window. Inside, it looked sterile and dull. He stood outside for several minutes, debating whether he should go in or not. He wanted to get rid of all those nightmares that haunted him, but he didn't know if he could face the questions that would arise.

Eventually he sucked in a deep breath and pushed the door open. He was greeted by the office secretary and was made to fill out some forms. Then he waited. He read the *Economist* and flipped through *Time* magazine. In *Time,* there was an article about an Afghanistan police officer who used to work for one of the warlords who grew opium. John closed the magazine and picked up *People* to see if he could find anything about Michael Jackson, but there was nothing. This gave John some hope. Eventually his name was called.

He was led into a small examination room and told to sit on the bed. The room had different medical charts posted on the walls. He leaned back and looked up at the white ceiling. After a while, the doctor entered.

"I need you to prescribe me some sleeping pills," John told her.

"You stressed?" she asked sweetly. John relaxed a little. She didn't ooze the sort of authoritative menace he associated with doctors. In fact, she was kind of pretty, with short, curly, hazel-coloured hair. Her face was round, and her cheeks were flushed. She wore deep-blue denim pants and a white blouse.

John nodded. "You could say that."

"Is it work?"

John nodded. "I'm a journalist."

"That explains a lot," she said, smiling widely. John couldn't help but smile back.

"What happened to your arm?" she asked, indicating the sling.

John considered lying, but decided he couldn't—not when the doctor seemed so sweet. "Well … it's difficult to explain," he started off. "I was shot by somebody."

The doctor nodded, seemingly unsurprised. "You mind if I examine it?"

John shrugged. She took off the sling and the bandage and looked at the wound. "It's healing nicely," she said. "You're very lucky."

John smiled. "Nobody has called me lucky in a long time."

She cleaned the wound and put on fresh bandages. "Let me take your blood pressure," she said. She strapped on the cuff to his good arm.

She asked him questions about his work.

He told her about the gangsters he was writing about, about Paul Gibson, how Ernest Hunter wanted him dead. For some reason, it felt good talking about it to a complete stranger, someone unbiased.

The doctor nodded and said, "Oh, I remember. I read that article about you. You were that reporter in Afghanistan, weren't you?"

John looked away demurely. "They should never have printed that article. I was in the hospital at the time."

The doctor undid the cuff from John's arm. "Your blood pressure is definitely high for your age. You exercise?"

"Occasionally."

"How much do you drink a week?"

"A little bit," John admitted.

The doctor frowned. "Five glasses a week? Ten?"

John suddenly became irritated. "Look, I came here about my sleeping, not my drinking."

The doctor stared evenly at John. Her smile and friendliness were gone. "Well, that could be a contributing factor to your inability to sleep well. I would recommend cutting down on the alcohol and taking a leave of absence from work."

John laughed, but his throat was dry and it came out croaky. "It's not exactly an option at this moment."

The doctor frowned. "What isn't? Cutting your drinking or going away? This could get a lot worse if you don't slow down."

"Look, I understand—really I do. It's just that I need to figure out who killed Paul Gibson and Ken Dzyinski before I get thrown in jail."

The doctor put down her notepad. "You realize the way you are pushing yourself, you could very well have a heart attack by the age of fifty."

John sucked in a lungful of air and held it. His immediate demise had always been something lurking in his brain—shot, stabbed, beaten to death, sure—but to think he could have a heart attack before he was fifty came as a shock. John tried to smile, to laugh it off, to think of some joke to make; but when he failed, he just nodded and said, "Okay, I'll do my best."

The doctor sighed. "I'm serious. You need to take better care of yourself."

She picked up her pad again and wrote John out a prescription. "Good luck," she said. "You can't just keep ignoring your health. I have office hours every Tuesday and Thursday. I don't normally accept new patients, but I'll make an exception for you."

John thanked the doctor and went to the pharmacy next door to fill his prescription. He then went home, popped some of the pills, drank what beer he had left in the fridge, and watched the afternoon news. He thought about what the doctor had said. If he somehow managed to escape jail time, he would go away, he decided. Maybe he would take Michelle on a cruise or go to California or the Caribbean—someplace warm and sunny.

When the program turned to sports, he went into his bedroom and passed out for several hours. He awoke startled and disoriented. He looked up at the ceiling until his breathing returned to normal. He thought back, but he couldn't remember what he had dreamed. He turned his neck and discovered it was still dark outside. He looked over at the clock and saw it was one o'clock in the morning. He closed his eyes and tried to get back to sleep but found he couldn't. He considered popping another pill, but then thought better of it.

He went to the bathroom, and when he returned, he sat at the foot of the bed, staring into the cavernous room. He slowly took a silver case from underneath his bed. He turned the combination lock and popped the case open. Inside was an old army-issue Glock handgun. It had been given to him by an American soldier in Afghanistan named Justin Clarke, just before he went on leave. Justin was a tall, bulky-shouldered man with a thick Midwestern accent. John didn't want to accept the gun, but the soldier said it was just for safekeeping while he was away.

The soldier had gone back to his home, some small town in Ohio. He had stayed there for a week with his wife and two young daughters. Then, before he could be shipped back to Afghanistan, he had blown his brains out. John saw it on the news a couple of days later. Another casualty. John had kept the gun, never really knowing what to do with it. He had contemplated turning it over to the US authorities, but in the end he had decided against it. He had felt it would have been an insult to the soldier's legacy to give it back. John had felt, for whatever reason, Justin had wanted him to keep it.

John had never fired a gun before, but he wondered how hard it could really be. He just had to point and shoot. The handle felt good in his hand, hard and cold and solid. But no, he was not a soldier. He was not as brave as Justin. What would he do with the gun? He slid the gun back into its case and put on a jacket to go outside.

The night was a dome of silver-blue light. Stores had long ago packed up for the night and closed their graffiti-riddled steel gates. There were only a few late-night stragglers waiting for night busses or waving taxis down. By the Old Winston bar, on the corner of Abbot Street, there was a crowd of drunken smokers talking loudly.

John walked past an old man who wasn't that old. He was scrawny, had long stringy hair, and was playing an old flute. He played it badly—melancholic note after melancholic note, sad and sour, and it filled John with a sense of loneliness and loss. Lying at his feet, the old man had a regal-looking German shepherd, who stared intently at John with large, sad, brown eyes.

Across the street, the lamps glowed illustriously. Taped up on to the lamps were photocopied posters offering rewards for people long lost and long gone. John walked along the lampposts looking at all the faces—black, white, Asian, Hispanic, Indian. These people were probably destined never to be found again. Their black-and-white replicas were forever stored away in the city's memory banks. The Downtown Eastside was where people went if they wanted to go missing, as much from themselves as others.

John turned onto Pender Street. The moonlight shone like a spotlight on to a man in dirty jeans and an old windbreaker. He was doing the spastic cocaine hop, arms and feet playing *rat-a-tat-tat* to a beat nobody could hear. John walked past two tall drag queens, arms interlinked, wearing glitter and silver jackets and golden necklaces, looking like Olympian champions. Somebody asked John for money, and John forked over a couple of bucks he had in his wallet. The man thanked John gratefully, bowing his head as he disappeared back into the shadows of the buildings.

John found himself at Rocky Moon. Had he meant to go there? He had no answer. He could hear the music from inside, a loud, thumping beat that somehow seemed to promise something intangible. Perhaps it was a hope of something so pulsating and so overwhelming, it sucked your entire being and made you dumbstruck for an hour or two.

John listened to the music for a while and then opened the door and stepped inside, into a flashy, neon-lighted world. He went up the steps, past the advertising on the wall. He paid his ten bucks and was searched by two bald bouncers.

The place was mostly empty except for a few permanent drunks and a couple of girls in the corner. One of the women seemed to want to compete with the strippers and was flashing the entire room.

The stripper was dancing lackadaisically to AC/DC of all things. She flipped her long sun-tanned body through the motions as if she was battery operated, wrapping her muscular legs around the pole, her slender fingers extended.

John sat down at one of the empty tables in the corner and ordered straight whiskey, watching as one of the girls stuffed a twenty into the stripper's g-string. John watched as the dancing girls, the massage girls, the girls serving whiskey shots, the girls taking orders, all made their rounds, circling predatorily.

John felt like he was a bad record, perpetually playing the same thing over and over and over again. Coming back to the beginning of his search.

The waitress came back with his drink, and John asked, "Is Michelle working today?"

The girl's eyes sparkled slightly. She had long blonde hair, tossed over her shoulders, deep eye shadow, and a thick red mouth. "What do you want? I can fix it up for you."

John gave the girl his Visa and started a tab. *Can you fix my marriage?* he thought. *Can you fix my nightmares? Can you fix my article? No, what I want, you can't fix*, John thought. "I just need to talk to her."

"She's off; I'm sorry," the girl said, tilting her head and thrusting out her hips, a sexy move, John was sure, she had practiced many times before. "You want a lap dance? A nice massage?"

John shook his head. He finished his drink and then went over to the bar. "Can I talk to Carl Dewitt?"

"He's not here. Something I can do for you?" the bartender asked.

"Tell him John Webster from the *Daily Globe* would like to talk to him." John handed the bartender his business card. The bartender narrowed his eyes and looked at the card dubiously. "Sure; no problem."

John went and sat back down, knocking a couple of drinks back, feeling slightly stupid. What was his plan anyways? To confront him about what he said to Alex Gibson? He knew he should have a plan. He had never freewheeled it in Afghanistan. He had planned everything carefully and concisely, leaving nothing to chance. John wondered why he was so reckless. Was it his desperation for a story? He couldn't find an answer.

John thought it was best if he just left. He saw no good coming from this, but for some reason, he couldn't make himself get up and walk out into the night air. An acute loneliness pinched at him. There was something about the whole setting that subdued him. He didn't quite understand: bars were meant as a gathering place, a place where everybody had a common theme, but John just felt sad and gloomy. It was the girls that did it for him—their bodies, their sensual promises just out of his reach.

A man slid into the booth beside John. It took John a moment to recognize the brutish, dense face: Keith Dowell. He was wearing dress pants and a tight cotton shirt. Chest hair was protruding from his collar. "What are you doing here?" he asked in his deep, baritone voice.

"I want to talk to Carl," John said.

Keith looked John over. "You're drunk," he said.

"I have evidence … if I go to the police."

Keith stared thoughtfully, not looking overly concerned. "What evidence?"

"Evidence he killed Paul Gibson."

"You're bluffing."

"Can you afford to take that chance?"

Keith shook his head. "Pity about your shoulder there."

John reacted violently. "Is that a threat?"

Keith got up, smiling menacingly, showing brilliantly white teeth. "If only you could see yourself … such a sad sight. It is unbelievable you are so full of self-importance."

Keith turned and started to walk away.

John got up unsteadily and followed him. "You won't think so when I bring your entire operation down."

Keith turned. He wasn't smiling any longer. "Let me call you a cab."

"I'm not getting into any cab you call."

Keith looked around. They were beginning to cause a scene; people were turning their heads, wondering what was going on. The bouncers began to close in on John. Keith said, "I'm your friend, believe it or not. I don't want any harm to come to you."

"You were the second shooter, weren't you? You and Carl," John said.

That was it for Keith. He nodded, and two bouncers took hold of John under his shoulders and dragged him to the door. John kicked and struggled, but it was useless against the bouncers' tight grasps. The bouncers pushed the doors open and carried John out onto the street. The wind had turned cold and beat against his body. He felt himself being put into a car as if he weighed nothing at all. The door was slammed shut. Panic ripped through his chest, and a swell of self-preservation hit his limbs. Before the car could drive off, John pushed the handle and tumbled out, hitting the pavement with a hard thwack.

He struggled to get up, but before he could do so, the bouncers were on him again. They tossed him back into the cab. John clawed his way to the door. One of the bouncers gave John a swift blow to the side of his head. The impact was about as hard as anything he had ever felt, and his view suddenly turned darkly myopic as he struggled to remain conscious. He sensed himself falling. He could smell the cushions—a mixture of dirt and lemon deodorizer—before he vomited. He looked up through the back window. He could see the faint silver glow of stars. Stars in the middle of the city? *How was that possible?* he wondered.

And he thought maybe this was how he was going to die. After all those close calls, those roadside bombs, those attempted kidnappings, those gun battles, he was going to get a sharp, cold, metallic pinprick in the back of his head; a single trigger would be pressed, and everything would be over. Because he had gone to Rocky Moon and asked for it. By going to the place he should have stayed away from. And as he lay there, struggling to remain conscious, he wondered if it hadn't been some sort of devious plan from his subconscious from the very beginning. Wiltore had been right after all—he had a death wish. It was his brain's way of saying it had had enough of the nightmares of living without Hayden, of struggling against the insurmountable, of living a life that had become paler and paler shades, shadows of shadows.

He heard voices talking quietly among themselves, and then he blacked out. He saw the boy again. He tried to tell him to run, but he couldn't speak. He couldn't move. Why? Why was he paralysed? He turned to William Russell, the camera trained on the boy, and he wanted to ask him … something. He couldn't remember what. Then he felt like he was falling, and then he stopped.

"We're here, boss," a voice said, arousing him from his sleep. John looked up. He was in the same cab as before. He sat up and recognized his apartment building. He tried to pay the cabbie, but the cabbie waved the credit card away.

"Already been paid for, boss."

John got out. He watched the taxi disappear around the corner. He went upstairs and lay down on the bed. He remembered the gun underneath him. He couldn't be tempted. He took the box and called another cab.

John told the driver to take him to Pandora Street. It was a little difficult picking out Michelle's house in the dim streetlights, but eventually he found it. There were no lights on and no sign anybody was stirring.

He told the driver to wait for him as he quietly went up the front steps and rapped on the screen door. Even as he did so, he wondered what he was hoping to accomplish. He waited for several minutes, looking back at the idling taxi.

He knocked, louder this time. He finally heard the muffled sound of footsteps and a voice, Michelle's voice, asking, "Who is it?"

"It's me, John."

There was a loud click as a bolt came undone and the door opened.

Michelle stuck her head out. John couldn't help but notice she was fully dressed. "What are you doing here?" Michelle asked, sounding annoyed.

"I need a favour."

"I'm out of favours. Good night."

John put a hand on the door. "Michelle, wait!"

"John, it's late. I need to go to bed."

"The police are going to search my apartment any day now. I need you to hold on to something for me."

Michelle raised her eyebrows, looking down at the case. "Illegal? What is it?"

John nodded reluctantly, shoving the case into Michelle's arms. "It's a handgun."

"Jesus," she said, looking down at the silver case. "What do you have that for?"

John shrugged. He didn't want to explain how Justin had given it to him for safekeeping. "I don't know really … I guess it's a comfort on some sort of level."

"John, I have a kid; I can't have guns in my house," Michelle said, trying to give the case back to him.

"Come on, it's locked up, and it'll just be for a little while, until this whole thing blows over."

Michelle hesitated some more, but eventually, after what seemed like forever, she nodded and started to close the door.

"Keep it someplace safe," John said, a little unnecessarily.

Michelle nodded, "Okay, I gotta go, John."

"I appreciate it—thanks," John said, turning and returning to the cab.

The Drop-Off

Wiltore and Lewis were sitting in the backseat of a squad car. Sergeant Damon Cook and Sergeant Devin Blake were sitting up front half-asleep. It was three o'clock in the morning, the sky was black, and everything was still. They were parked on Pandora Street in front of Michelle Lake's house.

Wiltore was always astounded how one block could be dramatically different than the one beside it. A couple of streets over, there were perfectly respectable houses, but here on Pandora Street there were collapsed fences, weedy lawns, tilted porches, and boarded-up windows.

"You got the subpoena yet?" Wiltore asked. They had applied to tap her phones, and they were just waiting on the judge's signature.

Blake half opened his eyes and looked at Wiltore in the rearview mirror. "No, not yet. Should come through any day now, though."

Devin Blake and Damien Cook had been partners ever since Wiltore could remember. They had both graduated from Simon Fraser University with degrees in criminology two years apart. Perhaps the only discernable difference was Cook had divorced his wife of ten years just six months ago. They seemed the natural partnership.

Wiltore took a sip from his coffee, now long cold. He was unconvinced the Lake woman knew anything. Blake and Cook had been staking her house out for the last couple of days, and they had invited Wiltore and Lewis along for the stakeout.

"Don't worry; it will be worth your time," Blake had told Wiltore when he had expressed his reservation. Blake had refused to say anything more, but he seemed quite pleased with whatever discovery he had made so Wiltore had agreed.

They had been there for a couple of hours, and so far nothing had happened. The lights were out, and there was no sign of movement. The whole street was asleep. The four cops took turns keeping a look out. Wiltore was getting tired when he saw a light go on in the top floor. He nudged Lewis, but she was already looking.

"Do we know which window is Michelle's?" Lewis asked.

Blake sat up in his seat and looked up at the light. "No, we know she lives with three others, but we're not sure whose room is whose."

Wiltore strained to see if he could see any movement, but the curtains were drawn and it was impossible to see anything.

Blake stretched and asked, "Wiltore, you still playing soccer?"

Wiltore looked out the window. "Sure—when I can."

Blake grinned. "We were thinking of playing."

Wiltore tried to smile, but he was too tired to make much of an effort. "You guys play before?"

Blake said, "We can hold our own, I'm sure."

Lewis tried to laugh, but it choked in her throat. "Better be careful, they're a competitive bunch."

"So are we," Blake said. "We don't like to be beaten."

Wiltore slapped Blake on the shoulder. "We'll hold tryouts for you guys."

There was a silence in the car. Lewis looked at the two cops in the front. "Don't worry; he's joking."

A taxi appeared from around the corner and meandered slowly up the street. The cops watched the car with fleeting interest until it finally came to a stop in front of Michelle's house, only a couple of car lengths away from them.

They watched as a dark figure emerged from the passenger's side and walked up the steps to Michelle's house.

"Can anybody make out who it is?" Blake asked, waking his partner up with a gentle nudge of the elbow.

The other cops shook their head in frustration. They watched as the man knocked on the door. Wiltore stared at him intently. He was tall and slender but with broad shoulders. He had a silver box in his hand. His outline looked familiar somehow, but he couldn't quite place him. Who was he?

Eventually Michelle came to the door. She was facing toward them, and her features could plainly be seen in the night. Wiltore hoped she would turn on some lights and the man's face would be illuminated, but there was no such luck.

Cook took out a digital SLR camera and snapped some pictures.

Michelle talked to the man for a while, and then the man shoved the box he was carrying into Michelle's hands. Wiltore wondered what was in the box. Drugs maybe? They waited some more.

The man turned and walked quickly down the steps. Michelle closed the door, and the man opened the taxi door. The inside light turned on as the man got in. *Finally*, Wiltore thought. The man turned to the driver, and then he glanced out the window.

"Son of a bitch!" Wiltore couldn't help saying. "John Webster."

"Who?" Blake and Cook asked almost simultaneously.

"He's the journalist for the *Daily Globe*," Lewis explained.

"So that's him," Cook said. "What do you think he gave Michelle?"

Wiltore shrugged. "No idea. Must be something illegal."

"I don't know," Lewis said hesitantly.

Wiltore, despite his fatigue, gave his partner an incredulous look that made Lewis raise her hands.

"Okay, okay," she said. "Let's look at the possibility, but rule nothing out."

"Well, what do you think it is?" Wiltore asked.

"It just seems unlikely Webster is involved in this, that's all."

Wiltore rubbed his eyes, feeling his shoulders tighten. "You still think we're wasting our time on him?"

Lewis looked away, refusing to give an answer.

A couple of minutes later, a shadowy figure emerged from the door. It took a moment for Wiltore to realize it was Michelle Lake. She was wearing a heavy jacket and a baseball cap. She shut the front door quietly and went down the steps to her car. Now all four cops were watching her as she started the car and slowly drove down the street.

Blake started his car and followed her slowly. "Told you it wouldn't be a waste of time."

They followed her as she turned left on Boundary Road and then right on Adanac, twisting down the narrow road. Traffic was almost nonexistent. Wiltore was afraid they would be spotted, such an obvious tail, and told Blake to stay back further. But Michelle seemed unconcerned about anybody following her. They drove on a few blocks; Michelle was slowing down. The police officers kept a respectable distance behind, watching the red glare from Michelle's taillights. They came to a small park. Michelle turned into the parking lot, and the cops drove on by.

Michelle parked her car in the parking lot and killed the engine. The cops circled the block.

"We'll get out. You guys wait here," Wiltore said.

"Okay," Cook said. "But don't spook her."

Lewis and Wiltore got out and backtracked down an alleyway, finding a lookout among some tall cedar trees where they could see the vague outline of Michelle. Wiltore looked up, cursing the lack of moonlight. There was no light anywhere, no lampposts. Across from the park there was a row of houses, but no light came from them. It was the perfect place not to be seen.

Wiltore watched as Michelle climbed out of her car, leaned up against the door, and lit a cigarette and put it up to her mouth; the bottom half of her jaw was illuminated in a tawny haze, giving her an eerie bansheeish look. She seemed to be waiting for something. She finished her cigarette and extinguished it under her foot. She moved restlessly around to the other side of the car, where she lit another cigarette. They didn't have to wait long: another car, a Toyota SUV, pulled up beside her, and a man got out. Wiltore tried to catch the licence plate, but he couldn't see in the darkness.

"Shit, you see who it is?" Wiltore asked Lewis, but she shook her head. Wiltore watched as Michelle greeted the man with a brief hug. Wiltore tried to see the man's face in the light of Michelle's cigarette, but he couldn't.

Wiltore was sure he had seen the figure before—not too tall, broad-shouldered. They talked for a while, and then Michelle popped the trunk of her car and took out a large duffle bag. The man bent over, inspected the contents, and then nodded. He went to his SUV and brought out his own duffle bag and gave it to Michelle. She put it in her car. The man said something to Michelle, but she shook her head. The man grabbed Michelle's hand. Wiltore unhooked his holster strap, but Michelle didn't resist. The man kissed her and took her into the back of his SUV.

"I'm going to get closer," Wiltore told Lewis, but Lewis put a hand on his shoulder.

"No," she said. "Let's radio Blake and Cook. They'll be able to run the licence plate."

"What if it's stolen?" Wiltore asked. He took his gun from his holster. It felt good to hold it in his hand. It felt powerful.

Lewis said, "Michelle used her own car. Don't blow this. Don't chance it."

Wiltore ignored Lewis and took off across the park. He was exposed in the open field. Grateful he kept himself in decent shape for somebody his age. Wiltore ran as quickly as he could, treading softly on the recently cut grass. He kept his eyes on the SUV for any sign of movement, but it was rocking gently back and forth on its springs. If anybody came out now, they would spot him for sure.

Wiltore passed through the playground and jumped into the empty swimming pool. There he stopped and crouched and looked around to consider his next move. He was about seventy yards away from the SUV. Would he be able to see their faces when they came out? In the darkness, he couldn't be sure.

Ervin wanted him off the case, did he? Well, Wiltore wasn't going to let them do that. No, he realized this was his chance to possibly crack the case wide open, and he wasn't going to let it go.

Wiltore looked around for someplace closer. The outhouse was only another twenty or so yards away. It wouldn't take him long to get there and would be a good vantage point. But how long did he have until the pair emerged from the SUV? Wiltore decided the longer he delayed, the chances of him getting caught increased.

Wiltore climbed out of the swimming pool, and keeping low, he ran to the outhouse. The run seemed to last forever, and by the end of it he was out of breath. He made it just in time as the man appeared from the SUV, zipping up his pants. He looked around the park. Wiltore hid his face behind the building. He counted two seconds and then peeked again. He could see the man who had emerged from the SUV clearly now. He had large, muscular arms and gold rings on each of his fingers. It took a moment before the name came to Wiltore: Keith Dowell, the manager of Rocky Moon. Michelle emerged from the SUV a little after. Wiltore couldn't see her face, but she didn't seem very happy. She marched without a word back to her car. She got in, started the engine, and threw the car into reverse. Keith Dowell watched the car disappear down the road before he climbed into his SUV and started the engine.

Wiltore took out his phone and called Cook. "Forget Michelle; follow the SUV. I want to know where he goes."

The Toyota SUV slowly reversed and pulled out of the parking lot. Wiltore watched it go before walking back to Lewis, who was still hiding in the cedar trees. "It was Keith Dowell, the manager at Rocky Moon," Wiltore said.

Lewis nodded. "What do you think was in the duffle bags?"

Wiltore studied his partner. He was still breathing hard. He could feel adrenaline running though his limbs. "You think it was guns?"

Lewis shrugged. "The obvious connection to Carl Dewitt? Can't think of anything else it would be unless they're doing something behind Carl's back."

"You still don't think Webster is connected to this?" Wiltore asked.

"Do I think he's part of the operation?" Lewis asked slowly, appearing to chew over the question. "Not wittingly, but perhaps you are right about him."

Wiltore tried hard to hide his smugness by lighting a cigarette.

They didn't say much as they waited to be picked up again. Wiltore started to pace around impatiently; he felt like getting back into the chase, a longing to be back in the car following Keith.

Neither Wiltore nor Lewis was dressed for the night chilliness, and they crossed their arms trying to fend off the cold. They walked out of the park to the intersection of the largest street, which was black and lifeless except for a family of racoons that waddled across the street.

Wiltore finished his first cigarette, kicking the butt to the curb, and started his second. Lewis watched him disapprovingly. "What?" he asked.

"Can I ask you a question?" Lewis asked, looking down at the sidewalk.

Wiltore studied his partner. "Sure."

"Was there a point where you decided family was more important than your career?"

Wiltore smiled faintly. "Both my father and uncle were cops. I guess I had good role models."

"You're successfully married, with three kids. Not many IGTF guys can claim that. You must have decided somewhere along the way you needed to make sacrifices."

"I dunno. I missed a lot of graduations and birthday parties. My wife, Christina, is a very amazing woman. My kids … I guess we don't have the best relationship, but I call them on Christmas." Wiltore rubbed his eyes. The adrenaline was beginning to wear off, and he was feeling tired again.

Wiltore remained silent after that. Lewis, perhaps realizing the significance of Wiltore's silence, didn't say anything either. Wiltore put out his cigarette with the heel of his boot. He looked across the street at the wooden-paneled houses crowded together and the dark hedges that needed pruning.

Eventually Cooke and Blake pulled up, and Lewis and Wiltore climbed into the back.

"So?" Wiltore asked, eager for the report.

"He went to an old warehouse on Lancaster Avenue," Cook said as they drove back to the police station. Their night wasn't done: they still had several hours of paperwork ahead of them, but none of the cops were thinking about that. "He wasn't there for long. He switched into a beamer and drove home. He's got this gorgeous place in North Vancouver. Must have this great view."

Cook put one hand on the windowsill and looked out the window. Wiltore watched him, wondering if he was picturing that view from the hilltop.

"It's a good thing you identified him," Blake said. "We never got a good look at his face."

Wiltore nodded as if the praise meant nothing, but secretly he was pleased. He was sure they would note it in their reports, and when Ervin read it, he wouldn't be able to kick him off the case. *Now,* Wiltore thought, *if he could just find the connection between Webster and the guns.*

Wiltore said, "We just have to find out who that warehouse belongs to."

Blake shook his head. "No need."

"Why not?" Wiltore asked.

"We already know. Gibson Investments Company."

The Lead

When Wiltore got home, he went to the bedroom to check on Christine. She was curled on one side in her cotton nightgown, her arms dug deep under the pillow, and her body was expanding and retracting with the slow rhythm of sleep.

Wiltore knew himself well enough to know his mind was too active to be able to sleep, so he went back downstairs into the living room and turned on the television to watch the news. The anchor was talking about a rebellion in some Middle Eastern country. The television changed to pictures of people marching in the street, chanting slogans and waving flags. Wiltore changed the channel and watched infomercials for a while.

He felt like running up the stairs, waking Christine, and telling her the good news, but he already knew what her reaction would be: *That's nice, dear.* After a while—and after watching a knife cut a tin can about a dozen times—he started to relax.

On the screen, a slim blonde wearing tight yoga pants and a tank top was demonstrating the abdominal accelerator.

"For ten minutes a day ..." she was monotonously explaining.

Wiltore went and got himself a beer from the fridge. It was times like this—when it was late and he was tired—that he would think about the time he volunteered to go down to New York after 9/11. How he had cleared the rubble from the Twin Towers. Now it was so long ago, so much in the past. Did it really matter anymore?

He would remember thinking it was odd there were still fires that needed to be extinguished, even weeks after the collapse—but then there was enough combustible material for the towers to burn on infinitely. In the next couple of weeks, he would find dozens and dozens of body parts. It was unbelievable how many limbs and heads he uncovered. Body parts after body parts.

John Webster had no right to be condescending; he wasn't the only witness of terrorist acts, Wiltore thought. He then wondered what Webster had been doing at Michelle Lake's house. What had he given her? He imagined John Webster charged, not just with contempt of court, but with trafficking. He wanted to see the look on Webster's face then.

On the television, the image had changed from the curvy, luscious blonde to a man in a lab coat selling pills of some kind. The deep, confident voice of the doctor snapped Wiltore back to the present. He thought about the break in his case. He thought about calling Ervin up and telling him the good news, but decided against it. It was late, and he would know soon enough.

Wiltore reviewed some of the evening's events in his mind. Lewis had wanted to get a judge to sign a search warrant for the warehouse, but Wiltore convinced her they shouldn't tip their hand yet.

Lewis bit her bottom lip, pouting a bit. "So what? We just wait while they deal drugs or—worse—weapons on the street?"

Wiltore shrugged. "I know it's not ideal, but we don't really have any other choice."

"But we do. We get the search warrant, find out what they're trafficking, and arrest them."

"Perhaps, but then what about Carl Dewitt? Or whoever killed Dzyinski and Gibson?" Wiltore asked.

"We all know the chances of actually solving either case is very small," Lewis said.

Wiltore turned to Lewis beside him. He wondered how she could possibly be giving up—especially now that they had leverage. "We leverage the small fishes against the big ones."

"You're always so patronizing—I wish you'd stop it."

Wiltore closed his eyes and took a deep breath before opening them again. "We were put together so you could learn."

Lewis was angry. Even in the dark, Wiltore could tell her face was a deep red. "Yeah?" she shot back. "What exactly have you taught me? We lucked out tonight."

There was a long period of silence in the car, worsened by the silence from the night outside. Wiltore was too mad to say anything and was afraid he would regret it if he spoke. After a while Lewis, perhaps realizing she had gone too far, said, "Look, we could cut our losses now and get those weapons off the street, or we could wait and probably not get any further."

"Lewis, we need to keep focused—get what we came for. We might be able to bust Michelle Lake and Keith Dowell and maybe they get five or six years behind bars, but Carl Dewitt will find another channel to distribute his stock."

"Cut them a deal. If Dowell doesn't break, perhaps Lake will."

Lewis leaned forward to the two officers in front, who had remained silent throughout the argument. "You guys don't have any take on this?" she asked.

Cook and Blake looked at each other. Blake finally spoke. "Wiltore is right. We need to be patient. If we don't progress, then we can always fall back on them."

That seemed to settle the matter as they drove back to the police station. They did their paperwork, and then everybody went home. They would all have to get up early—another big day ahead of them.

And now Wiltore was watching infomercials to try and calm himself down. He didn't know how long he sat there, but it felt good resting his eyes and resting his body in front of the television. After a while he crept upstairs to bed.

The Dinner Date

The bartender, a severe-looking man named Kirk, greeted John with a friendly, stiff handshake as John sat down in the corner of the Palace. It was dark and smelled musky. He surveyed the bar; it was surprisingly busy. He leaned his back against the wall, stretching his long legs out. He liked being against the wall so he could survey the entire dark, drunken canvas. He liked corners. He didn't know why, but perhaps it was because of all that time spent in Afghanistan and Iraq and all the other countries. He liked to have a sense of control, the ability to spot danger and escape out the back if the need arose.

But why in God's name hadn't he chosen somewhere classier than the Palace? When he had phoned Michelle, why had he just blurted out the first place that had come to mind? Why in front of all his colleagues? A stab of pain went through his stomach when he realized Liz might walk through the door at any time. He considered this for a moment, wondering if subconsciously that was what he wanted.

What if somebody recognized Michelle from Rocky Moon? Would they make the connection? Would they wonder what he was doing meeting a waitress who worked for Carl Dewitt? Would they think she was just a source, or would they think other things?

John ordered a whiskey. Kirk said something to John, but he only nodded his head in reply, unable to comprehend what he was saying. Kirk left, and John looked around nervously.

His phone rang. It would be Michelle telling him she couldn't make it. He knew it. But when he looked at the caller ID, he didn't recognize the number.

"Hello?" John said, answering his phone.

"Hey, it's Drake."

John looked around the bar instinctively, but nobody seemed to be paying him much attention. "Hey," he said, hoping he sounded casual enough. "What's up?"

"I have some information you might want. Something regarding our last conversation."

"Great; when can you meet?"

"How about now?"

"I'm sorry, I can't right now."

"You have something more important?" Drake sounded annoyed.

"I just can't—sorry. How about in two hours at Bloody Alley?"

"Okay; see you then." Drake hung up, and John put his phone on the table. He looked at the time. Michelle would be there any minute, that is, if she didn't stand him up. He ran his hands through his short hair. He was sweating, he realized. He couldn't remember the last time he had been so nervous about a date. He went to the bathroom and ran a paper towel across his face and neck. He looked at himself, criticizing the clothes he was wearing, his haircut, his unshaven face. He went and sat back down. He finished his whiskey and ordered another.

A blonde woman John recognized as an intern at the *Daily Globe* came over and introduced herself to him.

"Bryce Malcolm," she said, shaking his hand. She had a strong, professional grip. John looked up at her. She had a small round face, her hair tied back in a tight ponytail. She had on a striped sweater and a small golden necklace around her slender neck. She looked young, barely old enough to drink.

Bryce said, "You know you're sort of a legend in school. Your article about Fallujah is required reading at school."

John raised his eyebrows. "Really? I didn't know that."

Bryce sat down opposite John. She smiled at him, leaning her elbows on the table. "Has anyone ever asked you to speak to a class?"

John shrugged. "I think so—I'm not sure. I usually ignore those phone calls."

224 ◆   *Joel Mark Harris*

"Why? I think you'd be a great teacher."

John smiled graciously, glancing nervously at the door. If Michelle came in and found him talking to a pretty blonde, would she just walk out? He had blown one chance with her already. "I'm not so sure about that," John said. "I don't have much patience."

Bryce laughed as if it was a joke. "You were one of the reasons I decided to intern at the *Globe*."

John didn't quite know what to say to that. He wanted to tell Bryce to leave, but he didn't want to be rude and, also, he didn't want to annoy possibly his biggest fan. It wasn't often he was flattered. He looked at the clock on his cell phone. It was ten minutes past seven. He suddenly decided Michelle probably wasn't coming anyway. "Look," John said, "I should probably get going. But I'll see you around the office." John waved the bartender down and asked for the bill.

"I was wondering if you could help me out with my thesis," Bryce said.

John stared at her. "Wait ... you have to do a thesis?"

Bryce looked at him strangely. "Yeah, of course ... It's a master's program."

"A master's program? Why do you need a master's degree to write a newspaper article?"

Bryce laughed again as if John was being funny. "You didn't need to write a thesis, I take it?"

John shook his head. He was curious despite trying hard not to be. "What's it about?"

"It's titled 'Know Your Enemy.'"

John paid Kirk with his credit card. He wanted to leave, but he was too intrigued. "Strange title for a thesis, isn't it?"

Bryce smiled brightly, and John was acutely aware how beautiful she was when she smiled. "It's about how the western media report on Al Qaeda. How we add to the stereotypical image of an Al Qaeda terrorist. What we need is quality, in-depth reporting, something from somebody who understands the issues, something like Al Jazeera, but they can't get a broadcast licence in the west because they are perceived as Bin Laden sympathisers. It just adds to the us-versus-them mentality."

"Seems interesting," John said, just to be polite.

Bryce nodded enthusiastically. "My argument is you can't destroy Al Qaeda by military might—you can't destroy an ideology, just as we couldn't win in Vietnam. You can only conquer Al Qaeda by understanding them."

John smiled incredulously. "So you're saying instead of sending in the military, flood Afghanistan and Pakistan with an army of reporters?"

Bryce laughed, sitting back in her chair. "Yes, that's exactly what I'm saying."

John stood up. "I think it's a very interesting thesis statement, and I'll be glad to talk to you at another time, but I really have to go."

Bryce handed John her card. It was on thick paper and simply said in black type "Bryce Malcolm" and "Journalist." Underneath it gave her phone number and her website. John nodded, impressed, suddenly changing his mind about her. "You'll go far if you keep it up," he told her, and Bryce beamed as if she had just won the lottery.

"You think maybe I could persuade you to talk to my class—inspire the next generation of reporters and all that?"

John shrugged. "I don't know. Let me think about it, but to tell you the truth, I'm not sure I'd be the right person."

John left the Palace and crossed the street. From there he watched the entrance. He wondered if Michelle had already been and gone, and he had missed her again. Surely she wouldn't give him another chance—especially if she saw him with Bryce.

John paced the street nervously, keeping an eye out for Michelle. He hoped Bryce would leave and he could reenter, but she didn't seem to be done with her mingling. John looked at his phone: Michelle was thirty minutes late. He tried calling her, but there was no answer. He decided not to leave a voice message. She wasn't coming, he decided. But something—a small hope—made him wait a little longer. John stuffed his hands into his pockets, crossed the street, and almost bumped into Michelle as she came around the corner. She gave him a surprised look, and then relief crossed her face.

"I'm glad I'm not the only one late," she said, touching him on the elbow.

It took a moment for John to realize what she was saying. "Yeah …
yeah, I was catching up on some work. I tried calling you."

"My phone died, sorry. I just got off work."

She was wearing tight low-cut jeans that showed off her midriff, a
white shirt that flowed with her body, and brown Uggs, and she carried a
large leather bag.

They stared at each other awkwardly for a few seconds, unsure of what
to say, each measuring the other's reaction.

"Let's forget the Palace," John said, ripping his eyes away from Michelle.
"It's kind of a dive anyways—a place where broke journalists hang out."

"I don't mind," Michelle said, smiling faintly. "I'm sure I've seen
worse.

"No, at least let me try and impress you."

Michelle smiled, wider this time. "I'm not the type of girl you try and
impress."

"I'm sure somebody somewhere has tried to impress you."

Michelle shook her head resolutely, trying to stifle a laugh. "Nope, not
ever. You know nobody has ever even gotten me flowers?"

John looked at Michelle—her modelesque body. "I don't believe you."

Michelle laughed. John liked the sound of it. "No, it's the truth,"
Michelle said.

"So where do you want to go?"

Michelle shrugged. "I don't know—you wanted to go someplace
else."

John nodded. "Yes … that's right." He looked down the street in panic,
hoping something would present itself. He had no backup plan. A homeless
man walked up to them and said he would do a magic trick for cash. John
wanted to say no, but he was afraid of what Michelle would think so he
let the homeless man do his trick. Michelle seemed unimpressed, so he
shoved five dollars into his scrawny hand. The homeless man thanked him
and walked away.

John turned to Michelle. She was looking away, disinterested. He was
losing her, and so John said, "You know, let's get out of this area. I'm sick
of it."

He grabbed her arm and took her across the street, leading her blindly, running through the ghostly lamplight, past the rustic brick buildings, past the parked cars, and past the pink signs and the windows with sliced meat hanging on hooks. They walked over to Main Street, where there was a bus just pulling up to the curb. John took Michelle aboard just as the doors opened. He dug into his pocket for the correct change and dropped it into the meter.

They went to sit at the very back. The bus was only half-full, with people who barely looked up at the newcomers.

"Where does this bus go?" Michelle asked John. "Where are you taking me?"

John shrugged. "Have no idea—we'll get off at the last stop. How's that?"

Michelle laughed. "You're crazy."

"Believe it or not, you're not the first person to call me that."

He thought he really was crazy—in fact, he felt he had never done anything so crazy in his life, so purposeless. He should have been anyplace but on a bus. He should be in an office making phone calls, working on his story. That was when he remembered he was supposed to meet Drake McMillan in an hour. He laughed. It sounded strange and foreign to him.

"What?" Michelle asked.

"Oh, nothing—I just remembered something."

They sat feeling the vibrations of the engine beneath their feet and looking out as the city rolled by like an old movie reel—the tall brick buildings melted away to wooden family ones. John felt a strange sense of relief, a release of responsibility. The bus would take them where they needed to be. He slipped his hand into Michelle's, and to his surprise, she didn't let go.

The last stop was Steveston's Wharf. The temperature had dropped, and the wind made it chilly as it blew across the water, creating small whitecaps that splashed and shattered on the pier. They walked along the waterfront until they came to a cozy-looking seafood restaurant with a blue awning.

"This place is much too fancy for me," Michelle said, halting at the entrance.

"Let's just try it. If you don't like it, we can go someplace else."

But still Michelle hesitated. "John, before we go in … there's something I have to tell you."

"Tell me inside; I'm cold," he said, opening the door, and they stepped inside.

John asked for a seat in the corner. The table was lit romantically with candlelight, which flickered and swayed with any sudden movement. The waiter, dressed in dress pants and a chequered cotton shirt, handed John and Michelle menus. John ordered a bottle of wine.

"Wine?" Michelle asked, a small smile on her face. "You don't drink wine."

John shrugged. "Special occasion."

"Yeah, what's that?"

John shrugged again. The waiter came back with the wine and poured two glasses. John excused himself to go to the washroom. It was a multistall room, and John made sure it was completely empty before he locked himself into one of the stalls and sat on one of the toilets. He dialled Drake McMillan. Drake answered and told John he would phone him right back. John waited several minutes, pacing back and forth. Michelle would be wondering where he was. A man came in, used the urinal, and gave John a strange look before leaving.

Finally Drake called back. "Where are you?" he asked.

"I'm out in Richmond."

"Richmond? What the fuck are you doing there?"

"I won't be able to make it until later," John said.

"I risk my neck for you, and you're saying you can't make it until later?" Drake said.

"I'm sorry, but something came up."

"It's not more important than what I have to tell you."

John rubbed his head, which was beginning to pound. "Why don't you just tell me now?"

"You sold out to the cops, didn't you?" Drake demanded. "You think you can trap me?"

"No, Drake—wait. I'll be there; give me two hours." John hung up and went back to the table.

Michelle put the menu on the tablecloth, looking at it disinterestedly. She looked up at John and said, "What took you so long?"

"Oh—nothing. Just had to make a phone call."

Michelle folded the white cloth napkin in her lap. "So, I don't understand. Why did you want to take me for dinner so badly?"

John pretended to survey the menu before coming up with an answer. "There was something about you when I first saw you at Dzyinski's funeral."

"But you don't even know me," Michelle protested.

John smiled. "I know a lot about you—you work at two jobs, you have one daughter named Ella, I know where you live."

"You haven't asked me *the* question yet."

John frowned. "What question is that?"

"Why I work at Rocky Moon."

John was genuinely surprised. "Why should I?"

Michelle shrugged. "Everybody does—my sister, my parents, my friends. Why I don't get a respectable job. I told my family only about a year ago ... They weren't very happy with me. My sister threatened to call child services—take Ella away from me."

John nodded. "Yeah, I know what that's like." He told her about how Hayden wanted to stop him from seeing Byron.

"I don't understand," Michelle said. "Because you were shot?"

John sighed. "She's afraid I'll put Byron in danger ... I *do* see her point, I suppose."

A flash of anger flickered in Michelle's eyes. "No, that's bullshit. Fight her to the fucking end."

John gave a dry laugh. "I'm too stubborn to let her win—you should know that by now."

Michelle nodded. "No, I guess I do." She seemed to consider something. "But you gave up in Afghanistan, didn't you?"

John was saved from coming up with an answer by the appearance of the waiter. They ordered. John had the smoked salmon and Michelle a salad. John looked at her questioningly.

"I'm a vegetarian," she said.

John put his hand up to his forehead. "Why didn't you say something?"

Michelle shrugged, looking around the restaurant. "I tried ... I don't really mind. This is fine."

"It's been a while since I've been on an actual date." John looked down at the table, crumpling a piece of the tablecloth into his fist. "Actually ... before I was married, really."

Michelle blinked, reached across the table, and cupped John's hand. "You don't have to tell me—it's fine."

John smiled. "Thanks—I don't mind."

"No, I mean about Afghanistan."

John ground his jaw thinking about it. He had hoped to avoid the subject, but he supposed that had been wishful thinking. "Why are you interested anyways?"

Michelle leaned an elbow on the table and placed her slender chin on her palm. She eyed John in half-amusement as he squirmed under her gaze. She said, "You don't think it's interesting?"

"No ... no, I suppose, you know—it's just complicated," John said, crumpling the cloth in his fist harder. "There were a lot of factors.... My marriage was falling apart. I hadn't spent much time with my newborn son ... But most of all, I was tired of not making a difference, feeling I was just making a living off other people's pain."

Michelle nodded. "And what difference were you trying to make?"

John didn't say anything for a long time. He watched a venerable-looking middle-aged couple get up from their table and put on their jackets. The hostess bid them good-bye as they walked out.

"I knew a colleague of mine—a reporter for the *Washington Post*—who was killed by the Taliban. They made him kneel in front of a camera, and then some guy in a mask took the reporter and sawed off his head." John paused to take a gulp of his wine. "It was something from a movie, only it was real. I only saw the tape once, but now you can find it on the Internet, I think. It was gut-wrenching."

Michelle put a hand to her mouth. "My god, that's awful."

John felt the wine sink into his stomach. The restaurant had suddenly become cold and clammy. "I'm sorry ... we're in a great restaurant."

Michelle reached across the table and took his hand. "No, I asked. I shouldn't have."

John tried to think of something else now, but his head was hurting too badly to think clearly. "I don't know … to be used as a propaganda tool, to be more famous for your death than for something you did in life … to become an Internet spectacle my son would see.… That's why I never went back."

Michelle smiled, but it was a weak, unconvincing smile. Her eyes widened in sympathy, and then she looked down at the table, as if she didn't quite know what to say. In that moment, John reflected on how strikingly beautiful she looked.

John excused himself to go to the bathroom for a second time. He stared at himself in the mirror, at the tired, stressed reflection. He dug in his pocket, took some of the painkillers the doctor had given him, and downed them with a gulp of water.

He returned to Michelle. Their food had arrived. Michelle was picking at it in disinterest. John looked down at his own dish, but he had also lost his appetite.

He looked up at Michelle, realizing he had ruined the evening. He asked, "You want to just get out of here?"

Michelle took a bit of her salad and nodded. John paid with his credit card. He took the half-drunken bottle of wine with him, but left the food.

They took a cab back into town. John looked at his watch. He was going to be late for Drake. He wondered if he would wait. He thought about calling, but he decided against it while he was with Michelle. They didn't say anything for most of the ride. Michelle pressed her cheek up against the window glass, staring out at the passing blue night. John leaned his head back. The painkillers had set in, and he was pleasantly numb of most feeling. He was still clutching the wine in his hand. The driver turned off his radio and put on a soft rock station, which played softly in the background.

"One day I'm going to get out of here," Michelle said after a while.

John rolled his head to look at her. She still wasn't looking at him, perhaps transfixed at the moving images outside.

John said, "And go where? The suburbs?"

Michelle turned. "No. I'm going to go to someplace far, far away. India. Disappear from everything."

"That's right—you told me," John said. "What do you want to disappear from?"

"I suppose the question is what don't I want to disappear from?"

They didn't say anything for a while. John stared at Michelle. She suddenly seemed small and vulnerable.

"Is it bad?" he asked finally.

Michelle looked at him with big, opaque eyes. She then turned away. She didn't have to say anything to tell him it was bad.

"You know, you can tell me … as a friend, not a reporter," John said. "You know, maybe I can help."

Michelle shook her head. She looked close to crying. "No … you'll always be John Webster the reporter. Whatever friendship we have will always be secondary."

John rubbed his eyes and considered this. He supposed she was right, in a way: what other definition of himself did he have? Certainly not John Webster the athlete, not John Webster the university graduate, not Webster the family man. He was a reporter—that was it, but he was good at it. That knowledge was what kept him going.

John looked away, into the darkness and the tawny city glow and beyond that the dotted lights from the naked white mountains. She had shaken him to the very core. He was the war correspondent. That was it. Maybe that was why he perpetually looked for danger. That was why he followed gang warfare.

John protested again. "Maybe I can help. That's what I do, after all."

Michelle snorted. "What sort of world do you live in? This cerebral world of words? These people come at you with machine guns and knives, and you have, what?"

John stared at her. "Don't underestimate the power of communication and media."

"Your media and communication can't help me with the place I'm in."

"And how do you know unless you let me try?"

Michelle didn't answer but resumed looking out the window. John didn't press the issue. They stopped at Michelle's house.

"Well …" John said, "I guess I'll see you around."

Michelle nodded, her hand going to the door handle. She half-opened the door, but then she seemed to change her mind, turned, leaned over, and kissed John, pressing her mouth against his. She pulled back and smiled. "Don't worry about me; I'll get by."

"You want money? I can get you a plane ticket."

Michelle put her hand on John's cheek. She was warm to the touch. "I might have misjudged you—you might have half a heart after all."

John laughed. "I'll take that as a compliment—I have a feeling that's as good as it gets."

John watched as Michelle walked up the front steps to her door. He then told the driver to take him downtown. He phoned Drake's cell, but got no answer.

Blood Alley

Blood Alley wasn't too far from John's apartment. In fact, it was just off Carroll Street, next to Gaolers Meow. It was a typical Gastown alleyway, with crimson-coloured buildings, a brick pathway, and rusty wrought-iron fire escapes. The entrance was clearly marked with signs and cluttered with ornate Whitechapel-like lamps. He walked through the alleyway looking for Drake but didn't see him. The alley was tiny and lead to a dead end.

John came out of the alley. A man with a dark pinstriped suit and shiny brown shoes walked past him, and John eyed him carefully. Across the road, a figure curled up in a sleeping bag was in the entrance of an abandoned building. A short, pock-faced Asian man was leaning up against a lamppost, looking alertly around. John wondered what he was doing. Was he a drug dealer? A hired man for Ernest Hunter? Was he packing a gun? John wondered if he was getting paranoid. He never felt paranoid in Afghanistan or Iraq. There he trusted himself more.

John decided he had to move. The blood seemed to have frozen in his limbs. He walked around the block, intending to circle back. He walked past a pawnshop, a porn ship, a grocery shop, and a Chinese medicine shop. Light from half-lit road lamps reflected off the green and blue awnings. Steam rose from the gutters in sputters. A rancid, acidic smell wafted through the air—a combination of trash, of rotten food, of other things John did not want to discover.

There was fresh fruit and there was dead fish stuffed in ice on display in the windows. Somebody shouted something that echoed off the narrow buildings, but apart from that, the city seemed empty and was silent, like a ghost town. And hanging on the rows of buildings in deflated glory were neon yellow signs unlit, dead, or dying.

John came to the entrance of Bloody Alley again. He watched the entrance. It was a tiny alley, insignificant and useless really as anything except a tourist trap. He waited for Drake in the darkness. The small Asian man was still there, looking around, his hands in his pockets. He seemed to have no purpose. John tried to back himself further into the shadows, wondering what he was doing in the middle of the night waiting for a drug dealer. Would he show up? Was he annoyed at being made to wait? *The information he had must be good,* John thought.

A man and a woman walked from around the corner. They were both handsome and well dressed in dark clothing. The man had on a tailored suit and the woman a knee-high dress. They seemed to have come from some sort of party or a Granville Street club. They were talking loudly, oblivious to their surroundings. The woman stumbled and leaned heavily on the man, who also looked like he was about to fall over. He put his hand out against a lamppost. They laughed together.

John was watching the couple when a man with shoulder-length grey hair approached him, seemingly out of nowhere. He had wrinkly, rubbery skin, and the veins in his forehead were visible. He wore an old brown coat and tattered jeans.

John tensed up and held his breath. Who was this guy? Was it a trap? John prepared to run for it.

But the homeless man smiled. Half of his teeth were missing. "You live in the Woodward's building?" he asked.

John frowned, confused. "Huh?"

"I asked if you lived in the Woodward's building."

John looked at the couple, but they had passed down the street, still laughing. He turned back to the homeless man. He stunk horribly, but seemed harmless enough. "No," John said, "why?"

The man shrugged. "Just wondering. Have you seen the view from the top? I would like to see it on a clear day. Pretty impressive, don't you think?"

John found the glowing *W* in between the buildings. It always seemed visible. "I suppose so," he said.

"I've never been up to the top," the homeless man said. He paused ruminatively and then continued, "Don't suppose I ever will be. They've got security there. Stop people like me from seeing that view of our wonderful city."

John looked around for Drake, but he still couldn't see him. He wondered how a homeless man could think Vancouver wonderful; he didn't understand—it was cold and dark most of the time—but John didn't say anything.

The homeless man continued, "I used to live there ... of course, that was when it was a gutted building and we were squatting at the time, but you can't have everything, am I right?" The man gave a hollow laugh, his eyes wide with amusement. He seemed to be waiting for John to say something, but John just sighed, wishing he was at home in bed.

"I'm very sorry," he said. "But I'm waiting for somebody, so if you don't mind ..."

The homeless man frowned. "You don't want to hear about the Woodward's building? My parents used to shop there, you know. It's a fucking Vancouver landmark. I cried when Woodward's was shut down." The man paused. "You don't care?"

"No—it's not that. I just got out of the hospital, and I'm waiting for a friend to come any minute."

The man stared at John's arm as if he had only just noticed the sling. "What happened, man?"

"A car accident."

The man cocked his head. "Your name ... is it John Webster?"

John began to panic. He looked for the trap from the quiet nooks of the street and buildings. He expected a couple of big black SUVs to rumble around the corner and men with large machine guns to get out. John stuck his good hand in his pocket and started to walk away. Drake wasn't coming. The homeless man, however, followed him, seemingly unaware of his agitation, continuing to talk.

"The first time I was arrested, it was for shoplifting at Woodward's. I have fond memories, yes, sir. Then they built condos that nobody can afford. Something shuts down in this city—what do they do? Build condos. That's the city's answer to fucking everything."

John turned. "Please, just go away." John took out his wallet and gave the man what change he had left. "That's all the money I have. I'm sorry."

The old man took the change and put it in his pocket. "Relax, man. You're jumpy, aren't you? I just want to deliver a message."

John frowned. "What? What message?"

"Your friend says to meet him at Gassy Jack."

The man gave a large toothy smile as if he had been conning John all along; he then turned and walked away. John paused to take a deep breath. He looked around. The Asian man with pockmarks had disappeared. John was alone in the street.

John walked through the streets toward the statue of Gassy Jack. He desperately wanted a drink, anything to calm his nerves, but he forced his legs to keep moving. John arrived at the statue and looked around. A group of people were piling out of the bar, desperately trying to catch a taxi. John felt a little more comfortable. Drake or anybody else was unlikely to try anything with so many witnesses—drunk as they were.

Suddenly a man in a grey hoodie approached John. It was Drake McMillan.

John said, "You taking extra precautions?"

"You should too from what I hear," Drake said.

"Your messenger scared me half to death."

"Sorry—a client of mine."

Drake looked around nervously, and John thought, *apparently I'm not the only worried one.*

"Can you call the dogs off?" John asked.

"Kind of hard when you keep stepping in dog shit."

"Tell Hunter we can come to terms."

Drake shook his head. "You're asking the wrong person. I have no sway with him."

"You're the only one I trust."

McMillan peeled back his lips, making him look like a bulldog. "That's sweet, but Ernie is already suspicious of me." Drake paused, glancing over at the partiers, as if he was going to be overheard. "He didn't order the hit on you."

"What?"

"You heard me. It wasn't him."

"If not him, then who? Carl Dewitt?"

Drake shook his head. "No, he's only the arms dealer, the middleman. He's not a hit man."

"What about the police?"

"Man, if Ernie has police on his payroll, he's keeping it close. I don't understand … why even think that?"

"It's a hunch I have—I don't know."

"Somebody must have said something. It's a big thing. It's not something you decide one day."

"You wanted to meet just so you could tell me that?"

Drake took out a cigarette and a Zippo from his pocket. He slowly put the cigarette between his lips and lit it. "Somebody has put a price on your head."

"What?" John thought he had misheard him.

Drake looked at John with something that could almost be described as pity. "Ten thousand dollars for your death."

John forced a smile, although his stomach was in knots. "Ten thousand dollars? That's all a journalist is worth these days?" His attempt at a joke fell flat, and after that he didn't know what to say.

Drake took a drag from his cigarette. Ash fell to the feet of the bronze Gassy Jack. Drake said, "Ernie was furious—that's how I know it wasn't him. Said something about it was only bringing heat."

John stared at Drake carefully. He tried to read the drug dealer, but his face was hard and showed nothing. John said, "And no idea who put the word out?"

"No idea. Ernie doesn't know either. He seems to like you for some reason."

John sighed, crossing his arms tightly across his chest. He suddenly felt cold and empty, as if he was just skin, a shell, and everything inside him had disappeared. It was a funny thing—to have a numeric value assigned to him. Ten thousand was all. Ten thousand was how much his death was worth. Of course, in the Middle East, he had received numerous death threats, yet none seemed so ominous or so real as the one Drake had just delivered. Those things were expected in Iraq and Afghanistan; supported by the American military machine, they seemed like minor events. But here in his home city—the place where he had grown up—he had no place to turn.

"I suppose somebody is afraid I'll find something out." John racked his brain. It had to be Carl Dewitt—there was no one else.

Drake shook his head in disbelief. "All over a few newspaper articles. Doesn't make much sense to me."

"Okay," John finally said. "If you hear anything else, you'll phone me?"

John expected Drake to say something, but instead he ruminatively finished his cigarette in silence. John felt no need to move. No need to go home. He just felt tired now and craving that drink more than ever.

John looked around. Most of the bars had dumped their partiers onto the street, and the streets were now mostly empty except for the odd taxi that still trolled for passengers.

Drake flicked the butt into the drain. "What are you going to do?" he said.

John shrugged, staring at the fizzling cigarette, then up at Drake, who suddenly seemed more than just a source ... and more like a friend. He knew that was dangerous thinking and tried to push the thought from his mind, but it wouldn't go easily.

"Probably nothing—I don't know. The whole thing hasn't really processed."

"Maybe you should go away—lay low for a while."

John actually seriously considered it for a moment. Go to Mexico? Bermuda? He imagined Liz taking over the story with relish. "That's what everybody tells me ... But you know what? I just can't do it. It'd be too much like giving up."

"It wouldn't be giving up, just putting it on hold. These gangsters aren't going anywhere."

"Sure, I suppose. Let me think about it," he said, although his mind was already made up.

Webster went home. He tried to read a magazine, his legs kicked up on the couch, but his thoughts kept going back to Michelle. He replayed every movement she had made—flick of her hair, shuffling of feet, every piece of conversation she had said.

He eventually fell asleep. Again he was transported to another place and another time. It was hot and sticky out. The orange sun was large and wavering in the sky like a mirage, like it would suddenly blink out and swamp everything into a thick darkness. *If only*, Webster often thought.

He was walking around, laughing with William Russell. They bought apples from a vendor, a boy really. The boy smiled kindly at the two journalists—not the usual greedy, hopeful smile Webster and Russell were used to getting in Iraq, but a genuine, happy smile. The boy was handsome, with thick black hair, large eyes, dark eyebrows, and a small jaw. He was dressed in a white robe and seemed particularly interested in his two light-skinned customers.

"You American?" he asked, his English heavily accented.

"No, Canadian."

The boy looked at the journalists sceptically. "Never heard of it."

"It's the second biggest country in the world," Russell said. "We can fit ten Iraqs into Canada."

The boy laughed in disbelief. "Come on. You pull my leg."

"It's the truth," Webster said, smiling. He liked this boy. In Webster's experience, it was the boys and girls of this torn country who somehow, against all odds, managed to keep their juvenile optimism about the future. He wondered how they did it.

"If so big, why haven't I ever heard of it?" the boy asked.

"We have a small population—about the same as Iraq."

Webster could see the boy wasn't buying any of it. "It's okay to be American. We like America here," the boy said, spreading his arms wide, encompassing the entire market. "No need to make up countries."

Webster paid for the apples, and he and Russell walked a little ways through the bazaar, looking at the things for sale, at the colourful signs. Webster had just taken the first bite of the apple when the world around him suddenly erupted into a world of fire and fragments. He was thrown several yards, landing in a dried-up, empty ditch. He opened his eyes, spitting out the sand from his mouth. What had happened? He struggled to get to his knees. He looked around for Russell but couldn't see him. Everything was spinning around him. He heard shouts and screams—but they seemed dulled, distorted, as if somebody had put everything on low volume.

Webster looked around, slowly gathering his bearings. Miraculously, except for a few scrapes and cuts, he was uninjured. But his shirt and pants had been torn to shreds. The market had been totally flattened. Nothing was left but rubble and ash. He tried to run, but his legs were stiff and unyielding. He dropped to his knees, got up again, and then fell again. He looked up to see bodies scattered everywhere, some torn in half, some missing limbs, some with their heads ripped off. Blood was everywhere, running through the sand, drying under the Baghdad sun, making a reddish paste.

"Will?" Webster yelled, but he couldn't hear himself. "William? Where are you?" He looked through the scattered bodies. Was he dead? He started to search through the bits and pieces left. He almost tripped over a blackish mass, and when he heard a dull, painful moan, he looked down and saw, to his horror, it was a person. His skin had been completely burned away. Webster dropped to his knees, unsure what he could do. The mess of blood and muscle opened his eyes and stared at Webster with a kind of familiarity. Instantly Webster recognized who this mess had once been: It had been the boy who had sold them apples.

Webster stared at him. What could he do? He had no medical supplies, not even any water. Webster wanted to hold him, but he was afraid of touching him, of causing the boy more pain. The boy tried to say something, but only a small gust of air came out of his mouth.

"I'm sorry," Webster said. It was the only thing he could think of saying. "I'm sorry … I'm so sorry." And Webster started to cry uncontrollably.

The boy's eyes seemed to glow a little brighter (or was it Webster's imagination?), the same brightness that had attracted Webster in the first place, and then he closed them and his body went limp.

Webster woke up with a start. He was back in his cold, colourless apartment. It was early. Webster could tell by the tint of deep blue seeping into his apartment. He looked at the clock: five o'clock. He got up and had a warm shower, trying to forget his dream.

The Police

"Let me ask you a simple question: who polices the police?"

John frowned, unsure of how to answer. "I don't know ... I guess—the police, I suppose."

Cameron McCord put a single finger up in the air. "You would think so, but no. The answer is we do. The public. A police officer shot an unarmed man in Vancouver. You think the police officer was charged with murder?" He spoke to John like he was lecturing a bunch of journalism students—which he was sometimes invited to do. But John shifted in his seat warily. Cameron McCord, a media darling, was fond of lecturing. Normally John wouldn't mind a little posturing to get to the issue; however, the night before, he had slept even worse than usual—imagining all types of gunmen climbing up his building to kill him—and the last thing he needed was a lecture.

Cameron McCord was a fearless, cavalier lawyer for the Live Legal Society, a group of lawyers dedicated to social justice and doing pro-bono work for those who couldn't afford lawyers.

The Live Legal Society frequently took the Vancouver Police to the Human Rights' Tribunal or sued them in civil court over issues like police brutality, police shootings, and false arrests.

"I think what you're doing is admirable," Cameron continued. "Standing up for free press."

"I'm going to court later this afternoon," John said. "I still don't know what I'm going to say to the judge."

"I can help you out, if you want. I have a meeting—but I can reschedule if you need me."

John tried to smile. He imagined what his colleagues would say if Cameron McCord showed up by his side. One thing was sure: they would never let him forget it. "Thanks—but I already have a lawyer."

Cameron shook his head slowly, as if he was greatly disappointed. He was a hefty man with receding grey hair, small square shoulders, and thick grey eyebrows. He wore an oxford shirt without a tie. "Well, if you need me …"

"You think it's possible? Gangsters paying off police officers?"

Cameron appeared not to hear the question. "They had five witnesses saying the police officer was unprovoked. Of course, if it had been a civilian instead of a police officer, he would have been arrested in a New York minute and the book would have been thrown at him. Instead, reports were filed … the witnesses requestioned …"

John gave a long sigh. He wondered why he was even bothering. Was it simply to confirm to himself he wasn't following the crazy words of a paranoid businessman? Whatever it was, he was regretting the decision. John asked, "What are you saying? You think it's one big conspiracy?"

Cameron held up his finger again—a caution, John supposed. "No, not at all. I only mean to say it's possible. And I wouldn't be surprised if the police know about it already."

John looked at Cameron incredulous. "You're saying somebody in the police is keeping quiet about this?"

Cameron nodded. "Have you tried a Freedom of Information request yet?"

John shook his head. It would take too long, years probably before anything came to light. Hunter—or whoever was after him—would have killed him by then. John asked, "If the police knew about the allegations and were investigating them, who would know about it?"

Cameron thought for a while. "You could try Frank Mould."

"Who's that?"

"Deputy of the B. C. Police Complaints Commission," Cameron said, leaning back in his chair. "He's a good man, tries to do the right thing most of the time, you know? He's not an uptight bureaucrat like the rest of them."

"You think he would help me?" John asked.

Cameron shrugged. "He's your best bet, that's for sure." He looked up Mould's office number and cell phone and gave them to John. John thanked him for his time and stood up to leave.

"Sure thing," Cameron said. "Let me know if I can be of any help this afternoon."

John smiled. "I don't want to think about it—but yeah, thanks."

John left Cameron's office. He first dialled Mould's office number. He talked to a secretary, who put him through to Mould's voice mail. He then dialled Mould's cell phone. This time he got an answer, so he said, "Hi, this is John Webster from the *Daily Globe*."

There was a long pause, and John thought Mould had hung up on him. "Hello?"

"Yeah … I'm here. What can I do for you, Mr. Webster?"

"I was wondering if I could talk to you a moment about a complaint."

"Mr. Webster, now is not a good time—I'm sorry."

"When would be a good time?"

"I don't know … I'll phone you back," Mould said and then hung up.

John phoned him right back, but this time the phone went to voice mail. He cursed. He still stood in the doorway of Cameron McCord's office. He was in walking distance of the *Globe* office, and he considered going in to talk to Chuck about what he should do next.

He started to walk quickly, but at the traffic light he stopped. The Complaints Commission was in Victoria, on Vancouver Island. If he took the bus and then the ferry, he could be over there by the afternoon. In person, he might be able to convince Mould to talk to him. However, he wouldn't be back in time for his court appearance.

The traffic light turned green and the fellow pedestrians around him started walking, but John didn't move, staying poised on the edge of the sidewalk. Everybody streamed around him, and he felt slightly claustrophobic surrounded by these masses passing him by. He felt he was at a turning point in his life, that this crazy idea would alter everything from now on and the consequences were far-reaching and nebulous in quality.

If he took a seaplane, it would only take half the time. He might be able to make it back in time for the court. *Might.*

He hailed a taxi before he could think anymore and told the driver to take him to the harbour. John's heart was racing. He felt he was on to some exciting lead, a break, but he also knew he was only fooling his body. He was following the scantest of hunches—not even a hunch really. And for the first time, John wondered if this was just an excuse to get out of appearing before the judge.

He bought his ticket, and then he had to wait forty minutes before the next flight. He calculated it in his head. He would arrive in Victoria just after noon. That would give him just over two hours to track down Frank Mould and get back for the two o'clock flight so he could be in Vancouver by two thirty and make it to the court by three. It was doable, John decided. Just barely.

The flight from the city was spectacular. The day was clear. John wasn't bothered at all by the rattling and humming of the engine. He looked out the back of the plane and saw Harbour Center, the Woodward's building, the seven white sails like mountain peaks. This was the postcard version, the common reality of the city most people saw and most people thought about. John was content to watch and revel in the bliss of the buildings for a moment, admiring the sheen of the glass as it sparkled in the rising yellow sun. John looked at the water—a green-olive colour—and then back at the city, and he felt comfort in seeing the city dissipate further and further into nothingness behind him.

John landed and decided to walk to Fort Street, which was only several kilometres from the harbour. John passed the parliament building, with its green copper roof and bone-grey brick siding, reminding John of the Globe building.

John found the address he was looking for. It was an old concrete building, clearly marked. John took the elevator up to the third floor. The doors opened to a beautifully furnished room, with metallic lamps and polished hardwood floors. The secretary greeted John with a fake smile. She had big teeth and long blonde hair, tied up into a bun.

"You have an appointment?" she asked, scanning her computer.

John thought about lying, but figured it wouldn't get him very far anyways. "Well, no, but I need to see Mr. Mould urgently."

The secretary looked up from her computer. "He's very busy at the moment. You can make an appointment with him if you like."

"It really can't wait. I have a deadline to meet."

The secretary nodded again, smiling again. "Let me see what I can do," she said. She got up and walked down a hall. John watched her go until she disappeared around the corner. He looked at the time on his cell phone. It was already one o'clock.

He decided to call Chuck.

"Where are you?" Chuck asked.

"I'm in Victoria."

"In Victoria? What the devil are you doing there?"

"I'm following a lead." John explained how he was at the Complaints Commission.

"John, you need to get back on that plane."

"Chuck ... stall them, please. Get Mack to make a speech or something—I don't know. There must be—"

Chuck interjected, "You cannot be late for court today. They will issue an arrest warrant for you if you fail to show up."

"Just buy me some time, please. Half an hour."

Chuck grunted unsatisfied. "I don't know if they'll wait that long. You're playing right into their hands."

"They're going to stick me in jail anyways." John looked up. The secretary had returned.

On the phone, Chuck said, "You don't know that—the judge will probably be lenient. But you need to show up."

"Look, Chuck, I got to go. I'll phone you when I'm finished."

"If you're not back in the office in an hour, I'm giving the story to Cochrane."

"Okay, okay. I'm coming back."

"Right now?"

John looked up at the secretary, who was hovering over him expectantly. "Right now, I promise." John hung up.

The secretary said, "He's just on the phone right now, but he'll see you when he's finished."

John nodded and thanked the secretary. He hated lying to his boss, but he wasn't going back to Vancouver without speaking to Mould and he figured he could talk to him quickly and still be back in the office in an hour.

But after a while, Mould still hadn't come out of his office.

John asked the secretary, "Is he still on the phone?"

The secretary looked at John. Her smile had gone. "I'm sure he will come out of his office when he's done, sir."

John looked up at the clock over the secretary's desk. The time seemed to be slipping by him quickly now. He tried to concentrate on anything other than the clock. He looked out the window, which didn't have much of a view—just an office building across the road. He checked his e-mail on his phone. He had about two dozen or so messages. Most of them were from PR hacks, pitching him stories, but in the midst of scrolling through them, there was a subject heading that made his stomach knot: "I will kill you for what you did."

John stared at his phone for a second before opening the e-mail. It was from an obviously false account, but possibly traceable. He read the e-mail. It was more of the same drivel about he was going to kill John for what he wrote in the newspaper.

John put his phone into his pocket and picked up a magazine from the coffee table, but he couldn't concentrate. He looked at the pictures, but he recognized no shapes or figures; they were just blotches of colour.

His phone started to ring, and he wheeled back in his seat. He looked at the caller ID and was relieved to find it was only Chuck calling. He was about to answer it, but then thought better of it and turned off the ringer.

He asked the secretary if she would be so kind as to check on Mould and see if he was off his phone. She begrudgingly did so. She seemed to take forever, but when she came back she said Mould would only be a couple more minutes. A couple of more minutes rolled around, and still Mould didn't appear from his office.

John asked, "Is there a washroom around?"

The secretary directed him around the corner. John thanked her, but instead of heading to the washroom, he scoured the names on the door until he found Frank Mould's. He quietly opened the door and stepped in.

It was a small, cramped office with a tiny window at the end. Frank Mould was a large man with an oval head, a bushy moustache, and white spots on his pale skin. He looked up in surprise at John's stealthy entry.

"I'm sorry, Mr. Mould, but I really don't have much time," John said, raising his palms, trying to appear as unthreatening as possible. He sat demurely in the chair adjacent to Mould's desk.

Mould mumbled an apology on the phone and said he would phone right back. He put the phone back on the dock, a look of shock still on his face. "You must be John Webster," he said.

John nodded.

Mould said, "I thought you were in Vancouver."

"I was, but I flew over to see you. I thought face-to-face would be better."

Mould glanced at the door, as if was contemplating making a run for it. "I don't know if I can be much help, Mr. Webster."

"One of my sources says Ernest Hunter has a man on the police force. A man who is feeding him information." John didn't say anything more but let the accusation hang in the air. Mould didn't say anything for a while, and John couldn't tell if he was too stunned or just unsure of what to say.

"I seriously doubt that, Mr. Webster," he said after a while, shifting in his seat. "And I would be careful before you make accusations like that."

John nodded reluctantly in agreement. He wished he had a good reason to be making accusations, but even for him, an offhand comment by Alex Gibson wasn't much to go on. He said, "My source might be just trying to throw me off the scent; but nevertheless, I want to explore all possibilities."

"Who is your source?"

"You should know I keep all sources confidential. We can speak off the record if you want."

"I presume your source is a criminal himself?" Mould asked.

John ignored the question. "Your name was given to me by Cameron McCord."

Mould laughed lightly. "You must be scraping the bottom of the barrel if you're talking to Cameron McCord."

John frowned, rubbing his palm over his hair. Mould was probably right: he was desperate and not thinking clearly. Obviously Chuck would agree. "Regardless, he told me to come to you. There must be a reason."

Suddenly there was a knock on the door. It was the secretary, slightly red-faced. "I'm so sorry, sir. He told me he was going to the washroom," the secretary said, frowning at John. John held her gaze, trying not to look sheepish.

"It's all right, Courtney," Mould said kindly.

She stuck out a lip, almost like she was going to cry. "When he didn't return, I came looking … I can call security …"

"No, that won't be necessary, Courtney, but thank you. We were just finishing up."

Courtney closed the door quietly. They listened as her footsteps dissipated down the hallway. Mould leaned forward on his desk and rubbed the corners of his eyes, looking very tired. "I think you misunderstand my job here, Mr. Webster. We investigate complaints from the public— allegations of unlawful arrest, excessive force, that sort of thing. Our mandate does not involve investigations into police corruption or anything like that."

"Who does? The RCMP?"

Mould shrugged. "It depends. The police commissioner would probably have to request an outside investigation. The RCMP does have an anticorruption unit, which does the occasional investigation into police conduct, but we don't have an internal affairs department as such."

John sat back in his chair in disbelief. "So there could be rampant police corruption and nobody would know?"

Mould frowned, his cheeks sagging on his face. "Now let's not get ahead of ourselves, Mr. Webster. As I said before, the police aren't a bunch of thugs—you know as well as I do the vigorous training process they go through."

But John was not to be deterred. "What if I wanted to make a complaint?"

Mould frowned and shifted agitatedly, again glancing at the door. "You would have to have a specific incident."

"Would it be public record?"

"What are you getting at?"

John shrugged. "It's just a question."

"No, but the findings would be made public and are posted on our website—but I don't understand. I already told you we don't deal with that sort of complaint. Now, if you don't mind, I have some work I need to do."

John nodded and stood up, turning his cell phone back on. He was running out of time to get back to Vancouver, but he didn't want to leave without some answers. He would have to switch tactics. "I apologize for using up so much of your time, Mr. Mould, but this is important. You are familiar with the term 'fourth estate'?"

Mould shifted in his seat. "What's your point, Mr. Webster?"

"My point is that the fourth estate is a reorganization of the power and the responsibility the media have to the public—the same power and responsibility you have, Mr. Mould. People take us for granted, of course, not realizing how we affect their lives. But where would the public be without us?"

John could see Mould was unmoved. "Is that all, Mr. Webster?"

John nodded, feeling dejected. "Thanks for your time, Mr. Mould. You have been very helpful."

John took the elevator back down to street level. He was panicking now. He had nothing, and he was late for his court appointment. He looked around for a taxi, but when he didn't see one, he ran across the street to the next street over. Still no taxi. He cut into an alley. He was running out of breath. He saw a couple flag a cabbie down. He stepped in front of them and climbed in, ignoring the angry shouts behind him.

Court Appearance

There was no answer. Again. Charles sighed, put away his phone, and turned to Mack Carrington, who was looking all around, his hands stuffed deeply into his pants pockets. Robert Smyllie was looking equally dour next to Mack. They were on Howe Street, just outside the courthouse. Their hearing was in seven minutes and still no word from Webster.

"What do we do?" Charles asked Mack and Smyllie.

Mack looked at Smyllie and shrugged his bulldog shoulders. "We stall 'em," Mack said, turning and slowly walking back inside. Charles watched him go and then turned to look up and down the street, expecting Webster to sprint through the crowd of people any moment. Webster had never let him down before.

"Rob?" Charles rarely used Smyllie's first name, and it sounded foreign and uncomfortable on his tongue.

Smyllie turned. "Yes, boss?"

"We're going to stand together on this?"

"You know, boss, as well as I do," he said in his thick Glasgowian accent, "our legacies, and the reputation of our paper, will be defined by what we say in there."

Charles nodded pensively. "Okay, I'll meet you inside."

"Okay, boss." Smyllie turned and walked inside, leaving Charles alone.

Charles looked across the street toward the lawyers' local watering hole, the Hanging Judge. He so badly wanted to go in there and order himself just one drink, just one. He watched the lawyers through the large windows, drinking and planning their next move in whatever cases they were working on. He felt the invisible lasso tugging at him. Just one drink … He just needed to cross the street, push open the doors …

Instead, he took one more despondent glance up and down the street before going back inside the court. He took the stairs up to the second floor. His phone rang and for half a moment he thought it was Webster phoning, but he looked at the caller ID and groaned. It was Calvin Pommeroy the third, the director of the board and the largest stockholder. Charles was not going to answer. After all, what empty reassurances could he give? But then he thought better of it.

"Mr. Pommeroy, how are you?"

"What's going to happen, Charles?" Pommeroy asked.

Charles stopped at the top of the steps. "They'll give us a wrist slap, that's it." Charles saw no point in alarming Pommeroy now.

"This reporter … what's his name?"

"John Webster."

"Yes … He worth the trouble?"

Charles felt his hands go cold. He couldn't believe what he was hearing. "What are you asking, Calvin?" Charles dropped the formality, but Pommeroy didn't seem to notice.

"The board is nervous. Our stocks are down. We cannot afford a lengthy legal battle."

Charles didn't get angry, but instead spoke in an even-toned voice. He was used to such talk, and his answer came easily. "Sales have jumped 10 percent since his article about the shooting. It's almost guaranteed to win awards. Does that answer your question?"

"I'm afraid advertisers will be scared away from the controversy."

Charles rubbed his eyelids. Why couldn't he deal with Pommeroy later? "Advertisers love sales. And controversy generates sales," he said.

"I'm sorry, Charles, I don't know what to tell you. But the board will have to make some decisions."

Charles frowned. What sort of decisions was he talking about? "Calvin, I'll phone you later. Right now I need to concentrate."

"Of course, Charles. Phone me when the judge comes back with a verdict."

Mack and Smyllie were standing together in the hallway looking out the window panels, as if they too were just waiting for Webster to appear before them.

Mack and Smyllie turned when Charles reached them. Mack managed half a smile—no doubt trying to look hopeful, but he only succeeded in looking quizzical—and said, "It's time."

They went inside the courtroom together. There were a few reporters there—*Vancouver Times*, CBC, *New York Times* even—sitting unorthodoxically quiet in the back, like high school punks. Charles knew them all but gave no indication. They were professionals now, not colleagues.

Mack and Charles sat in the first row. Across from them was the government lawyer, a young-gun type, lean and sharp-chinned. Beside him sat Detective Wiltore and Detective Lewis. They didn't look in his direction, but stared straight ahead.

The sheriff came in and brought the session to order. The judge entered from the left. She was a small skeletonish woman with large bangs across her wrinkled forehead.

Everybody sat down, and the sheriff read the subpoena into the record.

The judge looked around the room with large cold eyes and asked, "Is Mr. John Webster present?"

Mack stood up. "Your honour, Mr. Webster has presently been delayed in Victoria, but he is on his way back to Vancouver as we speak."

The judge frowned. "Does Mr. Webster know the consequence of failing to appear today?"

Mack nodded. "He does, your honour."

The judge stared at Mack for what seemed like a long moment and then nodded. "Okay, let's proceed. Hopefully Mr. John Webster will be here in time to testify." The judge looked slowly around the courtroom. "I trust Mr. Charles Dana is here today?"

Charles stepped forward to the witness box. He tried to remain calm but was wishing now more than ever that he had gone for that drink. *Ten years of sobriety down the drain,* he thought. After he was sworn in, Charles sat down and crossed his legs. He tried to look collected and at ease, but the seat was hard and he felt cramped in the box.

The government lawyer approached. He said a few words and then asked, "Your reporter John Webster wrote an article titled 'Massacre in Langley Barn' on August 10, did he not?"

Charles nodded. "Yes, he did."

"In the article he uses one or more unnamed sources. You have been subpoenaed here today to reveal the name of the source or sources."

Charles leaned forward into the microphone. "I do not know the name of Mr. Webster's source or sources."

The lawyer stiffened his spine, his eyebrows raised in surprise. Apparently he had not anticipated this response from Charles. The lawyer glanced briefly toward the judge, as if for some sort of help, before regaining his composure. "Are you telling me, Mr. Dana, that you ran a story in your newspaper without verifying all the sources first?" he asked incredulously.

Charles took a moment to answer. The room was silent. "I have known John Webster personally for over fifteen years—we both worked at Reuters together. I personally recruited him to work for the *Daily Globe*. He is one of the most respected journalists in this country—among his peers and among the public. I trust him more than I trust my own wife."

There was a snicker from the reporters in the back. Wiltore turned to glare at them.

The lawyer would not be derailed so easily, however. "I am compelled to remind you, Mr. Dana, that you are under oath today. If I find out you have perjured yourself here today, I will make sure you are prosecuted."

Mack stood up and made an objection. "Asked and answered, your honour." But Charles waved dismissingly at Mack. Charles tried to ignore the crank that seemed to slowly tighten on his stomach. "It's okay. I am telling the truth. I am managing editor of one of the largest papers in the country. I cannot know every single source in the paper. We must have a level of professional trust with our journalists," he said.

There was another long period of silence in the room. The government lawyer seemed stumped. He finally slumped down in his seat, and Charles was dismissed. Charles was led out into the hallway, and there he was made to wait as Smyllie testified. The minutes he waited on the bench were probably some of the most excruciating of his life. He was not a fidgety person, but he found himself tapping his foot *rat-a-tat* on the carpeted floor. He heard the air vent turn on and off somewhere in the distance.

He wished he could peek in or put his ear up against the door and hear what Smyllie was saying to the court.

For some reason—perhaps it was the stress—his mind went back to when he was working at the *Wall Street Journal*. He remembered that after September 11 he would go to work every day and look down at Ground Zero, at the excavators clearing away the rubble, painfully slowly. He had been looking down at the same scene for a couple of months.

One exceptionally gloomy, oppressive Sunday morning, grey clouds hung over the skyscrapers of New York. Charles was the editor for the international bureau at the time. It was a slow news day, and he had been deciding what to put in the Monday edition. He found himself staring down at Ground Zero more than usual.

His phone rang. It was a shrill, unwelcoming sound in his office. *Ring ... ring ... ring ...* He snapped out of his vegetative state and went to his desk, but instead of answering his phone, he typed out his resignation letter. Once finished, he looked it over and then sent it out. He gathered his jacket and walked out, never to return.

It was the first and only time he had felt like a coward. He vowed he would never do that again. Never back out of anything ever again.

Suddenly the doors to the courtroom burst open. The reporters were the first to rush out. They pushed past Charles, who stood patiently, his hands in his pockets. Wiltore and the government lawyer walked out. Their facial expressions were unreadable. Mack and Smyllie were the last to appear. They stared glumly at Charles.

"What happened?" Charles asked.

Smyllie and Mack looked at each other and then back at Charles. Charles waited. It had to be bad. Mack was the first one to speak. "An arrest warrant has been issued for John."

Charles raised his eyebrows. "An arrest warrant?" he repeated in disbelief.

Mack nodded. "Failure to appear."

Smyllie looked down at his shoes. "I don't understand how he could be so fucking irresponsible."

Charles peeked into the now-empty courtroom. "Reckless is what you mean."

Smyllie mumbled in agreement. "If only he would listen once in a while."

They walked out of court together. Charles wondered if Webster's disappearance was his fault, if he had encouraged Webster's risk taking. Once outside, in the dotted shadows of the city, Charles tried to phone Webster again, but the phone went straight to the answering machine. Charles put his phone back into his pocket. He sensed Mack and Smyllie were expecting something from him, from the man who always knew what to do, but this time he had nothing and instead felt helpless and out of moves.

Byron

John thanked the pilot and closed the door to the seaplane. He looked at the clock on his phone. He had officially missed his court appointment. There was no point in rushing now. He wondered what would happen once he got back into the city. The strange thing was he didn't really care. He felt removed and detached from the whole situation, as if it didn't matter.

John hailed a cab and told the driver to take him to Queen Mary Elementary School. The driver nodded and pressed the gas slowly, and the cab rumbled into action. The news was playing over the radio.

"This just in: An arrest warrant has been issued for John Webster, a reporter for the *Daily Globe*," the reporter said over the airwaves. John felt his throat constrict. Was this real? Was this actually happening? he wondered. Then there was a commercial break. The driver changed lanes, two fingers on the wheel, apparently oblivious to the internal commotion happening beside him.

John's urge to see Byron was incredibly strong, like a drug compulsion. And it was even stronger now that he had an arrest warrant out on him. He wondered what Byron would be doing, what he would be learning about in school. He concentrated on what he would say to him. He wouldn't just show up; he would have a real plan this time. There was a ring somewhere, but it sounded distant and unclear.

"You're going to answer that?" the cabbie asked.

"Huh?"

"Your phone. You're going to answer it?"

John looked down to see his phone was indeed ringing. Embarrassed, he quickly stopped the ringing

The traffic worsened into a crawl. He looked out at the line of cars in front of him, feeling frustrated. He told the taxi to turn right down a side street that curled past some gigantic houses. He finally made it to Queen Mary Elementary. Byron's school was a large, ash-red building moulded with bricks and cement, and it had an oak shingled roof.

John paid the driver, got out, and walked the path up to the entrance. His phone rang again, and this time he decided he'd better answer it. It was Chuck.

"Webster, why don't you answer your phone?"

"Sorry—I was driving," John said.

"Where are you?"

"I'm just coming into Vancouver now."

"The judge has put out an arrest warrant for you, John."

"Yeah, I heard it on the radio." John looked around, as if the police would materialize out of the bushes.

"What are you going to do?"

"I don't know … I … have to think."

There was a pause on the phone. A car rushed past John with a loud whoosh. Chuck asked, "You're thinking of running?"

"No … no. I can't run. I have nowhere to go," but as John spoke those words, images of hiding places flashed through his head. Would Hayden keep him safe? Probably not. He then thought of Michelle. Could he trust her? Again, probably not.

Chuck interrupted his thoughts. "I'm glad, because that would be stupid. You need to turn yourself in."

"You're going to put Liz on the story, aren't you?"

"I have run out of options, Webster."

"Yeah, okay. I'll see you soon." John ended the call, feeling irritated. He stood still for a moment, deeply conflicted. He didn't know what to do. Should he turn himself in? He really had no other choice. But he decided he needed to see Byron first.

He pushed open the doors to the school and found himself in a long, colourless hallway. On the wall were rows and rows of student head shots.

They all smiled stoically for the camera, timeless, motionless, simple wall décor.

John found all those hundreds and hundreds of small pupils staring at him slightly unnerving with their fresh, almost embryonic faces. John had not stepped back into a school since he had walked out when he was seventeen, deciding he was done learning about obtuse angles, King Lear, carbon dioxide, Prince Edward Island, Billy Bishop, or *A Tale of Two Cities*. John had decided, rightly as it turned out, that a job with Reuters was more education than any classroom assignment could ever provide.

John admitted to himself later—much, much later—that he would never have had the guts to quit school had his father still been alive. His father would not have approved of his son dropping out of high school to pursue a career in journalism in the furthest parts of the world. John Senior had tried his hardest to appear upper-crust English his entire adult life, despite originating from the slums of Glasgow. John, unlike his theatre-loving father, didn't see much value in institutional learning.

John pushed through a set of double doors, following the sign that pointed toward the office. The receptionist was a Rubenesque woman with thick-rimmed glasses and misty eyes. She gave John a long, severe look, staring at his injured arm.

John put his forearms on the counter and tried to act as calmly and as naturally as he could. He asked the receptionist which room Byron was in, wondering if she was going to call the police on him.

Instead, she tipped her face down so she peered over her glasses. "And who are you?" she asked.

"I'm his dad," he said, and then, as if that didn't quite explain it, he added, "his father."

"Okay … what is the reason for your visit?" she asked, talking slowly, deliberately, as if he was a two-year-old.

"A family emergency," John said.

The receptionist nodded. "Okay, what's your last name?"

"Webster. First name John."

The receptionist typed something into her computer. John felt she was just stalling for time, probably pressing some panic button under the counter. They waited.

"109," she said.

John nodded a thank-you and walked down the wide, empty hallway. As he walked, he listened to sounds wafting into the hallway from the door cracks, sounds of scrupulous teachers lecturing and sounds of high-soprano voices, screeches, and laughter, all mishmashed together.

He eventually found the correct room. He stood outside it a moment before gathering his strength and knocking. A stocky woman with a round face and cropped brown hair opened the door slowly. She smiled hesitantly at John, eyeing him warily. Behind her, John could just barely make out a classroom of about twenty or so kids sitting obediently at their desks. He strained to see Byron, but the teacher slipped out into the hallway and closed the door behind her.

"What can I do for you, sir?"

"Are you Byron's teacher?"

"Yes, my name is Mrs. Nelson," she said.

"John Webster. I'm Byron's father. I need to speak with him for a moment."

Mrs. Nelson frowned, glancing back to the classroom. "Is it really necessary to disturb him?"

"Afraid so—family emergency."

Mrs. Nelson put a hand up to her mouth. "What happened?"

John was beginning to get impatient. "A car crash; his mother is in the hospital. I need … can I just see my son?"

"I have to say … Mrs. Webster warned me you might show up here. She made it abundantly clear you weren't welcome."

And just like that, John's story fell apart. He envisioned himself being handcuffed and put into a police cruiser while Byron watched. "Please, Mrs. Nelson, I just need a couple of moments … and then you can call the cops or whatever. Just one moment."

Mrs. Nelson smiled again, showing large teeth. He thought he saw compassion in her eyes, as if she understood all his pain and all his suffering. "Mr. Webster, I'm sorry, but I have very specific instructions."

John looked down at the floor and then at the door. He could easily push her out of the way, run to Byron, pick him up, and take him away.

But Mrs. Nelson seemed to know what he was thinking. "Go home, Mr. Webster. If you really love your son, you won't make a scene."

John nodded, not trusting himself to speak, turned, and walked down the hallway, but before he could reach the doors, Mrs. Nelson called out to him.

"You know, Mr. Webster, he brings all your articles to school … tapes them to his desk."

John stared blankly at her. He then managed a smile. With great effort, he turned away and walked out and across the street. He paced back and forth, stopping occasionally to stare at the school. Would Hayden come pick him up? Would she glide to the curb in her Lexus SUV? Probably. Byron seemed to live a life of controlled temperature. When John had been a kid, his parents didn't have a car, and he had walked everywhere.

As John waited, he wondered what would be the defining moment in Byron's generation. John supposed that was the greatness of youth and the future. You never really knew what shape the world would take. John was always struck with awe at how he had gone to bed one mild autumn day and awakened to the crashing of the Twin Towers and everything that went with it—the terrorist fear, Afghanistan and Iraq. Who could have guessed September 11, 2001, would be the day everything changed.

John sat on the curb, feeling the frustration build up. He watched the school. It was silent—an intimidating structure in the daytime stillness. The playground was void of children and lifeless as an empty shell. Only the occasional wind current struck and tore at John's face, funnelling through the quiet street, hitting the long slender spruce trees.

John began to accept his reality now. He wondered how long he would have to stay in jail for. Would it be months before Mack could obtain his release? What would he—forever the traveler, forever the wanderer—do confined in a small cement cell?

He felt his phone vibrate as he got a message. He took the phone from his pocket. It was an e-mail from Frank Mould, marked *Personal & Confidential*. He clicked to open it.

    Mr Webster, I couldn't put our earlier
    conversation out of my head, and so I did some

digging after you left. I have found no internal
investigation into the corruption of police officers.
However, I did look at some old records, and I did
find one complaint you might find interesting. I've
attached the document with this e-mail. Hopefully
you'll find it useful in your search. Please note
I am putting my job in serious jeopardy by doing
this, and I would appreciate it, as previously
discussed, if you would keep my name out of
print.

                    Thanks,
                    Frank Mould

John felt the excitement in his throat as he clicked open the attachment. It was a complaint form used by the commission, the logo on top of the paper. It was obviously photocopied or scanned and was handwritten. At the bottom, it was signed by Detective Clifford Wiltore. John almost choked. He read over the form; it was scant in details, but it was clear that Wiltore suspected some of his fellow police officers were taking bribes from gangsters. John had to read it over again just to make sure. It didn't name anybody specific and gave no indication of what had triggered Wiltore's complaint.

He closed the attachment. He suddenly felt faint and had to sit down on the curb, trying to connect the different pieces in his mind. What would make Wiltore go outside the police force? And what proof did he have? John had no doubt in his mind Wiltore would never talk to him.

John quickly dialled Frank Mould's number. His secretary picked up.

John grimaced. "It's John Webster from the *Daily Globe*. Could I please talk to Frank?"

"He's busy at the moment," she said frostily.

"Look—I'm sorry, I didn't mean to make you look bad," John said. "It was just I was on deadline, and I couldn't wait forever."

The school bell rang loudly and shrilly. The kids started to pour out of the doors—an eruption of babbling, excited energy into the playground, into the street, and into waiting cars.

The secretary said, "That may be, but he's still busy."

John looked frantically around for Byron. There were kids of all ages, colours, and weight classes, but John couldn't see his son. Voices and laughter floated toward John. The boys looked to be on some kind of marching orders, with their baggy shirts and denim jeans all similar in style and form. The girls—lacking in hips, but making up for it in height—were usually a few skips behind. They wore knee-high socks, tight sweats, and painfully bright-pink backpacks.

John said, "Could you just go ask him if he would mind being interrupted? Please?"

There was a long silence on the phone. John could hear the loud breathing of the secretary. He thought she was going to hang up on him, but instead she said, "Okay; hold on a moment."

A couple boys went to the swings and started pushing each other. A game of basketball broke out. The girls congregated at the cement steps, pretending they were ignoring the masculinity show.

John kept looking through the crowd. He contemplated just hanging up and trying Mould later. But he knew if he did that, the secretary would never forgive him and would probably never give him access to Mould. It would be best if he waited at least until she got back.

John became more agitated as the school crowd thinned and still there was no sign of Byron. He scanned the streets for any sign of Hayden or her SUV. If he was spotted by her now …

The phone clicked, and the secretary came back on the line. "He'll talk to you. Hold one moment."

John waited longer. Should he just walk away now? But just as he was contemplating walking to the bus stop, he saw Byron. He stared at him, breathless, his whole body cramped up. He was surprised that just the sight of his son would produce such a physical effect on him.

Byron was alone. He was wearing a navy-blue windbreaker, a large backpack on one shoulder. His head was looking down at his feet, and so John couldn't see his face; but his demeanour, his walk was distinctive.

He looked sad and defeated, and John wanted to run across the street to him and pick him up. Tell him everything would be okay, life would be okay—bumpy, sure, but okay.

"I thought you would phone," Mould said.

John almost snapped his head back. "Sorry?"

Mould cleared his voice. "I said, I thought I would be hearing from you."

"What happened to the complaint?"

"We forwarded it back to the VPD. I told you. We don't deal with that sort of thing."

"Did you at least talk to Detective Wiltore?"

There was an awkward silence. "No," Mould admitted.

"And you never heard back from the police?"

"No."

"You never followed up?"

John was still watching his son, who shifted the weight of his backpack and walked slowly down the road. For a moment, Byron was directly across the street from him. John could have called out to him in a voice almost speaking level and Byron would have probably heard him. But he did not, and he watched as Byron passed him, not noticing that his father was only yards away. Would Byron turn his head and see him? John willed Byron to look in his direction, but he just kept lumbering slowly on.

"Hello? You still there, John?"

John broke from his daze. "Yeah, I'm here—sorry."

"I don't have much time."

John was still watching as Byron slowly walked down the street toward his home. It wasn't too late; he could still run and catch up to him. John turned to look away. He said, "I'm sorry; I missed what you said."

"I phoned Benjamin Ervin, deputy chief of police about a month later. He said there was no evidence supporting Detective Wiltore's claim."

"And that was it?" John asked incredulously. "You believed him?"

"Why wouldn't I?" Mould asked. "He's the deputy chief of police."

"Did they do any type of investigation?"

"Of course, they did," Mould said irritably.

"Who did they interview?"

"Well, we didn't get into specifics."

John tried not to sigh. *Frank Mould would not have made a very good journalist*, he decided. "Tell me this, Mr. Mould—honestly. How hard do you think they investigated the detective's claim?"

"I have no idea."

"Don't you think Detective Wiltore probably made the complaint because he had exhausted all of his official channels? He probably came to you because he couldn't get the VPD to listen."

There was silence on the other end. "That hadn't occurred to me, no."

"Can you do me a favour?" John asked, exasperated. "Detective Wiltore won't talk to me, but maybe you can get some information from him—specifics about who he suspects are taking bribes—and then call me back."

"I don't know … If he doesn't want to speak with you …"

"Look, Mr. Mould, somebody has already tried to kill me. I need to know if they are police officers."

"That's impossible."

"Why? Why is it impossible? In Africa and the Middle East, it happened all the time."

"But this is Vancouver! We live in a civilized democracy. Those things just don't happen here."

"I guess we'll see."

After John hung up, he looked around for Byron, but he was already gone. The kids had all gone home, except for the ones playing basketball; and the school, once again, seemed empty and void. John called a cab, and as he waited, he wondered what he should do now. If he turned himself into the police, what would happen? He thought back to Cameron McCord's story about the man who was shot by the police. Perhaps drastic, yet he couldn't discount the possibility.

The cab pulled up, and he got into the back. No, he wouldn't—couldn't—turn himself in. He didn't trust the police—didn't trust Wiltore, didn't trust any of them. The taxi turned into traffic, stopping at a light. His mind churned with a thousand different scenarios, but it wasn't until he found his legs and arms guiding him that he realized there was only one place he really could go.

Manhunt

"What the hell are we doing here?" Wiltore demanded of the three other detectives. Detectives Cook and Blake shrugged. Wiltore stuffed his arms across his chest and waited. They were sitting in a colourless boardroom. A projector sat unused in the corner. They were waiting for Deputy Chief Benjamin Ervin.

After getting out of court, Lewis and Wiltore decided to look for Webster. Wiltore had mixed feelings about the way things had gone. He had stared intently at Charles Dana while he had been giving his testimony and—drawing on his vast experience in interrogation—was sure Dana had lied. Wiltore had put on the sirens, hoping to catch Webster at home. He hadn't believed Webster had gone to Victoria. Wiltore rang the buzzer, but there was no response. Wiltore and Lewis decided to wait in their car until Webster came home.

"You think he's going to show?" Lewis asked, relaxing beside him for the long haul.

Wiltore looked through the window at the brick building, wondering if Webster had barricaded himself inside. "I don't know—his fucking lawyer has probably phoned him already."

'You don't think he'll turn himself in?"

Wiltore shook his head. Webster was bullheaded enough to believe he could evade the police. "He thinks he's above the law—that he doesn't need to follow the rules like everybody else. That's what makes him dangerous."

The officers elapsed into silence. Wiltore saw a car pull up in front of the building and for a moment Wiltore thought it was Webster's car, but the man who got out wasn't the journalist. Instead, it was an older man with grey hair, a little shorter than John Webster.

Lewis asked, "Should we call him? Tell him to turn himself in?"

Wiltore shook his head. "If he doesn't show up in a little while, we'll try phoning. But for now, I think the best chance we have is to catch him unaware."

"But you think he's already been alerted?"

Wiltore shrugged, turning toward the street. "It's the best chance we have."

"And what if he doesn't show up?" Lewis asked.

"We phone for a search warrant and break the door down. Maybe we'll get lucky."

Wiltore's phone made a high-pitched ring. It was Benjamin Ervin. "I want you to report back to headquarters immediately," he said.

"But we're right outside of Webster's building. He could show up any minute."

"Just follow orders for once, Wiltore," Ervin said and hung up. Wiltore stared in shock at his phone for a moment, unable to comprehend what Ervin was thinking.

When they got back to the police station, Lewis and Wiltore found that Ervin had also phoned Devin Blake and Damon Cook.

"What does he want with all of us?" Wiltore asked, but nobody could answer.

Eventually Benjamin Ervin walked into the conference room with long, powerful strides. His uniform was neatly pressed, and he looked very dapper. He stared at each of the detectives, folding his hands together and resting them on the table. He looked down for a moment as if lost in thought. He suddenly shifted his neck upward.

"I want this reporter found. I want him behind bars," Ervin said finally. "And I want him found now."

Wiltore resisted the urge to yell at the deputy chief of police: *You idiot! What do you think I was doing?* Instead, he said, "I think we need to put some men at his apartment. He will need to go home sometime."

Ervin shook his head. "This is a man who's spent years avoiding detection in places like Iraq and Afghanistan. He knows how to blend in. We need to be a step ahead of him."

Cook cleared his throat and said, "Forgive me, sir, but what does this have to do with us? Are we being pulled off the Gibson investigation?"

Ervin frowned. "I thought we had come to the conclusion the killers of Dzyinski and Gibson were the same person."

"It's a theory … yes," Cook said cautiously.

"Then this reporter has some information pertinent to both cases. We need to find him. I don't want to read about any of this shit in the newspaper, you got that clear?" Ervin looked around the room again, his large brown eyes holding each detective's gaze for a moment or two.

Somebody is riding Ervin's ass on this one, Wiltore thought. He wondered who it was—no doubt somebody from the police board. The chief or the mayor maybe. Wiltore asked, "How much manpower do we have on this?"

"I have established a task force of twenty uniforms. I've sent them to his office, to his home—just in case he shows up." Ervin paused, scratching his neck. "Except he probably won't go to any of those places. That's the backup. You guys have been working the case. I want you to brainstorm. Where would a reporter on the run turn?"

Lewis was the first to speak. "He's pretty close to his editor, Charles Dana. He might try and hide out at his house."

Ervin nodded. "Okay, I'll send some uniforms. Anywhere else?"

Wiltore said, "There's this bar called the Palace that a lot of the reporters hang out at. He might try and meet somebody there."

"Who?" Ervin asked.

Wiltore shrugged. "I don't know. We could ask around and find out."

Lewis said, "He seems to have a close relationship with Michelle Lake."

"We could try her," Wiltore said, looking at his partner.

Ervin nodded. "Okay, any other suggestions?"

Cook asked, "You think he'll try to leave the country?"

Everybody turned to Wiltore—apparently he was the expert. "I don't know," he said. "But I doubt it. He could have backed off long ago and didn't. He's going to see this through to the end."

Ervin stood up. "Okay, then. Cook and Blake, you'll go the Palace—see what you can find out. Wiltore and Lewis, you'll go see what Michelle Lake knows."

Outside of the conference room and safely out of earshot of Ervin, Cook and Blake grumbled, "What are we going to do when we catch this guy?"

They got into the elevator together. The doors slowly shut. Cook pressed the button to the basement.

Lewis said, "Wiltore thinks Webster is protecting some criminals."

"It's not just that," Wiltore interjected. "I'm sure whoever Webster is protecting knows who killed Paul Gibson and Ken Dzyinski."

"What gave you that impression?" Detective Cook asked.

"Did you read Webster's article?"

Both Cook and Blake shook their heads. "No."

"Read it and you tell me Webster's source doesn't know," Wiltore said.

On the Run

John hailed a taxi and told the cabbie to take him to the airport. He watched the rearview mirror to make sure he wasn't being followed. The traffic was heavy, and it took almost thirty minutes for the taxi to pull up to the departures drop-off. *Much too long*, John thought. He tried to think of what moves the police would be making. He tried to deny it to himself, but he enjoyed this game: it made him feel young and vigorous. It made him feel important, as if what he was doing mattered again.

As John opened the door, he looked at his phone: five missed calls from Chuck. He made sure to pay the cabbie with his credit card.

"You don't have any baggage?" the cabbie asked, puzzled.

"No, I'm going to New York on business. I'll only be there a day," John said.

The cabbie nodded uncertainly, and John closed the door. He went inside and bought a plane ticket to New York. He then went to an ATM machine and took out four hundred dollars—all that was left in his bank account—thankful the police hadn't thought to freeze it yet. He folded the crisp bills and carefully put them in his pocket.

He bought a cappuccino from a small coffee shop and sat at a nearby table. He looked around tensely at the stressed travelers. Would a security guard recognize his face from a mug shot? Would a cop walk by and call for backup? He forced himself to sit and wait. Rushing wouldn't solve anything, and he might make fatal mistakes. He had to gather his thoughts.

His phone—which he had put on silent—started to flash. He didn't recognize the number, but he knew who it was. He answered the phone and said, "Do you know the worst conflict since the Second World War?"

There was a brief pause. John could hear loud breathing on the other end. And then Wiltore said, "You need to turn yourself in."

John got up from the table, intentionally leaving his wallet on the table. "You answer my question correctly, and I'll surrender."

"Mr. Webster, when will you realize this is not some game you're playing? You're hurting a lot of people here—now I know you don't realize it, and that is why I'm prepared to deal. But we need to know what you know."

John walked quickly out the sliding doors, across the street, and up a set of stairs to the commuter train, which would take John back to the city. He waited with about a dozen people along the track. "You haven't answered my question."

Wiltore sighed heavily. "You're serious? You'll turn yourself in?"

The train came, but John didn't get on. He watched as the other commuters piled on and the train pulled away again. "My word as a journalist."

"Vietnam."

"Wrong—try again."

"John, tell me this: what good can come of this? Where do you think you can go? What do you think you can do?"

"Somebody wants to kill me, Wiltore. There's a ten-thousand-dollar reward on my head."

"Ten thousand? Where did you hear that?"

"Why am I always one step in front of you?" John asked, wondering if Wiltore could hear the *whoosh* of the train.

"Perhaps because you're making it up."

"Why would I make something like that up?"

"Because I think you enjoy the limelight more than you enjoy reporting it."

John didn't say anything.

Wiltore laughed harshly and said, "You know, we're close to these gangsters. Couple of days, we'll make an arrest. I can protect you."

"Can you? From the police officers Hunter bought?"

"What are you talking about?" Wiltore sounded angry.

"I thought so too … until I saw the complaint you made."

There was a long, stunned silence on the other end of the phone. Then finally he said, "You're crazy. I never made any complaint."

John smiled despite himself. "Now who's playing games, Wiltore? Tell me. Who do you suspect?"

Wiltore stammered. His confidence seemed to have evaporated. "I don't know where you got that information from, but it's wrong. I am shocked you would think there is any police corruption."

John looked down the track. Another train was winding its way into the station. John took in a deep breath. He supposed he should not have expected anything less from the detective. "In case you were wondering, the answer is the Congo civil war. Over five million people were killed. I was there to witness it." John hung up. He pulled the battery from his phone and then slipped the SIM card out of its slot. He tossed the SIM card onto the track just as the train arrived. He pocketed the remnants of his phone and got on the train.

He looked out at the city as the train chugged along, wondering if this was going to be his last taste of freedom. The sky was so clear. He could see downtown perfectly, and behind the sky-blue mountains and smoky cloud puffs rolling languorously on and the harbour reflecting vivid shafts of light. *It was so perfect*, John thought.

He took the train to Broadway, where he got off, and then the bus to Pandora Street. He walked quickly, with his head down, crossing through alleyways, pausing sometimes to look back, but he saw nothing. He did not think too clearly of what he was doing or why. What would Michelle be able to do? Was it just a need not to be alone in this mess?

He went around the back and climbed over the fence. He suspected there would be somebody watching the front door. He tapped lightly on the screen. It had only just occurred to him: he had no backup plan if Michelle wasn't home. He frowned at the realization—he never would have made that mistake in Afghanistan. Always have a plan B. He was too old for this type of thing, he thought.

John got lucky, however. He saw Michelle come down the stairs, and he tapped lightly again. She turned and put a hand to her throat in surprise. John motioned her to be quiet by putting a finger to his lips. She went over and opened the door. She was wearing a plaid shirt too big for her and frayed jeans.

"What are you doing here? You shouldn't be here."

"I'm in a bit of trouble. Can you let me in?"

Michelle stepped aside and John stepped in, crouching behind a counter. Michelle looked around and then down at John, a perplexed look on her face. "What are you doing? Who's after you?"

"The police."

Michelle crouched beside John. "The police? Really? What have you done?"

"They subpoenaed me. I didn't show up in court, and so now there's an arrest warrant out for me. There's probably somebody staking out your house right now, just in case I show up."

Michelle put a hand to her mouth. "Jesus … What do you want me to do?"

"I need your help."

"For what?"

John looked at Michelle for a moment. He was hardly aware that his heart was beating fast or that he was breathing through his mouth. He thought back to what Drake had told him at Gassy Jack's statue. "Can you drive me to Andromeda?"

Michelle frowned. "You're going to see Ernest Hunter? Are you absolutely insane? He'll kill you."

"Not at his casino, he won't."

"No—I'm not doing it. You don't need me."

"I can't drive very well with my arm, and I need somebody I can trust. I also need an escape route, just in case things don't go well."

Michelle shook her head wildly. "No. You can't trust me. I don't know what makes you think you can."

John thought for a moment. "I don't know—it's just a feeling. I see the good in you. I see you trying to help out Ella. And I know you can help me out too. Please, Michelle."

Michelle didn't say anything for a long time. "Okay," Michelle said finally. "What do you want me to do?"

"Get your car and drive around to the alley. If you don't see me, that means you're being followed and just keep going."

Michelle nodded once and then reached her hand around John's neck and kissed him. She smiled shyly, got up, and walked out of the room. John listened to her quiet footsteps and then the door close.

John crept through the back door and across the lawn to the fence, where he waited for Michelle. He could still taste her lipstick. Her car pulled up, and he peered through the bushes. Nobody appeared behind her, and so he ran to the car. He got in and slouched so he couldn't be seen.

"Where's Ella today?" John asked.

"She's staying at my mother's."

John nodded. "Good. You still have my gun?"

"Of course—it's upstairs."

John made Michelle go get it. He listened to her light footsteps on the upstairs floor. She came back downstairs with a case.

"What do you really think you're going to do with this?" Michelle asked, handing John the case.

"I'm not sure," he said. "But it might come in handy."

They drove mostly in silence. After a while John, convinced nobody was watching them, relaxed a little. *This is the last place the police would look for me,* John decided.

"I don't know why I'm doing this," Michelle said, turning into the parking lot.

"You're doing this because you want me to find out who murdered Ken Dzyinski."

Michelle parked, but let the engine run idly. She rested her head against the backrest, jutting her pointy chin upward. "Would you stop that?"

John frowned, staring at Michelle. "Stop what?"

"I don't give a damn about bringing anybody to justice or anything like that."

John stared at Michelle, who sat motionless. "I don't believe you. You were at his funeral."

Michelle turned her head slowly as if by some unseen mechanical gear. "I was at his funeral because I felt guilty."

John still didn't understand. "Guilty? How?"

Michelle didn't reply. Instead, she reached forward, grabbing hold of the keys, and turned the engine off. "You're going to take the gun?"

John shook his head. "No, there's metal detectors. I don't think I would get very far."

Michelle nodded, opened the door, and got out. John did the same. They walked across the massive parking lot, full with rows and rows of cars. Halfway to the casino entrance, Michelle stopped.

"What's wrong?" John asked.

"It's dangerous for me to go in there."

"Why?"

She turned to face John. "Stop asking so many questions. Why can't you just believe me?"

John studied Michelle's narrow face, wondering what she was thinking. "I *do* believe you. I just don't understand."

"Maybe I'll wait in the car," she said.

John nodded. "Okay, I think that's a good idea."

Michelle returned to the car. John watched her in silence. She opened the door and slipped in. John wondered if she would drive off once he was inside. There was no time to think about it now, John decided, turning and continuing into the casino.

John walked the same path he had walked before, past the slot machines, past the roulette tables and poker tables. He walked down the hallway. He briefly wondered if he was walking to his death. If once behind those closed doors, Hunter, or somebody else, would put a couple of bullets in him.

He didn't stop walking, though. If he allowed himself to stop moving, the fear would paralyse him again. He would be like he was in his dreams, mute, unable to do anything. His only defence was to keep walking, one leg and then the other, and keep thinking—to see the angles and how to play them.

The same two massive security guards were guarding the door as before. They were dressed in black T-shirts and jeans. John stopped, unsure of what to say to them, but as it turned out, he didn't have to say anything. They nodded toward him and opened the door.

"Mr. Hunter is expecting you," one of the guards said.

John hesitated again. What was he doing? And in that moment, he remembered all the dark rooms he had entered into, all the uncertain situations; and so far, unlike some reporters, he had been lucky. He hoped his luck would hold.

John took a deep breath and walked into Hunter's small office. Ernest Hunter was on the phone, leaning back in his chair. If anything, he looked cool and relaxed. "All right … I got to go, see you later," he said, hanging up the phone. He shook John's hand cordially again. John looked around. The two of them were alone. It seemed odd. Where were all of his henchmen, his bodyguards? What did that mean?

Hunter turned to face John. "That was my son. He's just going into grade twelve. All that graduation shit, man. I'm so proud of him. You have a son, don't you?"

John sat down across from Hunter, still feeling cautious. He tried to remain calm and appear relaxed, even though his mouth was dry and his pulse was ringing in his ears. "Mr. Hunter …"

"Goddamn it, Ernie, I told you. I fucking hate this Mr. Hunter bullshit."

John shifted uncomfortably in his seat. "Sorry … Ernie. I need your help."

"Of course, what can I do for you?" he asked.

"You know who is trying to kill me."

Hunter held up his hands, palms upward. "I've been telling you all along. You just haven't been listening."

"I know it's not you … but I think it's somebody close to you. I think you know who it is."

Hunter seemed amused at this comment. "With all the affection I've shown you, I'm surprised you would think that."

John suddenly felt desperate and trapped, like he had never felt before. "You can call them off, if you want to … What would it take?"

Hunter didn't answer for a long time but sat deep in thought. John waited, and it didn't seem like he was going to get an answer. He studied Hunter, wishing he knew what was going on in his mind.

There was a knock on the door, and a man entered. Hunter frowned. "What is it?" he called out. A scrawny man slipped into the room. He was wearing dress pants and an open-neck oxford shirt. The man walked around the desk and whispered something in Hunter's ear. Hunter frowned even more deeply. He obviously didn't like what he was hearing. He turned and nodded. "Okay, thanks," he said, and the man slipped out of the room as quietly as he had come in.

"What is your relation to Michelle Lake?" Hunter asked.

"Michelle?" John asked, hoping he sounded innocent enough.

Hunter bit his bottom lip. "You know who I'm talking about. She's waiting for you out in the parking lot. We have her on surveillance."

John looked confused. Why was he so worried about her all of a sudden? How did she fit in? His mind was racing, trying to think. "She's a friend. I met her at Dzyinski's funeral."

"She was at the funeral?" he asked, scratching his head.

"Yes," John said, wondering what he had just done.

"And now she's helping you track down Dzyinski's killer?"

"No, I just needed a ride," John said, trying to sound as innocent as possible. He sensed he had somehow gotten Michelle into a lot of trouble, but he wasn't sure how exactly.

"A ride?" he asked incredulously. He paused. "She's your source, isn't she?" He smiled, showing large gaps between his teeth. His eyes, however, were opaque and flat as the black night sky.

John struggled to understand. What was he missing? "Source?" he asked. "What are you talking about?"

"You don't think I hear things? The police are looking for the man—or should I say woman—who served as your source for your newspaper article. Is she your deep throat, John?" Hunter laughed at his own private joke. He seemed to be enjoying himself, but behind that thinly veiled laughter was an air of menace.

"She had nothing to do with that."

Hunter pounded his hands on the table, rising out of his seat. "You take me for a fucking idiot, do you?"

John looked up at Hunter, trying to remain calm. *What was he missing?* "Of course not. But she had nothing to do with my article."

"You better tell her not to go home," Hunter said. His throat had flared out, and his veins were pumping.

"Ernie, please …"

Hunter frowned at John. "Get out, get out now!"

John held on to the side of his chair as if somebody was about to lift him from it. "Who is after me?" he asked. "It's the cops on your payroll, isn't it?"

Hunter backed away, startled. "I don't know what you're talking about."

"Ernie, tell them to back off. My lawyer has documents proving you ordered the hit on Dzyinski. If something happens to me, he'll go straight to the police." John stood up. He couldn't even convince himself of the lie he had just told. "Trust me, I'm not worth it," he said, walking out of the office.

John exited the casino as if in a daze. It took him a moment to catch his bearings. He felt as if everything around him was far away, not quite real. He leaned forward, his hands on his knees. Michelle pulled up in the car. John managed to lift the door handle and climb in.

"You okay?" Michelle asked.

"Yeah, fine." He closed his eyes. Relieved to be away from the casino, he concentrated on the motion of the car, the curvature of the rubber tires on the road. He wondered where they were going. He didn't care.

"What happened in there?" Michelle asked. "Were you successful?"

"I'm not sure," John said. His eyes were still closed, his mind still trying to process what had just happened.

"Michelle?"

"Yeah?"

John opened his eyes and turned to stare at her. "What mess have you gotten into?"

Michelle didn't answer right away. She stared straight ahead, seeming to concentrate on the road in front of her, the starting and stopping of cars, the passing buildings, the street lamps as they dissipated into the background. John waited, wondering what she was thinking.

"What do you mean?" she asked finally.

John frowned, feeling annoyed. "I mean, Hunter thought you were the source I used for my articles."

Michelle suddenly pressed the brake, causing the car behind her to honk. She didn't seem to realize it, however. "What the fuck?"

"The only reason he would think that is if you know more than you're telling me."

"I don't know anything." She looked at John, her eyes wide, pleading with him.

There was more honking from behind. A man in a yellow Ford gave them the finger as he passed them by. Michelle, however, didn't even notice the existence of the outside world.

"Maybe you should pull over," John suggested.

She nodded and pulled over to the curb, putting the hazard lights on. The traffic resumed its flow.

"What did he say exactly?" Michelle asked. Her cheeks were sucked in, and she had gone completely white.

"He asked me if you were my source, and he didn't seem to believe me when I told him you weren't."

"Fuck," Michelle said, pressing her palms into her forehead. "What am I going to do? He's going to kill me … I need to phone my mother. I need to tell her … I need …"

"Michelle?" John grabbed Michelle's wrists, and gently but firmly pried her hands away from her face. "Michelle?" he said again, gently. She turned to look at him. Her teeth were clenched, and her chestnut-coloured eyes were unrecognizable as anything human. "Forget I'm a journalist for a moment," he pleaded. "I'm your friend, but I can't help you if you don't tell me the truth." He let go of her wrists. She held her hands in the air, and then she lowered them slowly to her lap.

He put a hand on her cheek, which was flush to his touch. She looked up at him and pressed her flesh against his palm. He felt the air leave him, leaving him breathless, unable to move. He was surprised a simple touch could affect him like that.

"I tried to tell you to stay away from me," Michelle said. "You wouldn't listen. You were too stubborn to listen to me."

"I want to be able to help, Michelle."

With a sudden outburst of violence, Michelle took John's hand and pushed it away from her. "My boyfriend …"

"James?"

"Yes … James. He loved the casinos, loved to gamble. Played blackjack.

He would go every weekend. Then it became every day, until he hardly spent any time at home. I tried to talk to him, but it was impossible. This went on—I don't know how long. One day I came home to find our car gone. He had sold it to repay a gambling debt. That was the final straw. I left him and moved in with my mother. He phoned me a couple of months later to say he was in deep trouble and needed eighty thousand dollars." Michelle, who had held herself together well to that part, now broke into tears. They came fast and strong, large droplets, as if the storage of them had just been too much to bear. John looked around for tissue but couldn't find anything to offer her. And so he let her cry, waited for her. Eventually she wiped her eyes with her sleeve.

"The police found him dead a week later. They had tied him up and burned him alive. The next day Keith Dowell knocked on my door. He told me I would have to repay all the money James owed ... or he would kill Ella and me."

"How did you repay him?" John asked quietly, although he was sure he didn't want to hear the answer.

"I started off small ... transporting drugs from the dock ... Then it turned into guns ... I only looked once. They were big guns, heavy machine guns. It shocked me.... And then I saw your article in the newspaper, describing those guns ... and I knew it was those guns that had killed Ken Dzyinski."

John felt numb, unable to think. "Who gave you the guns?"

Michelle looked down at the floor. "It was always somebody different."

"And who did you give them to?"

"Keith Dowell, always. He would arrange a different meeting spot each time."

"And how much money do you still owe him?"

This sent Michelle into tears again. "He says I still owe him fifty thousand dollars ... I don't have fifty thousand dollars. Where am I going to get that money from?"

John was silent for a while, listening to Michelle's quiet sobbing. "You realize you'll never be able to repay him ... And if you do, he'll kill you."

"What am I going to do?" she asked, gripping hold of John's hand suddenly with incredible force.

"You need to go to the police," he said. "They are the only ones who can help."

Michelle suddenly turned on him in a rage. "That's your fucking advice? You don't find that ironic?"

"Go to Detective Clifford Wiltore. He will be able to help you."

"How do you know he's not banked by Hunter? They're all thieves, as far as I'm concerned."

John thought of something. "The night I phoned you from the bar. Whom did you tell?"

Michelle shook her head unconvincingly. "I didn't tell anybody."

John leaned in close to her. He could feel her panicked breath on his neck. "You told Dowell, didn't you? You told him where he could find me."

Michelle nodded curtly. "I didn't know he was going to try and kill you … I swear. He promised me I wouldn't owe him anymore."

John felt the anger swell up in the base of his spine, and he suppressed the urge to yell at her. "But he didn't keep his promise?"

Michelle shook her head, her eyes averted shamefully from him.

John felt the sudden urge to get out of the car, to get some fresh air. "I shouldn't have dragged you into this," he said. He reached into the back and took the gun from the silver case. "I need your cell phone," he said.

"Why?"

"I just do—don't argue."

Michelle handed over her phone. Her hand was shaking.

John asked, "Do you have Wiltore's phone number?"

"I have it in my phone," she said.

He scrolled through her phone and found it. He then took a pen from his pocket and wrote the number down on her hand. "Go to the nearest pay phone and give him a call," he said, opening the car door.

"Where are you going?" she asked, suddenly turning. "Don't leave me. Please … I didn't want to hurt anybody."

John didn't respond. He felt nothing for her. A dull numbing sensation had filled his entire body and coated his skin. Her voice echoed as if he was hearing her underwater.

John wriggled his injured arm free of the sling. There was surprisingly little pain; it felt stiff, but otherwise fine. He examined the bandage for blood and was satisfied when he found none. He placed the sling in the back of the car. What he was about to do would require full mobility of his limbs.

Michelle became hysterical. "He'll fucking kill me! You know he will. What about my daughter? Think of her!"

John got out of the car, his body seeming to move of its own accord. He shut the door behind him and started to walk quickly, in what direction he didn't know. He needed time to think. What was his next move? He didn't know. He started to run. Could he risk taking a taxi? No, he better not, he thought. He found the nearest bus stop.

Fear

"No, he hasn't checked in yet," the flight attendant said to Wiltore and Lewis, looking down at her computer. The two cops looked at each other questioningly. They had been almost at Michelle Lake's house when they had gotten a call from the chief of security, a soft-spoken man named Jessie White, at the airport, telling them John Webster had bought a plane ticket to New York about thirty minutes earlier.

Wiltore did a U-turn, and Lewis flipped on the siren. Wiltore pressed the gas pedal down, speeding along Oak Street out to the airport. It only took them ten minutes to reach the departures gate.

Wiltore handed the flight attendant his business card. "Okay, will you call me as soon as he does?"

The flight attendant, a skinny middle-aged woman with a drawn-out face, took the card with both of her hands. "Okay," she said. "You still want me to allow him through?"

"Yes, please. I don't want him to get spooked."

Wiltore and Lewis thanked the flight attendant. Wiltore called for backup, and while they waited, the two detectives split up and did a quick walk around the airport. It wasn't very busy for an afternoon, mostly businesspeople in crumpled suits with sleepy eyes coming and going, a few family reunions. Wiltore didn't see any of it. He kept his eyes alert for Webster; the adrenaline was keeping him going. Over the loudspeakers, flight attendants were calling out gate numbers. "British Air Flight 235 to Manchester is now boarding at gate F6."

There were a few sleeping bodies on the benches next to the international departures gate. Wiltore woke each person up, but none of them were Webster. Next, Wiltore went to the guards at the security checkpoint and showed them all a picture of Webster just in case he had slipped past the check-in, but the guards all shook their heads.

The two detectives converged again in front of the Bill Reid statue. Wiltore looked at Lewis, who shrugged. Wiltore pushed the urge to swear back down his throat.

"Check the bathrooms?" Lewis asked.

Wiltore nodded irritably.

As they walked back to their car, Lewis asked, "Should we wait for backup to arrive?"

Wiltore checked his watch. Webster's flight left in an hour. It was possible he would appear at the last minute and try to board ... But no, he still couldn't believe Webster would run. He tried to imagine himself in the journalist's shoes. What would he do?

He shook his head, realizing it had all been a clever diversion. "No, New York doesn't make sense. He's still here in the city somewhere."

Lewis shrugged. "Maybe he knows somebody there ... Maybe he just wants a safe place to crash until everything blows over."

"Let's go back to Michelle's place. Maybe we'll get lucky," Wiltore said, although he doubted it.

Just as they climbed into the car, his phone rang. "Detective Wiltore speaking."

"Detective? It's Michelle ... Michelle Lake. We spoke about a week ago at my diner. You remember?"

"Of course, Michelle. What can I do for you?" Wiltore made eye contact with Lewis and pointed to the phone.

"I'm in trouble. I need your help. Can I meet you someplace?"

"Sure, why don't we meet at your house?"

"No, not there. Someplace safe." Her voice was high pitched and stressed.

Wiltore frowned at Lewis, who was listening intently. He wondered if this was another decoy of Webster's. "Why isn't your house safe?" he asked.

"I did something stupid … John said I could trust you."

"Trust me? What do you mean? Did you talk to him?"

"I drove him to see Ernest Hunter."

"Wait! When did you do this?"

"Just now. But he spotted me and now he wants to kill me," Michelle said, in one extended breath.

"Michelle, you're not making any sense. Is Webster with you right now?"

There was a pause and Wiltore thought Michelle was going to hang up, but she stayed on. "I'm scared. There are people looking for me, trying to kill me."

"Okay, why don't we meet at the police station?"

"No, not there. I'm not safe there."

Wiltore sighed, trying not to let his impatience show. Webster had obviously infected her with his distrust. "Where is Webster right now?"

"I don't know."

"But he was just with you? He couldn't have gone far."

Another long, painful pause. Wiltore wanted to yell at her so badly … but no, she would tell him when she was ready. Finally, she said, "I think he went to the Rocky Moon."

Wiltore looked over at Lewis, confused. "Why would he go there?"

"I think he went to talk to Keith."

"Okay, stay put, Michelle. Don't move. I'll send somebody to get you."

"No, you don't get it, do you? I don't trust anybody else," Michelle said.

"You can trust me," Wiltore said. "I'll protect you."

"One more thing," Michelle said.

"What's that?"

"He's got a gun."

Wiltore frowned, glancing at Lewis. "Who? Webster?"

"Yeah … I don't know where he got it, but he took it with him … and I think he's going to get himself killed."

The Club

John got in line behind a group of college-looking guys who looked around half-intoxicated. They were talking excitedly about lap dances and porno movies. Whenever the door opened, John could hear the loud, thumping bass.

John dug his hand into his pocket. He was almost surprised to find his fingertips touch hard, cold metal. But then he remembered the gun and his purpose.

The college students paid their cover, and then, one by one, they were frisked. John looked around nervously. What was he doing? Was this really his clever plan?

One of the security guards, a thick-necked, muscular man, motioned John to step up with a bored flick of his wrist.

"Hands out," the guard said. John didn't move, frozen in his spot. The guard was more annoyed than angry. He said, "You, fucking stupid. Hands out of your fucking pockets."

The other security guard glanced over. "No, this one is on the list. He can't come inside."

"Sorry, bud," the guard said, and motioned for the next person in line to step up.

John pulled his gun from his pocket and waved it threateningly at the security guards. "Neither of you move," he said. He felt like he had in his dream, as if this really wasn't him. Someone else was saying these words, an actor playing himself in a movie. He was comfortably in bed, sleepily watching the action unfold.

The security guards froze wide-eyed. Somebody in the crowd screamed, and everyone scattered. One of the guards raised his hands and said calmly, "Okay, calm down. No need for anybody to get hurt."

"We're going inside to talk to your boss," John said. "Just want to talk."

The security guards nodded. John ushered them both inside. It was dark inside, and it took a while for John to adjust to the light. It was the same odious music playing over and over again. The advertising was blaring on the wall. Swedish massages. Growth hormones. Las Vegas trips. It made John sick all of a sudden.

John slipped his free hand into his pocket and pressed the speed-dial button on Michelle's phone. He could feel it vibrating on his thigh. He took a deep breath in and exhaled slowly. He really hoped this worked.

"Walk real slowly," he told the two guards. "Don't make any sudden moves."

They walked toward the bar. John hid his gun in his jacket. He looked around, but nobody seemed to pay him much attention. In the background, the song had changed to Joe Crocker; and on stage, the stripper, a pale brunette with large freckles, was doing her very best Kim Basinger impression. Top hat and all.

John followed the security guards behind the bar. The bartender was the same young guy that had been here before. He frowned at them but didn't say anything. The security guards knocked on a door.

"Come in."

Dowell was sitting at his desk. Dewitt was leaning over him, staring at the computer in front of them. They both looked up as the two security guards entered, followed by John. The room was warm and airless.

"What the hell?" Dowell said. "I thought I told—"

John took out his gun and closed the door behind him. "Put your hands where I can see them! Now! We are going to have a talk."

Both Dowell and Dewitt raised their hands slowly. They looked at each other, eyebrows raised, mouths open at John's audacity.

Dewitt turned and stared at John with large, black-pitted eyes. His surprise quickly disappeared and was replaced with mild contempt, his jaw pressed back against the rest of his skull. "Nobody points a gun at me and gets away with it."

"We already told you everything we know," Dowell said, his eyes on John.

"I don't think so," John responded. He motioned for the two security guards to sit. They did so. John moved his eyes across his captives. He had trouble thinking. All he could hear was the sound of his blood pumping loudly, and his breath was constricted. He wiggled his fingers, as they were beginning to feel stiff on the handle of the gun.

"You killed Dzyinski and Gibson," John said. "I can prove it."

Dewitt laughed loudly. "If you could prove it, then you wouldn't be here waving a gun around."

"Look," Dowell said. "The police are going to be here any moment. You better just hand it over."

John sucked in a deep breath of air, almost choking. "I know Michelle phoned you and told you where you could find me."

Dowell shrugged unconcerned. "We saw your interest in her—not that I blame you. She isn't too bad looking for a girl well past her prime. We told her to keep tabs on you and report back. She told us everything about you."

John felt his blood pump harder, and the thumping in his ears increased. "Who did you phone after? Who did you phone to kill me?"

"Why would we want to kill you?" Dewitt asked. He smiled as wide as a great white shark. "You're that fucking conceited? That full of your overblown self-importance?"

John took a step, levelling the gun at Dewitt's forehead. Dewitt didn't move, didn't flinch. His cavernous dark eyes betrayed nothing. He had stopped smiling, however.

There was a loud thump at the door. "Vancouver Police; open up!"

John looked around him at the supercilious grins surrounding him. He realized he was trapped. There was no way out of this.

"Identify yourselves," he yelled back, hoping to buy himself some time. *What if they weren't police at all,* John wondered.

"Police, open up." The voice was unfamiliar.

John looked back at Dewitt and Dowell. They were looking a little too smug for John's liking, a little too relaxed. What did they know that he didn't?

"I have four captives in here. I want to talk to Detective Wiltore," John said. He could feel his fingers start to cramp again, and he changed his grip on the gun.

"You don't get to call the shots, motherfucker! I'm going to give you five seconds, and then we're coming in shooting."

"I need identification," John said again. "Or I will kill one of my hostages."

John felt something swell in his throat. He tried to swallow it down, but it just seemed to sit there, causing his breath to cease. *They couldn't be VPD, they couldn't*, John told himself.

There was a pause at the door. John listened. The music was still vibrating in the background, but it seemed to have melted inconsequentially away. He heard—or thought he heard—the breathing of the men behind the locked door, their feet as they shifted balance.

"Detectives Blake and Cook."

"I want to talk to Detective Wiltore," John said.

"Enough; we're counting," said the voice from behind the door.

"I'll shoot," John said, pointing his gun at Dewitt's head. At least he could take one gangster out.

"Five ..."

John felt the disbelief of the moment. Of all the ways he thought he was going to die, this was the very last he could have imagined. And for some strange reason, he suddenly remembered a dream he had once had. It came back to him in a flash—the one where he was frozen, where he couldn't move, helpless as he watched the little boy as he cried out, then burst into flames, writhing in pain, his skin melting. The image came to him so vividly, so crystal clear ... he struggled to remain focused on the present.

"Four ..."

John turned his gun toward the door. He saw out of his peripheral vision Dowell make a move toward something under his desk. John swung his gun back on Dowell.

"Don't even think of it," John said.

Dowell raised his arms. "Okay, okay," he muttered.

But John could hardly see; everything was murky, like a reflection in the water breaking up. The boy was right in front of him, praying for help.

"Three …"

John, his gun still trained on the gangsters, walked around to the other side of the desk. "No sudden movements," John said, praying they would listen. He opened the top drawer and took out Dowell's gun.

"Two … This is your last chance, Webster."

John looked at Dowell and then at Dewitt, wishing he could understand what was happening. He suddenly imagined himself O.K.-corralling his way out of the office. He had never killed anybody in his life. How was he supposed to shoot somebody now?

"Okay, I'm putting the guns down," he yelled.

He dropped the guns and kicked both of them toward the door. There was a long pause, and John waited to see what the police would do next. He looked toward Dowell and Dewitt. They seemed unusually calm. Then something struck him: How had the cops known his name? Who had called them? Somebody from outside? No, couldn't have been … they had shown up too quickly.

"Carl? Keith? You in there?" the police officer asked from behind the door.

"Yeah, we're here."

"Everybody unarmed?"

John felt that something was happening that he didn't quite understand.

"Yes, he's dropped his weapons," Dewitt said.

"Okay then. We're coming in."

The cops kicked the door open. There were two men with badges hanging around their necks. They were dressed in identical black suits and had identical crew cuts. They pointed their guns at John. They certainly were cops, John decided. "On your knees," they commanded. "Hands in the air, now!"

John glanced behind him. "But what about …?"

"Just do it!" one of the cops yelled.

So John got on his knees and raised his hands. The two men relaxed a little, lowering their own guns. John still didn't understand what was happening.

"Who are you?" John asked.

The two men ignored the question, looking beyond John. John tried to gauge the detectives' moods and figure out what they were thinking.

Dewitt smiled and said, "Don't think I've ever been happier to see two police detectives before."

The two detectives turned toward Dowell and Dewitt. "What the hell happened here?"

"I dunno—he's crazy. He just came in waving a gun around," Dowell said.

The two detectives looked at each other as if uncertain what to do. John glanced over at the two security guards, who were still sitting in the corner silently.

"What should we do with him?" one of the detectives asked.

"He knows too much," Dowell said.

"What do you think?" Dewitt asked.

The detectives shrugged. "Wouldn't be hard. Easy to pass it off as an accident."

"Okay," Dewitt said. "Do it."

The two detectives pointed their guns at John. "Get up," they commanded, motioning with their guns.

John put up his hands. He felt his body going numb as the pulsing in his ears stopped. "Wait! You can't do this."

"Come on … don't make this hard … We can still make it look like an accident even with you fucking cowering on the floor."

"At least tell me … You killed Dzyinski and Gibson, didn't you?"

The two detectives looked at each other. One shook his head, lowering his gun. "Detective Wiltore was close to making arrests on both of them … They both knew about us, about our association … and we didn't know what sort of deal they would have made."

"And so you made it look like a hit?"

The detectives shuffled in their spots nervously. "Okay, enough. Time for you to fucking stand up," one of them said.

"What about Alex Gibson? Did you plan on killing him too?"

"If anything, he was more trouble than his brother. Unfortunately he disappeared before we could get to him," one of the officers said. "But don't worry, we'll find him."

"I know where he is," John said. "I could take you to him."

The two cops looked at each other again, as if uncertain of what to do.

"No, he's trying to buy time," Dewitt said. "Shoot him now."

John took a deep breath and stood up. He thought of Hayden … why hadn't he run to Byron when he had a chance? If only he had known that would be the last chance he would get to talk to him …

The two detectives raised their guns, but suddenly there was a loud crack and something exploded in the middle of the room. What was happening? He was back in Baghdad. Had to be. The market was crumbling apart. Suddenly the boy was lying right in front of him. Blood ran down the front of his beautiful white shirt. But this time, John was able to move. Why now? John wasn't sure. He ran over to him and gathered him up in his arms. He had such a small head, blue eyes, his hair strangely fluffy, like a Labrador's, his billowing cheeks set in a grimace.

"It'll be all right," John told him. "Don't worry; I'm here. I'll tell them. Tell them what happened. Tell them everything."

The boy managed a tiny smile. Or had John only imagined it? Then the boy groaned and grasped John's fingers and held them tightly. John started to cry. "I'm sorry," he said. "I'm sorry."

"John? … John? You okay?"

John opened his eyes. He was lying on his back, looking up at the bleak ceiling. Where was he? There was a strong stale smell in the air. He twisted his neck and saw Wiltore looking down at him.

"Paramedics are on their way. Don't move," Wiltore said.

"No, no, I'm okay." John managed to push himself up to a sitting position. There was smoke all around him. He saw several police officers. "What happened?" he asked.

"It's from the flash bangs," Wiltore said. "Luckily we got here just in time."

The smoke wisped away, and John saw the two detectives in handcuffs being led away by police in riot gear.

"That was quick thinking, phoning me," Wiltore said, taking out his phone. "I heard everything. Blake and Cook confessing to killing Dzyinski and Gibson."

John handed Michelle's phone to Wiltore. "Did you suspect them before?" John asked. His vision was still a little shaky, and his throat was sore and he had trouble speaking.

Wiltore didn't answer for a while, lost in thought. "Yes and no." He paused again. John waited. "It's complicated," Wiltore said. "I found Dzyinski knew things about my investigation that weren't public knowledge. I knew it had to be someone from my unit. Blake and Cook were the most likely suspects."

John touched his forehead. It was beginning to throb. "Am I under arrest?"

Wiltore laughed airily and shook his head. "No, for the time being, you're safe. We have what we need. Your source is safe too."

Two paramedics entered and knelt by John.

"I'm fine," John protested.

Wiltore touched John lightly on the shoulder. "We'll be in touch," he said, and with that, he turned and walked away.

The Interview

John woke up feeling well rested. He kicked off the sheets and swung his legs off his bed, all in one motion. He looked around his bedroom and was surprised to find light seeping in through the curtains. What time was it? How long had he slept? His clock said nine thirty.

He got up and stretched, running his hands through his stubble, doing a mental tune-up. He had gone to bed late and had forgotten to take any painkillers or sleeping pills, but to his surprise, he found he had slept soundly—not a dream to be spoken of.

He went to the bathroom to urinate, wondering when the last time was he had slept so well. He studied himself closely in the mirror, unafraid of what he might see: he needed to shave, but apart from that, he looked good and, perhaps more important, youthful.

John had a quick shower, enjoying the intense warm water running down his body. He then slipped on some clean clothes and went to the corner store to buy a newspaper. He was satisfied to see his story was splashed over the front page. He walked a little further to buy a coffee and some breakfast from a restaurant on Abbot. The day was cloudy and grey tones had set over the city as the autumn season drifted inauspiciously in. John found himself welcoming the change, the dying of the leaves and the palette of colours that came with it.

John thought about the interview he had in the evening with CBC. He finished his breakfast—he would read the rest of the paper later—and headed home. He had a lot to do before he went to the studio. Ever since his dramatic showdown at Rocky Moon, he had been inundated with interview requests.

His phone rang. It was Charles Dana. He told John the deputy chief of police, Benjamin Ervin, was holding a press conference later in the afternoon.

John smiled. "I wonder what he's going to say."

"No idea," Chuck said. "You want to cover it?"

"Can't," John said. "I have a doctor's appointment this afternoon. I might be getting rid of my sling."

"That is good news," Chuck replied. "Phone me later and tell me how it goes."

John promised he would and hung up. Before his appointment, however, he drove to Michelle's house. When he knocked, the fat, old man opened the door. He was wearing the same sweat-stained shirt he had been the first time John saw him, and John wondered if he ever got out of the house.

"I was wondering if Michelle was home," John asked.

"Michelle?" he asked, his eyes rolling upward in thought.

"You know, the MILF?" John said, slightly bashful.

"Oh yeah," the man said. "She moved out."

"Moved out?" John asked, surprised. "Did she leave a forwarding address?"

The man shook his head. "No, sorry … I don't think so." He paused, a large frown on his face. "Are you John Webster?"

John nodded.

"She left a letter for you."

The man disappeared into the house and moments later reappeared with an envelope, which he handed to John. John thanked him and returned to his car. There he opened the envelope.

Dear John,

I finally bought tickets to India. I don't know how long I'm going to stay, a couple of months. Forever, perhaps. Nobody will be able to find me here. I have finally realized my fears … yes, I realized it was fear that was holding me back—well, more accurately, you made me realize that I was afraid to pursue my dreams. My only regret is that I failed to persuade you to come with Ella and me, but in the end, I know my breath would have been wasted on you. No, scratch that—I have two regrets. My second is that I didn't have the courage to tell you this in person. I have to write my thoughts, let them flow on the paper. It's that old, old fear thing again. Why does it creep along with us, attached to us like our shadow? Why can't it just leave us alone? Why can't we tell each other what we think and what we feel? I have a tendency to allow myself to be shoved in the background, to be the backup plan, the girl you call late at night when your date doesn't show up. Well, John, I can't do it anymore. I can't be that person.

You would like India, I think. But I understand you must do your own thing—even if it destroys you. I pray it won't. I hope you catch the killer. I hope your article wins a Pulitzer, if that is what you want. I hope it touches people the way you want it to, but most of all, I hope you find your answer. I think, however, you're looking in the wrong place. You won't find your answers in the Downtown Eastside or in Afghanistan or Iraq or in any other physical place. You can only find them within yourself. Good-bye, John, may we meet again.

Michelle Lake

John read the letter over several times, each time getting a bit more of a sinking feeling in his stomach, realizing he would never see her ever again. He bit down on his bottom lip, feeling an emptiness well up inside him, a shortness of breath.

But then, wasn't this for the best? What sort of future did they have anyways? If she hadn't run, she would have been picked up by the police, possibly murdered by some gangster. Yes, this was the best way, the only way.

He wondered if INTERPOL would ever find her, bring her back. He doubted it. Finally he crumpled the letter up and threw it out the window. He then started the car and drove away.

Webster drove downtown to the CBC building. He parked and went up to the top floor, where all the television interviews were done. As the interview was being set up, Webster decided on a whim to call Hayden. He wanted to patch things up. As the phone rang, he wondered if he would have a chance to speak before she called the police.

The phone rang a couple of times, but instead of Hayden, Byron picked it up.

"Hi, Dad. I saw your article in the newspaper. I cut it out and put it on the fridge."

"It's on the fridge?" Webster asked, surprised.

"Yeah. It's pretty long and covers most of the fridge."

"Byron, if you turn on CBC News tonight, you'll see me being interviewed."

"Really? That's so cool, Dad."

Webster saw the producer waving at him. "I've got to go, Byron, but I'll call you real soon."

"Okay. And, Dad?"

"Yes?"

"I'm really proud of you."

Webster smiled. "Thanks, Byron. I'm proud of you too."

The interview started, and the host, a man in his mid-thirties named Ian Lamb, started by introducing John Webster as an award-winning journalist who had covered all the major conflicts in the last ten years. Webster smiled, trying not to blush under the hot lamps.

Ian Lamb asked a lot of questions about what it was like covering wars in the Sudan, Iraq, and Afghanistan, before moving on to the state of organized crime in Vancouver.

"Do you think we need to take a hard look at corruption in the Vancouver police force?"

Webster paused for a moment before answering. "I think we always need to be vigilant. And, I mean, that is the journalist's job—to be vigilant, whether it is keeping tabs on a politician, the army, or the police force."

"You were shot once, almost killed several times," Ian Lamb said. "Wasn't there a time when you said to yourself: this just isn't worth it?"

Webster tried to laugh, but then just shook his head. "No, I always knew the story was a good one. It was worth covering. I think the city needs a witness, because if nobody documents these things, then they will go unnoticed. I think people in their busy schedules, their busy lives, tend to forget that there is a large world around them with large problems, and it's my job to remind them."

"What makes you do it?"

Webster paused again, looking into the dark camera lens, knowing somewhere out there, Byron would be watching this.

"I don't know … possibly it goes back to my time in high school. I think I was in grade eight when I turned the corner in the hallway on my way to math class, and I saw a group of older kids picking on one of my classmates. Now, I didn't know this kid very well—and I've forgotten his name—but he was a scrawny kid with large glasses, just the type bullies pick on. I watched as the older kids started shoving him, closing in on him like a bunch of sharks, and I felt I should at least stand up for him. So I went over and stood next to him, and the older kids started taunting and jeering me. I grew scared that they would beat me up, and so I ran away … and afterward, when I was crying in my mother's arms because I felt so ashamed for what I had done, for not staying there and standing up to those bullies, I vowed never to feel that ever again."